A Note on the Author

John MacKenna is the author of twenty-one books – novels, short-story collections, a memoir, poetry and a biography – and a number of radio and stage plays. He is a winner of *The Irish Times*, Hennessy and Cecil Day-Lewis Awards. He is also a winner of a Jacob's Radio award for his documentary series on Leonard Cohen and a Worldplay Silver Medal (New York) for his radio play *The Woman at the Window* (RTE Radio 1). He teaches Creative Writing at Maynooth University and at The Hedge School on the Moone.

Also by John MacKenna

Novels
Clare
The Last Fine Summer
A Haunted Heart
The Space Between Us
Joseph
Hold Me Now

Short-Story Collections
The Fallen and Other Stories
A Year of our Lives
The River Field
Once We Sang Like Other Men

Memoir
Things You Should Know

Non-fiction
Castledermot and Kilkea:
    A Social History
Shackleton: An Irishman in Antarctica
    (with Jonathan Shackleton)
The Lost Village
I Knew This Place (Radio Essays)

Children's Books
Turkey's Delight
South

Poetry Collections
The Occasional Optimist
Ten Poems
Where Sadness Begins
By the Light of Four Moons

Plays
The Fallen
The Unclouded Day
Towards Evening
Faint Voices
Sergeant Pepper
Over the Rainbow
The Woman at the Window
My Father's Life
We Once Sang
Redemption Song
Lucinda Sly
Between Your Love and Mine
    (with Leonard Cohen)
The Mental

We Seldom Talk About the Past

Selected Short Stories

John MacKenna

NEW ISLAND

WE SELDOM TALK ABOUT THE PAST: SELECTED SHORT STORIES
First published in 2021 by
New Island Books
Glenshesk House
10 Richview Office Park
Clonskeagh
Dublin D14 V8C4
Republic of Ireland
www.newisland.ie

Lyrics from 'Boogie Street' reproduced by kind permission of Leonard Cohen.

Lyrics featured in 'The Fallen' are from 'Somewhere a Voice is Calling', composed by Arthur F. Tate with lyrics by Eileen Newton.

Print ISBN: 978-1-84840-803-6
eBook ISBN: 978-1-84840-804-3

Typeset by JVR Creative India
Cover design by Fiachra McCarthy, fiachramccarthy.com
Printed by FINIDR, s.r.o., Czech Republic, finidr.com

Front cover image: Turf Field in Ireland
Image credit: Tristan Hutchinson/Millennium Images, UK

New Island received financial assistance from The Arts Council (An Chomhairle Ealaíon), Dublin, Ireland.

New Island Books is a member of Publishing Ireland.

10 9 8 7 6 5 4 3 2 1

For my friend and agent, Jonathan Williams

So come my friends, be not afraid, we are so lightly here,
it is in love that we are made, in love we disappear.

Leonard Cohen, 'Boogie Street'

Contents

Introduction

The thing that first intrigued me about short stories – in the beginning O'Connor, O'Faolain and Lavin, borrowed from my parents' bookshelves; later Chekhov and Carver – was the sense of absence they brought, the inconclusiveness, the wonder of the unfinished. I've always thought of short stories as photographs. We see what we see, but what came before the moment and what follows the moment can only be guessed.

That sense of absence and want has been a huge part of my own stories – the missed opportunities, the empty chairs, the might-have-beens. Indeed, one of the stories in this selection is 'Absent Children', one of five stories with that title that I've written over the years. This may stem, in part, from the loss of a number of my siblings, still-born children, buried at the bottom of our garden.

Selecting stories from collections that range back over more than thirty years has been difficult and intriguing. The stories speak for themselves but a short account of their roots may clarify some aspects for the reader.

The pieces I have chosen begin with the title story from my first collection, *The Fallen*. It's a tale inspired by a First World War headstone in the cemetery in Athy, Co. Kildare. Out of that one stone and that one name grew a story narrated by two voices, a story of love, loss and futility.

'The Unclouded Days' and 'Hewer' are from the same collection. Both are inspired by events in the area of south Kildare in which I grew up. The former began life as a stage play, based on real events from the 1930s. 'Hewer' grew out of a phrase thrown by a teacher at a fellow student in my schooldays.

The next three stories, 'The Things We Say', 'A Year of Our Lives' and 'Over the Rainbow', are drawn from my second collection. That book was written in the aftermath of the end of a marriage, a two-year period spent living alone in a cottage on the edge of Mullaghcreelan Wood – a time that also inspired my novel *Clare*. As with 'The Unclouded Days', 'Over the Rainbow' began life as a one-man play, but there were aspects of the character that didn't fit on stage, so I reworked the narrative as a long story. Often, the process of writing, rehearsing, rewriting and performing brings on the urge to find a new medium for a story – to expand (or contract) the work from play to story or story to play.

'Husband,' from *The River Field*, is a glance into a future that may await any of us. 'Laburnum' came from a dream – an imagined encounter in the garden of the Church of Ireland rectory in Castledermot. In that dream, I came face to face with my schoolboy nemesis, a teacher whose cruelty was often beyond words. This occurred in the shadow of the wonderful laburnum tree that reached across the rectory wall for years.

'Breathless' grew out of the tragic trail of disappearances of young women in a geographical triangle that touched on my home area. The four women in the story are not based on real people, but the ordinariness of their lives and the brutality of their disappearances are paralleled in the story. Again, this began life as a stage-play.

'The Low Terrace' takes its title from the colloquial name for the street on which I was born and grew up, Abbeylands in Castledermot. The story is a mixture of memory and imagination, an homage to the people among whom I grew, a retelling of aspects of our lives. Memory is a place I've often gone to for stories – reality fictionalised or reality remembered in memoir.

'Sacred Heart' was inspired by a walk my daughter and I took on a beach in North Carolina. It comes from my most recent collection, *Once We Sang Like Other Men* – a body of work inspired by the notion of retelling the stories of the twelve apostles in a contemporary setting and written in the shadow of my brother's death.

'Friends' is the only story in this book whose genesis is unclear, even to me. It began with a character and that character brought his own story – not one with which I was particularly comfortable but discomfort and dis-ease are wonderful and challenging places from which to write.

The final three stories, 'Resurrection', 'Absent Children' and 'My Beloved Son', are from *Once We Sang Like Other Men*. 'Resurrection' was inspired by the notion of a child taking the words of a priest literally and expecting the resurrection of his dead father, but it's also about that first call to short-story writing: the intrigue of the uncertain, the unsolvable mystery that can destroy a relationship.

'Absent Children' is a continuation of my fascination with the notion of childhood and absence, inspired, I believe, by the fact that three of my siblings died at birth and were buried in our garden, at some kind of peace. Their unbaptised state meant they were refused burial in sacred ground. But the story is also prompted by a period I spent house-sitting for friends in a dwelling on a river bank – a setting I found increasingly depressing and dangerous to my mental health. Landscape, mostly for the better, has always been a central part of my work – another character in stories. If we lose touch with the soil, we're lost.

When I wrote 'My Beloved Son,' I had a sense of the completion of a circle. It took me back to some of the work in my first collection and it seemed a fitting story with which to end the *Selected Stories* – everyman and everywoman coming face to face with the heartbreak. As Jackson Browne wrote in his song 'For a Dancer,' 'in the end there is one dance you'll do alone.'

John MacKenna
July 2021

The Fallen

For Frank and Breege Taaffe –
from whose home the Hannons went
to join the fallen

I wore a lavender skirt that night, a slate and brittle blouse. There is a lavender skirt thrown across the chair. A different skirt. Outside, the dark says autumn. A thick mist trembles into drops on the lead pipes. It pip pip pips the last few feet into the gutter in the yard. I turned from this same window on that night. A night in summer. I looked at what I appeared to be. I knew exactly what I was.

The road outside was just as quiet then as it is now. But that was a different quietness. That was the stillness of a summer evening as the gardens burst into a bloom of sound. The click of forks echoed, turning out the last settle of the deepest frost. A neighbour, borrowing, shouted, her voice rebounding from wall to wall along the gardens. Carts rasped in the alleyways as drivers backed and worked the loads of dung between the creaky gates. Girls with arms of precious roses hurried from place to secret place. The heels of love began to sound again. The heels of love were mine.

Here. I am here. Over here on the angle of the cobbled paths. Behind me the trains thunder. I despise the angle but I welcome the grass that is thick and long, cut once, perhaps, in eight or twelve seasons. I welcome that softness and the softness of her footsteps, unheard now by those she passes in the street. Her resolute body unseen. Her faint laughter reaching only me and my words are caught only by her. And, perhaps, by the other old soldiers grown tired in their graves. Men who still remember little things. Obscurities. The shining promise of a blade. The glisten of skin, caught, at last, after all the talk. The button blaze. The lightning smile.

Did we pay too much for the pleasures we got? The things that mattered then seem of no consequence any more.

What you want is my story.

My name is Mary Lloyd. I was born near Castledermot in the County Kildare on the seventeenth of June, 1890. I was the youngest daughter of three. My father was a farm labourer who could turn a pair of horses with a twist of his wrist and a cluck of his tongue. He cut and kept the ditches, weaving alder, sally, elder into fences every spring. He carted grain to Hannon's mill. He ploughed the acres pair by pair. We rarely saw him in the summertime, except in passing, when he'd lift us on the chest-nut backs and trot us to the road. My mother was a seamstress. Her customers left their cloth in a shop in the town and we collected it after school, carrying the bundles carefully, up and down Fraughan Hill.

By the time I was ready for work my sisters were mar-ried and gone. I travelled twelve miles to find something new. From the side of Fraughan, through Castledermot on a fair day. The cattle milled on Hamilton Road, dropping their thick necks to drink from the Lerr. Farmers and jobbers and huck-sters pushed and jostled on the Square. They glanced at me. I waited hopefully, for some remark, a whistle or a gesture. They were too busy with their money. I walked through Hallahoise, past the woods at Mullaghcreelan, by the gates to FitzGeralds' castle, on through Kilkea, Grangenolvin, to work in a bakery in Athy. I was sixteen then.

I did my work in bakery and shop. I danced. I sang. I walked with other girls on summer nights. Out past the pond at Bray and back the Castledermot road. Board dances and house dances marked the seasons of my life. I would dream men's tongues along my breasts, their lips about my nipples. I had my share of men. They had their share of me. I was twenty.

I'd see him in the street. Him and his wife. She was young. Almost as young as me. And hard. I could hear it in her voice when she spoke in the shop. They moved from Barrack Street to a cottage on the Dublin road, across from where I had my digs. I'd see him in his garden among the daffodils and dahlias. Everything in that garden had its place. The rows and lines reminded me of my father's garden, of his fields all ploughed and set. There were apples and cherries where the drunken bees hummed and fell. But it wasn't just a garden of lines. There were clumped and clustered flowers where you least expected them. They took you by surprise. And all the plants and slips in pots along the gravel near the door. All waiting to be sown or given out to people in the town.

I wonder where a passion like mine starts. How does it grow? Does it run in the blood or does it just get out of hand till it's beyond control? Is it like sap rising? Is it something that insists on being heard? I know it stares. It stares till the stare is returned. It flames until it burns its root and then it goes on burning. It outlasts time and place. I know all this because this passion for him carried me beyond any love I had accepted in the past.

I'd walk the roads I knew they'd be walking. I'd stay at home, miss dances with the other girls if I half-thought he'd be there burning twigs or leaves in late October. I'd talk to his wife for ages in the hope that he'd arrive. I'd stand at the gate and stare across at him. I knew how foolish I must look but I didn't care. I was twenty-two.

I'm Frank Kinsella. I was born in this town on the seventh of October, 1880. I was an only son. My father was dead by the time I was born. He was never talked about and I never saw any reason to enquire.

I left school at twelve and started work for the Lord Kildare. The FitzGerald of Kildare. I set my mind to like the work. I walked the six miles out and back. I did my work. I was never late and I never missed a day. I listened well to every word that I was told. I watched what the other gardeners did and I knew his garden backwards by the time I was sixteen. I knew every strain of apple; every pear along the castle wall; every breed of rose; every vine in the greenhouses. Azaleas, magnolias, hydrangeas. The cypresses, the oak, the ash, the elder and the clematis. There were winter mornings at Nicholastown when the frost was as thick as cream. There were evenings when the rain was like bamboo rods across my back on the straight beyond Grangenolvin.

I'd salute Lady Nesta on the driveway. I'd stop to talk to Lady Mabel on her horse. I remember Lord Walter framed in the stable doorway with a light behind him like a golden blanket, soft and clean. It was Christmas time.

It was Christmas, too, when I met my wife. At a dance in the town hall in Athy. There she was in a crowd of girls. Her face was young and clear. It was like the light in the stable yard. And her hair was wild and brambled. She had a smile as bold as brass. We were married the following autumn. New suit, a ten-pound note and two days off. Lord Walter promised to put in a word about a cottage on the Dublin road. He was as good as his word.

She was hard at times but so was I. I could swing a fist with the best of men on Barrack Street. But she could soften too.

If you asked me to name a time, I'd go back to a summer morning. It was four or five o'clock. We'd been to a dance somewhere near Baltinglass and we were freewheeling down from Mullaghcreelan. The light was just coming up and it was a warm morning. Sometime in the end of June. We weren't even tired after all the dancing and a ten-mile cycle. We were laughing as we reached the bridge above the Griese. We stopped and I lifted her onto the parapet above the river. I climbed down to pick a water iris from the bank. The river was down to a trickle and the bank was cracked and baked. I remember my boots made an impression on the mud. I looked up. She was perched above me. And then a man rode past, dismounted, pushed open a gate into a field and wheeled his bicycle across the grass. He had a small white box tied to the carrier. We watched until he disappeared into the ruins of a church. I climbed back up and handed her the irises. She dropped them slowly in the water and we watched them sail between the rocks and out of sight. Oh, she could soften too.

She never loved me the way I was in love with her but I accepted that. I saw this as how our lives were going to be. The same as everyone I knew. She could be soft but the softness disappeared and she had a habit of denying the memories I had. I'd remind her of things and she'd pretend to remember nothing. She'd be angry if I went on about it. I never understood how she could swear the past away. And once she started that, I knew I loved her as little as she loved me. I'd think to myself that she could change as much as she liked and so would I. But she should leave the past alone.

At times she'd say she was bored. Another time it was loneliness. 'You have the garden,' she'd say. 'The garden doesn't mean the same to me.'

One of her brothers would cycle in in the mornings and they'd cycle out together. After work I'd call to her father's house and collect her. Winter and summer she'd be there, curled up like a cat beside the fire. Once or twice, when it was raining, she said she'd stay. Then more and more I'd hear that story. 'You go on,' she'd say. 'There's no sense the two of us getting wet. I'll stay the night.'

Never once was I asked to stay. She never suggested it and her father and brothers made no move. I knew they'd never have me sleeping under their roof. As far as they were concerned, she was still one of them. I'd go home and walk around the garden. I remember one wet spring evening in particular. I walked around and around the cottage, up and down every path. There was a fine rain falling and there was a yellow light from the sun over the Laois hills. Around and around I walked. Other times I'd check the potato pits or heel in cabbage plants. I'd smoke a pipe. Some nights I'd sleep there in the chair. I'd wake at two or three and toss another sod on the melted flames. In the end the winter won. The blankets burnt with a better heat. I could imagine then.

She came some Saturdays. I'd arrive and find her there. The house would smell of bread and her. The hearth would be swept. I always kept it swept but this was in a different way. More complete. The windows would be open and the washing done, flying a flag of possibilities. She'd stay till Monday. I'd begin to tell myself the past was past. And then I'd find her gone again. I'd say nothing and neither would she.

Sometimes, I think, she was on the edge of touching me. I don't mean touch. I don't mean tease or sting. She was on the edge of explaining what was there or what was missing. Or so I thought. I never could be sure.

One Wednesday, the end of April, I drove a cart into the town to collect some seed from the railway station. I saw her father and her brothers at our gate. They had her dresses and her coats across their bicycles. One of them was coming down the path, his arms spread out. He had a mirror and a picture in them. They knew I saw them and they stood like frozen cattle, watching me. I jigged the horse and carried on.

She came to see me once after that. One evening of that week. We talked about nothing. She walked the garden with me. She was full of chat about the flowers and the plants. She'd touch my sleeve. She'd sweep the hair back from her face and stare at me, a thing she hadn't done for months. She was a girl full of courting tricks again, except I knew she wasn't. There was nothing to it. She was safe. Her bits and bobs were gone by then. She was as safe this last time as if it had been her first. And then they came to bring her home.

I'd meet her on a Sunday, safe between her brothers, on the steps after Mass. The way they carried on, you'd think I was something to be afraid of. As if by then I even cared.

The whole town knew. I'd hear it in the bakery and in the shop. Every tongue had a different twist. It was because of this or that. Because he wouldn't touch her. Because he never stopped. There were always two sides at least, and every side was talked about and twisted. It wasn't that she was telling anyone. She'd still come into town but she talked as much to me as anyone and there was never a word about him or them. And he never talked. I never saw him talk to anyone. But that didn't stop the hints. By May the whole town knew.

What could I do? I was caught. Marooned. Too soon to try to make a bridge but the gap cried out for me to fill it.

Through May his garden stayed untouched, and then one evening after rain I saw him, scythe in hand, the nettles crashing from the ditch. The drops reared up and shone in every light. His sockets were still and his arms moved in them, floating rather than flapping. His head was half bent. His body was as hard as granite. I leaned across our gate and stared at him. Every now and then the blade would catch the stony wall and rasp and spark. Then it swished the wet and stinging greenery. I could hear the clean, flailing sound as clear as water. He was silent in his work; each swing was measured as he worked along the garden, never going back, the nettles laid as neat as corn across the grass.

I loved him then, by Christ I loved him then.

I wanted those arms to disentangle themselves from the work of scythes, from whatever memories of pleasure or pain that kept them straight. And I didn't care what it was that had driven them apart. Too much pain. Too much demand. I could coax or satisfy. Listen, I wanted to shout, I'm not afraid of what the people think or what the people say. I've watched until I know the flex of every sinew in those arms. I know the stoop, the stretch, the walk, the watch.

My name is Mary Lloyd. I start my day at six. I try to meet you or to see you as I leave for work. I rarely do. I carry bread from bakery to shop. I think about you. I think, she's the one that left but it's me that you ignore. I've seen you talking to her, hung there between her brothers after Mass.

Frank Kinsella, my name is Mary. Mary Lloyd.

I'd drive the four-pronged fork into the bitter earth. I'd push the tines a foot below the soil. I'd stoop, as I had stooped all day, and then I'd lift and free the prisoner of a winter I'd allowed to drag itself into the summertime. I'd speed the rhythm gradually. I'd thrust, then push, then stoop, then lift. And thrust and push and stoop and lift. And thrust, push, stoop, lift. Thrust, push, stoop, lift. I dug my way out of the past. I dug myself a shallow grave from which to breathe, in which to rest. I thrust and push and stoop and lift and then I hear this voice that frightens me because it seems to come from nowhere.

'My name is Mary Lloyd.'

'I know your name.'

'Tomorrow is my birthday. I'll be twenty-three.'

I smile, I can think of nothing to say and so I smile.

'I'd like it if you'd walk with me. If you have nothing else to do.'

I smile again. I say, 'Of course.' I have no idea why.

My name is Mary Lloyd, I say, as I walk back from work. I hurry now along the cobbled street. I am anxious to be out of these working clothes. I brush the flights of flour from my hair as I walk. I smile at people. I want to stop and tell them about the possibilities and still I do not want to stop. I want to hurry. I nod and rush on past the Railway Bar, across the bridge, out by the manse and through the yard into the house. I prepare myself. I wear a lavender skirt. My blouse is a slate and brittle grey.

We walk across the town. I don't care who looks or what they say or what it means. Neither, I'm sure, does he. I talk. It is uneasy talk but I go on talking and he laughs. Sometimes he smiles but his smile is as uneasy as my talk. Mostly he laughs. I can recall every moment of that walk.

We go on walking several nights a week. On Sundays we cycle out between high ditches. He calls for me. Comes and stands at the gate. Leaning across his bicycle, he talks to the woman of the house. He says goodnight at that gate. And sometimes, when I am early, I stand at his gate. Once he invites me in to smell the roses by the wall.

The summer passes. What do I notice? Fifty factory girls are burnt alive in England. I read about them in the newspaper. They are not me. I notice his garden. I notice how his face will cloud and clear. I notice her whenever she's about. She smiles at me in the shop.

I travel home one Saturday to see my sister's child. I travel back on Sunday afternoon. I ride in a sidecar to Kilkea and walk the rest of the way to be in time to meet him after tea. That evening we walk out past Lord's Island. We walk beyond the horse bridge, across the fields along the Carlow road. We perch on a half-built cock of hay and gradually slide until our backs are resting on the scattered wisps. He talks and talks instead of touching me.

That night I notice the dahlias touched with rust inside his gate. Lying awake, his plant of stock outside my window, I think how I would relish sin. But he has been so rigid in his hard, red boots. His collar starched and done. I wish that I could dance the seven veils. I think about how he went on talking while the possibilities narrowed and shrank with the light.

Walking back along the railway line, he'd told me. I remembered word for word.

'She never loved me the way I was in love with her but I accepted that was how our lives were going to be.'

I waited for the rest. I waited for the recognition that I knew he had to have. If he couldn't put the words in place, if he couldn't give, at least he had to recognise what I was telling him with every gesture. I waited for him to say she had never loved him the way he knew I did. I lay and smelt the stock in the blue-black night. I imagined his tongue on mine, his fingers travelling between my thighs, his lips collapsing on my skin. In the end I knew there was a depth of pleasure and I knew as well that he'd never say that kind of thing. Not this side of whatever grave he'd already dug. Was that to be our only bed?

I envied her her passion.

If she'd talked of it. If she had put some shape on it. If she had turned to touch. I talked and talked in the hope that she'd grow tired of my talk and, despairing of ever kissing me, kiss me then.

I envied her her passion.

If she had skirted it. If there had been a breath. I strained and strained to say something. To move. To step out of that grave. I tried at night to put the whole thing into words. I wanted to unhook the lust from its silent pier. But then, I thought, I know nothing about that sea. What am I? A silent inland walker, scrabbling for some other words to say the words for me.

One morning I went and sat on the low wall at the road. I measured the steps that would take me to her window. I counted the possibilities. I decided on bringing her to my house. I rehearsed the possibilities. I went back inside and lay down and felt her touch in my own. I felt the possibilities seep away.

But I envied her her passion.

I thought the smell of stock must smother her in what I felt for her. Did it not tell you everything, Mary? Mary Lloyd.

I envied him his strength.

Never mind the strength to work all day and then to work on through the night. I envied him his strength to take whatever came. To let her go when she decided she was gone. And I envied him not taking what was there of me. He could have done at any time. He need never have asked. I envied him that. In spite of everything, he must have known that I was his. I envied him his strength and damned him into hell for it.

I looked at him and saw a blind and stumbling plough horse. I thought of how my father turned his horses with a twist but I couldn't turn him any way. He was too heavy to ignore. Too set to change his ways. His boots were like brown lead feathers. His eyes were set on the end of some long drills that stretched like graves and graves and graves.

I envied him his strength, but Christ, I wished that he could sense the lust, the passion trapped in every breath I drew. Could he not feel it in my fingers; hear it in my darkest gasp; smell the smell of love that frightened me with its strength? Could he not untie the harness and touch me, just this once? Could he not take some lessons from the songs he hummed or from the thoughts his body sowed in me?

I waited.

We talked about the earliest dead who had fallen in France. They were not me.

After the harvest, after apple picking, he kissed me and I eased his hands about my body. He talked about breaking from the pier. I didn't understand but urged his fingers on. He was changing, becoming another man. I thought about the curves of his body and the curves of mine. I thought of this in the early frost, hurrying to work. I thought of it in the warmth of the shop. I gave myself to it. I drew his tongue between my lips and refused to let him go. When his touch was not enough, I touched with him. I no longer cared about the smile his wife carried. I smiled myself.

Sometimes we talked about the names we'd heard. About the dead swept back on a tide of blood at Mons. About floundering sailors from the *Cressy* and the *Hogue,* sucked into the icy sea. I felt the blood pumping like water in a millrace. I felt his mouth suck my breasts between his lips. My blood drove towards one moment; all day it drove towards the moment of release.

And then he told me he was going. I asked him why. It seemed too simple to ask that question but I had the right to ask him why. I had nothing else to say. He just smiled. A wry smile. A mirror of his smiling wife? I knew then that when we'd touched we'd hardly touched at all.

Mons, Ypres, Paris. What had these to do with me?

Nothing. And nothing to do with me. They were places where things were clear. In a minute of foolishness I had told her part of what I thought. If I went, there was some chance the past would change here the way it was changing everywhere else. I had this vision of coming back and finding my wife gone, dead, something unforeseen. Something would happen that could never happen while I was here. I believed that. She looked at me when I said that. There was something of that other, brassy look. There was no anger. Just sadness.

Nothing will change unless you change. We could go and live in another place. There's nothing here that I can't live without. I'd be happy out of here. And I have no need of rings or churches or words. None. I could gladly go without them all. You've never changed. Your wife won't be gone. She won't be dead. But there are other things that could die. Will die. Things are changed already. Why? I have the right to ask you why.

For once I thought that touch instead of words would stop the questioning. We were under the chestnut. It was raining. If I was to tell her why, what would I say? I had no idea why. It might be to escape. Or to evict. My fingers moved with ease, my tongue was sure. The rain dripped in a great circle from the widest branches while we lay in their umbrella. There was no escape. Her breath quickened and then became a question. Why?

There were other mouths that called me traitor from the corners of the street, from black doorways, from the market crowds. I never raised a fist. I ignored the mouths I could have bruised or broken easily. But I felt no satisfaction knowing how they longed for pain and were denied it by my fists hanging limp. If there was a betrayal, it had happened a long time ago.

I had no interest in the tunic or the buttons or the guns. They were part of a cause. I wasn't going for a cause. I wasn't going out of reason but out of hope.

What did I hope? That if I went I'd come back a different man. If nothing had changed, at least I would have changed. And coming back, I'd find the same woman.

But did I believe? I believed that she'd remain. But her question dimmed and quenched the hope.

'Do you believe in everything you've said?'

'I believe you will remain.'

'What else do you believe?'

I'll tell you now. I've said it often enough to myself. I'll tell you now. I believe in the beauty of your breasts, in the form of your shoulders, in the sickle of your thigh, in the ease of your hands, in the power of your eyes, in the fury of your hair, in the storm of your whisper, in the passion of your thought.

'Do you believe in everything you've said?'

'No. I don't believe in me. My past is a nightmare. I have never told you that. First there is penance. Then sleep. Then this dream.'

'Is that the truth?'

Part of the truth. The truth has nothing to do with us. The truth has all to do with me. Everything we have done has been true. The places have always been true for me – fields, gaps in ditches, trees that were one way in winter and one way in spring. Ways that you lay or laughed or walked. Ways I prepared for meeting you. These have all been true. There's no question about these. But I have no answer about why. No answer for myself, much less for you.

'When you smile your mouth reminds me of your wife's.'

That might be what you see but that has nothing to do with the truth.

'I saw no hope.'

I told no one until the thing was settled but already they knew. I gave my notice. Lord Walter asked me to think again. He said there were people he knew and then he said the job would keep.

I put straw on the pits. I got my uniform. I tied the last of the dahlias. Collected my wages. Cycled down the castle avenue without looking right or left. At home I washed in the starry yard, put on my uniform and called for her. I walked to her door and knocked. The stock was still in flower. They asked me in and ignored the uniform. We walked across the town and back. Sat on the low wall until Sunday came.

The night before he left we danced at the town hall. Sneering, I said, 'Why don't you wear your uniform tonight?' For once I saw the pain and it frightened me. I drew back from saying any more, afraid I might have said too much. What did we do? We danced every dance while the music was playing. The music of fiddle, melodeon, piano and drum. We swung with the crowd without hearing the music. I was stunned by the speed with which certainty had arrived. Danced to the waltzes when the waltzes were playing, nodding at faces that passed in the crowd. There was Robert MacWilliams and Christopher Power, faces that passed as we swung around. He kept his distance but this moment of passion lasted as long as the music was playing. And then the music stopped. The faces grew voices, the movement was over and bodies jostled towards the cloakrooms. We were part of the crowd again. Faces smiled. Mouths dribbled short ashy cigarettes. I handed in my ticket, took my coat and put it on before we walked down the stairs. Stepping out into the night, I felt neither cold nor warmth. Loud men shouted in Emily Square, peeling their bicycles from the layers against the wall. Girls laughed and waited, uncertain whether to go or stay.

We walked up Offaly Street towards the park. The cold, hard park with its shiny brown bark and its thinly frosted grass.

'Would you not bring me home this once?' I said.

'What did you say?'

'Would you not bring me home? This once.'

I brought you … home.

Instead of passion there was panic. He saw how easy the whole thing could have been. How simple. But he dared not recognise it. Too late for that. And I dared not say anything. Isn't that the way it was that night? Whatever our bodies did, no matter how easily, could have been done much better a thousand times after that. And whatever it was that they failed to do could be changed if there was time and ease. They did their work. The sweat of terror made the bodies slide together. It might have smelt of ecstasy but we were terrified. Our bodies ground on because it meant we had nothing to say and less time to think. And he was thinking, as I was, how this might have happened before and how easily it could have been another day on which we'd rise and go to work and come back home and go to bed. Had I not said all that? The truth was evident but there was no place for it now. I stayed and watched him dress. Had this been some kind of sweet, pale honeymoon?

We walked to the station. Him in his uniform. Me in my dancing dress. There were others there in their regalia. Their wives and sweethearts dressed for the day.

Mick Lawlor. William Wall.

I kissed him then. There on the top platform outside the stationmaster's house. We leaned against the iron footbridge and kissed. He saw, again, how easy life can be. His body hard between my twisted skirts. Until the train began to move.

Outside the station, in the silence after he had gone, I heard somebody whistle, a young shop boy on his bicycle. A song the band had played the night before: *Night and the stars are gleaming, Tender and true; Dearest! my heart is dreaming, Dreaming of you.* The walls closed in. I saw the throng. I smelt his sweat and I heard the music clearer than when it played. Every sense I'd stifled came alive. His smell, his touch, his taste flowed from every pore and left me sick.

I woke up. It was another day. I had to work. I realised he had gone. I dressed and walked to the shop. Where was he now? Still in Dublin? Halfway across the sea? Somewhere in England? Certainly no further than that. I expected him to come lumbering into the shop, embarrassed, saying he had talked with Lord Walter and things had been worked out. He was going back to gardening. He was looking for a cottage in Kilkea. It might take time but then we'd move.

I was in the bakery when one of the girls called to me. There was a man in the shop wanting to talk to me. I recognise him. Noel Lambe. He says Frank has left a key with him. He'll be keeping an eye on the cottage – sleeping there now and again. He's to give me anything I want. I'm to go there any time I want. I can stay there if I like. That's what he's been told to tell me. I have only to let him know. Any time. All as matter of fact as that.

I carry bread from bakery to shop. I chat. I clean the windows in the street.

I wake up. It's another day. I have to work. I wait and wait.

Little things that never bothered me before begin to bother me now. The weight of these boots. The way the collar scuffs my neck. The task of writing and what to say and how to say it.

'We have arrived here safely and we are training. It's not as bad as you might think. I suppose Noel told you what I said about the house. Whatever is there that you might want is yours to take.'

I don't mention moving in. I try to come to that from several ways but I can't.

I sit out in the barrack yard and try to think of other things to write. I look at the nail of moon caught on the edge of a hawthorn bush. Beyond it the lake water is dark. Darker than the Griese. But the thorn reminds me of a turn on the castle avenue. This is England. That was home. I start thinking of fields. I think of how she nested in the hollows of my body. I think of how I wound my arms around her and nested in the hollows of her body. Her breast was in the hollow of my hand. There was a particular smell from her hair. Maybe of apples or rain. I started to say that to her and then some people passed and we went back to our bicycles and she tossed my hair with her fingers.

I don't mention any of this in my letter. This has happened. She knows that. Why write it? I tell her the food is good and the lads here are a decent crowd.

I wake and it's another day. I walk to work. I stop at his gate and notice that Noel has scuffled all the weeds. They lie in neat piles along the edge of grass. Today he will come and burn them.

I wake. This is not another day.

We cross the English Channel. It's not as bad as people say. They tell us Ypres was the worst but they tell us too that English, Irish, Germans, sang together at Christmas time. I write and tell her this.

'A happy, happy New Year.'

I am surprised at what I've written. I leave it so.

I wake and it is spring. The snow melts into isolated spots of snowdrop. The crocuses in purple-yellow dot the ground around the apple bark. And then it snows again in wintry narcissi. The evenings lengthen, carts of dung arrive from the countryside and back between the creaking hinges of town gates. Young girls I last saw as children walk with boys, out the Dublin road to Ardscull and back.

And then it is summer. I tend his garden in the evenings. Noel comes and cuts the grass. The roses rear above the walls, sweet pea rambles across the gable. I wash and clean the floors. I open drawers and find his shirts in neat lines. They smell of winter. I hang them on the line and it gives me pleasure to see them threshing in the warm wind. I leave them out overnight and tell myself as I walk to work that he is home. I almost see the smoke from his chimney. That evening I fold the shirts and put them back inside their drawers.

Noel comes and limes the walls. We sit in the kitchen talking. The sun seems caught on the hills of Laois, unable to sink. It throws a long bolster of light across the table. I ask Noel if he knows why he went. 'If you don't know, no one does,' he says. His words give me some feeling of closeness to Frank. I know what he says is true. If I don't know, he doesn't know himself. And it doesn't matter, anyway. All that matters is that next summer the three of us will sit here and then the pair of us.

His letters come. I write to him. I read his words.

We heard a story down the line today about two blokes who were sentenced for desertion. They were strapped to the wheels of a gun and shot. I don't write about that kind of thing. We hear these stories, we talk about them, but I don't write of that. I write and say things are going well. I say the weather is improving. I am glad to hear the garden is doing well and glad about the lime. The cottage needed that. I mention people I know, fellows I've met – Larry Kelly and Stephen Mealy.

In April we were at Ypres. The gas crept like stink from a tomb. We passed these men lying in the grass. Their eyes were bandaged. We could hear their screams long after we had lost sight of them. Somebody said, you can't fight that bastard gas. I didn't write of that.

I remember the autumn by its fruit. I picked the low apples. Noel climbed for the high. I came home one afternoon and found a basket left at my digs, a basket of pears sent from the castle. I walked with the other girls on October Sundays. To Bert Bridge, to the Moat of Ardscull.

At Christmas I went home to Fraughan Hill. The house smelt of damp timber and the fire shot sparks across the stone floor. I told my mother about Frank. She smiled and said nothing. On the morning I left she said, 'You'll be all right.'

We had an Easter of daffodils. They trembled and shivered. I picked some and put them in a vase on his table. I left them there, even when the petals nodded, frizzled, stumbled and fell. I left them for a very long time.

There were other things I didn't write about. I met this chap with his fingers cut so deep that they hardly seemed to be a part of him. I asked him how this happened: stretcher bearing. No stretchers left. He and the others carried the wounded on sheets of corrugated iron. He lost the use of his hands but he went on carrying with stretcher sacks tied around his neck. He told me he had carried a man two miles to the medic. Already there were thirty or forty bodies surrounding the trestle table where he worked. Still men, men screaming. The medic worked on, his vest blood-soaked. The bodies came and went, the dead and the dying. The rest were shipped further back.

The funerals begin. In the afternoon the shop shutters bang. Small cards with scrawled words appear all over the town, on doors in Barrack Street, in Leinster Street, around the Square.

I break the last branch of bloom from his lilac tree and take it home. The scent fills my room for three nights and then the bells fall apart.

One afternoon while we were marching, very close to the front, we saw a horse galloping towards us. His innards were trailing like a second tail. Then these men appeared. They came in twos and threes, the walking wounded. They came without rifles, many of them shirtless. They reminded me of people I had seen at gravesides, people deep in shock. They ignored us and went on walking, sometimes linking like drunken men on the Barrow Bridge, stupefied beyond recognition. Further along the track I saw a piece of flesh. I recognised it. Torn from the horse's belly. We went on marching.

Later, lying in a trench, waiting for the whistle, I thought about all this and then I thought of her. I knew then I would write and tell her everything – but first about the horse, the wounded, the raving mad.

His laburnum flowers fall, their golden rain scattering the grass. I get more letters from him now, full of the things he sees, the things he smells, the sounds of shells and guns and human voices. He tells me everything.

'My darling, Last week, Sunday I think, we came upon this village. It's hard to believe but it's still in one piece. It was raining when we marched in, far back from the lines. A bit like Ballitore on a wet evening. No one about. Four of us went to this little café place and sat there drinking wine. We stayed there while it got dark. You get used to wine. It's nothing like the pint of stout in Maher's but better than a lot of things I've drunk out here.

'There was this woman behind the counter. She sat there the whole afternoon and evening. She was sewing. When it got dark she lit a lamp and I could have sworn she was you. I know what you're thinking, so much for all this wine, but I swear, with the light and the colour of her hair, it could have been you. I was just sitting there watching her, and thinking to myself that I've forgotten a lot about you. About the way you look.

'The clearest memories I have are of the parts of you I saw the least. Your face only came back to me in her face and hair in the light of the lamp. You must get a photograph taken and send it to me. Then I can remember all of you. Like I say, there's parts of you I have no trouble remembering at all.

'I know what you're saying to yourself – this fellow is getting very forward.

'I've been thinking, too, about the things I'm looking forward to going back to. I made a list of them the other day. November mornings cycling out to Kilkea was the first. And then the blossoms in the castle yard. And summer evenings coming in the road when the cuckoo is raising a row in the fields. These are going to be the same as they always were. I've noticed that. No matter what changes for me over the years, no matter what sort of time I'm going through, these things always keep their magic for me.

'There's other things that will never be the same. And the things between us, they'll never be the same, only better.'

I went down to Carlow to have that picture taken. It was a Wednesday afternoon, a half-day in Athy. I took my bicycle and went alone. I was put standing in front of a tree painted on canvas.

I spent one night in a shell hole, out in no-man's-land. The artillery went on firing, the thunder never stopped. I lay there with my companion, a dead machine gunner.

When I got the photograph I put it in an envelope and sent it off to him with a letter I had written but would never dare to read.

'My dearest Frank, I've had the photograph taken and I enclose it here. I cycled to Carlow to have it done. The man there was very nice. He said all the girls are having it done. I went down on my birthday. Imagine, I am twenty-six. The photograph came on the train this evening and I collected it on my way home. I shouldn't say this, but I like it. I hope you do too. Is this the way you remember me or the part of me you've forgotten?

'It's terrible to hear what you have told me about the war. Everything is quiet here now. Sometimes I think the worse the things you write about, the better it is. I feel nothing will happen to you while these things are in your letters.

'Every week now some house in the town has a black ribbon on the door and the telegram boy from the post office is dreaded when he appears in any street.

'After I read your letter, your last letter, I laid it out on the bed in your room and took off all my clothes and stood in front of your mirror and looked at myself. I was thinking of how little we've seen of one another's bodies and thinking about what you said about being different. I think you're right. But I was thinking, too, that the braver and bolder you get in your letters, the harder it is for me to be any way bold in mine. And to think I was the one who was always wishing you'd do those things to me when we were out walking the Carlow road. Now I can only wish you were here to touch and kiss me the way I know you're thinking when you write your letters. You have so little time and I have all the time in the world. Don't worry, I was on my own in the house when I did that.

'I wait every day for your letters. I keep them all. I think, sometimes, you must be out of the war, the way you write such long and lovely letters. Everything here is waiting for you. Noel has the garden in fine order. The house is shining inside and out. I've painted the gate bright red. I hope you won't mind that. Everything is ready – the house, the garden, me, my body. Everything is waiting for you.

'I love you.'

I heard of a stretcher bearer who went out seven times yesterday. Each time he brought back a wounded man. The eighth time he was killed.

'My darling, I was thinking today about all the flowers I've put in that cracked jug on your kitchen table since you went away. Crocuses and snowdrops; lilacs and dog daisies and cornflowers and roses; water irises and wallflowers and dahlias now. I've picked them everywhere. Out the Barrow line, at Mullaghcreelan and Ardscull. In your garden and along the roadside out past Bray. I even brought a spray of fuchsia from Fraughan Hill.

'I wonder what flowers will be in it when you come home. Whenever it is, even in the depth of winter, I'll have flowers in it for you.'

We push to a new front line. For a time there's relief. Something new promises, but then this line, these trenches, become the same as all the others. We have been in them before or someone else has. Our lines weave. Here we are at the front line, a mile away some other uniforms are moving cautiously.

There are always stories here. New stories come with every telegram. With every corpse a story comes. One week there are four men from Barrack Street, four doors with black ribbons, eight windows with the curtains tightly drawn. Schoolchildren walk from the other end of the town to gawk. They have never seen so much death before.

I begin to fear for something. It seems there is nothing to stop this rush of dying, nothing to say the next black ribbon won't be fastened to his door. I have to get away. I leave early and travel with Noel, on his cart, to Castledermot. I walk from there. I stop to throw a penny into the Lerr at Hamilton Bridge. I wish for luck and life. For him.

Near the top of Crop Hill I meet my father taking a horse down to the forge. I walk with him. A shire horse. Brandy.

'This is the heaviest horse we've ever had,' he says. 'And he's as quiet as a lamb. Do you remember Bess when you were small? I used to put you on her back.'

I remember. Black, brown, grey and bay with a star on her forehead. 'She'd be nothing to this fellow,' my father says. 'Skin and bone.' The huge feather-feet fall as lightly as a bird's. The horse steps daintily until we reach the open forge. I stand and wait. I rename the bits of harness that my father taught us all: the cheekpiece, the blinker, the brow-band, the peak, the haims, the pad, the loin strap, the crupper strap, the quarter strap, the breeching strap, the bellyband, the girth, the trace bar, the rein, the bit, the noseband. I have remembered every one. I repeat them to my father and he and the blacksmith clap. The horse turns and shifts uneasily.

Walking back, my father questions me, as he did when we were children.

'Would you give a horse a long drink, now, after a hot day's work?'

'No.'

'And which comes first, the food or drink?'

'The drink.'

He laughs. 'You remember well, I taught you well. I doubt your sisters would remember the half of it.' And without pausing he says: 'What about this chap of yours?'

I tell him almost everything, but not the important things.

'You'll find it hard, the two of youse, when he comes back. Things like that are all very well until they look like being permanent. Can you deal with that? The sneers and the priest coming twenty times to your door? That'll be the easiest part. Have you the stomach for all that? Has he?'

'We have now,' I say. 'He mightn't have had a while ago, but we both have now.'

'Well,' my father says, 'if you're bent on staying with him and if the pair of youse are in love, you'll be all right. You've nothing to worry about in your mother nor me.'

I laugh and say: 'Doesn't news travel fast?'

'Faster than you'd think,' he says, and we walk on laughing and I'm so happy that I've come back here.

I get back to Athy on Sunday night. I sit in your kitchen and put things in order in my mind. You have my photograph. I have your house. Your wife has nothing. I smile.

The summer passes. Every weekend I walk or cycle some place. Sometimes with Noel, sometimes with girls from work, sometimes on my own. I walk around Kilkea a lot. There and in your house is where I find it easiest to be with you. I talk to you all the time. I take plants from the fields and tell you what they are. I point the differences between the spear thistle and the creeping thistle. This is the evening primrose and this is the hawk's-beard. My father told me those. There are places where I can talk to you and say things I may never say to your face.

The summer ends and then the autumn.

I never wonder at his luck in being alive. I believe he will never die. Always he has some stories in the post of death, of bravery, of miracles.

'We went back to that village, to that café I wrote about. The woman is still there. She hasn't changed. She hasn't aged. She wore a brighter blouse this time. I took it as a sign. I have to laugh to think that someone like me, who never looked up from the ground, is seeing signs. And out here of all places. But I believe that nothing that has happened – no torn limb, no frantic horse, no soldier screaming, no shell that leaves me in an open grave with corpses all around – can come between us.

'The woman in the café lives, she dresses brightly, she smiles, I suppose she loves. All this a few miles from the front. She is the same as she was and so are you.'

'I have to write to tell you this. Today in the shop some women were talking about someone they'd heard was killed. One of them turned and said: "And how's your Frank?" I could have cried. "Your Frank." I laughed and said you were fine, that you'd be all right.

  'And this woman said: "Of course he will, hasn't he you to come home to? Why wouldn't he be?" I think that was the happiest minute of my life. And you do have me. And I have you. And every night now I leave a space for you beside me and every morning I wake up in your space.'

The summer has passed and the autumn. Sometimes I wonder at my luck at being alive, at escaping without a scratch. Sometimes I am convinced I will never die.

His letters come. I find them on the windowsill in the hall when I get home from work. The envelope is always fat and full of paper, sometimes a dried flower that I put into a book I keep. Sometimes I send a pressed flower back. But never one from his garden. Always wild flowers.

'Today is my birthday. I'm writing this in a garden or what remains of it. It's a garden on the edge of a town and it looks down across a valley. It's like looking out from the clear patch on the side of Mullaghcreelan, down across the castle and the houses in Kilkea. But here there's no village, just a clear valley of fields, without a tree. There's a river in the bed of the valley, as wide and cool as the Griese.

'I was here last spring when the place was paved with flowers. I prefer it now. It has the bite of home. We're billeted here but I've taken my blanket out into this garden to sleep. You get used to sleeping under the sky but here it's quiet. If the wind blows right, there isn't even a muffle of the guns.

'Lying under a tree at the end of the garden, I remember nights when we were out the Barrow line and, strange enough or maybe it isn't, I remember our last night. Our only night inside. My only regret is that the nights were too few and the distance seems so far. But not too far. This is the quietest, the happiest birthday of my life.

'I love you.'

I carried that letter to work with me and read it in the yard when things were quiet. I carried it home and that evening I went and sat in the room where we had lain and I read it and read it again. I wanted to write something like that but now, at such a distance from him, I could feel his passion flowing and mine was drowned.

'I've been thinking hard about things, now that I have the chance to. I thought maybe it was the great hate that made everything seem in its right place. But that can't be it because there's little or no hate here. None of us feels hate for whoever is behind the big guns. We feel panic sometimes and we feel helpless for men who are dying in the dark, men we can hear shouting and can't reach, and we feel disgust at what the human body can look like, but we feel no hate. I've never felt as free of hate. I think it's the pain all around us that makes other feelings so important. That's what it is – the pain.

'Then the other feelings are more important than they were. You see a man get hit. You see the blood draining out of him the way we'd drain a lake. You see the life going with it. You look, when you have the time, and you see these things. You see a skin disappear and another one replacing it. You know the man is changing in a way you never get to understand but you recognise the change. It can happen as sudden as a dam bursting or it can be as slow as a summer evening. But you know death is coming on, it's like a mist. You see it and you don't. And you think about the other things that are draining out of this man. The love he wanted to talk about. And you realise there's no other time than the time we have now. You are in a trench and as fast as anything you're somewhere else.

'I'm back with you on the haycocks out the Carlow road or in a field at Mullaghcreelan but this time I don't talk on and on. This time I kiss you and touch you and I forget the shells and the bullets and the mist that's always hanging over us.'

I read his letters. I keep them till I've finished my meal and then I take them across to his cottage and I read them in his room. I sit in his kitchen and write these letters in my head, letters I've been making up all day at work. Letters about the parts of me he barely touched. I write about the feelings and when he must do these things and how. But when it comes to writing the letters down, putting them on paper, they seem foolish. They never seem to have the ease of his.

And so I write: 'Everything here is as it was. Noel has all your apples in. They're laid out on the scullery floor on sheets of newspaper. The ones that weren't ripe are in the kitchen window. They catch whatever sun there is and I come and check on them in the evening.

'Noel laughs and says I should move in altogether and be done with it. The girls in work laugh, too, when I talk about you. "You're twenty-six," they say. "You'd better settle down. Get the house and then he'll have to take you!" I laugh at that. I think I'll wait. Do you want me to wait? Will it be as easy when you get back here?'

I ask the question more of myself than him but I am pleased when his answer comes in a torrent of words I wish he had used when he was here. His words explore each part of me.

'I want you to know these things. I came out here to take stock, to gather strength for going back. I have no fear of that. I don't care about the mouths that mouth. I care for our mouths and for the way they meet each other. For the way they meet strange parts of the body and don't find them strange at all.

'If a man here can be twisted, be hung from a stump or blown onto the top of a wall and left for days, he loses his life. We lose our respect for the unimportances. We put this aside and carry on surviving and when this war is over, we'll put it aside and return to living.

'For me that means going back to the castle, cycling out in all weathers, working hard. It has nothing to do with what people say.

'For me it's getting back to the cottage. It has nothing to do with where the cottage is.

'For me it means my body and yours – the dry smell of your hair, the wet smell of me in you, the dark smell of the shadows your breasts make in the lamplight, the clean smell of us standing naked together wherever we want it to be. None of this worries me because I've been doing this for the last months, years, and so, I know, have you. We know each other's bodies. They will meet like friends and lovers who don't hesitate. They will find their way without more than the slightest touch to guide them.'

When I touch, my touch is of his hands.

'The thing I miss, apart from you, is trees. I'd love to climb a tree again and feel the particular way a tree is. There are no trees where we are now, only the occasional stump.

'I feel myself growing surer each week. I see men that we buried reappear. These are men without legs. Men whose heads are found elsewhere. I see men running, men I know to be dead. They go on running in the smoke, their faces dead. They fall eventually but by then the life is gone out of them. I see a man running on one leg. For a long time he thinks there are two and he goes on running perfectly. And then he sees and he falls, crying, and we leave him there. We go on running because we have two legs under us and we want to keep them there.

'We rest against a parapet of flesh, of men gorged each into the next. I hate all these things – the shells, the gas, the buried and unburied dead – but it's the rain, puddled, dammed and trapped in trenches that hurts the most. It seeps in through the boots, through the ankles and the knees. Joints ache. Coats, soaked and muddy, dry and melt and dry again. Fresh shell holes smell of powder and then of rain. The water appears like holy wells around our feet. It comes from nowhere. We hear of thousands, hundreds of thousands, dying. We see them. We see the enemy from time to time but I hate only the rain.

'The lists go up on every side.

'We find a pair of legs, their owner is running somewhere, running on into the smoke.'

'My darling, I have read and read your letter until every page is tattered from turning and carrying. I don't care to leave it anywhere that someone might see it, so I bring it everywhere with me.

'When I read where you had written about me being your wife, I stopped. It was like a dream. Had I been asleep and missed out on that? I wondered. And then I realised what you were saying and that was even better. You say that since the night when we slept here I have been your wife. For me I have been your wife since very early on.

'And when you wrote all those things you think about, I knew exactly how you felt and I did what you asked. It was a sunny afternoon and I cycled out to the bridge at Kilkea and crossed the two fields and lay in that place where you asked me to and I knew you were there. It was the way you wrote it would be.

'When you come back, that will be the first place we will go together. I love you more than everything and I often think that this war, this separation, was worth it after all because I know you're not gone.

'I love you, my darling. Mary Lloyd that now thinks of herself as Mary Kinsella.'

When we went forward we had blackened faces. It was night. We cut through wire. There were fewer flares than usual – a blessing. We came upon them suddenly, three young men, much younger than we were. They threw up their arms and we bayoneted them. Very little time to stop. We went through their uniforms. Then up and on across another no-man's-land. More muck, more sockets in the earth and legs and fingers pointing nowhere. Then up and on.

I thought I saw a level spray of bullets. I couldn't have but I thought I did. It started away to my left and neatly mowed through two of us. I was running, the other man was crouching.

It tore my legs from just above the knees, it shot his head away. His lungs released a flow of air, a belch out through his open neck and he went down.

I thought of how the pain was less than I expected. I thought of how passion seemed less possible without my legs. I tried to picture her pushing me about in some stiff chair, lifting me like a bladder onto our bed. I was a different man and the future took on a different sense; it drained of any colour.

I had suspected this all along. I could look now and weigh the options for myself. And I could go on looking because by then I was dead. My body was half-sitting, my open eyes stared straight ahead as my comrades raced by.

Of course the letter came to her. I could only laugh. And then they brought him home. She followed him along the street, between her brothers. He came in a box off the evening train, down past the shuttered windows and back again in the morning. Through the welcoming gates. She followed him and I followed to the top of the bridge and watched from there.

An army grave. She'd be buried with her own. I knew his grave was far too small. There was no crevice where I might knead my body between the earth and skin. I wished they'd left his bits in France. To have him lying at the head of the street while I pressed my naked self against the cold wet window as if he was there, out there, beyond it.

I set myself to live within the bounds that I had set myself. I turned myself on you but reaching back became a crime.

I have become content with naming things that marked our past, reverting to my former self: daffodil, wild violet, primrose, the cherry tree, bluebell, lilac, the golden rain, the marigold, the apple fruit, the rusting dahlias underneath.

His wife was there behind the hearse. One wife.

I saw no hope beyond the bounds that I had set myself and that is why I despise the angle now. I see the possibilities when they are gone.

If you can touch, then touch me now.

Daffodil, primrose, wild violet, the cherry tree, bluebell, lilac, the golden rain.

Across the street the laburnum bends, a kind of light.

The marigold, the apple fruit, the rusting dahlias underneath.

I press myself against the window and watch the ghostly danc-ers pass.

    Frank Alcock.
    Martin Hyland.
    John Byrne.
    Mick Lawlor.
    Willie Tierney.
    William Wall.
    Owen Kelly.
    Thomas Fox.
    Stephen Mealy.
    Joseph Hickey.
    Larry Kelly.
    Patrick Leonard.
    Martin Moloney.
    Robert MacWilliams.
    Martin Maher.
    Christopher Power.

Laurence Dooley.
Thomas Ellard.
Norman Hannon.
John Hannon.
Henry Hannon.
Thomas Hannon.
Frank Kinsella.
And Mary Lloyd.

I push my naked body through the glass and join the dismal dead who pass.

The Unclouded Days

My son drove me home from Dublin tonight. We talked for a while and then there was nothing to say. Not an uncomfortable silence, just nothing that needed saying and no need to say anything else. The doctor had nothing much to say either. Things were under control, he said. Meaning that things are lying low. That phrase struck me driving between Kilcullen and Castledermot. The moon had been lying low and then, quite suddenly, it had climbed high enough to sweep across the fields at Hobartstown.

'Drive on into Carlow and back the Mill Road?' I asked.

He nodded and we drove past the turn for our house and out the main Waterford road, on into Carlow and then we cut back across country and came at the village from a different direction.

The moon was well up by then and the fields were wintry pale, even though the night still had summer hanging in the westerly breeze. Big shadows ballooned from the trunks of chestnut trees. Not a cloud anywhere on the vast horizon. Just that magical light in the sky. What I'd have given to walk out across one of Emerson's fields, my shadow smoothing the ridges and drills before me. I could have done. I could have said to him to stop the car but I didn't. I sat back and watched the white light floating by. And then we were back here, at the house, and I was walking inside and my daughter-in-law was already wetting tea and my grandchildren were calling from their bedroom and I put the pale fields in the back of my mind because I was glad about this reprieve.

I have cancer of the throat. Not that you'd notice to look at me but it's there, working away like worms under the earth, and when it's ready I'll know, long before the visit to the doctor or the next bout of chemotherapy. I'll know. But for now, for tonight and tomorrow and the rest of this week, I'm still all right.

I'm lying back now in my own bed in my own room in this house I bought in nineteen forty-nine. I live here, with my son and daughter-in-law and my two grandchildren.

They've made great changes to the place, worked hard for what they've got. They broke out the back wall, went up a storey, built on three bedrooms and a bathroom. I have my own space. My own room. My own shower. I have privacy when I want it and company when I want it. The grandchildren, they're nine and five, come in and give me kisses goodnight.

I bought this house for the garden. It had grown wild by the time I moved in but I changed little, I loved its wildness. I cut back here and trimmed there and pruned in bits and pieces and, almost overnight, the garden John Wortley had made thirty years before was alive again. The house was secondary and it stayed that way until I married in the summer of nineteen fifty-two. After that the house came back to life.

I still look after that garden. A young chap from the village comes in to do the heavy work, digging and the like, but the rest is left to me. Fruit bushes, fruit trees, vegetables. I do all those. Last summer I put a swing in the branches of one of the plum trees, for the children, and I have a patch of grass at the far end, for them to play ball on; they love that.

On fine days I go out there and sit and read the paper. If the throat is up to it, I'll wander down to the gate and talk to people passing by on the road. They used to ask me did I not mind all the changes in the place. I'd say, why would I? There's many a man less sick than I am, many a man younger than I am, ended up in the County Hospital because no one wanted to look after him, I'd say. I'm glad to see the place alive and thriving, I'd say. I waited four years to buy this place and now my son and his wife and my grandchildren are here. That's worth more than keeping things the way they were. No point in looking back.

I was never one for that myself. The odd day I'd sit out in the garden and doze or the occasional night I'd lie here and drift back but not too often. And when I do, I think more about the important things that happened than about what I said or did. Mostly. Like, if I was to think back now, I'd say: last year, the Pope's visit; nineteen sixty-three, Kennedy's visit. That's how it would work.

Once in a blue moon I will go back, methodically. The Cuban missile crisis; the Emergency; the constitutional referendum. I lived through that and I can hardly remember a thing about it. I taught it for forty years, forty sets of young fellows and young ones, and it means nothing to me. With the exception of one thing. Summer of nineteen thirty-seven. One person. Alice Moynes. I suppose I was never a government man, never a church man, never even a history man really. More my own man.

Or was I? Last Good Friday, I sat out in the garden in the sun. I was just back home from hospital then, the first time in fifty-odd years that I wasn't in the church on that afternoon. I felt I'd won some kind of battle. After all that time. But despite it all – the church-going, the history-teaching, the political nonsense I listened to – I was still my own man. And I got more out of taking the grandchildren to the shop on a Friday, for that white chocolate they like, than I did from the serious business I was supposed to be an expert on.

Lying here, with the moon going down past Prumplestown, I'm happy. To hell with this growth in my throat and the new blocks in the bedroom wall and the fact that next week it might all be different. That doesn't worry me. And tomorrow I'll collect the children at ten past three and we'll walk back here together and I'll have the spuds washed and ready when half past four comes. And that gives me more satisfaction than names and dates and vicious politicians or dead soldiers in pointless ballads. Not that I don't remember anything. I do. Sometimes.

I never saw the point of wearing widow's weeds, dressing in black for all that time. A certain degree of respect, if that is the correct word, a public face on it – yes – but no point in taking the whole thing to extremes. You have your innings and then it's time to carry on and for others to carry on.

Independence is what I've valued most of all. Being able to do what I want to do when it pleases me. I enjoy people. Thoroughly enjoy them. But I enjoy my independence, too. It's something I've savoured from the moment I got it back. But then I was always rebellious, oh not openly so but the strain was always there. I don't know where it came from. Certainly it didn't come from my parents. But it was there, right from the start, running under things.

I was an only child but things were very strict for me. I had madly religious parents. Not that I didn't like them, love them. I did. I was extremely fond of them. But there were things I felt uncomfortable with, from as far back as I can remember. The claustrophobia of the thing. Not the family, of course, but the religious aspects. Not that I even knew, not as a teenage girl, why I felt as I did. It just seemed that as I grew I became more and more aware of the pointlessness of it all, of the religious wall we could neither climb nor break through.

There was the incessant hectoring of people. In the markets and fairs of towns. My father preaching and my mother sitting at a wheezy harmonium, belting out those hymns, some of them bloody awful. Most of them. Oh there were some pleasant ones, good tunes, and I did enjoy singing them. Sometimes I loved singing them. But mostly there was nothing else in the whole farrago for me. I could see that my father was wasting his time. That was a part of it, a frustrating part. My parents, who were so kind to me, to everyone, wasting their time on a pointless exercise. Protestantism, fundamental Protestantism in Ireland in nineteen thirty-seven. Show me anything more ludicrous, more hopeless than that!

I told myself I would never, never get caught on that tread-mill of preaching, teaching, singing, standing on wet street corners singing. And what did I do? I ended up on an even worse treadmill of boredom. Sheer bloody boredom. Married to a bank manager who didn't believe life existed fully beyond the bank counter and, if it did, it was there to further his banking career. The golf club and the bridge club were sub-offices for him. Every friend was a potential client and every social occasion was an opportunity to canvass business. Oh he was pleasant, witty in a dry way, but there was always the edge. The ulterior. Not in a cunning way. To say that would be to be unfair. It was just that he lived for his work.

God, I hated those golf outings and bridge evenings and bank dinners and presentation events. I developed the art of sitting at a bridge table and playing quite well while my mind was far removed. My first pleasure was in relishing the fact that the others could have no idea just how far I had strayed, how totally I had escaped. You can look someone straight in the eyes, speak to them in an intelligent way, watch your cards, and yet your mind and body are elsewhere. You can be sixteen and swimming stark naked in a clear river, somewhere in south Kildare, with the water lapping the pebbles and your skin touching the water irises while you're making a perfectly acceptable play in some smoky hotel dining room. The human mind is a wonderful, wonderful thing.

You don't remember the name of the river immediately but you can feel it. Smell it. Oh, the smell of a river bank! You no longer smell the perfume or the cigar smoke in that room; you no longer hear their voices. The conversation comes and goes and you join in but it comes and goes in some remote place in your mind.

That evening, that place, those people, mean nothing. But fifty years earlier is as clear and fresh as rain. Moments come like pictures on one of those modern television screens. Crisp. Clear. Full-coloured. You can reach in there and touch things, feel them.

Occasionally, now, when the river doesn't come, I do find myself back on the streets with my parents. Back on that little box we had, with those religious mottoes on the side. *Jesus is Love. Drink and never thirst again. God loves the Sinner.* I could never remember the other, the fourth. Something about the arms of the Lord. I think.

I was back there the afternoon my husband was buried. All our friends fussing about the drawing room, offering sandwiches and tea and port. I sat there, having a perfectly coherent conversation and smiling and feeling relieved that I was free again, relishing the thought of the next day and the next and the next and the independence they'd bring. And everyone was talking so quietly and not wanting to upset me and suddenly there I was, back in some village, standing on my little podium, singing as clearly and freely as I ever had.

∼

Lying here, with the moonlight draped across my bed, I believe I could still walk the biggest of Emerson's fields without a trace of tiredness. I used to believe I could do all sorts of things without a problem, even when I was a young lad. I remember arriving for football matches in Castledermot, looking at the big empty field and believing I could easily outrun anybody on the other team and score points from any angle. Time and again I'd believe that. I was the eternal optimist in that regard. It could always be done and I was the one who could do it. I could jump farther and higher than I'd done the week before. I was high-jumping over a few branches the day I first met Charlie Donnelly. Now there's a man I haven't thought of in a long, long time.

That was nineteen thirty-seven. The end of June. I was working on Emerson's farm for the holidays. My exams were finished, the end of my second year in university. I was what, eighteen? Eighteen. It was my third year on Emerson's. I'd cycled out there the day after I got home from Dublin to see old Mr Emerson.

'Of course, Martin,' he said. He always said that. Every year, when I asked about a summer start. I'd been working there since I was fifteen. I knew all the men out there, they were friends of my father's, played billiards with him.

'Back for more punishment,' they said when I arrived on the Monday morning. It was the wettest June anyone could remember. Emerson's had three new tractors that summer and they were stuck in the barn. The horses were out again.

I was sent to one of the outfields to fix up the laths on a shed, pull down the rotten timber, nail back the loose stuff. I had the day to myself.

'Bring out your lunch bag, stick at it till it's done,' Mr Emerson had said. 'You needn't come back in here, just get it done and then skedaddle.'

It was a bigger job than I'd thought. Best part of a full day's work but I kept at it. It was good to be inside while the rain belted down on the tin roof. When the breaks came, I'd go out-side and do what needed doing. I was a conscientious worker. Maybe that's why I was sent out there. At lunchtime the sun came out and I pulled down a few branches from a chestnut and made a rough high jump. I remember tucking my trousers into my socks, preparing myself for the first jump and then soaring way over the modest height I'd set myself. I pulled two bales of straw out of the loft and stuck the uprights into those; I was get-ting more ambitious and I believed, firmly, that I'd crack some kind of record if I kept at it. I was lost in what I was doing and then I heard a shout behind me.

'What a'ya at there?'

This big, grey-haired man in a dirty shirt and rubber boots was standing at the corner of the shed.

'High-jumping,' I said.

'Ye'll be for the high jump if Emerson gets ya,' the man said.

I knew that was nonsense but I pulled the branches out of the straw anyway. That was the effect he had on me. Immediately, he sat down on one of the bales and pulled a bottle of tea out of his pocket.

'Sit down and ate yer stuff,' he said.

I sat on the other bale. Two farm workers sitting in the brief sunlight. The man wolfed into his bread.

'Did you start today?' he asked.

'Yes, just this morning.'

'Just this morning. And what's your name?'

'Martin Neill,' I said.

He chewed another mouthful of bread.

'Martin Neill. You must be Paddy Neill's young lad, that works in the beet factory.'

'Yeah,' I said.

The man spat sideways and drank from his tea bottle.

'And what are ya doin' with yerself?'

'I'm in the university, in Dublin,' I said. I suppose I thought he'd be impressed.

'In the university, mind. And what are ya at there?'

'I'm studying history.'

'History bejasus. And do they teach ya anything about tractors there?'

I thought he was joking. I laughed.

'Tractors?'

'Aye tractors.' There wasn't a hint of humour in his voice.

'No, they don't.'

'Did you see the three tractors above in the barn?'

'Yes,' I said.

'Three of the finest tractors in Kildare, locked up in a barn because there's water in the low fields and they're about as useful as a prick on a snowman. That's fuckin' progress for you. That's what the industrial revolution done. Three fuckin' tractors, one more useless nor the other. What do you think of that?'

I remember mumbling, having nothing to say to his tirade.

'I suppose you're right.'

He looked sideways at me.

'Course I'm right.'

Then he chewed on another mouthful of bread. I wished he'd go off and let me get on with the work. There was something about him that was venomous.

'Karl Marx,' he said, when he was finished chewing. 'Now there was a man. *Das Kapital*. That's the book that has it all.'

There was a silence. He was looking at me.

'I never read it,' I said finally.

'Never read *Das Kapital*,' he roared. 'Never fuckin' read it.'

'It's not on our course.' It was a lame excuse. I knew that as soon as the words were out.

'You never read *Das Kapital*,' he said, ignoring me. 'Not let inside the Catholic University, I s'pose. D'ya see, that's the way of it. The Protestants have the land and the Catholics have their little university and they'll kill one another to hold onto what they have.'

Again the expectant silence, the stare.

'Maybe so.'

'Just fuckin' so, just fuckin' so. And I s'pose you come out here to see how th'other half lives?'

I had him there.

'I've worked here the past three summers.'

'Lookin' in on how the rest of us survive.'

'That's bloody rubbish,' I said.

'And when the nights draw in you'll be off back to Dublin.'

I had him again.

'I have to go back in October. I have no choice.'

But the victory was empty. He ignored what didn't suit him.

'Gettin' fuckin' jumped-up ideas, hah?'

'I've no jumped-up ideas.'

'Like your father. You didn't lick it off the street. Another jumped-up fucker!'

'Fuck off yourself,' I said and I gathered my lunch bag and walked into the shed.

The man stood at the door and roared in after me.

'Why don't you run back up and lick Emerson's arse. You should have plenty of practice. You think you're out of it, son; you're out of fuck all.'

I sat in the shed, knowing I was trapped. To walk out would be to face him again. He gathered his bag and his bottle and strolled across the field, making sure I saw him all the way.

That was Charlie Donnelly, though I didn't know his name then. All I knew was what I'd heard and what I could see. The shambling, grey-haired man who had come and gone like an angel of blight.

I remember breaking the chestnut branches into little pieces and flinging them in every direction. I could never take a jump that summer without expecting him behind me. Or so it seemed and yet I haven't thought about him for years, not in this way. Maybe there's something in that.

When I was first diagnosed, when I first heard the news, in that hospital in Dublin, when the word cancer was first mentioned, I remember thinking it didn't sound all that bad. The doctor was reassuring. Treatment. Monitoring. Good general health. Progress. All the phrases rolled out and I felt reassured. Happy almost that I was in such good hands, glad to be of assistance to that man in his chosen vocation. And afterwards, walking down Grafton Street to get a bus to the station, it struck me. I met a woman and, for twenty seconds, I was sure this figure weaving through the crowds was my mother. The image. Dead. But there she was. And even when she passed, she still looked familiar. And there was a man beside me in the bus to Heuston, white china skin, who might, for all the world, have been old Mr Emerson when he was laid out.

Ghosts, I thought at the time, coming halfway to meet me.

Thinking about Donnelly this way is a bit the same. Remembering that conversation, if it was the conversation we had. Is that the next step? Now you see us. Now you hear us. Now you meet us.

If I should die before I wake …

~

That summer, my father decided we were moving out of Dublin. Of course, he discussed it with my mother but he was the one who said to me: I've decided we're moving out of Dublin.

We were travelling on for Jesus.

My uncle, his brother, agreed to take on the running of their printing business himself, at least for the summer. We let our house in Terenure and went west. Well, through Blessington and Naas and Kilcullen. I was accustomed to summer preaching. My parents did it every summer. On the corners of the streets of Dublin. But now that I was finished school, my father said, it was an ideal opportunity to move farther afield. To give ourselves a greater commitment.

Preach to the unconverted somewhere in the wilderness between Dublin and Laois, my cousin Lesley said.

It was a wilderness to me but I found the whole thing exciting. Getting away from Dublin. Fields full of flowers, fresh water in the rivers, country roads I could bicycle through. God knew what.

Not that it seemed like that at first. We had an old Ford, everything piled in. And the rain, my God how it rained that June. Staying the first night in Blessington. And then Naas, Kilcullen, Carlow. Creaking stairs; high old beds; the same bedspreads; the rain, everywhere. And all these quaint villages. Moone. My God, how that made me laugh. Timolin; Castledermot; Ballitore; Levitstown; a place called Jerusalem; another called Palatine; Knocknagee.

We stayed in digs while we looked for something more permanent. With families who needed the money but were wary. My father would seethe, quietly, in his room while they prayed the rosary downstairs. My mother would try to mollify him. Once we spent the night sleeping in the car, after he had burst into someone's kitchen and railed about the true path to Jesus. I remember running through the rain while the man in that house told us we'd burn in hell and my father stood in the yard exhorting him to get down on his knees and embrace Jesus.

But we all loved that time. My father relished the challenge. My mother loved the country. I was seventeen. I was free.

We went to look at a cottage in a place called Maganey. My father had decided we would base ourselves in the area. Convert south Kildare, Carlow, Laois, west Wicklow before we moved farther afield. It was a battle plan with him. A year and then a decision on whether to continue or retreat to the weekend streets of Dublin.

Maganey was a road off a road off a road, somewhere between Athy and Carlow. The cottage was a small one. Two bedrooms, kitchen, living room. Outside loo across the yard. Corrugated-iron roof. All freshly painted. Neat. A lovely garden full of the most old-fashioned flowers.

We drove out from Carlow with the auctioneer. Passing a public house he said, this is Maganey. A public house and of all things, a station, a railway station. And that was it.

The cottage was almost a mile away, down two roads. The Barrow flowed behind it, three fields distant. The sun was shining on the iron roof, shining after rain. I could see my father reading biblical significance into this shining, burning light. I could almost see the flaming angel of the Lord reflected in his eyes. Somewhere on that roof, close to the chimney, the Guardian Angel had descended and was hovering again, as he had done in Bethlehem. And then it began to rain again.

Inside, we could hardly hear ourselves because of the noise of the rain on the roof.

'Furniture,' the auctioneer shouted. 'Furniture would soak up the sound. Make the world of difference, Mr Moynes. That's all you need. A few chairs and tables, bit of floor-covering and you wouldn't notice a thing!'

And then he stood in the doorway of the kitchen and told us that he knew why we were in the area but his was a policy of live and let live and he bore no ill will to anyone, church or chapel.

'We all have to eat and the place is for renting,' he said. 'Six months or twelve and then an option to buy. That's the situation. No ill will.'

He left us to talk it over and my father smiled.

'It's all money to him,' he said. 'Roman Catholic or Protestant, all solid silver.'

We took the cottage. While we waited for furniture from Dublin, we went on living in digs, travelling from market to market, standing on street corners preaching, giving our tracts to anyone who would take them. My mother pumping the organ; my father perspiring, even on the coolest days; me singing and handing out leaflets. The country was full of competing preachers. There was a general election and a constitutional referendum. I knew nothing of the pros and cons and my father dismissed it as the work of Caesar.

'We're of another King and Kingdom,' he'd say to people. I thought that rather rude. They normally took our tracts without complaint. I'm sure they never read them but they took them.

Once, in Carlow or Tullow or somewhere, when my father had said his piece about that other King and Kingdom, a man caught him by the collar and shouted at him.

'Well, why don't you go back to England then, you black bastard.'

Every market was thronged with competition. Politicians and stallholders and ourselves. All of us selling a line on something or other. I could see that clearly. My father couldn't. I think, perhaps, my mother did. We were all there as a form of entertainment for people who had little or nothing else to entertain them.

Once, we stood in the empty Square in Athy, not realising everyone had gone to watch a shop being demolished. It had burned down the night before. It was an endless round. Tuesdays in Castledermot; Wednesdays in Athy; Thursdays in Carlow; Fridays in Tullow. An endless round of rain and noise through that June.

And everywhere the same kinds of people. Small farmers; farm labourers; hucksters; travelling salesmen; conmen; destitute families; children skittering home from school at lunch-time. The same traders doing the same rounds as ourselves. We'd nod and chat to each other. All of us in the same line of business. The regular traders would give us mugs of tea, we'd share our sandwiches.

If the sun shone and we wanted to swim, we'd still be there; if the rain fell, as it did, we'd still turn up. All of us labouring ever onwards. Christian soldiers; soldiers of Mammon. Did it matter a damn? All of us part of the same travelling show.

~

One of the men on the farm told me Donnelly's name. I didn't ask for any more information. When I got home that evening, my father was in the garden.

'God bless the worker,' he said.

I asked him if he'd ever heard of Charlie Donnelly. He leaned on his spade and took his pipe from his pocket. He fiddled with it, the way he always did when he was about to talk about something he disliked.

'Ah yes,' he said. 'Charlie Donnelly. I know him all right. He come up here forninst Easter time, from Kilkenny direction, and he wasn't a wet week in the place when he come out here one evenin', out here to the house, wantin' me to get him a start in the beet factory.'

I remember the way my father lifted the spade and drove it deeper into the wet clay, making a steadier support to lean on. He had a habit of doing that too. As a child, when someone came to the hedge, I'd know if my father was going to talk for a long time or a short time by the way he drove a spade into the ground.

'No, I'm wrong in that,' he went on. 'He came out demandin' a start in the factory. I told him straight out that it's layin' men off we were, not takin' them on. "As if the fuckin' jobs were yours to give," he says to me and then he starts spewin' out of him like a cesspit. In the end I had to tell him to shag off with himself, in case yer mother heard him. The next thing I know, he's up workin' in Emerson's. I thought Mr Emerson had better sense nor to take on someone like that. But that's him. Why did you ask?'

'No why,' I lied. 'I just met him. I just wondered.'

My father never mentioned him again. But every evening he'd be there in the garden when I got home. We lived out beyond Castledermot then, on the Athy road, a place called Mullaghcreelan. We had a cottage and a cottage acre and my father would be out there every evening. He made the neatest, straightest drills I ever saw.

When I was a small boy, I'd hear him in the garden on spring mornings at half past five, before he cycled off to work. I'd wake and the fork would be rasping into the ground and he'd be whistling and I'd creep over to the window and pull back the curtain and, as if I was letting more light in on the garden, he'd always sense that I was there and he'd turn and wave and I'd wave back and then I'd pull back the curtains and lie in bed, listening. And the next thing I'd know was that my mother was calling for me to get up. I'd look out again and the garden would be empty.

That garden was different from this one. You could see right across that garden. No trees, no shrubs, plain vegetables with a half-dozen apple trees on the back ditch. If I looked out this window I'd see shadows and trees and dark-branched moonlight across the path. This is a complicated garden. My father's garden was simple. But not my father. I knew that all along. He was straight and he was as reliable as a level but he wasn't a simple man. He'd say things that you wouldn't hear from other men. Like one evening, maybe two weeks into that summer, he was tricking with me.

'How long are you out in Emerson's now?' he asked.

'A fortnight.'

'A fortnight. And it hasn't stopped rainin' one day. If you're not careful, Mr Emerson'll be blamin' the rain on you and lettin' you go.'

And then he got serious and he leaned across the table.

'D'you know what I miss about not bein' your age again?'

'What?' I said, expecting a smart remark.

'I miss one evenin' like this. After rain. This time of year. I was walkin' along a headland and I brushed agin the corn, green corn, and the smell, the wet, fresh smell that come up off it nearly made me cry. And that same evenin', cyclin' in past the Big Bush, it started rainin' and I took shelter under a whitethorn an' the rain come down through it and brought the smell of the May with it. I miss that more nor I miss anythin'.'

I stared at him but there was no mirth in his eyes. He was open to me. I sat there waiting for him to say something else and wishing that he wouldn't. I didn't want that moment broken and still I was afraid he might say something else and I wouldn't know what to do or say. And then he relaxed and took out his pipe again.

'You tell me the tractors is tied up,' he said.

I nodded.

'I suppose yis have the horses out?'

I nodded again.

'Did they set you to tackin' the horses yet?'

I shook my head.

'They wouldn't.'

There was no sense of derision in that remark. It was just a fact.

'That's a skilled job. Not anyone can do it. I remember and I a young lad, twelve or thirteen, I used to go over to Delaney's at the weekend and they'd set me to tackin' the plough horses, big, heavy horses. I'd have to stand on a box to get the tackin' over their heads. Gentle as lambs they were. Isn't it strange, too, the way nature can put the kibosh on progress?'

'How do you mean?'

'Goin' back to the horses. And there's another thing. I see young lads inside with us, in Carlow, young lads your own age, from the town, and they get up in the mornin', get up on their bikes, cycle out to the factory, do the shift, get back on the bikes and cycle home, and if you asked one of them to kick a football or run after it even, they couldn't. And they'll tell you that's progress, every man ownin' his own bike!'

He laid his pipes on the table, the pair of them, and took his penknife and cleaners from his waistcoat pocket.

'And these politicians is the same. There's half of them sayin', oh we have to have a new constitution, we have to make changes, go with the times. And the other half sayin' leave well enough alone. And the thing is, the thing is, Martin, that the two lots of them believes completely in what they're sayin'. I don't know.'

I watched him snake the pipe-cleaner through the shaft, settling himself, now that the rain was down and the garden was out of bounds.

'I'll tell you though, there's one man in this parish that'll see no change and that's the parish priest. I was tellin' your mother. And I comin' home this evenin', cyclin' through Castledermot, he come out the gate of the parochial house and he flagged me down. "Have you seen any sign of these travellin' preachers?"

he says to me. "I haven't, Father," I says. "I heard of them but seen no sign." "They're a danger to the parish," he says. "Are they, Father?" says I. "They are," he says. "And I was wonderin' if yourself and a couple of the other men in the billiard hall might be prepared to do somethin' about them?" Well, I looked at him, Martin, straight in the eye and I said: "Father," I said, "I hope the days of runnin' people out of places and burnin' them for what they believe is well dead and gone." Well, he wasn't one bit pleased, Martin. He turned on his heel and was back up the drive, with the door banged behind him, before I even had time to get me leg over the bar. That's one man that'll see change over his dead body.'

He worked on his pipe quietly and then he looked at me.

'Have you seen any sign of them?'

'No,' I said.

'Ah, well, you won't. Them people now wouldn't want to get their nice clean clothes dirty walkin' across mucky fields. But sure why would they? Unless they're goin' to stand on the walls of the sty and preach to the pigs!'

He chuckled quietly to himself and tapped his pipe on the range door. I can still hear that soft, warm chuckle.

He never came to me, I never saw him on any street after consultations. I saw other people, other men I worked with, teachers I taught with. Often. I dreamed one night that I was in Naas and a bus pulled in beside me and all these people I'd known, people I'd grown up with, got off it. Eight or ten of them, all long dead.

Another time I dreamed I was in a big shop in Dublin, one of those fancy places that smell of heat and perfume, and all the other shoppers were people I'd known who were dead. I remember waking in the hospital and being surprised that I was still alive.

But my father never came to me, never rounded a corner in a crowd or drove past me in a coach full of American tourists and here he is, him and Donnelly, mortal enemies, word for word in my room.

Maybe the doctor was wrong. Or maybe I'll never die. Maybe they're all coming over to see me, to whisper in my head, because I haven't kept my appointment with them on the other side. Wouldn't that be good?

~

I've never wished for children but had I had a child I should certainly have had two. There are problems being an only child. Certainly in being an only daughter. The closeness of the family was wonderful but it could be lonely. I was not an adult that summer, not in the way my parents were. I envied them their commitment to faith. Occasionally, I doubted my mother's sincerity. Not that she ever said or did anything. It was an intuitive thing on my part. There were moments when she seemed not to be there on the same level of intensity as my father. Not that she could have been. No one could. He was, I suppose, fanatical in some people's eyes. Living so close to him, I didn't see that but I've seen it in other circumstances since. I saw a hint of it in my husband's attitude to business. But that was a different feeling. I was less concerned with it because I found it less interesting. Uninteresting. But with my mother I sensed something, thought I saw something without being able to pin it down. Perhaps my own feelings were hers, blown-up, exaggerated. Fulfilled. Yes, perhaps my doings were the fulfilment of her secrets. But in the day-to-day travelling and preaching there was never a moment I could point to and locate the root of revolt.

Instead, we travelled together and when we arrived in a town we each had our responsibilities. My father would unload

the harmonium and set it up; my mother brought out the leaflets and pamphlets and I put out the box with the mottoes.

He always began with a prayer and then we sang. My mother's
voice was weak and squeaking. My father's was flat and tuneless. I
kept the hymns and songs together. My voice would lift clear of theirs
and I especially loved it when I was allowed to sing alone. I loved the
performance, the audience, the opportunity to be seen and heard for
myself. On those occasions, I was free of whatever hold they had on
me and, paradoxically, I was never lonely. That was my medium.

I remember clearly getting back to the cottage one evening
and finding a letter from my cousin Lesley in Rathfarnham.
She was coming down for the month of July and two weeks
in August, she said. I could hardly wait. Living in Dublin, I saw
Lesley all the time but, suddenly, her coming down seemed the
most promising thing ever.

I could introduce her to the country. To my fields, my
roads, my walks, my river. It wasn't that I wanted a position of
superiority. It was just an opportunity to share these things with
another girl. To say: this is what I've found.

I can still recall the excitement of that evening. Vividly.

~

My father never mentioned Donnelly to me again. Never. He'd
said his piece and there was no more to be said. I had to make
my own way from there. Reach my own conclusions.

I'd keep out of Donnelly's way as much as I could. Sometimes
in the evenings, when I went down to kick football in the field,
he'd be there, sitting on the wall, watching, and the next morning there'd be a gibe.

'Yis couldn't kick shite. The boys down our country'd bate
yis before breakfast. Wimmen, oul fuckin' wimmen.'

I did well in keeping clear of him but in the early part of July we were set to cleaning out a scrub wood on the out-farm near Maganey. I cycled out ahead of him and got working immediately. Not because I wanted to but to keep out of his way.

When he arrived, twenty minutes after me, he sat on the ditch and watched me.

'What are ya at?'

'Mr Emerson said we're to stack this timber,' I said.

There were logs and poles on the headland.

'Mr Emerson,' he said, laughing. 'Mr Emerson my arse. Tell me, did anyone ever call you Mr Neill?'

'No,' I said, carrying on with the work.

'No, nor no one ever called me Mr Donnelly. Forty-seven year old and no one ever called me Mr Donnelly.'

He came and stood on the end of a pole I was about to lift.

'And do you know what makes him Mr Emerson? Do ya?'

I said nothing but he went on, as if I wasn't there at all, a cigarette hanging from his lip, jiggling as he spoke.

'Fifteen hundred acres, that's what makes him Mister. Fifteen hundred fuckin' acres. People is afraid of him because he has land. They nod and blink to him wherever he goes. I stood up to the likes of him and I got pissed on and shit on and I learned my lesson. Now I do what they expect.'

He lifted his foot and spat the cigarette into the grass. He walked up to the ditch again and sat down.

'But I know him and his likes for what they are. It's all money, land and power in the end. Emerson and his likes have the land and that's their power. The priest and the minister have the pulpit and that's their power. I have nothing but I can shite on the farmer's grass and rub it on his door and I can pull me wire and there's nothin' the priest can do about it. That's my way, boy. I'll take the church shelter of a wet mornin' and the wage packet of a Saturday and fuck them all.'

He stood up again and walked over to where I was stacking logs. He leaned across the timber and looked me straight in the face.

'Never trust them. Education counts for nothin'. They'll savage yer bollocks off if you give them half a chance. They'll shit on you, so you shit first.'

His tone was almost intimate and then he spat again and pulled off his coat and set to carrying timber.

When we stopped for tea he asked me whether I'd seen or heard of the travelling preachers. I told him I hadn't.

'They're all the one,' he said. 'Priests, politicians, preachers. Powermongers the whole fuckin' lot of them. They've no time for me but they want my money, my soul, my vote. Whatever little I have they want. But you mark my words, son, put all these Christians in the one ring together and they'll ate one another's arses.'

What was it about Donnelly that made him confide all this in me? Much of it was confidence. He hated my father and he had no time for me but he was prepared to tell me this. Or perhaps I was the only one who'd listen, out of coldness if not interest, without answering back or walking away. I can hear that whispered tone of voice as he leaned across the poles.

'Education counts for nothin'.'

Maybe it was meant to put me in my place but I didn't think so then. It was more of a warning. Or maybe it was both.

I made my parents sit in the car when we got to Maganey station. I was the only one on the platform, waiting, watching for the train that Lesley would come on.

The porter looked out from his office and smiled at me. I smiled back and then walked the length of the platform. The track stretched straight for half a mile towards Carlow. Back towards Athy, the direction from which the train would come, the tracks ran straight beneath a bridge and then curved away between trees. I measured my steps the length of the stone walkway singing in time.

All things bright and beautiful, all creatures great and small. When I turn the train will be in sight. I turned, the track was empty.

All things wise and wonderful, the Lord God made them all. I shall turn and walk back and then the train will be here.

The purple-headed mountain, the river running by,

The sunset and the morning that brightens up the sky.

Oh, when will this train ever arrive?

The cold wind in the winter, the pleasant summer sun,

The ripe fruit in the garden –

There it is, the engine black and massive, the carriages snaking uncertainly, unsteadily, behind.

Oh God, I hope she's on it!

And there she was in a waving arm and blowing hair and a shout that was filled with laughter.

Did I ever hear her laugh so much as in that first afternoon? Afterwards, there seemed to be so much of a serious nature to talk about. Of course we laughed again but in between the serious talk of two young women. And later still, Lesley took everything so seriously. Love. Marriage. Money. Home. Living. Death. If I were to say that first afternoon together was an explosion of mirth that preceded a lifetime of longer and longer periods of seriousness, I would be giving it an import that comes from hindsight. But I have often thought about it. We were never as innocent with each other as we were that afternoon when she got off the train. Open, yes. Intimate, yes. Close, yes. But never as laughingly girls again as on that cloudy afternoon – the last cloudy day of that summer.

We stood and hugged and chattered and eventually my father came to take us out to the car. I think he thought we had both fallen under the train but, instead, he found us gabbling among Lesley's luggage.

~

It was sometime in that early part of July that the parish priest began to talk about the travelling preachers. I still hadn't seen or heard them. It must have been July because by August we were working Sundays and going down to Levitstown for Mass. We had a dispensation, the weather had been so bad. But the first time I heard him preach about them was in Castledermot, so it must have been July.

I was sitting in the men's short-aisle, I always sat there with my father. It was a strange place to hear a sermon because the pulpit was side-on and the gallery floor cut off any sight of the priest's head. You heard a voice coming out of this pair of shoulders, you saw the hands waving but that was all.

What did he say? He used the stock phrases he always used but he used them with venom. More venom than normal. Yes, yes, he talked about people being attracted, no lured, how could I have forgotten? Lured by the new and the unfamiliar. That was the one weakness of the human character. That Sunday. He began in that quiet way that warned us all of a storm.

There were travelling preachers in the area, going from place to place.

And then the pause and the correction.

No, let us not call them preachers; let us call them what they are. Proselytisers. And these proselytisers are fastening onto the weak, the gullible, the naive.

And then the turn of phrase.

From Baltinglass comes news … of a family lured away. A complete family.

And then the punch.

With the exception of one seven-year-old girl, who, having just made her First Holy Communion and filled with the power of the Holy Ghost, said no. No. To the lure. No. To the new. She said no. She is in the care of an aunt while approaches are being made to her family.

And the plan.

These proselytisers have a plan. Of course it is unclear to those of us in the aisles. But the Holy Father has spoken many times of it. He has stressed the need to be wary.

My father gently bumped his knee against mine. I looked at him. A smile flitted across his face.

'This is for me,' he whispered out of the corner of his unmoving mouth.

'Those not for the Pope are not for his church.

Those not for the church are not for Christ.

The Devil works in circuitous ways.'

'He must,' someone behind us whispers, 'if he bothered with Baltinglass.'

As if he had heard. Could he have? The priest whirls and peers into the men's aisle.

'You men at the back are not listening!'

That desperate silence.

'It is not my job to tell you how to react.'

He turns back to the body of the church.

'You are good people but you cannot allow your faith to be threatened. I will monitor. I will advise. I hope you people are prepared to defend your parish and your faith.'

Is that what he said or is that some composite picked up and stored cynically in the meantime? That or something very like it. A wonderful man to let the last syllable of echo die before continuing. Better nor any preacher or missioner, the people said.

No, I'm being unfair. I couldn't remember that, not the very words. But maybe I'm entitled to that bitterness. It ill becomes me, Father, wherever your shade is now, doesn't it? You could strike me dead if I wasn't already close to it; stick me to this moonlit floor. But I don't think so.

~

I don't believe I allowed Lesley the time to unpack her bags before I had her out into the garden, across the gate and into the fields to show her the places and smells and sights I had become familiar with. It seemed that the summer, the real summer we dreamed of annually but rarely got, had arrived off that train.

The next morning the sky was a blue tarpaulin. I took her down to the river where the reeds grew high. I had made a narrow pathway through them to a flat, grass bank. The water was five feet deep. Ideal for swimming. And how pleased I was, too, that here was another real singer. I would no longer have to fight my father's flat-ness and my mother's squeak alone. I told her about the characters we had come to know at the markets. Not at all like the people in Dublin, much more volatile, much less predictable. I knew Lesley would love them. And I knew my parents were pleased that she had come. They saw her as a surrogate sister for me. They could relax in my regard, at least in the coming weeks.

I took Lesley to see the water irises that first morning, too, on the bend where they grew. All I had ever seen were garden irises. But these were special. We gathered them and brought them back to the cottage. I put a huge jug in our bedroom window, a blue glazed jug, and their yellow flagged heads rose beautifully in the sunlight on the sill. And out beyond them was the corn, turning late and slowly. Lesley would be here for what the local farmers said was the height of the year, the golding of the fields. And day after day there wasn't a cloud anywhere. We would waken at five or six to heat in the room and heat in the garden.

And then I woke one morning, just after five, to the swish sound of a paintbrush on the front wall of the cottage. I got out of bed and walked into the garden. My father was busily white-washing the wall. But why? It had been bright and white already. And then I saw them, the dark letters through the wet wash. Odd letters, tall, crooked, black. Indecipherable now.

'What did they say?' I asked.

'It doesn't matter,' my father said, smiling.

'This happened during the night. What did they say? You have to tell me.'

My father shrugged and went on whitewashing. My mother came through the door, carrying a cup of tea for him.

I remember turning to her and shouting: 'You have to tell me.' And then I turned back to my father. 'If I'm to be part of what you're doing, if I'm to sing and preach and work with you, then you've got to treat me as an equal now. I need to know what it said.'

My father put down the brush and turned to me.

'It said: GO BACK TO DUBBIN,' he laughed.

My mother giggled.

'You think that's funny,' I said. 'All right, it's amusing but it's not funny.'

My mother went on laughing.

'Why would anyone do this?'

'It's happened before,' my mother said. 'Many places. Our first house in Dublin, our car, the organ, walls. You don't think about it.'

'But I don't understand why,' I said again.

'Anger,' my mother said. 'Blind anger. People hear us and listen and other people are angry with the listeners and we're the ones they vent that anger on. It means nothing. We had a newly painted fence once, a picket fence, at our house in Bray. The night we'd finished painting it, it was daubed. So we painted it again. It was daubed again. We painted it a third time. It was torn down and every stick was broken. In the end it didn't matter. The Lord provides. We'll sing and then we'll eat.'

We sang, the three of us. We stood in the garden and sang and Lesley came and watched from the doorway. Half-asleep, she looked at us and laughed. And we all laughed then. I don't remember ever being happier.

We just stood there. No audience. No message. Nothing. Just standing there singing. I believed then, for that moment, that nothing could stop us, that what we were about was correct. And I sang and sang like I'd never done before. I remember the moment, even though the song is gone.

~

I remember the way the weather took up. Anyone who lived through that summer will remember it. One week we were tramping about in eight inches of mud and a few weeks later there wasn't enough water to go round. The weather lifted like fog, up and was gone. And we were left with days of sun and heat that stretched as tight as a tent from dawn to dusk.

And we were out there working every hour of light that God sent and beyond. You'd see the dim lights of the tractors dragging up and down the hill fields at all hours. On nights like this, when the moon was full, you wouldn't need lights. Just the chugging out in the countryside and the shadows thrown from the machinery.

We worked shifts those weeks, to catch up with what had been buried by the rain.

I can remember shop assistants stopping on the road at five or six in the morning, on their way home from dances, and shouting at us.

'Go on yis boys yis, quare few wans askin' for yis in Carlow.'

They'd climb onto the ditches and wave till we waved back. 'Get up and ride them maaaaachines!'

By then we'd have been in the field for an hour.

I got home late one night, well after twelve, and found my mother waiting up for me. There was an envelope on the table. It was from the university. I'd passed my exams. I knew I should have been delighted. I was, I suppose, and my mother hugged me and she woke my father to tell him the news, but afterwards, lying in bed, I found it hard to be excited by it. Out there in the fields history meant nothing. It had no place. Its pointlessness, uselessness, was as clear as a ditch when you were out there working in the middle of crops and seasons. I think I lost faith in history from then on. I held onto it, to earn a wage, but no more than that. It was never a living thing again. It wasn't that the moment was of such importance, just the point, the night, where my interest finally ran out. No more than that.

In all my summers on Emerson's, I'd never seen work like we had that summer. I'd be out there in the morning to see people cycling to work; I'd see women on their way in to the town to get the messages; I'd see children straggling along the roads on their way to thin beet; I'd see courting couples walking out the roads after tea; I'd see poachers cutting across the fields in the half-dark, and still I'd be there.

I remember stopping the tractor one evening on a headland, getting down for a break. Or do I actually remember this? Have I put it in place? Have the years of putting dates and places on things worked their way into me?

No, I believe I remember this evening.

I stopped the tractor on a headland and got down and I saw two girls crossing the other headland with towels under their arms. I wanted to shout something smart at them but I couldn't think of a word to say and I kept thinking that if Donnelly was here he'd have some smart remark on the tip of his tongue.

Eventually I thought of shouting: I'll be free in two weeks' time if you're interested, but by then it was too late, even if I'd had the courage. They were gone through a gap in the ditch on their way to the river.

I climbed back onto the tractor and carried on working and this bit I do remember clearly. I looked at the sun where it sat in the sky and thought to myself that it must be half past eight and I was delighted that I could feel myself so much at home in the fields that I could tell the time with accuracy and, at the same time, I felt a terrible sense of waste of time sliding by me, out of my control. I suppose I'm only lucky I don't have that same feeling now.

~

The wonderful thing about Lesley was that she had no interest whatsoever in religion. Not even a pretence of an interest. She travelled with us, gave out leaflets, sang with us but she thought the whole thing was a complete hoot.

In the evening we would walk down to the river and swim, not another sinner about. When we'd finished in the water we would towel each other's bodies dry. While I towelled her she would tell me about a boy she'd met, from St Columba's, how she would meet him at weekends in Rathfarnham. He was in his final year and that autumn he was going to Trinity to study medicine. She would talk to me in a deep, intimate tone that drew me in to the secrecy of their relationship. I'd find myself sitting closer to catch every breath, every syllable.

She had met him at a Christmas party. He was so beautiful, she said. That was the adjective she used. In anyone else's mouth it would have sounded strange but from Lesley it sounded perfectly natural, correct. She told me his eyes were brown.

'He does all the things you'd want him to do,' she said. 'He listens and he laughs and he treats me like a human being. He doesn't expect me to be foolish or fawning or skittish.'

She told me they'd met every day during the holidays, until she'd had to come down to us. Before that she'd gone up to watch him play cricket at weekends. Seeing him was what she missed most, she said.

One evening she spoke particularly intimately and I remember sitting as still as a stone, waiting for each twist in the tale.

He had taken her, it seemed, in his father's car, to the Sally Gap. They'd gone swimming there, in the rain, without any clothes and afterwards he had dried her down with his shirt and it had been lovely.

'We've been to bed several times since then,' she said.

I caught my breath at the wonder of her frankness, at her daring to do that, to say it.

'I can't wait till he gets his rooms in Trinity,' she said. 'Then we won't have to listen for the sound of his father's car or for his sister.'

God, I envied her. I'm not sure whether it was her boldness or her willingness to tell it all so openly but I envied her.

On evenings like that she'd towel me slowly and show me how he had kissed her and touched her. I was half in love with that boy myself and half in love with Lesley. There was no awkwardness in the things she said or did. I learned so much from her in the most innocent way. No, not innocent, guiltless way. It seemed she was as one with her body as I was with the river. She told me never to accept less from anyone than I was prepared to give.

'There's pleasure on both sides, Alice,' she'd say. 'You know that now. Our mothers would like us to think otherwise and so would a lot of boys I've met, dozens of them. But not now.' And she'd laugh hoarsely. 'Never accept less than you're prepared to give.'

She spent evenings showing me how to kiss, how to touch, how to insist on being myself in search of my own pleasure. All I wanted was to find a spot to bring it all to fruition.

I remember some conversations clearly; some are a blur. But I do remember the sandy spot at the river with the weeds and the rushes growing high. We'd made a narrow entrance so that we couldn't be seen from the field or the road. The river was sunk in weedy banks but the water was clear and deep.

We'd swim and when we'd finished we'd throw our togs in, in case my mother noticed they were dry. We'd throw them in and dive from the bank. I can still feel the rush of coolness from my fingertips, along the rest of my body as it cut through the water. It might be ten o'clock by then, the sun gone down, the night cooling but the water still warm.

Nothing mattered. I loved the days and the singing because they led to the nights and the water and my body at ease in there, at ease in a different world. And then the drying off. Lesley easing the towel about me, caressing me. Everything was perfection. This was how life was meant to be. I'd lie on the bank or sit on the grass and Lesley would embrace me lightly and fondle my breasts and I hers. We would lie together in the twilight, touching so gently at times I was never sure if we had touched.

And then sometimes we would jump into the dark water and I would relish the happiness I had. I imagined that ecstasy was just around the corner. I was convinced of that.

~

One Sunday in the throes of the harvest we cycled down to Levitstown church. We had a dispensation to work on Sundays, in case the weather broke, and we'd go to Mass in Levitstown at half past nine because the church was nearer than Castledermot. The parish priest had driven out to say Mass.

I can still remember the dead, stale smell of sweat in that church. Even where we stood, Donnelly and two other men and myself, at the back porch, the smell was heavy and stifling.

The Parish Priest stood for a long time in the pulpit, in silence, letting the importance of his presence sink in and then he began to speak slowly, methodically; he was playing the patient man, the caring shepherd that Sunday.

He allowed us to know a secret, as he often did. Many people had been to see him about the travelling preachers; they were worried. He would tell us what he had told them. He would point us to our faith, our priests, our Pope. He would point us to our God. He reminded us that ours was the one, holy, Catholic and Apostolic church. He refreshed our memories on the oath we took each Easter Saturday when we rejected the Devil and all his works and all his pomps.

'What more can I do?' he asked quietly. I am one man. You are the people, the people of God, the people of the church of God.'

I had heard all this before but not what followed.

'You must do, you must do what you think fit in defence of your faith. You must decide and you must …'

He let the words hang, I remember, for five seconds, ten, fifteen. People shifted, coughed and still he waited, until the silence was restored. And then he launched his attack. These people had no fear, he said, they had come to the very church gates in Castledermot. They were arrogant, conceited, proud and dangerous. They masked their bitterness in sweet music.

I remember the rest or the gist of it.

'Eve was fooled by such sweetness. Will you be?' He pointed to the front seats.

'Or you?' His finger wandered across the raised faces.

'Or you?' He pointed to the back of the church.

'The people of God must protect the church of God. I cannot do it for you.'

And then that long silence again before he slowly blessed himself and people knelt in their own sweat.

We got away after Communion, pulled our bikes out of the tangle of handlebars at the wall and cycled away from the church, back up towards Kilkea and work. As we pushed up the hill Donnelly pointed to a small, corrugated-iron-roofed cottage.

'That's the so-called den of iniquity,' he laughed. 'That's where them people live. Yer man don't like them preachin' and he don't like them livin' that close to a church and, fuck him, he doesn't want a penny goin' to them. That's the nub of it!'

Donnelly stood up on the pedals of his bike and bellowed back towards the church.

'I'm your priest, you're my people, get out there and kick the shite out of them for me.'

We cycled on, turning left and freewheeling towards Emerson's outfarm.

'Mark my fuckin' words,' Donnelly said. 'I'd like to be in on the kill for this one.'

Was I chilled by what he said? I don't think so. Not then. It meant nothing at the time. I kept clear of him, worked day and night, sweated and pushed and pulled. Did what I was asked. Worked from dawn to well into the darkness. Waited for the last patch of corn to fall.

We finished the harvest on a Saturday morning. I remember sitting on a trailer behind one of the tractors and gate after gate was open from field into field. Everything was cut and dry.

Emerson brought us in for a slap-up feed and then let us go home. As soon as I got back to the house I took a basin out the back and had the first decent wash I'd had in weeks. There hadn't been any point in it up to that. One day's sweat poured into the next.

The feel and smell of a fresh shirt was a reward in itself. And then up on the bike and into Carlow.

I thought about going to the pictures but I stood in Tullow Street and sucked in the fresh air. My first free night in months. No more hay, no more straw, no more barley, no more wheat, no more tractors, no more trailers, no more work. Too fine to be stuck inside. I wandered around the shops, bought myself a new pair of boots, put them on the carrier of the bike and then I decided to cycle out to Castledermot, up to McEvoy's shop. I'd celebrate. I'd buy myself a bottle of lemonade, maybe two, maybe three!

I remember coming in the Barrack Road, through Prumplestown, past Copes' Mill, pushing the bike as hard as I could. Riding and riding and riding, pushing myself, getting some idea of what it must be like to be a kite. There was a light, warm wind in my face and my hair was blowing back and I bent over the handle-bars and stood on the pedals and I began to move faster and faster. I pushed with all the strength I had, bursting my heart and lungs to go as fast as I could and when I could go no faster I sat back, arms out and freewheeled, looking out across the fields on either side. Everything there was cut and dry, too. I closed my eyes for eight seconds and opened them again and shouted across the empty ditches. I was high up in the blue above that road, I was up there flying, soaring on the warmth of air, flying, flying, flying, there was no other word for it. I was that kite in the sky. And I can remember clearly, with a cold accuracy, that coming through Carlow Gate, into Castledermot, the kite came down to earth again.

The streets were empty and I thought to myself – where are all the fellows and girls I grew up with? And I knew where they were. Down the River Road or in the Laurels, easy in one another's company and there was I delighted because I had a new pair of boots on the carrier of the bike. I remember slowing to a crawl and thinking what a fool I was for working all year to pass exams and then working all summer to get money to work for another year at more exams. I had five weeks left to get to meet Ann McDonald or Betty Hardy, that was the truth of it.

I pushed on up Athy Street and into the Square and then I stopped. There were these people, a man and a woman and two girls, on the platform beside the pump in the middle of the Square. I stopped the bike and stood watching them. The man was talking about Jesus and then he finished and the woman started playing an organ and they all began singing. I stood there staring at this gorgeous girl with dark hair. I knew there were three or four fellows standing on Copes' corner, smoking, watching me, but I didn't care. I stood there watching and listening and the girl's voice rose free and singing. 'He walks with me and he talks with me.' That's all I can remember of the song, the hymn. Even then I don't think that much sank in.

I'd stayed to watch them pack their bits and pieces into their car. I was in a daze going home. I realised they were the preachers but that was of no importance to me then.

I cycled home that night. Through Hallahoise and down Mullaghcreelan. I lay in bed in the half-darkness and tossed and turned. I thought about getting out the bike and cycling over to where they lived but then I thought better of it.

I remember getting up, opening the window of my bedroom, staring out into the darkness and then lying down again.

I tried to remember the words of the hymn, some phrase of it. It was important to me because I was in love with that girl and her voice was in those words. I was filled with all the passion of a young man. I strained and strained to make contact with the girl. I believed

I could, if I only tried hard enough. I held my head between my hands and whispered some imagined phrase into the pillow and the words became hers, the voice was hers. I touched my body with my hands and they became her hands. And afterwards, lying half-asleep, I imagined her there. To have someone like that to be beside me, to wake beside her, to have her there. Just to have her there.

The next morning was Sunday. I was up before anyone else. I was in Castledermot half an hour before Mass began. I hung around outside the church, waiting for them to arrive. In the end, I had to go inside. I stood in the porch, listening, knowing that if I heard one sound of them I'd be gone out of there. I don't think I even waited for my dinner that day. I cycled down through Kilkea, across through Levitstown, down past their cottage. Slowly. The windows were open but the front door was closed and there was no car in the yard. I cycled down to Levitstown Bridge and up again and down again. In the end, I threw my bike across a gate and climbed into the field behind their house. I crept as close as I dared.

The yard at the back of the cottage was empty but for one blue, summer dress hung out on a wire fence to dry. I listened for a long time but there was no sound from the house. I crept closer and stepped across the low wire on the back ditch, crossed the small lawn and stood transfixed. This was the dress the girl had worn in the Square in Castledermot. Did I dare to touch it, to be that close to something so close to her, something so intimate?

I've often thought about that in the times since then and I know there was no decision because there was no choice. I reached out and touched the light material. I forgot about the place I was in, about the chance that someone might come from the cottage, the possibilities of being caught. I touched the cloth but that wasn't enough. I felt its texture but that wasn't enough either. It wasn't the cloth that was important, not even the dress itself. It was what it meant. Whose it was. I took the dress in my hands and buried my face in the warmth of its folds, in the scent of her body, in the folds that folded about her flesh. I was lost in the world of her body.

Of course, sense prevailed or cowardice and I put it back on the wire and re-crossed the ditch and went and lay on the hill that overlooked their yard. I lay there watching the house, the yard, the dress. I lay like a stone, watching and listening. I could hear every sound, every wasp, every bird. I could smell the smell of the clover. I strained and strained to be with her. But it wasn't enough for me any more. And nobody came.

~

A week from the end of that August I began to face the fact that I would soon be alone. Lesley would go back to Rathfarnham and I would come down to that river alone. But I was determined to enjoy every minute of that week.

We went down to swim every evening. The wild flowers were slightly frayed by then – frayed by heat. The sky darkened a little earlier but stayed a constant shade of plunging blue.

We were totally at ease with each other's bodies by then. Not even at ease – easy. We swam and floated and dived and I never felt any need to turn away from Lesley's body or from my own.

We had become aware of a boy watching us from a hill two fields away. He had been there the previous Sunday night and again on the Monday and Tuesday. We laughed about him. As we walked from the cottage to the river we would stop from time to time to watch him. He was too far away to see clearly but we knew he was watching us.

His face seemed as brown as walnut and his shirts were white. As white as snow, as white as May, as white as Queen Anne's lace. I watched him with a particular interest, expectation. I expected, as we swam, that he would come through the weeds but he didn't and I was disappointed.

That Friday afternoon, we drove Lesley to the station at Maganey. The platform was as empty as it had been the evening she arrived. After the train had left I watched it out of sight and then rushed back to the car. I could hardly wait to finish my supper and I was down in the field on my way to the river. And there he was on the hill. I walked particularly slowly.

Come down from your mountain and meet me, I thought.

But the figure stayed there, like Lot's wife, on the hill.

Oh stay there; you may be nobody worth meeting.

I slipped into the water and out again and stood on the bank. I did something I had never done when Lesley was there, I walked to the edge of the weeds and grasses. I knew I could be seen from the road but I could be seen, too, from the hilltop. He must see me.

I stood there, at the edge of the field, and dressed very slowly.

I missed Lesley, of course I missed her, but I felt an excitement. Something was going to happen. I willed it. Something was going to happen. Something was going to happen.

~

A letter came to our house one afternoon in that first week of September. It was delivered by a young lad on a bicycle. The same letter came to every house in the parish. It was signed by the parish priest. And the Church of Ireland minister. If only I'd kept it. Wouldn't it raise a few eyebrows now? But I can remember the gist of it. I went over it often enough afterwards. It talked about the value of tradition. About people answering different bells but believing in the same Christ.

We'd never heard this kind of talk before. Never.

It talked about two families in Baltinglass and one in Athy being 'led away', that was the phrase that was used. It said the time might soon be ripe for action. But not yet. Approaches were being made to the families. But the time might soon be ripe.

I read the letter when it came and I read it again when my father came home from work and I read it half a dozen times that night but still it had nothing to do with the people I'd seen in Castledermot. These people it talked about had nothing to do with the girl I'd watched dressing on the bank. I sat on the hill that night. Waiting. Sweating.

~

Of course he was there again the following night. I determined to catch this boy, to confront him. I set out as I always did, went through two gaps in the hedges and, once I was out of his sight, I cut back across the edge of the field, out onto the road and up the back of the hill on which he was sitting.

I ran up that hill and my heart was fluttering with fear. And hope. I remember thinking I was totally insane.

~

I saw her leaving the cottage, crossing the fields, but she disappeared. I sat waiting, knowing she must reappear but the minutes dragged away and she didn't and the thought struck me that she had finished with swimming. I felt as though my whole life had been leading to this moment and I was faced with emptiness. With nothing. I had never felt a bleakness like that moment. Never.

~

He was standing on the hilltop when I came up behind him. I thought at every instant he would turn around and see me but he didn't. I had practised, all the way up that hill, what I would say and I said it. Loudly, for all the world as if I was as bold as brass.

'Like David and Bathsheba.'

He started and turned, his face was white beneath the sunburn.

'You frightened me,' he said.

'I thought you were here to watch me,' I said. 'You have been watching me, haven't you?'

He was silent.

'Well haven't you?'

'I saw you in Castledermot, on the Square, singing,' he said.

'You've seen me swimming too,' I said, laughing at his unease. 'I saw you watching me. Do you want to come and swim?'

'I can't swim.'

'Well, walk with me then. Come and keep me company. If you want to.'

He didn't move.

'Perhaps you'd rather sit and watch from here.'

He seemed, at last, to come to life as I turned to walk down the hill.

'No, no, I'll walk with you.'

'Good.'

I took a chance and glanced at him. The paleness was still there beneath the colour. His hair was short and brushed back. His shirt as white as it had seemed from the river bank. He wore scuffed, white canvas shoes. We walked in silence, down the hill and across the field towards the river.

~

I walked her to the river. She changed into her swimsuit while I sat on the bank, feeling foolish. I watched her turn and dive and roll in the water. It was as if ... as if she'd been born in that river. Afterwards, she came and sat on the burnt grass and slowly dried her hair.

I sat there, watching and listening.

She asked me if I knew the story of David and Bathsheba.

I told her I didn't.

'I thought of it every evening while you were sitting up there,' she said.

I mumbled something.

When she had finished dressing, she asked me if I would walk her home.

We went on walking and walking and I kept expecting her to say goodnight but instead we walked and walked and, before I knew it, I found myself in her parents' house, sitting in their kitchen, talking to her father.

He asked me about university, about my studies, about summer work on the farm, but there was no mention of religion.

~

I think my parents were pleased to see me with someone for companionship. I imagine they expected Lesley's going would upset me greatly. I remember my father spoke not a word about Jesus that evening, not to him. I was so relieved.

He called for me each evening, after that, and we went to the river. I began teaching him how to swim. In the end, in desperation, after I'd thought about it a hundred times at night, I found the courage he never would have and I kissed him.

After I had done it, I remember feeling a little angry that everything should have been initiated by me. I told him.

'You should have been the one to do this,' I said.

'Should I?' was all he said.

'You're the one who's close to the land. I'm the preacher's daughter. I'm not supposed to know anything about this kind of thing.'

He laughed at that. A wry laugh but it angered me even more.

'Are you happy just to sit there,' I said, 'and have me come running to you?'

'I didn't mean it to be like that,' he said.

I shouted at him then. We were sitting in the twilight, on the river bank.

'You must do what you believe in, that's why my father is here, that's why I went looking for you, that's why things happen. Because people make them happen. If you sit up there on your hill nothing is ever going to happen. You must know that.'

He was frightened. I could see.

'I didn't know what to do.'

'Of course you did! If you wanted to do something you'd do it. You do want me, don't you?'

God, I still remember that silence. That awful bloody silence and then my uncertainty. I thought he whispered 'Yes' but I wasn't certain.

'You know what David did when he wanted Bathsheba?' I asked.

He shook his head.

I knew I must tell and tell him in the way I had always seen that story, tell him in every detail. I stood up and looked across the darkening river so that my face was turned from him.

'It happened one evening, when David had risen from his couch and was walking on the roof of his palace, he saw a girl bathing in the river. Her name was Bathsheba. Even from that distance, he fell in love with her. He stood there and watched her bathing and in his mind he wanted her more than anything in his life. It didn't matter that he was married or that she was. He stood there watching her and he knew he must have her. In his heart, he came down from that great height, from his power and his palace, from what people expected of him. He overcame people's ideas and his own doubts and his soul went down to Bathsheba on that river bank. She must have felt the power of his passion surround her and swallow her. She stood there on the bank and she dropped her hair from her fingers and let it roll over her shoulders and David came and took the strands in his fingers and felt for the shape of her face through the hair.'

I turned back towards him then and he was standing directly behind me. He did what I had wanted him to do, he took my face in his hands, felt for the shape of my face through my hair. But I went on talking. I knew I must.

'Once he had done that,' I said, 'once he had broken the barrier that other people saw between them he saw there was no barrier at all. It was as easy as that. And he realised she already sensed what he felt. He felt the strength of her shoulders and knew she could carry whatever weight might fall on them because of what they were about to do.'

He spoke, again in a whisper, but this time I heard.

'And what did they do?'

'She went with him and slept with him. But once they had decided, that became easy. It became as easy as David running his fingers through her hair. As easy as that. My father tells that story as an example of sin but I don't see it that way at all. I see it as a story of passion that would out. I see it as a very beautiful story. It is a very beautiful story, isn't it?'

He said nothing. Instead he kissed my cheek.

'And as true now as then,' I said quietly.

He kissed me again and I opened my lips to his, as Lesley had taught me. We stood there, deep in that one long kiss. My hands were by my side. I slowly reached back and opened the buttons on the back of my dress. His hands slid from my hair and brushed the dress from my shoulders and then he knelt before me, slid down my body, his tongue tracing a course down my throat into the river bed between my breasts. I bent to kiss him and we fell onto the golden grass and I could smell the black river and his clean hair and I could feel the sweat that was his and mine.

The same young fellow who had delivered the letter from the parish priest came two days later to tell me I was wanted in the parochial house. My mother was out at the time and I didn't tell her when she came back. I got out the bicycle and went into Castledermot.

I was left sitting in the parlour for twenty minutes. It smelt of dampness and floor polish.

Twice the housekeeper came in and told me the parish priest was a busy man but I was to wait; I wasn't to go without seeing him. In the end, he arrived.

I stood up and he motioned me to sit down again.

He stood at the window, behind me, looking out across his lawn to the Laurels. He thanked me for coming to see him, congratulated me on passing my examinations, told me I was a bright lad, a lad who had worked hard and made the best of the educational opportunities that had come my way. That was a good thing, he said. A positive thing.

'*Educere*,' he said, 'means the leading out of the potential of the mind.'

How many times did I use that same phrase myself in the years since – and hate myself for it?

'Opening to new ideas,' he said. 'Isn't that what it's all about? And assessing the danger of the new when that danger arises. You're a lucky chap, Martin. Your family has worked hard for you, worked hard to get you where you are. They're working hard to keep you there.'

His tone was warm, understanding.

I found my head falling lower in expectation of the lecture about ingratitude that must follow but he was even better than I'd imagined.

'And the people of the village,' he went on, 'they're proud of you, Martin. In a few years' time, when you're a teacher, they'll say:

Martin Neill, yes, I went to school with him, played football with him, I grew up with him and he's a schoolteacher now.'

That respect, he told me, that position brought responsibility. I was at an age where I was beginning to notice girls and that was as it should be. Without that attraction, where would the human race be? And he laughed. He understood these things, just as he understood three, or was it four, years earlier – as if he didn't remember – when he'd given me permission to work on Emerson's farm. The Emersons were a good people, decent people, who recognised religious differences and were prepared to respect them. Live and let live, he said. His voice was deepening, darkening. The storm was upon me.

These proselytisers, he thundered, were a different matter. They lured people, ensnared them.

He appealed to me to be sensible, to think of my career, my faith, my future. Not to risk everything for a few hours in the company of a girl who was being – and I remember this phrase – 'dangled as a lure' before me, being used to trap and ensnare me.

I hardened my hands into fists. If this goes on … I thought … but his voice became soft again.

'Think, Martin,' he said. 'This is a slippery slope. First your virtue goes, then your faith, then your hope and then everything is gone. Self-respect is lost irretrievably.'

He sighed a deep sigh and walked past me into the hallway and disappeared. I sat there, angry and sweating. Wanting something or someone to attack. I heard footsteps in the hall. The housekeeper.

'He says you're to go,' she said.

~

There is one incident which I have preserved and taken out into the light of my recollection only occasionally. I have never been sure whether that was because I wanted to ensure its value lasted by not over-examining it, becoming overly familiar with it, or because I found it more daring, more assertive than any other thing we did in our time together. Perhaps it is a little of both.

We had come back one evening from the river to our cottage. My parents were out, visiting someone in Carlow, I think. I took him to my bedroom, to my bed, for the first and only time. We made love, if that is what we did, yes, we made love, quickly, silently, breaths held, listening for my father's car. It must have been quite late because a light shone across the hallway, from the kitchen, into my doorway. It must have been very hot, too, because my window was fully open and I could hear every sound from the roadway. He was so tense. I listened to the cricking of the laburnum pods in the front garden, to the cracking of the roof timbers in the hot darkness. I cupped his seed in my hands to keep it from the white sheets. I poured it slowly onto my skin and rubbed it on my stomach.

I watched him rise and dress and then he watched me.

Another evening we came back from the river, again my parents were away. The front door was daubed with tar. That time it said: DEVIL WORSHIPPERS. When my father returned he helped him clean the tar away. They worked by the light of a storm lamp. I can still see them in the light, standing in their shirt sleeves in the doorway, moths flying about them, scraping off the thick tar. People cycled by in the darkness beyond the light. I remember the sounds of bicycles and then voices falling silent.

~

People always said they could hear my father's tone of voice in mine. I could never hear it until one evening, a week or so after I'd gone in to see the parish priest.

My father was out in the garden, digging potatoes, when I cycled into the yard. He called me over to look at the potatoes, firm in their bed of clay. I helped him carry a sack of them into the shed and he started talking while we collected the fork and some empty sacks from the garden.

'My job is as safe as houses,' my father said. 'There's nothing that boyo can do to touch it.'

Somehow, I knew he knew about my meeting with the priest.

'He has no say in the beet factory. None,' he went on.

We were standing in the darkness now, in the middle of the half-dug garden. I couldn't see my father's face, just hear his voice, and I began to recognise a turn of phrase, a tone of voice that we shared.

'Oh, I know, I know nothing about this girl. She could be the grandest girl in the country for all I know. I'm not saying she's not. And I'm not telling you not to see her.'

He seemed to be speaking out into the fields, into the trees beyond our back ditch, to someone out there.

'I started out as idealistic as you but I lost it along the way, I lost it because I had to lose it. Just remember in two or three years' time, when you're looking for a teaching job, that's the time this man's words could echo far and wide. But it's up to you. No one can tell you what to do, there's no one can make your mind up for you. You have to look at this from every angle, see it every way and then make up your own mind. Maybe the best thing to do is what you want to do but don't be seen doing it.'

He paused for what seemed a long time and then went on.

'But maybe not. You make up your own mind. Decide yourself. Think it out.'

I wanted to hug him and kiss him and tell him he'd lost nothing. But I didn't. He walked away from me; his big boots were almost silent in the fresh clay.

I knew what I'd do. I'd cycle over the next evening, Wednesday, and wait for her at the cottage. She'd be down with her parents at the station in Maganey, collecting their pamphlets. When she got back we'd cycle over here together. I turned to follow my father inside. He was waiting at the gable of the house.

'If you want to bring her here, if that's what you decide, she'll be welcome. Your mother and myself, like.'

I have often thought since, how rarely I saw the sameness between us. But I did that night. It was a night like this but without a moon. A night when you saw things as straight as a road and as firm.

~

That evening, when I took him to my bed, is not the only one I hesitate about. There was another which I almost never look at now. Not because it upsets me any more; it did for a long time but not now. Now I look at it with distaste but it has lost its power to frighten me. I am too old to be frightened by it in the way I was when I was seventeen.

It was a Wednesday evening. Once a month, on a Wednesday evening, we drove to Maganey station to collect boxes of pamphlets which came on the late train from Dublin. The porter would have them waiting at the doorway to the platform, my father would tip him and load them into our car.

That Wednesday we drove down as we always did. There were a great number of people in the station yard. Many of them I recognised, men from Castledermot, women and children, too. They seemed to be standing about, aimlessly. My father walked through them towards the door. The boxes of leaflets were there as they always were. My mother and I sat in the car. I noticed the porter staring through the ribbed glass of the ticket office. As my father bent to lift the first of the boxes it seemed as though he was swallowed by the crowd. They swirled about him, shouting, screaming. My mother and I jumped from the car but two men held us back. The crowd was in a frenzy. One man, in particular, I could hear above the others.

'We're a Catholic people,' he was shouting. 'We've had enough of your carry-on. You've stolen enough children from their faith.'

His voice seemed to come first from one part of the crowd and then another, as if he was running about, urging them on. Suddenly he appeared where we were standing, beside the car. He screamed into my face, his mouth inches from mine, spit spattering my face.

'Youse can get yerselves back to hell. Out of here. You'll steal no more children! You hear, none!'

The crowd surged and I knew my father had been knocked to the ground. My mother was crying but I began to scream at this man, at the crowd, at the men holding us.

'Let him go,' I screamed. 'Let him go, you bastards.'

I tried to break free but the man holding me laughed and shouted: 'Shut up, you little fucker. Count yerself lucky.'

And then there was smoke and I realised these people were burning our pamphlets. A woman reached into our car and took my mother's Bible from the seat and it was thrown into the crowd and then onto the fire. My mother and I were bundled back into the car and the crowd opened and I could see the flames dying down. Children were running about, collecting stray leaflets and throwing them onto what remained of the fire. My father came staggering back. His face was ashen. I thought in that moment that he was about to die. He sat into the car and mumbled, 'Christ preserve us all. Bless us.'

The engine started and we began to drive away. A stone clattered on the roof and then another and another and another and another and my mother was weeping.

~

When I got to their cottage there was no one there. I left my bike in the yard and walked up the field to catch the last of the sun. I was lying out seventy or a hundred yards into the field to get the last of the coppery rays. I must have been half-asleep because it was nearly dark and I heard a banging in the yard and the sound of glass breaking. I ran down across the field, over the back ditch and around the side of the house. The front garden seemed to be full of people, men I knew, shopkeepers, farm workers, men from Castledermot. There were more of them inside the house. The windows had been smashed, the front door kicked off one of its hinges.

I started shouting at them, for all I was worth.

'What are you doing here, for Jesus' sake?'

'Get outta here,' someone said.

I turned to the man nearest me, he was smashing a chair off the front wall.

'Did the priest put you up to this?'

A voice from behind me made me turn; it was Donnelly.

'Fuck off outta that, ya little bollocks.'

'What are you doing here, Donnelly?' I shouted.

'You learn to run with the hare and hunt with the hound, sonny. I always tould ya that.'

'You're a traitor,' I said.

He stood right up to me, his face to mine.

'Safer with the hound, boy,' he said and then he smashed his forehead into my cheek, I heard and felt the bone crack and as I was falling his boot crashed into my stomach.

'Now who's a fuckin' traitor, hah? Get outta here if yer not able for it.' He began kicking and kicking and shouting at me. 'Bastard, bastard, bastard, bastard, bastard.'

Every scream was a kick, into the stomach, the face, the testicles, the back. As I rolled under his kicks I saw a man at the window of her room, the room where I'd lain with her. He was bundling clothes through the broken pane. Donnelly picked up one of the blouses and dangled it over me.

'Did ya fuck her, did ya, did ya? Ya did, didn't ya? Ya fucked her.'

He dropped the blouse onto my face and began kicking me again. And then he stopped. There were lights in the yard, a car. The men surged towards it. I heard voices. Warnings. Threats. I turned to see what was happening. The crowd was shouting at the car, at the people, at her parents, at her. She broke through, running towards the house and then she saw me and ran in my direction. Donnelly grabbed her and held her back.

'Go on, fuck her now, go on.'

I thought he was going to kill me. His eyes were burning in the car lights. I began to crawl away, towards the fields, the darkness. He pushed her to the ground and kicked me again. I began to vomit.

He leaned over me.

'The next time it'll be yer fuckin' neck an' yer father's.'

I kept crawling and crawling until I was behind the house, I crawled through the wire fence and stumbled into the field, I ran and ran. I don't know how but I ran and ran up onto the hill.

I could see the house and the yard in the lights from the car.

The crowd seemed to slip away into the darkness. I saw the three figures moving about the yard, collecting clothes, piling them into the car. I knew I had to go down, explain to them that this had nothing to do with me. But I was afraid. I was afraid the crowd would come back. I was afraid of Donnelly. But I had to tell her, explain to her, and then I saw two figures in a gateway a hundred yards down the road, two figures lounging across a gate and I sat on the hill crying. I pressed a cloth against my mouth. A blouse. Her blouse. There was blood on it from my mouth.

I watched them get into the car and drive away.

I sat there for a very long time. For hours. In the end, I went down to collect my bike. It had been thrown over the back ditch into the field. By Donnelly, I've always thought. A last act of kindness to make it easy for me.

I cycled home and hid the blouse under my pillow.

The next evening, when I got back from Naas hospital, my clothes were all washed and ironed and neatly laid out on my bed. The blouse was there, too. Washed, ironed, left unstitched.

I kept that blouse for a long, long time. I told my wife it belonged to my mother. And then, eventually, it disappeared.

~

After that evening we went and stayed with my cousins in Rathfarnham. After the terror, things settled down. My father returned to his printing business and we moved back to our house in Terenure. He continued preaching but stayed in Dublin.

My parents died. I married my bank manager and my bridge and my golf. Lesley married her doctor. A different one.

A number of times I travelled to Waterford by train. Newbridge, Kildare, Athy, Maganey. I often thought about getting off the train and enquiring.

I could have written. I'm sure a letter would have got to him. I never did. When I put something behind me I have done with it.

I sang at my father's funeral and never sang publicly again. I had done with that, too. It's best in the end.

Hewer

He stood in the rectangle of shadow where the sun from the door and window had not reached. He felt the softness of the shavings under his feet. Felt them as he had done for years. The workshop was quiet. The two men who had come in that morning had gone home. Home, he knew, to change their clothes, put on their good suits, wash themselves before they came back with the crowds after tea. He had wanted to do the work himself but the boys had insisted and the two men had come in at nine.

He ran his hand along the tight-grained wood as he did when he had finished a job himself. He loved the feel of the strong oak under his pushing fingers. No matter what the job, it always had the feel of something masterfully done. All the more so because of the finality of the thing. Something so conclusive must be as near perfect as didn't matter.

He walked about the workshop, passing in and out of the sun that rested easily on the warm floor. He found himself dragging his hand along the timber, losing concentration. The work would be good. The boys knew what they were doing when they asked Tommy and Mick to come in. They had known her as long as he had himself. It had been as important to them to do it properly as it would have been to him. The timber sat perfectly, board into board. As yet there was no lining. He was glad of that. He preferred the feel, the smell, the rawness of timber. They would put the sawdust in later and then the soft white material. They would staple it neatly, ready for the morning. He had done it himself countless times.

When his sons suggested having the men in to make the coffin, he had argued. It was his responsibility, he said. If he had made coffins for the town, he could make one for his own wife. But they insisted. Now he didn't mind. It was fine work. He looked at the curved head, viewed it from the doorway. Fine work.

When he stepped into the late sun he left the workshop door ajar, as it was always left. The warmth was unseasonal for March. For almost a week the skies had been clear and the sun hot. He scuffed the ground at the wooden water barrel. It was flaky with dryness, half-empty.

'Hewer of wood,' he said aloud.

He looked about him, afraid that he might have been heard. The garden was empty, even of birds. He whispered the words again. There had been a time when they set him aflame with hatred. Sullivan, the teacher, had thrown them at one of the boys, trying to make little of him.

'Your father is a hewer of wood, boy. Remember that.'

He had wanted to go down and beat Sullivan's head in but she had cajoled him into doing nothing.

What are words? she'd said. Who cared what that lout said? Let it rest.

And he had done nothing.

Years later they laughed about it. A compliment, she said. But he still nursed the sting of the condescending remark. He could imagine the biting, twisted lip as the words were hurled. He could see the compliment, not in the words, but in what he was, hewer and shaper of timber, maker of worthwhile things. Even in death what he made was beautiful, solid. More solid than the words of a man in a schoolroom.

He was at the end of the garden now, among the rhubarb stools. The great leaves would spread out through the
summer and dance in the pelting rain. At night you'd hear
the rain beating on them. That and the creak of the firs and
the roar of the trains picking up speed. Sounds of the night,
winter and summer.

He turned to go back into the house. A corner of the
garden shone in the very last rays. He had been digging there
earlier in the week. The first turnings. There were colours
beyond the rainbow thrown off the clogged earth, drowned
in the darkness of the laurel hedge. The cleanly cut sides of
the grass path led him back to the wicket gate and the yard.
He glanced into the workshop as he passed. The fresh shavings
were darkening, curling.

He lifted the old latch on the scarlet pantry door.

'Is that you, Pop?'

'Yes.'

'There's a cuppa here, if you want it.'

He went into the kitchen. Tim was standing by the table.
Peter sat at the fire.

'I'll have it so.'

'Before the crowd come,' Peter said.

'Aye, they'll be up soon, I'd say. Soon as the Angelus is gone.
Everything ready?'

'Yes.'

They drank their tea.

'Is the work all right?' Peter asked.

'It's fine. You were right. The lads did a proud job. I shouldn't
have kicked up a fuss. I just thought I'd like to do it but you were
right.'

They said nothing. He was glad they didn't patronise him.

'Where's Susan?'

'She's upstairs,' Peter said. 'Putting in the rest of the flowers.'

'Her mother was good to take the children.'

They finished their tea. Tim cleared and washed the dishes.

'What time is it?'

'Just six.'

'They'll be here soon.'

'Yes.'

Susan came into the kitchen.

'I just put in the rest of the daffodils, they're lovely. If you want to go up and have a look … before the crowd.'

He pushed the door in and stepped onto the scrubbed boards. There seemed to be flowers everywhere. Daffodils, tulips, freesia. Two tables under the window were covered in a cloth of petals. There were arrangements on each side of the bed and along the old mantelpiece over the blocked chimney. Susan had made a flame of the place.

This was what she had wanted. Flowers, flowers, flowers, when she died. He crossed the room and touched the back of her left hand. The blue veins grizzled against the tip of his finger. He closed his fist over hers.

Walking to the window, he looked through the firs to the cathedral. He no longer felt uneasy with his back to her. He had done last night. As if it was too early to turn away. But now he stayed at the window until Susan came into the room.

'Is it all right?'

'It's grand, girl, grand. The way she always wanted.'

'There aren't too many?'

'Couldn't be.'

She smiled at him.

'Only for you,' he said.

Susan crossed to the bed and touched his wife's hair.

'She looks grand.'

'Aye. But she got very old near the end. She was the same all her life until the last few weeks. Even the colour sort of went out of her hair.'

'She was beautiful.'

The heavy smell of tobacco filled the hall and the sitting room. Susan and Tim were in the pantry, drying the last of the glasses. Peter was crating the empty bottles. He could hear the gentle clink from the yard. Tommy and Mick would be gone from the workshop.

'There was a huge crowd.'

He didn't answer. He was thinking about how well loved she was.

Susan came in from the pantry.

'Are you all right?'

'Grand.'

'Can I get you something?'

'No, I'll just sit here till you're ready. Maybe we'd say a few decades before we go to bed.'

'Of course. Do you want to start now?'

'No, no, there's no hurry. I'm not a bit tired.'

They wound their way through the last prayers of the trimmings and got slowly to their feet.

'You'll have a cuppa before bed.'

'If the rest of you are having it.'

'Of course.'

He was lying in one of the single beds in the front room. Tim was asleep in the other. Peter and Susan had the side room. It was coming light. He looked at his watch. Gone six. He held his breath for a long time. This was only the second night they hadn't shared a bed. Last night and tonight. Never while she was alive, right up to the end.

He got out of bed as quietly as he could.

'Where are you going?'

'Out for a walk, just for a walk. It's bright.'

'You're all right?'

'Grand.'

'Do you want me to come?'

'No. I'm grand.'

'You're sure?'

'Yes.'

He put on his trousers and shirt and sports coat. He waited until he was out on the landing to put on his socks and shoes. It was light now and warm. Gently, he pushed in the door of their room. The two neighbours who had been there through the night remained as they sat. The room smelt of daffodils. He looked at his wife. She was blue and fragile.

Outside he could smell the summer coming. He walked across by the cathedral and out the Dublin road. He was glad to be clear of the town. When he got to Tullabraugher Protestant church he cut across the fields. About him, among the scattered mangles, sheep lay still. Bunches of daffodils gawked over the low stone wall of the churchyard. He went up the slope until he was out on the hill. The spire of the cathedral hid the house. Straps of smoke held the sky above the roofs. But it was not as he had hoped. He could not recapture the warmth of the days when they had come out here, when she was a thin, hard-breasted girl in nineteen forty. Out from the town on her half-day. Up through the trees and out of sight of the road. Those trees were gone. He closed his eyes but all he saw was the flowered room and the blue body.

Stupid, he thought, standing here in a damp field on a March morning. He wanted to be one with a memory but that wasn't possible in the house. The boys were good to him but they knew nothing of the real woman. How could they? Nor would they want to. It was a part of the past, of a passion that had nothing to do with family. It was too artificial up here. He had put too much store by it. You couldn't recapture everything at one time in one place. He had come up here expecting his ghost and hers to be waiting for him. But it wasn't like that. He should be satisfied with the peace that was in the house. But he had hoped for something beyond that. And he went on half-hoping as he crossed back between the sheep and out onto the road.

As he walked he tried to recall that impertinence of her girlhood. The carnival dances. The way she was always almost eager for him to see her body. But he couldn't feel what it had been like. He could see but not feel. All he felt was the frazzled vein.

Susan was in the pantry.

'You went for a walk?'

'I did.'

'Is it warm out?'

'Yes.'

'That's good.'

'Yes.'

'The others are still asleep.'

'Do you know what?' he said eventually. 'She'd like to have been buried at night.'

'Did she tell you that?'

'No, I just know it. She was mad after carnival lights, strings of coloured bulbs.'

Susan waited for him to continue but he was silent.

'You must have had a wonderful life when you were young.'

'I'm only realising how far it went in such a short time. You think you can always go back to things because they happened to you but they get dried up and tired. There's nothing worth looking at. And then it all sinks in and the pomp and carry-on isn't enough. The church and the prayers and all of that.'

Susan watched him, saw his sadness turn to bitterness, slowly. Like him, she was afraid.

The Things We Say

It wasn't my idea to come back here on our honeymoon. I'd have chosen somewhere that wasn't home but my husband was so enthusiastic about the prospect of spending time in the place where I was born and grew up that I finally agreed and, anyway, it wasn't as if we needed privacy or anything like that. It was a holiday, I suppose, as much as a honeymoon.

Not that it all began auspiciously. Among the people on the bus that took us the last sixty miles to my village was Robert Holland. He didn't speak but he stared at me so that my husband noticed.

'Do you know that man?' he asked.

'Vaguely,' I said. 'He came on holidays to the village when I was a kid.'

'He must have been impressed. He hasn't taken his eyes off you.'

I laughed it off and hoped nothing more would come of it.

How long since I last saw him? Five or six years? Not that there was anything sinister in seeing him, just an ominous feeling that may turn out to be completely unfounded. There was nothing worth mentioning to my husband, nothing that I could explain, nothing that would make any sense in the cold light of day. It was all wrapped up inside me, still is, maybe always will be.

And then the bus was clattering into the village and my mother was on the Square. My brother was cycling down the hill, late as usual, and taking the bags on his bicycle.

Walking to the house, we heard two cuckoos calling from the fields near the cliffs.

'That's for good luck,' my husband said.

'Is it?'

'Of course it is. It has to be.'

Immediately I regretted my curtness.

'Yes, good luck and good fortune,' my mother said.

The wiser woman.

My brother was at the house before us, the bags upstairs, glasses and a bottle of wine on the kitchen table. My mother looked over the photographs from the Registry Office, hiding her disappointment. My brother toasted our good sense in keeping things simple and inexpensive. My husband talked about the two cuckoos again. My brother said they were devious birds, untrustworthy. My brother who is so like me.

'I saw Robert Holland getting off the bus,' he said, once the birds had been dismissed.

'Yeah.'

'He wasn't here at all last summer. He must be back to do something on the house. It needs painting.'

I nodded.

'Do I know him?' my husband asked.

'The guy on the bus,' I said.

'Another broken heart she left behind,' my brother said.

'Not true,' I said, laughing. 'And now we're going out for some sunshine. Tomorrow it could be raining.'

We walked through the village, out onto the coast road, past the Martello tower and on to the sleeping-ground hill. The sleeping-ground runs down the back of the hill. Green mounds and grey stones that finally melt into the dunes at the beach.

I took my husband into the sleeping-ground and showed him my father's grave. And then we walked down to the dunes, passing Mrs Holland's grave. But I said nothing. We waded through the heavy sand on the dunes and then back up the hill, climbing into the fields and walking along the clifftop and into the lanes that twist back into the village. While we were walking, the sky changed. It sucked up the spray from the cliffs, turned the white water grey and spat it out again. We sheltered under a wall blackened with rain, hunkering on the grass.

As the rain grew harder, we crouched lower and then my husband lay back and pulled me down on top of him, opening my shirt and sucking my breasts, pushing my jeans down until his fingers were inside me, until I wanted him inside me, until I'd opened his jeans and I was fucking him. Until we both came, his hands showering me with flowers and blades of grass and clay, his face flecked with rain and sweat. We lay there for a long time afterwards, letting the rain puddle on our skin. We might have been discovered but that didn't worry me.

'You're my saviour,' my husband said.

I smiled at him. 'How?'

'Every time we fuck in a place like this, somewhere that we don't expect it, it brings me to the edge of madness and then you bring me back again. When I come in you, I'm saved from something I don't understand, something that seems to be waiting for me. I just know I am.'

I smiled at him again.

Sometimes he says things like that. And sometimes they stop me up short and sometimes, like today, my mind is somewhere else and they just about reach me.

And then, tonight, when I came up to our bedroom, my old room, after my mother and brother had gone to bed, my husband had lit candles. On the windowsill and the bedside table and the washstand. We sat on the bed and he ran the backs of his hands up and down my face, very slowly. I like it when he does that.

'Save me again,' he said. 'Be my saviour again.'

He kept saying that while we fucked again and I tried to be quiet when I came, biting into his skin, biting as deep and as hard as I dared.

And then we both fell asleep. I must have woken after ten or fifteen minutes. The candles were still burning and my husband was lying with his arms thrown across the bed.

My crucified saviour, I thought, and I smiled.

I was ten the first time the Hollands came to the village. I shared this room with my sister then and we had a candle for light. I'd see the Hollands in the village. Mrs Holland was elegant and slim and dark. Her husband was grey-haired and tanned but his tan was different from the burned skin of the fishermen whose boats lined the quay. His was an even colour. Robert was a child of my own age.

The Hollands bought a house on the other side of the hill. Some weeks I'd see them every day – at the shop or buying fish on the quay – and sometimes I wouldn't see them for days.

'The English,' my brother called them.

When I heard them talking, in the shop, I knew what he meant. Their accents were English, very English. They stood out and, as a result, people either avoided them or were drawn to making them feel at home. We seem always to have been like that in the village. There's no middle ground. In everything there are extremes, no middle ground. Perhaps it's the lives we've lived on the edge of the land and the edge of the sea.

Whenever the chance came, I'd watch Mrs Holland on the quay, dressed in her kaftan. She had a confidence and grace that I admired but never achieved myself. She was the kind of woman I'd have gone on admiring had she lived. Sometimes I'd see her on the beach in her swimsuit. She and her husband swam several times a day, strongly along the line of the coast while I kept to my depth, but then I was the only swimmer in our family.

'Sea people never swim,' my brother would say. 'Better to go down quick and be done with it.'

I spied on her when she sunbathed on the rocks. I was enthralled by her long brown legs, her plunging swimsuit that seemed backless, her ease with the elements. She was elegance.

The Hollands came back every summer after that. When I was fourteen I thought they were the most perfect and most beautiful family in the world. That was the summer my father died.

I rarely talk about my father, not because I have no clear memories of him, I do, and not because he wasn't important to me, he was, but because he was always part of whatever certainty there was in our house and I still think of him as that. As whatever quiet certainty there is behind my life, even now.

The Hollands came up to our house the day my father died. They spoke to my mother and brother. They offered the use of their car for the funeral. And Mrs Holland spoke to me. I don't remember what she said; I don't think I heard the words. I was mesmerized by the reassurance of her tone. I felt everything would be all right. She sounded so certain that I couldn't doubt her.

Later that summer my sister went away to stay with my aunt and in the same week the electrical storms began. We always had storms in the summer but these seemed to come every night. I'd lie in the darkness, terrified, and then the light would snap and unsnap, a second of light which unveiled shadows, faces, figures. My father's face? His outline? His hand on the window-sill? I wanted my father to come back and I dreaded his arrival. I wanted to call out to my mother but something stopped me. And then, reacting to my silence, a figure in the doorway. My brother. Holding me in his arms. Shushing me gently. Singing quietly. What was it he sang? I can't remember. Jesus, I can't remember. But he was there when I fell asleep and he was there when I woke, curled in a blanket on the floor beside my bed.

The storms went on. Night after night, into a second week and a third.

'They'll kill us,' I said, one night when the sheet-lightning rose out of the sea and dipped the village in a wash of blue and white.

My brother took me to the window. 'Sit there,' he said. 'Don't move. Count to twenty and don't move. Just keep watching the back field.'

And then he was gone, reappearing at fifteen in the yard below, climbing the stone wall into the small haggard behind the house, parading around there, dressed only in a blanket, while the sky and the land were fused in thunder-flashes. And then he climbed on to the wall and dropped the blanket and stood there, naked, with his fists driven up into the night while the noise and the light poured over him.

I slept soundly that night and every other night of that flashing summer. Most mornings, when I woke, my brother's blanket was curled on my bedroom floor.

And here's my sleeping husband. I'd like to tell him of how my brother saved me from the dark and the light, but he'd think my brother was mad.

Anyway. Anyway, time to blow the candles out.

The same small field. The same stone wall. The same window-sill where I sat and counted to twenty. But what was the song? Tomorrow sometime, when the chance comes I'll ask my brother if he remembers. Or maybe not. He'd be embarrassed and he'd deny the whole thing happened and that would destroy so much. He'd dismiss the whole thing in the way I dismissed my husband's talk about the cuckoos being lucky.

Why are we like that? Is it an ocean cynicism? Does it come with the uncertainty of the sea? Or is it just us? Just this house, this family? Is it because we had so little that we pretended we needed nothing?

No. That's not entirely it. I wanted things. When I was eight or nine I wanted to fly. I desperately wanted to rise up over the village and see beyond it. I'd watch the black shadows of the swallows zipping across the back yard and I'd wish my shadow could be that fast. Here and gone. Gone somewhere new and exotic. Or just gone. And there were other things. I wanted my father back with us. I wanted Mrs Holland's elegance. I wanted to slip in and out of places without drawing attention to myself. I wanted to be beautiful. Most of all, I wanted to escape and, at the same time, I never wanted to leave.

But nothing happened. Summer ended and it was time to go back to school. Life went grinding on. Winter storms. Skeletons of boats thrown up on the beach. Spring threatening but never coming and then summer again. The buses running twice a day. Day trippers. The Hollands arriving. School closing. Walking the quay wall with the other girls. Watching and waiting. The summer withering. The last of the summer buses. The Hollands walking the beach for the last time, swimming their last swim. Tying their cases on to the roof rack of their car, waving goodbye. And then the quay was empty, apart from the trawlers, and it was time for school again.

I was fifteen. Sixteen. Seventeen.

Anyway. Anyway, time to blow the candles out.

I can hear my husband breathing. That makes me wife again. It feels the same as it did and yet there is no comparison. Being married then was much the same as now. And then it changed. And this may change. No matter how good things are they may not be good enough. I learned that and it stalks me now. The better things are, the worse they may be when they're gone.

Sometimes I think the black days are our safeguard, the days when there's nothing to do but let him sink until he's ready to come back up without any help, until he's able to do it. I've learned enough to know I can't rescue him. Those may be the times that save me, if I ever need saving. Those may be the memories that will keep me afloat if I'm thrown back on my own. Those are the saving graces, not the days when he's flying, when his happiness is intense. The times when he's inside me, when he's a different person, when he doesn't speak because he's lost in me, are useless afterwards.

That kind of exhilaration comes back to haunt. It's the memory of blackness that helps, that proves life can be better. What would he think, this husband who tells me fucking with me makes him feel like God on the edge of creation? He smiles when I joke about creation but he doesn't really listen. What would he think if he knew I store up the sensations of exclusion because I know I may need them someday? Of course I admire his appetite for passion but I'm grateful for the balance that keeps me in control.

The sky is cloudy but there's a full moon behind the cloud. The yard is more sallow than white but everything is clear, right across the fields and down to the shore. The light isn't brilliant but it has a kind of serenity. Isn't serenity enough? I thought about that on the bus coming out here. My husband asked me a hundred questions about the village, about growing up here, about the people and the places I knew. He was like a child. And then he asked me to take him to the first place I'd ever made love, to take him there and fuck with him.

'Why,' I said. 'It's not jealousy, is it?'

He looked hurt when I said that, as though I hadn't understood. 'Of course not. I just want to be everywhere that's you. Your house. Your room. The place where you first made love.

The place where you were born. The place you went to school. That's all.'

'I lived here for eighteen years,' I told him. 'How long have we got?'

He smiled at that. 'Just that once,' he said. 'Just that one place.'

And when we came up to this room, tonight, when he took off my clothes, when we lay down together, I said, 'Here, this is where I first made love.'

'Tell me about it,' he said.

And I told him a story. About a boy who'd followed me around all that summer, my seventeenth. Robert Holland. He'd come for the summer with his parents, as always. But this time it was different. His mother had changed. She was no longer elegant. She was ill and haggard and wasted. She was dying.

Mr Holland went everywhere with her. They walked the beach, slowly. To anyone who didn't know them, they looked like a couple lost in conversation, as indeed they were. But, to those of us who knew, everything had changed. They walked too closely together. They were wrapped up in each other. Her faded body seemed to fold itself into the shadow of her husband. They were holding on to whatever little was left to them and the closer they walked the wider the gulf that was before them. Even then, even as a young girl, I had some notion of that. I might not have understood it completely but I suspected the horror that lay ahead for them. To see that once elegant woman being carried by her husband against the wind told everything.

I stopped watching them. I couldn't bear to see her melting away. I avoided the beach at the times I knew they'd be there. I never walked to the side of the hill their house was built on. I tried to forget what Mrs Holland had been and what she was.

But Robert was watching me, following me. And I was sorry for him. I made a point of talking to him. It was difficult.

I'd known him so long and never spoken to him, beyond a word on the road, and now, wherever I went, he was there. Waiting for me to talk. So I did. Not that we ever talked a lot. He was as shy as I was and the silence helped both of us. We both knew how much effort was involved and we both respected the other's fear.

Afterwards, I wondered about that time. About Robert and his parents. Did he feel excluded by his parents or was he terrified of watching his mother's life drip away? He seemed to avoid his parents as much as I did. He hung around our house a lot. My mother fed him. And then it happened. We were here together one afternoon. Alone. I came upstairs to get something and he followed me. I turned around and he was standing in the doorway of my room. It just happened. No great event. He knew less about it than I did. I wasn't leading or being led. It was just something.

'Did you love him?' my husband asked.

'I felt tenderness towards him. I felt sorry for him. I liked him. He was handsome. He still is, you've seen that.'

And I told my husband about the rest of that summer. About how I went on sleeping with Robert Holland. About how we learned things together, simple things about each other's bodies.

And then his mother died.

'They buried her here in the village, in the sleeping-ground,' I told my husband. 'She was thirty-eight years old.'

I cried, remembering her. Such a beautiful woman and the terrifying sadness she left in her wake. So different from the feelings when my father died. Such a sense of complete waste.

'Everything about her was wasted,' I said. 'Her body, her grace, her possibilities.'

'I'm sorry,' my husband said. 'I shouldn't have asked. It was none of my business. I didn't mean to do this.'

And he rubbed the backs of his hands against my face, very slowly.

'Save me again,' he said. 'Be my saviour again.'

He kept saying that while we fucked.

The things we say, the questions we ask each other, fearing the truth, yet hunting it down to its bitter end. But some of what I told my husband tonight was true and the rest wasn't worth telling. Not because I'm ashamed of it but because he wouldn't understand. Just as Robert Holland didn't. Just as his father didn't – not really. But Mrs Holland would have done, I know she would.

Still, it wasn't all my husband's fault. All this remembering. There was Robert Holland on the bus. Mrs Holland's grave. And the small inscription at the foot of her headstone. The inscription I'd almost forgotten. Let me tell my husband now. While he's sleeping. Then he can hear whatever he needs to hear and the rest can go unremembered.

Mrs Holland was dying. That much is true. Everyone could see it. To see her husband and herself together was to see that. Where once they had complemented each other, they now, literally, leaned together with an awkwardness I can't describe. People passing, people who knew the situation, were uneasy. We felt as if we were intruding. I think Robert felt that way too. He wanted them to have whatever half-chance remained to remember and relive the past.

Maybe I knew, with the intuition of the young, that he needed someone to get him through that time. And, maybe, I was flattered by the thought that I could be the one. We were there for each other. Maybe it was as simple as that. Sometimes the most clichéd explanations are the truest.

He might have stumbled across someone else and so might I but we didn't. We spent those weeks walking, swimming, kissing,

talking when we had to, when there was nothing else to do.
Once or twice he came up to my room, when the place was
empty, and lay with me on my bed but he seemed to have no
energy, no passion, no desire to do anything. We'd lie face to
face cocooned in our separateness, everything that his parents
weren't. Whatever satisfaction existed stemmed from his sadness
and my attempts at comfort. He was concerned with his dying
mother and I was concerned with myself. We were only slightly
concerned with each other.

And then his mother died, one morning in July.

I went up to their house that afternoon. The curtains were
all open. Even the window in the dead room was wide to the
breeze from the sea. I'd never seen that before. My father, like
everyone else who died in our village, lay in a dark room that was
perfectly still. Mrs Holland lay in a room that filled and emptied
with the swing of the wind and the stuttering of the sea. The sun
streamed across the floor and on to the brass bedstead. Everything
was white with light and her body seemed to be nothing more
than a flimsy transfer on this cotton sheet. I had to look carefully
to be sure she was really there. Her skin seemed to appear and disappear as the wind filled and emptied the room. Was this a body
or a ghost? Was this the woman I'd known or a reflection off the
sea? One thing I did know – she was no longer beautiful. There
was an emptiness in her face. No trace that life had ever been
there, no sign of beauty. Nothing of her left.

Mrs Holland was buried in the sleeping-ground the following afternoon. No church, no prayers. Her husband read a poem
at the grave.

Years later, I heard someone read the same poem on the
radio and discovered it was 'Crossing the Bar'. I went to the
library and found it and copied it. I still have it somewhere in a
drawer. I know that late that night, the night of Mrs Holland's

burial, there was an orange sunset that bled the whole sky out over the sea. And, later still, there was the evening star above the house where the Hollands had lived for so many summers, the house where she had died.

I didn't see Robert in the week after his mother's death. I waited for him in the place we normally went but he didn't come and I didn't dare go up to the house again. I did go to the sleeping-ground most evenings, partly to visit his mother's grave, partly in the hope of seeing him. Even then I thought it strange that I should be drawn to where this woman was buried. I rarely went near my father's grave but somehow there was something about Mrs Holland's youth and beauty that said, Come and look and savour the tragedy. I think I almost needed her, needed to be near her, needed to breathe the dead air and watch the dying flowers on the dry sands. I can't explain this. I was young, I was impressionable and I was lost, but those are facts and they don't explain a lot.

But it wasn't evening, it was morning when it happened. A bright blue and yellow morning, just after seven. A morning at the start of August, when summer crams everything into a final thrust of heat and the particular light of the season. I'd woken very early and couldn't sleep again, so I went swimming and now I was making for home, crossing the sleeping-ground. And then I saw Mr Holland. He was standing in a dip in the ground, about fifty yards from his wife's grave, not even looking at it. Instead, he was watching me. I stopped when I saw him, the red towel I was carrying trailing in the seagrass that keeps the graves anchored to this earth.

'Don't stand so far away from me,' Mr Holland said.

I moved towards him but very slowly. I was a little frightened.

'Stand here,' he said, pointing.

I went and stood beside him.

He was silent.

I could barely hear his breathing. Short, soft breaths. I wanted him to speak, to say something that would break this terrible silence. I wished someone would come and disturb us but I knew the beach behind me was empty.

He stood there, staring out past me, across the waves of sharp grass, breathing those soft breaths. I thought he was going to die. And then, suddenly, he had my hand in his but nothing was said. I waited for him to do something. I expected him to scream or to cry but he didn't. Nothing. Breathing. The sea away behind me. The sand beginning to dazzle as the sun moved higher.

'Are you all right?'

I heard my own voice and was surprised by its strength and calmness. He turned, only slightly, so that his face was close to mine. I expected his eyes to be filled with tears, but they weren't. I thought he might kiss me but, again, I was wrong. Instead, he stared at me and then knelt down slowly and let go of my hand.

'Let me see you,' he said, in a whisper. 'Please, let me see you.'

I dropped the towel I was holding and undid the buttons on the front of the light dress I was wearing over my swimsuit. I rolled the dress off my shoulder and it fell, loosely, down my arms, only catching at my waist.

'Let me see you,' he said again.

I pulled the straps of the swimsuit off my shoulders, first one and then the other. I stopped for an instant but only an instant and then I peeled the damp swimsuit from my breasts and stood there, facing him.

'You're very beautiful,' he said.

'Am I?' My voice, but I couldn't believe I was speaking.

'Am I?' I asked again.

'Very.'

I took his head in my hands and pressed his face against my belly. I felt the unshaven skin against my skin. My fingers were tight in his hair.

'You smell of life,' he said, the words coming up, muffled by my belly. 'No, you smell of sea. You smell of salt water.'

I held him to me a little while longer and then relaxed my hands. The wind was blowing against my skin, lighter and cooler than it had been. I thought of two things. I thought of rain. I wished it would rain; I wanted it to rain on me. I had almost forgotten that Mr Holland was still there. I wanted to feel rain on my skin, I wanted to sense rain running off my shoulder, making streams on my body. And then I thought of possibility – the possibility of my life. For the first time, maybe the only time, in my life I felt that I was in charge of everything that would happen to me. I was mistress of my destiny.

Mr Holland had eased himself away from me. He was sitting back on his hunkers, his eyes on the ground. I think he had forgotten me, too. I pulled my dress back over my shoulders and buttoned it. The cotton felt strange against my breasts but I left my swimsuit about my waist. I did all this very slowly and then I picked my towel from the sand and walked away.

I didn't feel power over him. I didn't feel remorse. I felt released from childhood and, despite everything, I've never regretted what happened that morning. I've never seen anything wrong in it. For either of us. What was I to him? An angel of life, an attempt at reaffirmation? Perhaps. But my wings were too light to carry him out of that place and state. My wings were new. If I could have saved him I would but I didn't know how. I wasn't even aware that he needed saving. But I can't blame myself for that.

It was the evening of that day when Robert Holland came to our house. My mother and brother had just gone out. I think he must have watched and waited until I was alone. I was sitting in the kitchen, reading, in the dusky light and he walked in, without knocking, and stood at the table.

I put down my book and stood up but before I could speak he took me by the hand and led me upstairs to my room. He undid my buttons and let my dress fall to the floor. He kissed my belly and eased me on to my bed, kneeling beside me and easing his hand inside my pants, beginning to slide his fingers inside me. I closed my eyes and let him go on masturbating me. I didn't want him to stop and I was already too far gone to do anything for him. I just wanted his fingers inside me, I wanted him to go on stroking me. I wanted to come. Then I'd do whatever he wanted. Then. But for now it was me.

Suddenly his fingers stopped. My first thought was that my mother or my brother had come into the room. I opened my eyes. We were alone but Robert was standing up, glowering.

'I saw you,' he said. 'I saw what you did.'

He started to cry.

'Don't,' I said. 'Lie down with me.'

He spat on me and walked out of my room. He went so quietly that, for a while, I thought he was outside my door, but he was gone.

I saw him again during the rest of that summer. Of course I did. I saw him the next night and the next and every night for the next two weeks. I saw him coming in on one of the trawlers in the twilight. I saw him talking with the fishermen and the police. I saw him walking to his house where he had stayed every night since his father went missing. My mother had sent my brother up to invite him to stay with us. He thanked her but said he was all right where he was. I never saw him during the day. He was out on the boats, searching. My brother said the body would turn up in ten or twelve days but it didn't. It never appeared. Nor did Robert the following summer. The house stayed locked and shuttered.

After that he came back only at odd intervals and when he did he always spent the first few days walking the beach and the rocks, searching, it seemed to us. As if he didn't believe we had kept watch all that first winter. As if the trawlermen didn't check their nets carefully.

But his father's body never appeared and then it went beyond the time when it might.

'For such a strong swimmer to do that,' my brother said once.

'Maybe he cut his wrists,' my mother suggested.

'No,' my brother said. 'I've seen that done. He wouldn't have got out far if that was the case. He'd have been washed in before the week was over.'

I left the village that autumn, husband. I began the journey that took me to you. Eventually.

Three summers afterwards, when I was back here with the man who was to be my other husband, I saw the stone on Mrs Holland's grave. 'In loving memory', and all the rest. Name. Dates. And, on the base of the stone, her husband's name and one line: 'May he find peace'.

'There's a life out here that I've never seen anywhere else,' you said to me last night, when we were walking. 'It must be the sea and the wind and the openness to the world across the ocean. This whole world.' But the sea has nothing to do with life, I thought. But I didn't say that. I'd said enough already.

'You smell of life,' he said. 'No, you smell of the sea.'

May he find peace.

May all of us.

And love.

A Year of Our Lives

She is walking through the woods with the children. They know these woods so well. The children chase and gallop ahead, sliding on the hardened frosty grass where the sun makes no impression. She walks slowly, her hands driven deep in her pockets. She walks steadily. The children pause at the end of the pathway and look back at her; she motions them on – up the hill to the summit. They trot away, their voices slipping sporadically through the trees. She reaches the end of the path and turns to follow them. And then she sees it. A thin blue rope sagging from the heavy branch of a sycamore. It dangles three feet above the ground, its end tied in a thick knot. It has probably been there all summer. Small children have clung desperately to the knot, older ones have sailed effortlessly across the path, wrapping their legs around the rope, calling for someone to push them.

She shivers but she isn't cold. This is barely controlled shaking. Walk on, she thinks, keep walking, follow the children. But there is no escape from the rope, it becomes another rope, one she has never seen, one that haunted her teenage years. It becomes the rope that Mary Noonan spoke of, the story that Mary Noonan whispered in the midnight dormitory, the horror that Mary Noonan never told to any other girl in the school. But she and Mary Noonan had talked, their beds head to head in the darkness. Mary Noonan who arrived after the Christmas of second year, a late boarder. A girl who seldom spoke in the daylight hours. A girl whose father had died suddenly over the holiday, the nuns said.

Where is Mary Noonan now? They kept in touch till marriages took them to opposite ends of the country. Mary Noonan who had been a friend but whose story had given her nightmares for years and is reappearing now in these frosty woods. As if she needs it. God knows, she doesn't need it now. That voice, that country voice coming, one night, out of the darkness.

'You know my father died at Christmas?'

'The nuns told us.'

'I found him.'

'That must have been terrible,' she'd said, having no idea how she'd deal with even the thought of her own father's death.

'It was Christmas morning.'

'Jesus.'

'I never told anyone here about it,' Mary Noonan had whispered. 'You wouldn't tell, if I told you, would you?'

'Course not.' And she never had.

'He was always on the piss,' Mary Noonan had told her, rolling on to her tummy and whispering quickly. 'He kept selling fields and drinking the money. Long as I remember our farm was always getting smaller. One day a field'd be ours and the next day someone else's cows'd be in it.'

She remembers nodding in the darkness, rolling on to her tummy, finding the light of Mary Noonan's eyes, wanting to reach out to her but not daring.

'Last year there was nothing left to sell but that didn't stop him. He'd be off for days and then I'd find him asleep in the car on my way to school. He'd be halfway down our lane. And then he went on the piss on Christmas Eve and didn't come back. Christmas morning my mother sent me out to look for him, to get him home, not to let him near the church in case he'd make a show of us. As if anyone didn't know already. For fuck's sake, everybody knew.'

Even now she remembers her chill at Mary Noonan's directness. It signalled something awful.

'The car was at the bottom of the lane,' Mary Noonan had said. 'But he wasn't in it. I opened the door. His overcoat and short coat were in the back seat. I went down the lane, on to the main road. I thought he might be walking ahead of me. There was no one else around but it was getting bright. I could hear the wind humming along the telephone wires. I always try to make out the sound, to hear the people talking, to hear the voices in the wires. I can nearly hear people talking all the way from America, saying "Happy Christmas", and things. Do you ever do that?'

'No,' she'd said.

Mary Noonan laughed quietly. 'Well, I do. Anyway, I saw something, on a pole a bit down the road. It was kind of like a shadow till I got closer and then I saw it was a person. I thought it was a chap from the telephones fixing the wires but then I saw that whoever it was was hanging from one of the rails that's nailed across the top of the pole. I couldn't see the face, it was turned away from me, but I knew who it was. I screamed and screamed and then I ran, past our lane, to Parkinson's. The two lads drove back with me. When they saw him, one of them said: "How the fuck did he get up there in the dark?" And then they reversed the car and brought me home. They told my mother. She said nothing. After the guards came, they cut him down and the ambulance took him away. The guards drove us to my uncle's house. When we passed the place there was nothing left but tyre tracks in the grass and a bit of rope still in a knot on the crossbar.'

And then Mary Noonan had been quiet for a while. Finally she'd spoken again. 'He was a bollocks. I'm glad he's dead.'

He might have been dead for his daughter but the unseen man had not been dead to *her*. Most nights that term she dreamt of him, dangling from electricity poles on her road, in the school grounds, even in the dormitory. Sometimes, in her dreams, she was trying to untie a knotted rope from the bar on the end of her bed. A thick black knot that could never be undone. She had woken sweating, the sound of Mary Noonan's quiet breathing at her head. Eventually, the nightmares faded. Until now.

The children are dancing on the summit, waving their arms, urging her to run the last forty yards.

'Come on,' they're shouting. 'Come on, come on.'

And she is running.

He is jogging through the woods, as he does every morning. Sometimes the long way round, sometimes the straight run to the hilltop and back again. This cold, dry morning he feels good. He is rested. His head is clear. He is running well, ready for whatever ambushes the week has planned. His strides are easy and sweeping, his feet bounce off the frosted grass. It's as though his body is floating above these legs, above legs that are younger and faster than they should be. His breath comes out like diamonds. The sun is genial in the gaps between the trees. It's glint and haze and glint and haze up through the trees to the brilliance of the hilltop.

He rests, breathing deeply, looking out over the smocked countryside, picking out the landmarks – the moat, the power station, the sugar factory – and then he's off again, down the steepness, his strides controlled, loosening into the mottled forest and along the wide avenue until he is out into the car park near the road.

Monday morning car park, after the night before. Wads of sodden tissue in the grass after the late-night couples on the way from the discos and bars. He slows to a walk, knowing the corners under the trees, counting the discarded condoms. This is something he does every morning now. Seven this morning. The scattered rubbers with their bulbs of dull semen give him hope. Reassure him. There is life out there, still going on. Passion still running wild. Couples are still fucking in cars, their mouths locked together, coming noisily, quietly, without caring. As long as this goes on, the struggle continues. He starts running again, across the car park, on to the road, towards his house.

xii

She's lying in this bed, in this room, in this house. His house. A house she hardly knows. It's late in the afternoon, the day after Christmas, and the light in the sky is helpless. This is an eastern sky. Her bedroom looks on to a western sky – lighter and brighter later. But this has nothing to do with the feeling inside her. Sufficiency. Satisfaction that they've finished, that she's come, that their bodies are apart. She feels easy. Rested. And certain that this will never happen again. She has no regrets about her generosity to him. Just certainty.

She remembers other times when they made love, when they fucked – in the weight of a hot open field the summer they married; in the kitchen while her parents talked upstairs; under a railway bridge in a blizzard, their bodies boiling in the freezing afternoon. She's not surprised by the distance of all this. Why shouldn't it be distant? Those were other people. She closes her eyes momentarily, opens them again, turns the bed-clothes back and steps away quickly. She finds her clothes in the dusk, prepares to leave. Already she's thinking of something else. Something more important now.

Suddenly he's awake, completely awake. The woman's pale skin is gone. The large beautiful eyes are gone. The breasts, pressed against the dress, are gone. As soon as he's conscious he remembers these things and as soon as he remembers he's aware of their absence. It all happens in an instant.

The screen hisses mesmerically at him. Rubbing his eyes, he pushes himself out of the chair, presses the 'off' button on the TV set and then the 'rewind' button on the video. Later. He'll return later to the would-be lovers in the summer wood of *A Month in the Country*. Later.

Outside, the winter afternoon settles grimly. Inside, the fire is a collapsed purple parachute on the grate. Is it the ash or the dusk outside? These faces. Faces pressed against the wire of some death-camp. Deep eyes calling but he hears nothing. He sees them speaking, trying to tell him something. Trying. To tell him something that must be told. Must be heard. The eyes like dulled love bites, peering. He hurries into the kitchen and lifts the phone. He listens. Nothing but the monotony of the tone. No language. No voice. Nothing.

He stands in the cold kitchen, scanning the wilting Christmas cards, listening. Willing someone to speak.

i

'What did you want doing that for, with a lovely house, a lovely home? Would you not get together, the two of you, sort it out? How can you turn your back on all this? We went through this, you must remember that. Times when I was on the batter and she'd raise hell and rightly so, but we got through it.'

'It's not easy for a woman to start again. It's all right for you but you should think of the other side. It's all right for you to walk away.'

'The kids won't thank you for it. You might think it's all as smooth as ice now but by God they'll see it otherwise. Wait till you see what it does to them. No one will be laughing then, I'm telling you.'

'All the outside influences, that's what I blame.'

'And that fellow. Are you bent by any chance?'

'You can only swim so far against the tide.'

'For Christ's sake, you got through the hard times, what're you doing now? It's downhill all the way.'

'We counted on you. We always thought you were solid as rocks, we never saw this coming. You were always there to be relied on. I can tell you this is some shock.'

'I can only hope they won't despise you in the end, that this won't put them off the rails. That's my only hope for you.'

'Why don't you leave it for a while, see how things go? You owe these years to the kids.'

'It's not the same when you close the door on your own, no one else to share a house. It's not the same at all, you never get used to it.'

'How do you mean things'll be all right? They won't be all right, how could they be?'

'Every couple goes through things like this. You have to give one another enough room to get out of the way. But that doesn't mean throwing in the towel. You don't just turn around and say, "That's the end of it." Not with children, you can't do that. Jesus, you might as well lay them in a coffin as that.'

'All the work the two of you put into the place. It's all right talking about this, that and the other but it'll never be the same again. You had your noses out of the wood, kids well on their feet.'

'Too much time spent with other people.'

'Listen, you'll hear it all. They'll say you couldn't ride him, wouldn't ride him, wouldn't let him ride you, that you were riding half the town. They'll say anything.'

'You'll be kicking stones out there, with your feet in the fire.'

'No one will ever trust you again. No one. No one trusts a woman who can't keep a family together.'

'Do you know how lonely it is? Do you know how hard it is to start again? I think you've had it too easy.'

'Take a holiday, a bit of time apart and you'll come back like it was new.'

'The kids might look like they're okay but in a year or two years, it'll surface.'

'I hope this doesn't catch you when you're least expecting it – you could go down when you're least expecting it.'

'Listen to me. If you had no choice, if you had to work this out, you'd find a way to sort it out. Wouldn't you, in all honesty? I don't want to be critical but you would, wouldn't you?'

'Things'll never be the same, don't tell me nothing's changed. Every fucking thing has changed. Everything.'

ii

He sits, waiting for the traffic to clear. Cars and vans and lorries backed up from the railway gates. He turns the key and the engine dies. He rolls his window down on the dry day. Not spring yet but getting there. And then he notices a woman at the surgery gate and something about her look tells him everything. He feels the pain again. The pain from a long time ago. A different kind of distress. A suffering he could only marvel at, about which he could do nothing. All that pain, spread over him across the childhood years, is here in this one face now. All of it in one morning. The doctor may have put some name on it, prescribed something for it, calculated some time for it but the look is there and he is terrified. By this woman's pain and by his own. Her face says no.

He sits in the jammed traffic. She stands by the surgery gate. Both waiting.

In the late afternoon, just before dark, she is walking past the hoardings around the town hall. Her eye is taken by the neat black graffiti on the newly painted boards:
'Ger loves Sally so fuck off & leave them alone.'

She smiles. For a moment she considers stopping and completing the haiku. She searches for something appropriate.

That night, in bed, she rearranges the words in her head:
'Ger loves Sally so

fuck off and leave them alone.'

She sleeps and wakes.

In the electric lit bathroom, she writes the words, just beside the mirror where the children won't see them.
'Ger loves Sally so

fuck off and leave them alone.'

And then she adds her final perfect line.
'Dante. Beatrice.'

iii

She stops the car on a wide stretch of roadway, turns off the engine and sits in the quietness. The rain darkens the door of the day, insinuating itself into the bare bushes on the roadside. One of those days when it isn't raining but there's rain everywhere. She winds down the window and listens to the songless road, the leafless sighing and sucking of the trees. And then she notices the gulls circling above this inland countryside. She gets out of the car and walks to the breast of the railway bridge. The gulls are suspended above a blue tractor, hanging effortlessly as the tractor ploughs its way up and down the sodden fields. A kiss of elation touches her heart. The birds flagging a new season, the plough burrowing for something that will come good.

She imagines the washed blackberry flowers climbing this bridge. She sees a day with the tar swimming on this road. She remembers a shoeless afternoon, carrying a prized poached trout from the river, wrapped in her white handkerchief. What age was she then? Younger than her daughter is now. She is back cycling on a late summer day, dismounting at the foot of Mullaghcreelan to walk the steep three hundred yards, and two fox cubs, mottled by the capsizing sun, are rolling on a bank beneath the trees.

A car slows at the foot of the bridge and comes up the hill.

This, she knows, is a new year. The electric wire above her head is singing, the trees are beginning their wombing push.

The car passes. Two faces peer at her. They see a woman leaning against a parapet, watching a blue tractor turning the earth inside out. What don't they see, she wonders? They don't see the bruises on an uncertain heart.

He hates the random way that March deals its moods. The sudden slapping rain as he races from the car and fumbles for the door key in the dark. And as the key turns the rain stops. He steps inside this house that was once his home. The cat follows expectantly. Why else should he be here, who else will feed her? He flicks the kitchen light, finds a tin and spills it into her dish. He leaves her eating, wanders through the house, drawing curtains, switching on lights.

Back in the kitchen, he lifts the cat, strokes her, carries her to the door and puts her down in the garden. She looks at him and then saunters away. He goes back inside and closes the door. He is standing inside an empty house. Not so long gone but long enough to be uncertain. He feels the need, the need to stay. It would be good to stay the night, he tells himself. Good for passers-by to see a car outside. No one will know.

He walks through the sitting room and pauses outside the closed door of a bedroom. He dares not open it. That is not the place to sleep. Not now. Not any more. He walks into his son's bedroom. The light from the hallway is a dim sheet across floor and bed. Slowly he takes off his clothes. Very slowly. He stands naked in the middle of the room, uncertain. Then he turns back the quilt and slides between the cold sheets. He stares at the ceiling. There is nothing in his head. Only the fact that he is here again. He looks about him, at the walls covered in maps. Scotland. Iceland. The United States. Reproductions of medieval maps. Kilkenny. Galway. A hand-drawn map of this town.

He closes his eyes to blot out the picture, the curving coloured streets. This house. A huge red arrow pointing to it. He begins to shake. A terrifying coldness rocks him. He breathes deeply, evenly, trying to control himself. He breathes in. Breathes out. Breathes in. Deeply, deeply. The soft smell of Olbas oil comes from his son's pillow. He lays his face in the scent, in the pillow, in whatever there is. He hears a noise in the room. The sound of his own, deep, breathless sobbing.

iv

She watches her daughter standing among the daffodils in the garden. The child is lost somewhere, unaware of the flowers about her or the trees budding above her shoulder. She stands in her bedroom doorway, wanting to walk across the garden and wrap her arms around her daughter and pour her love over the child. She wants to keep on pouring until every crevice in every bone is oiled with the love she feels for her.

But she is afraid. Afraid the love may fall like a weight on the child. Afraid her daughter may take this pouring as something else. Afraid some iota of the doubt the child's father thrives on may raise its smiling head in her daughter's life. Afraid the warmth may be lost.

She steps quietly out of the doorway and begins to cross the lawn. The child turns to her, watches her approach and then opens her arms to her mother.

The small boy's question comes back to him hours later.

'If you had three wishes and you couldn't wish for three more wishes every time you got to the third wish, what would you wish for?'

He reconsiders now. For you, for her, for us, for happiness, for courage, for escape, acceptance, certainty, a new car, an old car, a dog, a tidy garden, a welcoming home. Peace for the world, joy for the world. Understanding of the world. Some way of finding a wish to begin with.

When you're old enough, he thinks, I'll explain this to you.

v

He cleans his house thoroughly. He rearranges the photographs on the shelves. He spends a long time planning where he will plant the cherry blossoms. Next year they will bloom here. This house is everything he wanted.

Today he hates it.

She wakes from her dream. She cannot remember anything other than the terrible fear but now the sun is up. She closes her eyes, certain that when she sleeps, she will not dream again.

vi

Early in the morning he starts work on the shambles of a garden. The rambling half-acre that was part of the initial attraction. Now it's a battleground scattered with the implements of war. The lawnmower abandoned near the gate, victim of the clumped, hummocked grass that has been uncut for years. What seemed wildly pastoral a month ago is now merely wild.

And somewhere in this chaos his son has seen the possibility of a football pitch. By the weekend there must be order. He leaves aside the clippers, abandoning the tedious business of trimming for the more satisfying task of slashing his way through the nettles behind the shed. The air grows tart with the smell of broken nettle stems. He sweeps the blade through the air. Again and again the acid breath comes from the shadow of the wall. Sweep and slash and sweep and slash and then, in the corner of his eye, a red gash on the end of the blade. Bird? Animal? He mouths quietly, Shit.

The scarlet flitters from the hooked blade, somersaulting back into the grass. Peony rose.

He breathes again.

Overgrown peony rose slashed and cut with all the rest.

Early in the morning she drives out of the empty town. Mist squats in the fields. She turns off the car radio. Who needs news on a day like this, a day already gathering heat. Bad news has no place in such a day and nothing can match the still beauty of the morning. She rolls down her window on the warm breeze of the countryside. Glancing in her mirror, she smiles at the two sleeping children behind her. Washed and dressed and ready for the day ahead and already exhausted. And just as well – sufficient unto the day is the intoxification thereof! Her smile becomes a quiet laugh.

Then a bird touches the windscreen, its wings brushing the glass as a leaf might, rising as a leaf might in the draught of the passing car. Rising and rising and then, in the rearview mirror, tumbling and falling into the road.

She slows and stops the car. She checks that the children are still sleeping. But everything has happened so gently, sweep and fall of ounces of feather, that nothing breaks their dreams.

She walks back along the road quickly. The green and yellow bundle lies on the black tar. She bends and lifts it in her palm. Still warm, the skin unbroken, the wings and feathers all in place. Breath of life, she thinks, and she breathes on the bird.

The feathers come to life but not the bird. She lays it in the thick branches of the roadside hedge, its head resting on a wild woodbine flower. Green and yellow too.

vii

She's standing in the kitchen, drying the last cup. The afternoon house is quiet. Empty. Not an empty loneliness, more a silent satisfaction. Hot, quiet, solitary. Nothing is oppressive. The emptiness and silence amount to nothing. The cup in her hand is shining. As a child, when it was her turn to dry up, she'd shine each cup and plate and saucer and put them high on the dresser and then she'd sit and admire them, the light spangling across them. Now she hangs this final cup from a hook on the shelf and watches its gentle swing.

Reaching up, she pushes the kitchen window wider. The laburnum is still yellow on the lawn. She notices a leaf on the windowsill, behind a candle. A dead leaf that fell from a sprig of something or other and lay there for a long time. She lifts its rusty shape and her heart falters. The sunshine has ironed a perfect leaf on to the light wooden sill. She hunkers down to examine the leaf, the fractured pattern of its edges.

He knows this is one of those days. He must keep moving. He must keep doing. He draws the sheets from the bed and piles them on the floor; strips back the pillowcases; pulls the duvet from its cover and piles the linen into a bundle, ready for the wash. He pushes the windows as wide as they'll go. Stooping, he takes three paperbacks from the floor beside the bed. A cup is glimpsed under a chair. He reaches in and takes it out, expecting a ribbon of tea around the edges. Instead there is the orange dye of his daughter's night-time drink. Her lips against the rim, fair hair thrown back, her eyes. Her mother's eyes.

viii

She lets the photographs slide across the kitchen table, sixty photographs spilling from a wallet made for half that number. They skid and flicker in the sunlight from the open back-door, a shuffled pack of queens and knaves and jokers from another August afternoon. A dry church porch, its top carelessly clipped; grey leaves from the previous winter still swirling in the frozen print; helianthus; familiar faces. Dead faces. Her own face. She studies it for a long time. The same face. A different face. And his face. Was there deceit even then? In the smiling, wily eyes?

Her eyes move across the other faces. The obviously dying, the surprisingly dead. Was it an afternoon like this one? No. Much less sunny. Much cooler. Some things, at least, have improved. She smiles a dry smile at the thought.

The stones spill out of the plastic bag, across the Formica table of the rented holiday home. The children are hunkered on their chairs on either side. They begin sorting the stones they want for their collections. He takes one stone from the pock of sandy colours. A stone the size of his bent thumb. A round stone that reminds him a little of the earth seen from space. One side a smooth blue, the other a cracked grey. He puts the stone in his jeans pocket, thinking he will give it to her when he returns the children.

Later, walking the clifftop, he takes the stone from his pocket. It looks inconsequential. He puts it away. Tomorrow he will skim it across the calm sea-water and then regret its loss.

ix

He stands in the yellow kitchen, looking across the garden. His eye is drawn back from the hills beyond the valley, back from the valley itself, back to the branches of the twisted evergreen behind the garage; from the mass of the tree to the figure in the flat branches at the top. His eight-year-old son squats in these branches, his green peaked army cap pulled low, his binoculars tight to his eyes scanning the fields for something, someone. For a German infantryman or a Japanese sniper. Or for something less real. For something unspoken and unspeakable at his age.

He cannot avoid the thought that his son is there, in the high branches, for some reason other than play. And then he remembers his own boyhood hours, spent alone in the Rocks or in the furze bushes on Rice's hill. Simply for fun. But it wasn't simply for fun, was it? It was for something else. For escape from something, he knew that. And in search of something never found. He looks at his son in the tree and sees two boys. One is mortally wounded by what went on around him, the other is still capable of laughter. He leaves the kitchen and crosses the garden. He waves to the small boy and then begins climbing through the raw branches, emerging on to the plateau of soft palm. He sits by his son, looking out across the fields.

'There,' he says quietly.

The small boy peers through the binoculars. 'Where?'

'There, behind the gate, far end of the field. Look. See. There.'

Together they watch the sniper, who doesn't yet know they have his measure.

It's late, very late, and the rain is still falling straight on the glass roof outside her bedroom window. It has been falling like that all evening. Straight and hard. But she has only just noticed, now in the silence after a night of bitter talk. After explanations to people who have no right to expect explanation. People who expect because they qualify as family, extended family. People who spent the hours explaining why they were right and she was wrong. Children. Family. Home. Friends. The years, what about the years, you can't undo the years, they said. You can't just sweep them away. The words came, like the rain, straight and hard and bitter.

In the end, in order to escape, she faced them down. 'You don't mean children or family,' she said. 'You mean your-selves. What this will do to you. Isn't that the point of it? Well, isn't it?'

And they looked at her, like horses watching a road, nod-ding, seeing but incapable of sorting one thing from another. And when she left they followed her to the car, asking her back. She drove away, leaving them in the porch light, the vellum faces following her departure.

Now she gets out of bed and opens the connecting door into the conservatory. The rain batters away. She slides back into her warm bed, lies in the almost darkness and remembers a night when she went out, long after midnight, and stood naked in the pouring rain, letting it massage her hair and skin and eyes.

But not tonight. Tonight she is too tired for that. She lets the sound of the rain go on falling in her head but she is too tired to make anything more of it.

x

Suddenly, this afternoon, there is sun. The apples feed off it. They flicker and flash in the garden. She takes a bowl from the garden and goes out to collect them. Each one is fingered, tested for hardness and ripeness. The chosen few are lifted carefully, turned and snapped from the branches. She smells their smell from her fingers. Each one is placed carefully in the bowl. Sometimes the sun off the skins is blinding. She chooses the last apple carefully and takes it to where she can sit in the hammock and enjoy the sharpness of its flesh. She lies back, savouring the taste of her garden.

A question comes, creeping from some corner, brought out by the pungent apple smell: What, after all this time, will it feel like to kiss an unfamiliar mouth? She cannot imagine its taste. She recalls the terror of adolescence, facing the first kiss. The expectation and trepidation. They return but there is a sunny anticipation, too. She closes her eyes and smiles and knows hope, again.

There it is, among the brittle sycamore leaves. The house. The long-remembered house where, as children, they stole apples. The house whose orchard was only part of the temptation. The orchard in which the woman walked every afternoon. The woman whom they watched from the sycamores. The woman who walked so casually among the apple and plum and pear trees, her sallow hair piled high. They had sat in these trees, three boys, waiting for her to go inside, waiting to steal the apples. Watching the woman who walked the afternoon. And here is the house again, among the curtained branches, here where he left it thirty years earlier. And he is surprised.

He stands among the trees, not daring to walk any nearer, not daring to check whether the wall is still intact, the orchard still standing, the house still alive. These things matter but they are too precious to be tried. He stands quite still and remembers the woman walking the orchard and wonders, as he has often done, whether her husband came at night and took her hair down from its nested curls, feeling it plunge heavily through his fingers, or whether she unpinned it for him in the yellow light of their summer room. The sun catches his eyes and he is blind for a moment and then the wind hoists some leaves across the light and he can see again.

Were they even in love, those people in the house? Perhaps not. Yet how could anyone not love that woman in the orchard? In the end it didn't matter whether her husband had been as fascinated as he by her hair, by her slow walks through the garden. There had been a fascination. That was all that mattered then, and is all that matters now.

Over the Rainbow

How do you choose a place in which to die? You know the how and you know the why but you can't decide on the where. No, let me rephrase that. How do you choose a place in which to kill yourself when you know the how and the why? But I'm not being entirely honest with you there either. How do I choose a place in which to kill myself? I know the how and the why, it's just the where that's the problem.

When I was a small boy *The Wizard of Oz* was legendary in our family. My parents had been to see it eight or nine times during their courtship and my father was forever telling me it was the best picture Hollywood had ever made. Best story, best make-up, best acting, best music, best set, best everything. He promised that if ever it came to a picture-house near where we lived he'd be sure to take me to see it.

I must have been about seven-and-a-half or eight when it came to the Ritz in Carlow and we were all set to go. I remember the evening. We were just about to leave the house, it was after tea, when someone called. Some farmer who wanted a valuation done; someone who wanted a site measured; someone who wanted to look at a house – my father was an auctioneer – and it was a question of business before pleasure, so we didn't get to go. But my father promised there'd be a next time. And sure enough, a couple of months later, the picture turned up in Bob's place in Athy. But this time there was no question of going. This time it clashed with some political dinner dance or other and, my father explained, being an auctioneer in a small town he couldn't afford to offend any political party. You never knew when you'd need a favour done, he said. You never knew when you'd need a planning permission pushed through and so he never missed a political dinner dance of any persuasion.

It must have been shortly after that when my father started to tell me these bedtime stories about the Wizard – they began as simple stories but they soon grew into a legend themselves. That winter, whenever my father put me to bed, he'd tell me these stories about how he and I set out for Carlow to see the picture. But we weren't taking any chances. We left the house just after lunch-time. And we weren't travelling in the normal fashion. Nothing as mundane as a car. In the story, my father explained that we had a barge moored on the local river and we were travelling to Carlow in this. He told me how we went down and untied the barge – it was called *The Yellow Brick Road*, and he'd always say, 'I'll tell you why later on' – started the engine and chugged down the river.

In the first adventure he told me about, we were wedged under a bridge out at Halfmiletown. The water was too high, the bridge too low. Just as it seemed we were about to be foiled again, my father had a brilliant idea. He jumped off, raced to a nearby house, returned with a shovel and shovelled rocks and clay and sand into the river, building a dam, and the water level fell, the barge scraped through and we sailed on.

A week later he came up with an adventure where we were attacked by a monster as we crossed the Mill Pond. My father dispatched him with a blow from the shovel. As he told the story, I could see the monster's huge empty eyes as it slid back into the black water.

A few weeks later a third episode was added. This time we were attacked by pirates – they had discovered why the barge was called *The Yellow Brick Road*, all my father's money had been turned into bars of gold and hidden in the hull – and I fought them off while he sneaked aboard their three-master and brought the three masts down with three huge blows of the shovel. I could hear the timber creak and snap, I could feel the splash as the pirates dived off our barge in panic.

Each episode ended with us arriving in Carlow, tying up on the Barrow track and my father taking me ashore to a sweet shop where I was laden down with sweets, ice-cream and Corcoran's lemonade. Then we hurried down Dublin Street and Tullow Street and into the Ritz where the lights were just going down.

Always, at that point, my father would cross and turn off the light in my bedroom so that there was just a glow from the bulb on the landing. He'd come back and sit on the side of my bed and there, on the end wall of the room, I'd see a flickering screen with Dorothy and Toto and the Tinman and the Lion and the Scarecrow and the Yellow Brick Road stretching away for miles. And my father would start to sing in his low, broken voice about the dreams we dare to dream and the clouds and the troubles that melt away like lemon drops.

I never remember any more of that song because by then I was always fast asleep.

When I was twelve I was picked to play for the school football team. I was a pathetic footballer but they picked me anyway. I was put in as a half-back, I think because the backs were tall and the midfielders were strong and the teacher reckoned, if the worst came to the worst, they could kick the ball over my head and keep me out of trouble. I remember rushing home, full of excitement, to tell my parents. My father seemed as proud as I was. He said this was the beginning of a great career and he'd be sure to come and see me play.

Our first game was against some Christian Brothers' school from Athy or Carlow or Portlaoise or somewhere and the team was let out of school at a quarter-past one. We marched down to the field and got togged out. I remember the pride of pulling on the number five jersey. I ran around the pitch with the other boys but, once the game began, it became obvious that I was being outplayed. The boy who was marking me was bigger and fitter and faster – better – than I was. At half-time, as we were standing in the centre of the pitch chewing on our quarter oranges, the teacher came and asked if I'd mind giving someone else a run in my place? I was surprised I'd lasted even that long.

I went and sat with the other boys on the sideline. About six or seven minutes before the game ended, I saw my father arrive and stand behind one of the goalposts, talking to some of the other parents.

When the game ended and I'd togged in, I went to meet him. He told me I'd played brilliantly. I'd been outstanding, he said. His eyes were moist with drink. When we got home, he told my mother the same story. I was superb, he said, and it was only a matter of time before I'd play for the Lilywhites. I didn't tell my mother that he hadn't bothered to come and see me play. Not because I was afraid of the row or because she might be upset. It wasn't that. And I didn't tell my father that I knew he hadn't thought it worth his while to be there – not because he might be upset. It was just that even then, even at twelve years of age, I couldn't find the strength, I couldn't find the energy. I was too full of pain and hurt, even at twelve years of age, to tell him how I really felt. But I never, ever, ever forgave him for what he'd done to me.

When I was in college there were a number of guys in my year, in my class, who were gay. I always made a point of not being seen with them, not being associated with them. Once, a mutual friend of one of these guys and mine asked me if I'd talk to his friend. He had some problem or other and he seemed to think he could talk to me, that I was the confessorial type. I listened to him, I don't even remember what his problem was, and threw in whatever clichés came to mind and when he was about to leave, just by way of winding things up, I told him to be careful. I had no idea what I meant by that and neither, I'm sure, did he but it seemed an appropriate way to finish the conversation.

Waiting in the hospital for the results of my tests, I was sitting in a small waiting room. One other man and myself. We got talking. He was gay and he had full-blown AIDS. He talked and talked. He told me he'd been in a steady relationship for the previous seven years. No hanging around toilets, no going to clubs to pick people up, no promiscuity. His partner and himself had even bought a house. A small house with a little garden. A house on a quiet street. The kind of street where kids play football in the afternoon and elderly people stroll down for the papers on Sunday mornings.

He put me straight. He said, 'When you go down for the results of your tests, when you go into the office – if there's one person there you're okay, if there's two people you're fucked.'

It wasn't that he was trying to make me more nervous than I was. It was just that he had this information and he was passing it on. He'd grown up in a small village, like me. Two sisters, his parents and himself. When he realised he was gay, he said, the thing that worried him most was the fact that he might never have that warm family situation that he'd grown up in. But, when he told them, his family had been completely supportive. His partner and himself would go and stay with his parents for weekends. They'd go and visit his sisters and their families.

Everything he'd ever hoped for or dreamed of had come true. And then this.

I remember walking down the corridor from the waiting room to the doctor's office and playing that game we'd play as children when we'd pluck petals from a flower and say, He loves me, he loves me not.

Walking down the corridor, every time I passed a door I'd say, There'll be one person, and then I'd pass another door and I'd say, There'll be two people. It went on and on like that – there'll be one person, there'll be two people, there'll be one person, there'll be two people – until turning a corner I bumped into some nurses and lost count. And, anyway, I realised how childish a game this was. Whatever result, whatever verdict was waiting for me, was already there, sitting in a folder on that desk. Nothing I could do – no game – could change whatever was waiting. So I walked on, knocked at the office door and went inside.

There were two people waiting for me. There were two people.

A few weeks later I came back to the hospital for some more tests and I met this same man I'd met in the waiting room. Simon was his name. It seemed like a chance in a million but then, when I thought about it, it wasn't. Not any more.

Every time I'd come to the hospital I'd call to see him. And then I started calling because I wanted to. Because I enjoyed his company. Because I was his friend. His partner was dead by then.

One weekend, about a month before Simon died, I called and took him out for a drive. We drove out of Dublin, out through the Wicklow mountains, through the Sally Gap. It was a warm afternoon late in summer. We just sat in the car and watched the scenery passing by, saying nothing. When we got down to the coast I parked the car and we got out and walked on this huge, empty beach. Not another soul on it. Not another sinner, Simon said. We walked slowly, right out on the tide-line. At the end of the beach there was a rocky inlet and we sat there and took off our T-shirts to catch the last of the sun. And while we were sitting there, some emotion – but emotion doesn't do it justice – some feeling welled up in me, overcame me and I walked across behind where Simon was sitting and kissed the back of his shoulder. For a few seconds I thought he hadn't noticed because he went on sitting there, staring out over the flat sea, and then he turned around and reached out and touched the side of my face. He ran his fingers down across my neck, across my nipple and down on to my belly. And then his hand just fell away.

I kissed his mouth and his cheek and his neck. We were blood brothers.

Perhaps that was the place to die but I wasn't ready to let go.

Anyway, enough of this maudlin talk. Do you remember the summer of 1976? The warmest summer in living memory. It was also my last free summer. I'd grown up in a family constricted by rules, in a village constricted by rules and this was my last chance to break free. I headed for London. I got a job as a kitchen porter in a hotel – which meant I swilled out the piss from the toilet floors in the morning and washed the salad in the afternoons and sometimes the two seemed to criss-cross. But the money was too little and the weather too hot to be stuck inside, so I spent my free days scouring the building sites for a start. After three or four attempts I came across an English gaffer and I asked him for a start.

He looked me up and down.

'What's yer name then, Paddy?'

'John,' I said. 'My name is John.'

'All right, Paddy, can you dig?'

'Yes, I can dig.'

'Can you carry the hod?' He was matter of fact.

'Yes, I can carry the hod.'

'You 'fraid of heights?'

'No.'

'All right, Paddy, we'll give you a week's trial.'

All that week I was first on the site in the mornings. No digging was too hard, no hod too heavy, no height too great, no overtime too demanding. I was twenty-four – young enough to believe in my own strength, old enough to know when not to push it. The gaffer was impressed. At the end of the week I was made permanent.

It was a lunatic summer. It was also America's bicentennial year and London was full of Americans who'd come over to escape the bicentenary and ended up bringing it with them. Of all nights, I picked the fourth of July to go to see *The Mousetrap*. I remember sitting in the theatre at the interval, surrounded by Americans, thinking, If only I could figure out who done it I could leave happily now. But I couldn't figure it out so I had to stay to the end. After 'God Save the Queen' had been played, about fifty blue-rinse Americans stood at the back of the theatre and sang 'The Star-Spangled Banner'.

As the summer wore on, the weather got hotter and the shorts on the girls in the streets got shorter, their blouses got skimpier. Some time in late July a new bloke – another Irish bloke – came to work on the site. On our first day together we were a hundred and fifty feet up in the air, sitting on a steel girder, eighteen inches wide, dangling from the end of a crane, trying to manoeuvre it into place when suddenly he began to scream. 'Jesus Christ, look at the meduccets on that. Aw, fuck me, look at them, look. Ah baby, I'd be dug out of ya. Baby, come on up here, I wanna make love to you.'

He was pointing at a girl in the street below us. I kept thinking, If Jesus is even slightly offended by all this then it'll take just one slip of the crane-driver's hand, one puff of wind and we'll both be wrapped around a cement-mixer and there'd be no more meduccets, no more fucking, no more anything, just the long brown box.

But either Jesus wasn't listening or he wasn't offended and we survived. But as the summer went on and we got higher, my friend got louder and louder. And it was always the same cant – I wanna make love to you.

On my last Friday on the site the gaffer took me out for a drink. He brought me down to a pub called The Blue Coat Boy, a traditional-looking place. We walked through the bar and into this small backroom. There were half a dozen snooker tables crammed in and twelve to fourteen blokes playing. They ignored us and we sat chatting. The gaffer told me if ever I came back to London I was to look him up and he'd guarantee me a start.

While we were chatting some music began to play and the lights came up on a tiny stage in the corner. A girl came out and began to dance. I could hardly hear the music over the clacking of the snooker balls. Then the girl began to strip. She unbuttoned her blouse, kicked off her shoes, dropped her skirt, removed her bra and peeled off her pants so that she was dancing there stark naked. But that wasn't the interesting part. The interesting part was that through all this the blokes went on playing snooker, arses in the air, eyes on the table, not paying her a blind bit of notice.

Then the music ended, she stopped dancing and bent down to pick up her clothes and was about to walk off when, from a doorway behind us, there was a raucous shout.

'I wanna make love to you.' My mate from the site lumbered in, swept his hand across a table, scattering balls and gestured to the girl.

'I wanna make love to you. Come on, baby.'

It was that kind of lunatic summer.

Speaking of love. Have you ever noticed how easy it is to fall in love but how difficult it is being in love? I mean, if we made a list, all of us, about the things we associate with falling in love it would – with one or two personal exceptions – be the same list. You hear a song on the radio, a love song, and it seems to speak to your particular situation. You turn an aisle in the supermarket and there, at the other end, is the object of your affection. You imagine they must hear the beat of your heart. You drive into the town where they work and your heart runs amok. You see a car in the street, the same colour and make as your loved one's, and you step into the traffic to check the number plate. You telephone them on some pretext of business and you try to make the phonecall last, in the hope that they'll hear the 'I love you' in your voice. You write a letter, always late at night, and then you post it immediately because if you don't you never will. You see. It's the same for all of us.

We met through committee meetings, my lover and I. We were on the same committee, working for the good of the community. We always seemed to be the first to arrive and the last to leave and if ever we went to someone's house for coffee we seemed to be the ones who ended up doing the washing-up. We went away one weekend, to a seminar in Wexford, and on the Saturday afternoon, when our lecture was over, we had an hour to kill before dinner and we went down to the beach for a walk. Going down some steps in the rain we both lost our footing and held on to each other for support. That electric feeling when you hold the hand of the person you love. You want to go on holding it. You want to transfer that feeling. You never want to let them go.

When we got back from that weekend, I wrote one of those letters. I finished it at a quarter past two and then I went out in the rain and posted it. I knew if I waited till morning I'd lose my courage.

We spoke on the phone, two days later, and there was no mention of the letter. Had I said too much? Too little? Had I not made myself clear? You called the next day and this time you talked about the letter. You said my feelings were reciprocated. That was the phrase you used. Every cliché became a fact. I was walking on air. I was ten feet tall. The person I loved loved me.

We arranged to go away for a weekend together. I booked a chalet by the sea. It was one of those weekends when everything that could go wrong did go wrong. The car gave trouble; it rained all the time; the heating in the chalet didn't work. We spent the Saturday afternoon walking up and down the beach. It was pouring rain, blowing a gale, freezing. We went on walking up and down and up and down that beach. Afraid to go back to the chalet. Afraid of what might happen. Afraid of what might not happen. In the end, the cold and the dampness drove us back. We lit a fire, cooked a meal. We talked and talked and talked until there was nothing left to say and then we kissed. That first kiss undammed everything. Made everything possible, probable.

When I think back on that weekend, I think of the taste. The taste of the sheets after we had made love. The bitter after-taste of wine from your tongue when we kissed.

We'd meet whenever we could. Sometimes our half-days coincided and we'd make love in my bed in my room. You may laugh, you may be offended, but when we made love it wasn't just sexual or sensual or spiritual. It was like the perfect prayer. Every time we made love was like the perfect prayer.

One weekend at the end of the following summer we drove back through the village where I'd grown up, out to a hill a few miles beyond it, where I'd played as a child. It had been very fine for several weeks and then it had rained for a couple of days and now it was fine again. As we walked up through the woods the pungency of the undergrowth, of the clay, of the trees, was alive. And then we came out on the hilltop, above the timber line, and everything was hot and dry and bright. The tops of the trees were about ten feet below where we sat. It was as if I could step out and walk across them, the way I'd walk through clouds in a dream. I pointed out that you could see five counties from the top of that hill.

Everything was laid out below us like a rainbow of colours. The yellow of the corn, the gold of the stubble, the red of ploughed fields, the green of pasture, the grey of the road, the blue of the sky, the hundred shades of the trees about to turn. All this laid out beneath where we were sitting.

I turned to you and said I'm giving you all this.

You smiled at me and said How?

I'm going to put all these colours into a ribbon and tie it in your hair, I said.

You stopped smiling. And what'll you do then? you said.

I'll untie the ribbon and let your hair fall down over your soft blue eyes.

Perhaps that's the place to go back to. To die.

My lover telephoned. She asked me to come and meet her in her office.

It was an October afternoon. There were two steaming mugs of coffee on the desk between us. Behind her was a window and across the road was a park. I could see the trees through that window. It was one of those October days when everything is still. But every now and then a breeze would riffle through the trees and a blanket of leaves would come down and then everything would be still again.

She told me she hadn't been feeling too well; she'd gone for a check-up. Nothing out of the ordinary. And the results had come back that morning. And she was HIV positive.

I knew, as soon as the words registered, I knew without having to take any tests myself, without having to see a doctor or visit a hospital, I knew I was HIV positive myself. I knew. Not in my head or my heart or my soul but literally in the blood that was running through my veins. And when I knew that, I said to her, Let's stop pretending, let's stop this charade, let's tell everyone who's involved, everyone who should know. Let's tell them. Let's start living one life instead of these two lives we've been trying to keep together and keep apart.

She just sat there and shook her head. She told me she needed time to herself, to come to terms with this. She needed room for herself.

She shook her head. She asked me to give her time to deal with this.

I said I would but I knew while I was saying it that in the days and weeks ahead I'd telephone and write, that I wouldn't be able to give what she asked for, what I'd promised. I knew, too, that in asking for time we had come to an end.

It was getting darker by then. I could see people hurrying from the other offices. Hurrying to their cars. Hurrying to get home, to get to the pub, to get to meetings. Just as we had done. I thought how simple it would have been to put on our coats and scarves and walk hand in hand across the park. What a simple, ordinary thing and yet we had never done it in public and wouldn't now.

We both sat there and it got so dark I could no longer see the features of her face, just the outline of her hair against the window. She made no move to go and she didn't ask me to leave and I was grateful for that. I thought, as long as we can stay in this room, in this darkness and quietness, nothing that's happening out there beyond the trees, no sickness that's growing inside us can do us any harm. As long as we can hold on to this time, this darkness, then everything will be all right.

I have no memory whatsoever of leaving her office that evening but I do remember clearly thinking, feeling, that as long as we had this we had everything.

Afterwards there came the anger. I blamed God, you, medicine, me. I'd get into my car and drive at eighty-five, ninety miles an hour along narrow country roads. I'd drive at ninety miles an hour down narrow roads, around blind bends. Sometimes I'd close my eyes and press the accelerator to the floor. I didn't care who I killed or who killed me. I'd drive flat out with the car windows open and I'd scream and scream and scream.

Fuck you, God, fuck, fuck, fuck, fuck, fuck you for what you've done to me. Did you see me on the street? Did you pick me out of the crowd? Did you say, There's a bastard whose broken every rule in the book; there's someone who needs to be taught a lesson. Did you say, I'll give this bastard a dose he'll never forget, I'll let him die in agony? Did you put the finger on me and say, He's the one? Well, fuck you, God.

And then I blamed you. You could have been the one to say no. You could have been the one to say friendship, nothing more. You could have been the one to point out that we weren't in a position to get involved like that. But blaming you lasted about as long as it takes me to say it. Then I blamed medicine. For days I'd sit in my room and hear all these voices going round and round inside my head. I'd close my eyes and see these faces. I got to know these people, these executives of medical companies. I got to know their faces, their voices, their suits, their haircuts, their monogrammed briefcases. I could see these people sitting around boardroom tables in penthouse offices and I knew they had a cure for the HIV virus. I knew it was sitting there in some formula on that table but all I heard were their voices going on and on. Talking all the time about ballpark figures.

We wait till Europe and America catch up with Asia and Africa, they'd say. That's where the money is. Give it till another eight, say ballpark figure ten, million people are diagnosed positive, then we move. We wait till the straights catch up with the gays, they'd say. Then we can go with this. Wait two, three, ballpark five, years. If we do that, if we time it right, they'd say, laughing, we make enough money not just for ourselves and our kids but for our grandchildren to retire. I'd hear all this, day after day, going round and round inside my head and there was nothing I could do to let it out, no valve that could release the voices and the faces. And I'd think of people like you and me and Simon, depending on these bastards.

And then I blamed myself. I had three or four days free that Christmas and I'd get up early in the morning and go down to the kitchen and clear the table and then I'd lay out all these blank sheets of paper with a calendar in the middle. I became determined to work out when, exactly, I had contracted the virus.

It couldn't have been this week because you were away on a course. It couldn't have been that week because I was on holiday. It couldn't have been this week because we didn't meet. In the end, I narrowed it down to one week. It couldn't have been the Monday because, when we made love, I wore a condom. Same thing on the Tuesday. In the end, I narrowed it down to the Thursday of that week. By then you were on the pill and we were safe.

I remembered that day so clearly in every detail. We made love in my bed in my room that afternoon. While we were making love the front door bell rang. I'd left a note pinned to it saying that I was unavailable until half-past six and anyone who wanted to see me should call back after that time. I knelt up and looked through the net curtains of my bedroom window. I saw a figure scuttling through the gateway and then I turned back to look at you. Your mouth was slightly open and your tongue ran across your bottom lip. Your hair was streaked across your forehead. I bent down and ran my tongue between your breasts. Your skin tasted hot and salty. My tongue continued across your belly and into the wet warmth between your thighs.

Eventually, I got back to blaming God.

One dark afternoon in January I walked into the church, up the centre aisle on to the altar, up until my face was pressed against the tabernacle door. The church was empty but I don't think it would have mattered then even if it hadn't been. I pressed my face against the metal door and shouted. Why did you do this to me? Why, why, why, why to me? That most pathetic of questions to which there is no answer because there is no valid question in the first place.

And then I tried to pray. I'd get down on my knees beside my bed and close my eyes but nothing would come into my head. Nothing. No words. Nothing. And when I'd open my eyes I'd see you lying there in my bed. In the end, I went back to those childhood rhymes:

Now I lay me down to sleep,
I pray the Lord my soul to keep,
and if I … die … before I wake …
and if I die … and if I die.

When I was growing up in the fifties there was still a shadow of TB hanging over our village. There was a family living near us, a Church of Ireland family, the Somervilles, and they had four daughters, Mary and Anne and Emma and Kate. Mr Somerville worked as a farm labourer just outside the village. Three of the girls died of TB. First Anne and then Mary and then Emma. Kate was the only one to survive.

I remember, as a child, sometimes we'd drive by their cottage and their washing would be hanging out and my mother would refer, disparagingly, to TB sheets.

Once Mr Somerville's name appeared in the local paper for some minor offence, not having a light on his bicycle or something like that, and my father read out the report and sniggered and said, That's TB for you, bad blood will out.

I knew I had to tell my parents about my situation. I drove over one Sunday for lunch and when we'd finished the meal we sat in the kitchen drinking coffee and then I told them. I told them I was very ill and that I wasn't likely to recover. And then I told them I was HIV positive. I swear, as soon as that registered with them, I could see the look on both their faces, I could read their minds like a book, as soon as it hit them. HIV positive. That must mean some kind of sexual perversion. I could see both of them reacting in the same way. It wasn't my illness or possible death that was of primary concern. It was this sexual thing. This perversion.

After a time my father turned to me and said, Was it Kate Somerville? Jesus Christ Almighty, I hadn't seen Kate Somerville in what … eighteen, twenty years, and this was the best he could do?

Later that afternoon I was standing in our sitting room, looking out across the lawn from the back window. That strange room that smells, paradoxically, of furniture polish and dust, that damp room that is only ever used on Christmas Day and Stephen's Day. The door opened behind me and I knew by the footsteps that my father had come in. I heard the creak of the leather armchair near the fireplace as he sat down. He cleared his throat and I knew he was going to speak. I remained at the window, my back firmly to him.

Do you remember the day after your ordination? he said. Do you remember when we came back here to the village? The pipe band was out to meet us, there were bunting and flags and banners all the way down the street and the footpaths were lined with people. And do you remember the three of us walking down the street after the band, you in the middle and your mother on one side of you and me on the other? And do you remember what I said to you? I said, you're no longer our son, you belong to God now.

His voice faltered a little then but he soon found it again. This … this … this thing, he said, this … sin has nothing to do with your mother or me, it's between you and God. And you have nothing to do with us.

I wanted, there and then, to remind him of that afternoon, that football match when I was twelve years old, but I didn't.

When all this happened I could, I suppose, have spoken to some of my confreres. Some of them might have been sympathetic. Some would have pointed out how many commandments I had broken. I had failed to honour God. And my father and mother. I had, I suppose, technically committed adultery. I could have gone to the Bishop. It wasn't that I was afraid of what he might say. There was nothing he or anyone else could say that would come even close to touching me now. He might even have been sympathetic. He might have left me in my parish for four or five months and then quietly shipped me off to some convent as chaplain. The nuns would have welcomed me, prayed for me, nursed me and buried me. But I don't want that.

I've always been conscious of my body, of keeping myself in trim. I can still do my press-ups, push-ups, running on the spot. I still look after myself. But in the last few months I've started watching my body for signs, for sores on my skin, for cuts that won't heal. Watching. I don't want to end up like Simon, not able to do anything for myself. I don't want to end up in a sweaty hospital bed some summer afternoon, lying there when I know I should be out running through the forest. I don't want to lie there knowing the angel of death is loitering outside the door. I want to go out and meet the bastard halfway. More than halfway.

I know how I will kill myself and I know why, and it has just been a question of deciding where.

In the end I chose this church. My church. My altar for the past eleven years. Isn't that what it was all about? Isn't that why I was here every morning at eight o'clock; isn't that what people came for on Sunday? The blood sacrifice? By the time I'm finished here they'll be buying a new carpet for the altar, at the very least. I can see my confreres wading through my blood to get to my body. There'll be no hushing it up. No smuggling me into consecrated ground under false pretences! No humbug from my parents or the Bishop. None of that.

I've written you one last letter, my beloved, my lover, my heart in this heartless world. You take the ashes and scatter them wherever you choose.

I know why I'll die and where. And how. I've seen enough of this in the line of duty to work it out. Wouldn't Judas have traded his rope for a Stanley knife. Two quick strokes and you're on your way. Virtually painless. Money back guarantee but there's no going back, thank you.

Step one. The ritual. And the practicalities. Roll up the sleeves. Better still, remove the shirt. A few well-chosen words. This is my rejected son, who would have been better off becoming an auctioneer like me, marrying and fucking within the sanctity and safety of the marriage bed.

Jesus Christ! Blood. Blood. Blood. As good as the guarantee.

And this is my beloved son in whom I am disappointed but I will send down my own Son to meet him outside the gates of paradise.

Oh, Christ. Jesus, Jesus, Jesus.

Not that I have any faith in paradise. Not any more. The only thing I have any faith in is that afternoon when we sat in your office and I watched the trees and the leaves and the darkness coming down and I thought: if we can just hold on to this, we can hold on to everything.

Husband

When Liz got home from work her husband was sitting in the garden, in his favourite spot, on the bench beneath the big sycamore. He was sitting very straight and very still, staring out across the vegetable patch and the raspberry canes, focusing on some distant place beyond the end of the garden and the snowing whitethorn hedge.

At first she didn't see him. Having come into the kitchen and dropped the shopping bags heavily onto the breakfast counter, she flicked the switch of the kettle and turned the radio on. Later, she would think it ironic that Mozart's 'Piano Concerto No. 21 in C' was playing. *Elvira Madigan* was the first film they'd seen together and her husband had been enthralled by the music.

The groceries put away, she made herself a cup of coffee and went into the dining room to find the newspaper. And still she did not know he was there. She had left her crossword half-done and was determined to finish it before tea. She sat with her back to the window, labouring over the last three clues, determined not to resort to her thesaurus. The Mozart ended and the announcer introduced Bach's 'Sheep May Safely Graze'. She looked again at seventeen across, where 'elucidate' was suddenly obvious, and once that was apparent, 'ductile' and 'quaint' were equally so. She wrote the –int with a flourish and, throwing the newspaper onto the table, sighed contentedly as she downed the last of her coffee. Only then did she turn to look across the garden, only then did she see him, his back set rigidly, his feet firmly planted on the ground, his face turned to the north, watching for that something that she could never see. She felt herself go cold.

Anne felt herself go cold. The moment she stepped into the kitchen and saw the open door, her heart tripped and her back turned to ice.

'Oh Christ,' she said out loud. 'Oh, Christ, Christ, Christ!'

She had left him sleeping in his armchair in the bay window, warm in the late afternoon sun. She had gone upstairs to vacuum and then the phone had rung and then rung again. How long had she been? Twenty minutes, half an hour, no more. She was sure the back door had been locked, as sure as she ever could be. She'd cleaned the grate and taken the ashes out in the morning, brought in the washing, collected the post from the box at the gate and then locked the door again. Hadn't she?

'Please Jesus, don't let him be gone far,' she said as she stepped into the yard, scanning the garden, hurrying past the empty shed with its open door, and down through the orchard to the gap they had used years before to escape into the fields beyond. But the gap was blocked now, overgrown with brambles and may bushes. The bile rising in her throat, she turned and ran between the trees, out onto the drive and down to the open wooden gate that swung aimlessly onto the road.

'Fuck.'

Running back to the house, she grabbed her keys and bag from the hall table and got into the car. Driving along the avenue, she glimpsed something moving between the birches, slowed, ground the gears into reverse, but what she had seen was nothing more than a shadow of the bay tree.

Out on the road, she couldn't decide which way to go. Left was open countryside, right was the road into town.

If he were seen in town, someone would recognise him, someone would bring him home, someone. If he got to the woods there was no telling where or when he'd be found, or if. She put that thought out of her mind and turned the car for the open road, driving fast between fields that were hurrying to cover themselves in the flimsiest of barley dresses. Glancing continually left and right, she blessed the farmer who had levelled the ditches and converted the countless fields into open tracts that offered no hiding place to a man trying to lose himself when the things he had known were already lost to him.

Liz closed the patio door quietly, the handle clicking smoothly into place. The birds went on singing in the ditches around the garden. Her husband went on sitting as he had been, poker-straight, his sight line still snagged on a distant bush. She moved tentatively down the bark-mulched path, waiting for him to hear her, waiting to become the distraction that would catch his attention, but he remained unaware of her presence.

She stopped a half-dozen steps from his seat and watched the revenant of someone she used to know. What did she recognise? The ray lines darting from the side of his eye, the dark channelled furrow down his forehead. Lines and gouges and this vehement silence that refused to even acknowledge the birdsong or her presence.

She moved closer and sat beside him on the narrow wooden bench that sagged with their weight.

'You came back,' she said.

He looked vacantly at the place her words had come from, then looked away again.

'Does anyone know you're here?' she asked, and before he could speak, answered her own question. 'Of course not.' They sat together in the early summer sun that dipped and danced between the frayed clouds. Around them the hawthorn choir built melodies, pointing and counterpointing, a soloist rising only to be drowned by the surge of other voices. She thought of Edward Thomas's blackbird and all his other birds of Oxfordshire and Gloucestershire.

'I used to think the birds sang for pleasure,' she said. 'You were the one who told me they sang for power.'

The sun disappeared, only to reappear almost at once, shadowing the freshly cut grass. He lifted his hand and wiped something from his jacket.

'Are you all right?' she asked.

'All right,' he said.

She nodded and sighed.

'All right,' he said again.

'Good.'

'The moon will be here in a short time now.'

'I suppose it will.'

'It'll be all right.' She turned to him. 'Why did you come back?'

His brow furrowed in the light of the sun but he said nothing.

'You're all right there, aren't you?' she asked.

'All right.'

'I'm popping back inside. Do you want to come with me?'

He looked at her, then brushed his hand across his jacket again, but he made no move to follow her.

'Don't be late,' he said. 'Your mother never sleeps till you're in.'

Anne stopped the car on the roadside and got out. A sudden sweep of sunlight galloped across the empty fields, billowing the ground and blinding her. She shaded her eyes with the back of her hand and sat back against the wing of the car.

'Where the fuck are you?' she said out loud.

And then the sunlight was gone and she covered her face with her hands, breathing deeply, smelling the soap from her palms, allowing herself, for that instant, the remembered indulgence of her morning shower. Uncovering her face, she swept the landscape slowly, methodically trawling the emptiness for some sign, some stumbling figure coming out of the tide of early dandelions, some hand waving helplessly far out in a sea of grass. But there was no one, nothing to do, just the emptiness of a triangular field running down to the vast shadows of two trees on the bank of a river that was hardly deep enough to drown in.

And then her phone rang and she fumbled the passenger door open, pulling the mobile from her bag, spilling money, mints, plastic cards across the seat.

'Hello.'

'Anne?'

'Yes.'

'This is Liz.'

'Yes.'

'Paul is here, with me. Well, not with me. He's in the garden. I'm looking out at him now. He's sitting in the garden.'

'Thank God!'

'Where are you?'

'I'm out on the Barrack Road. Driving. Looking for him.'

'He's fine.'

'How long has he been there?'

'I don't know. Not long. I saw him five, six minutes ago. He was here when I got back.'

'I was working upstairs. Not for long.'

'I know. It's okay. He's okay. Don't worry.'

'Thanks, Liz. I'll be over – give me ten minutes.'

'Take your time. I'll look after him. He's very placid, very much in himself; there's no problem, seriously.'

'I'll be there.'

'Okay. Drive carefully.'

Liz put the phone back on the table and stood at the door, watching her husband. But there was so little to see. A rigid figure, with a transfixed look that might have passed for determination had she not known better. The feet so resolutely firm on the same ground he had once dug with such fervour, clearing, weeding, composting, drilling and raking, sowing and tending. Morning and night in the late summer and early autumn, overseeing the harvest of his labours, sharing his excitement with the children. And then, one spring, she'd looked out into the garden and realised that he was gone, that their marriage was over, that he had left her. And year by year she'd returned more and more of the garden to low-growing grass, so that now the vegetable plot was a delicate patchwork that might comfortably fit on the large kitchen table.

The garden he'd known had grown away, the man she'd married was missing in action, every design they'd been familiar with was lost beyond recovery. All she saw, when she looked at the figure sitting beneath the tree, were haloes and auras, betrayals that might have been confusions, and bewilderments that might have been mistakes.

Anne sat in the car, checking her eyes in the mirror, wondering if the lines about them said enough, or possibly too much, about the past thirty months. Not that there was much she could do about any of it now.

Turning the key, she opened her window, pressed the CD button and looked again, across the suddenly vast and indifferent fields. Beth Nielsen Chapman's voice drifted into the warm air outside, something about years, how they take so long and they go so fast.

'Too fucking true,' she said ruefully, and, sighing deeply, turned the key again till the engine crooned.

'He's asleep upstairs,' Liz said.

She led the way into the dining room. Through the window, Anne could see late shadows stretching across the garden.

'How did he get here?'

'I have no idea.'

'Whenever I take him out for a drive, whenever we come out this way, I always ask him if he remembers living here. I tell him this is where you still live.'

'It was the place,' Liz said. 'It was the place he came back to, not me. He has no idea who I am, that's patently obvious. But he found his old seat in the garden, and when he came in here, he came in of his own accord. And then he went upstairs and got into bed.'

'I'll go and wake him,' Anne said.

'You don't have to.'

'He could sleep for hours.'

'It really isn't any problem to me, unless you want to wake him. I've put some dinner on; you're more than welcome to stay and eat. I'd like that.'

'Are you sure? You don't have any other plans?'

'I'm sure.'

'Would you mind if I checked on him?'

'Not at all, follow me.'

Liz led the way up the wide stairs. 'He can't get out,' she said. 'There's a dead bolt on the front door; the only other way is through the dining room.'

Liz opened a door at the top of the stairs and Anne stepped into the big, bright room. Her husband was sleeping soundly, the lines and frowns washed from his forehead and eyes, his hands unclenched.

'He's fine,' Liz said and then, as if correcting herself, 'isn't he?'

Anne nodded as they stepped onto the landing, leaving the door open.

'I'm really sorry about this. It's only the second time he's done it in, what, two-and-a-half years?'

'Nothing to be sorry about. I really don't know how you deal with the constant pressure. Is he ever violent?'

'No, never,' Anne said quickly. 'Never, there's nothing like that. Mostly he doesn't even talk to me now. It's just silence and … unease, I suppose. No emotion, nothing like that.'

'I often wonder,' Liz said. 'The children tell me, of course, but I do sometimes wonder.'

'There's no reason for you not to call.'

'I don't think he'd want me calling, not if he knew.'

'But he wouldn't know,' Anne said quietly.

'Maybe his coming here today was a kind of invitation.'

Liz smiled. 'Perhaps it was. But I doubt it.'

The women ate on the patio. Evening trailed into a night that was calm and close, the light from the garden lamps falling in flat pools on the blossoms around them. They talked about flowers and gardens and work. Occasionally one or other of them went upstairs to check on the sleeping man. Liz opened a second bottle of wine as the moon rose above the sycamores and the talk turned to death and release.

'I think I'm almost ready for that,' Anne said. 'I told myself at Easter that if this summer was a good one, if he was well enough to go places with me, if we could get out and go for walks, if we could get to the sea, if we could go back … to places we'd … been together when … well, you know …'

'I know.'

'I thought if we could do those things, I'd be happy to let him go. But he may not want to go, he may not be ready to go for years. It's not as if he's capable of deciding that, or anything else, is it?'

Liz shook her head before she spoke. 'Perhaps he came back here subconsciously today, to see something he's getting ready to leave?'

Anne said nothing. She doubted that was why Paul had travelled the two miles between one house and the other, but she didn't feel it her place to say so. Instead, she glanced at her watch.

'What time is it?' Liz asked.

'Just after one.'

'Will he wake now?'

Anne shook her head.

'Looks like we're here for the night, then,' Liz said. 'I have just the thing.'

She went inside and came back with fresh glasses and a bottle of liqueur.

'I brought this back from Greece last year,' she said. 'I was saving it for something. Why do we have this mania for saving things?'

'I don't know,' Anne smiled. 'For hope?'

Liz poured generous measures of the liqueur. 'I'm not so sure,' she said.

The two women drank in silence.

'If that's not to your liking, leave it,' Liz said.

'No, it's fine, I've never tasted it before. I'm sure it could do some damage to the grey matter.'

'So they say. Strange, isn't it?' Liz said, pointing to the upstairs bedroom. 'In all his life he never drank, and yet it's gone for him so soon. It must have been hard for you, in the early stages, when he knew what was happening.'

Anne nodded.

'I know, from experience, that he wasn't a patient patient.' She giggled at her own pun.

We fucked a lot, Anne said, but not out loud. We fucked to forget that he was forgetting. We fucked as if every time would be the last time until, finally, it was. And every time, I wanted to feel him inside me for as long as that was possible. Sometimes, I imagine I still do.

'I shouldn't really talk about him this way,' Liz said. 'It's unfair. It's better that we don't. It's your life and his, to whatever extent. It's a different time.'

'I don't mind talking about him,' Anne said. 'Really, I don't. It's good to talk to someone who knew him when he wasn't the way he is now. When he was whole. So many people never really knew him then. They look at his drawings and I tell them which buildings he designed and I know they can't believe me.'

Liz refilled their glasses. 'He's had so many lives,' she said. 'His time as a boy, his student days, his time married to me, his time married to you and now this twilight time when he's not anchored to anything.'

'I think he's very anchored,' Anne said quietly. 'He mentions the children sometimes, talks about them as though they're still young. Sometimes in the evening when we walk in the garden, he stands at the top of the lawn and asks me where they are and I explain to him that ours is a different garden from yours. I don't tell him they've grown up, as that wouldn't mean anything. But I think his coming back here was another chain to that anchor.'

Liz nodded, shrugging her shoulders. 'Are you warm enough?' she asked. 'I could get you a jumper.'

'No, I'm fine. Thanks.'

'What do you think of this liqueur?' Liz asked, the words stumbling slightly over one another.

'It's different.'

'It's disgusting. I have just the thing to bury it.'

She went back into the house and returned with brandy glasses and a bottle of Cognac.

'That should do the trick. The devil you know and all that. You pour.'

Going inside again, she put on some music. It streamed quietly through the open doors.

'That won't wake him?'

Anne shook her head.

'You talked about hope,' Liz said, taking a sip from her brandy glass. 'Do you still have hope for him, in spite of the emptiness? I don't have to live with the emptiness, and I don't think I could. There was an emptiness when we went our separate ways, but I imagine it was of a different kind. I could still see him, be angry with him, make him angry with me, until over the years it became less important, faded away. But you have to live with this hollowness, day in, day out.'

'I don't think about it. I do what has to be done. There are times when it's almost possible to forget, like when we're sitting together and I'm reading and he's watching the birds in the garden. Times like that have their own normality.'

'But then there must be other times, like this. When he escapes, when you have to search for him, when there's no normality in anything.'

'That rarely happens,' Anne said quickly, too quickly.

'I didn't mean it to sound accusatory. I meant there must be times when you wonder if there's any way out of this …'

The sentence went unfinished.

Anne looked away, across the shadowed garden, into the darkness that leeched the light from the open door.

'I suppose I try not to think that far ahead,' she said sadly. 'Maybe I haven't had to, or maybe I've chosen not to.'

The two women sat quietly, notes and phrases drifting up into the night sky like smoke.

'"How sour sweet music is when time is broke and no proportion kept."'

'The music's beautiful,' Anne said. 'What is it?'

'Mascagni. The 'Intermezzo' from Cavalleria Rusticana.'

Silent again, they suddenly heard the music lift in an immense and passionate wave, swelling and trailing above the garden, where it hung for a moment, and then for a moment longer, until finally it washed back gently over them.

'That's the most beautiful thing I've ever heard.'

'It is beautiful, isn't it?'

It was sometime after five and light was fingering the sky. They were still sitting at the table, drinking large tumblers of water.

'I have to go to bed,' Liz said. 'My eyes are closing. You can have my bed, that's where Paul's sleeping. It's just the way it happened, where he went.'

Anne laughed. 'It doesn't need explaining.'

'Of course.'

'I'll probably just crash on the couch in the dining room, if you don't mind.'

'No, fine, absolutely. But you're welcome to sleep upstairs.'

'If he wakes early, he may want to go home, to our house. I won't wake you.'

'All right.'

'But thank you, again. It can't have been easy … you know. Thank you.'

Their bodies arched uneasily as the two women hugged, and then Liz was gone.

Anne woke to the sound of gentle, hesitant music. She lay on the couch listening. Sunlight lapped from the garden, through the open doorway, music following. The slow, uncertain, disconnected notes of 'Greensleeves'.

Walking barefoot across the room, she stepped into the lemony day. Her husband was sitting at the patio table, last night's accumulation of glasses lined up before him, tapping out each note with a teaspoon. Stopping, he poured a thimble of water into one of the glasses and sounded the note, listening closely, tapping again, listening, his head bent close to the table. He straightened then, and for a moment was very still, before the tune began again.

'Alas my love you do me wrong ...' Anne softly sang to herself while her husband played on, a one-man band, making a bewildered, irregular and desolate music.

Laburnum

The local paper was waiting for me when I got in from work. I don't mean the freebie rag that passes for a paper where we live, I mean the local paper from back home. The real paper. My father sends it every week. Among other things, it tells me who I should write to, to sympathise, and who I shouldn't expect to see around the village when we go back in the summer. I left the paper unopened until the children were in bed, something to look forward to. When my wife had gone out to her swimming session I spread it out on the table in the kitchen and started with the local notes. When my wife returned, I showed her the photograph.

'So that's him,' she said.

She had never seen Cooney, though she knew him quite intimately, from my descriptions. He had been the scourge of my childhood. Before I was even born he'd fallen out with my father about some court case or other. My father had appeared as a character witness for someone Cooney was prosecuting. After the case Cooney had come up to our house and, finding my father out, had been abusive to my mother. Insults were traded for a couple of weeks and then both sides settled into life-long silence. And now he had retired as principal in the local school and was pictured at his presentation.

'I expected horns,' my wife said.

'He was too clever for that.'

'Well, at least he won't inflict himself on any more kids. That's something.'

'He should have been fired years ago. The abuse we took from him was unbelievable. I don't know which was worse, being in his class or the fear of going in,' I said. 'I can laugh at most things but there wasn't even black comedy in his case, just plain malice. Can you imagine what it's like, when you're nine, being told by your teacher that you're dog-ignorant and that it's hardly surprising, given your pedigree. It was all insinuation. You were being hurt but you couldn't see the wounds, just feel them.'

'Well, he's gone,' she said. 'No point working yourself up about it.' And she went off to make some tea.

When we'd finished the tea she asked me if there was any other big news. 'No,' I said, flicking through the paper and stopping, again, at the photograph of Cooney and all the village dignitaries.

'Don't start again,' she said.

'I just want to see who was there.'

I looked at the faces. Some familiar, some unfamiliar. The parish priest, the new principal, the area inspector, the other teachers, a few parents, the county councillors.

'There's another interesting man,' I said, indicating the local rector.

'Why?'

'He was once my prospective father-in-law.'

'Tell me more.'

'Another time,' I said. 'It was a strange situation. His daughter was a strange girl, very strange.'

'Attractive?'

I nodded.

'But very strange.'

'And she didn't marry you.'

This summer we went back to the village for six weeks. My uncle was in hospital and my father needed help with the farm.

The children loved the freedom of the place and my wife was within driving distance of friends in Dublin. There wasn't an awful lot to do; I was there for reassurance. My father, as usual, had things ticking over nicely.

One weekend my wife took the children up to stay with friends in Meath. I was left to my own devices. After tea, on the Saturday, I walked down to the village for the paper. I was late. All the shops were closed. I decided to walk to the end of the village and back across the fields. The place was all but deserted. A few teenagers were lounging on the wall of the rectory and, above them, in the lowest branches of the huge laburnum, three or four others were swinging noisily. The place was obviously unoccupied. It was June, the rector was away on holiday. I hadn't been in the grounds in almost fifteen years. On an impulse, I decided to go in. The girls sitting on the wall ignored me, the boys in the branches sniggered and carried on with their swinging. The windows were still the same shabby maroon I remembered. Always in need of a coat of paint. Always slightly faded.

Between the garage and the house there were roses. Blue Moon. Above them was the window that had, once, been the light of my life. I peered through the grubby panes. Everything was covered in dust sheets. Perhaps the rector had grown more prosperous. Or less. As I rounded the corner I heard a shout and then another and then a flurry of jumping and running and laughter. I turned to go back and, as I reached the gable, I saw a figure crossing the gravelled yard. It was Cooney. As he walked, the delicate flowers from the shaking tree continued to fall about him. I thought they would never stop. The evening was still and they came down straight between us.

He spoke almost immediately. '*Laburnum anagyroides.*' He pointed with the walking stick he carried. I remembered that tone of his voice immediately.

I said nothing.

'The largest I have ever seen. The fullest flowers and the stoutest trunk I have ever come across in this species. I come here to enjoy it, to savour its strength and beauty and stillness.'

I waited for some cutting comment about the boys who had been playing in its branches but instead, as if to illustrate his disdain, he poked at the fallen petals about his feet. Then he walked the few yards to the house and rested on the sill. I could imagine him doing that every evening.

'It's a different world in here,' he said. 'The quietness. I tried it in my own garden but it isn't the same. There's something about the atmosphere in here. Different from us. I believe it comes from generations of quiet certainty.' He went on poking at the settled yellow flowers. 'But imagine living here and never seeing this tree at its most splendid.' He shook his head.

I stood my ground, waiting for him to finish, certain he had no idea who I was. He wouldn't have seen me in twelve or fourteen years.

He picked a flower from the sill. 'A lot of people mistake this for mimosa but it's not.' He got up slowly and walked towards the gate. I allowed him out of the yard before I followed. I had nothing to say to him. When I reached the gate I saw that he was standing, with his back to me, on the path outside. I pulled the iron bars shut behind me.

Cooney spoke without turning. 'Were you ever in there in your time?'

'Not really,' I said.

'Every summer, for four weeks, I go in. While they're away. It's a holiday in itself. A different world.'

He walked away. I heard young voices sniggering in the graveyard across the street. I pushed the bolt home on the gate. My hand was the colour of rust.

We were back in the village at the end of the summer for my uncle's funeral. Someone mentioned that Cooney was failing and, coincidentally, the following evening, as I drove along the River Road, I passed his daughter pushing him in a wheelchair.

A month ago, my father mentioned on the phone that Cooney was dying. He'd been moved to a hospital here in Dublin. I thought of calling to see him. My wife said I should.

'He knew you that evening. He made his move, his gesture. It was more than you expected. You should bury the hatchet at this stage, for God's sake. Just drop in.'

'I'm not sure,' I said. 'I'd have nothing to say.'

'Bring him a book, a gardening book. I'll come with you if you want.'

'I don't think so.'

'Try,' she said. 'You mightn't even get in. Leave the book at least. Let him know.'

'No,' I said, finally. 'He probably doesn't even remember that evening. He may have thought I was someone else. I'd only confuse him. I'd better not.' But, instinctively, I knew he remembered. 'Anyway, Jesus, when I think of what he put me through in school,' I said, frantically searching beyond that summer evening and hearing, again, his words spat at the nine-year-old me. 'No, leave the vindictive bastard as he is. There's no point, I couldn't carry it through. Let him go.'

Breathless

A light suddenly shatters, splintering down the side of Rice's Hill, between the few remaining furze bushes, tumbling into the mirror of the river, smashing that too, throwing beams in all directions. Morning has fractured and night is over.

Look carefully and there are five pairs of footwear scattered in the grass. Silver stilettos, white runners, brown walking shoes, black boots and a tiny pair of pink Wellingtons, with elephants on the side. Suddenly, as if spirited from nowhere, three women and a teenage girl come walking through the dewy field, as if unaware of one another, bent on finding their shoes.

'They used to crucify me,' the slight woman says, but to herself. 'Something about the arches, I don't know what it was.'

The young girl pushes past her and picks the runners from the ground.

'They weren't the best pair in the shop, but I got a staff discount and that …'

Her voice trails away as someone laughs from behind her, the voice of a red-haired woman.

'Surrounded by shoes. There must have been twenty pairs scattered all over the place, everywhere you looked, shoes, shoes, shoes.'

And near the ditch, the fourth woman, fair-haired, quietly spoken, takes the silver stilettos from the grass, wiping them dry.

'I got these for a wedding,' she says. 'My first cousin's wedding. On my father's side – my father's brother's daughter.'

The red-haired woman is still laughing, speaking quickly, twirling as she does so, as if trying to include the others in her conversation.

'The right one of this and the left one of that and one of a pair in the wrong box and the sales assistant, as she liked to call herself, standing behind me going *tsst tsst tsst*, like I was taking the last place in the last lifeboat off the fucking *Titanic* and leaving her behind.'

'These fitted fine in the shop,' the slight woman says, as if ignoring the other three, 'but once I wore them for more than twenty minutes, my feet felt like they were ready to fall off.'

The young girl – how old is she, fifteen or perhaps sixteen? – kneels on the grass and holds her runners close to her face. We need a name for her. Something plain, something ordinary, but there are no names to give. A name would be a certainty and there is no certainty here. We can't even be certain that we're hearing or seeing what we believe we hear and see.

'I bought these and then I bought a football shirt for my little brother,' she says, but no one listens because the red-haired woman is still laughing, still talking.

'And I wouldn't mind but half the shoes weren't mine. I'd only tried on eight or nine pairs. The rest belonged to someone else. She was just too fucking lazy to tidy the place, it was like she expected me to do it for her.'

The girl looks up, as if trying to find a face that's interested, and then continues.

'I just tried them on and they fitted, were comfortable, really, really snug. It was like I'd been wearing them for months. I put the old ones in my locker in the canteen,' she says, but still no one is listening.

The slight woman sits on the damp bank and pulls on the black boots.

'I'll bet they still fit like a glove when I put them on. I can wear them for a while but then they cut the feet off me. A friend of mine one time bought a pair of shoes for a wedding and she had to take them off in the church, halfway through the Mass, they were that bad.'

The girl smiles, diving into the silence that follows. 'My father used to say every pair of shoes takes you on a journey. When we were kids, he'd tie up our laces and say: Let's hope today's a long journey and a happy one.'

As silence closes again about the women, suddenly each is aware of the other three, and all of them wary. It's the red-haired woman who finally speaks, smiling again.

'The gas thing is that I was thinking about leaving anyway. Be careful what you wish for, you might get it. Of course, thinking about something and doing it are horses of a different colour. Plus, if I'm honest, I was probably thinking of leaving from about eighteen months into the marriage. But I think that's the way with a lot of people. The other gas thing is that this was only the second time in my life that I got my picture in the local paper. The first time was at a night out in one of the local pubs: there was four of us, scuttered, and we looked it. But to make things worse, we were all over the shop, like we had moved when the picture was being taken. But we hadn't, it was the way they printed it. Each of us with three eyebrows and our mouths up around our noses and our noses pushing up our eyes. Plus, whatever way it happened, it looked like I had no top on. He looked at it and went *tsst tsst*, like he was a fucking teacher or something, and says: You look like a whore, like you were gagging for a ride. I said nothing but I thought about it, all that night and all the next day when he was at work. And I thought, You fucking bastard. It's all right for you to call me a whore when we're in bed and you think it does something for me, and it's all right for you to laugh and call me a ride in front of your mates, but it's not all right when it doesn't suit you. But that's the way he is, just the way he is and I don't know why. Could never put my finger on what it was that changed him. Anyway, this is not about him. This is about me. Me and my body. Bodies are funny things. We're never satisfied with them; well, I wasn't anyway. I wanted to change these. Not that I want to be going around with a pair of Dolly Partons in front of me, like outriders in the President's cavalcade. But I'd like to have something … out there … you know. But that's another thing – it depends on how you're feeling, doesn't it? It depends on the way you see yourself. Even blind people must have days when they think they look great, and days where they feel like the sweepings off the hairdresser's floor. And that can't be down to looks, can it? I mean, a blind person saying How do I look? is talking through their hat, aren't they? It's all in the head. Same as the rest of us. Not that I'd want to be blind. Deaf before blind and dumb before deaf. That's the way I'd have it. And I have it now: dumb, deaf and blind. Sort of. Not that it feels the way I imagined it'd feel, if I'd ever thought about it, which I didn't.'

She looks at the others but they seem not to know what to say. And then she laughs out loud.

'Just forget it. Forget it. If Alice was here she'd be laughing at me. There you go, she'd say, there you go complicating things again, making mountains out of molehills.'

'I often wondered about that,' the young girl says quietly.

'About what?'

'About how blind people know whether they look good or not, you know; whether their teeth are clean or their hair is straight or their shoelaces tied.'

'They wear slip-ons,' the slight woman says.

'Huh?'

'All blind people wear slip-on shoes.'

'Do they?'

'Yep, unless they have guide-dogs that are trained to tie laces. The problem with Labradors is that they can't do that, their paws are too big, too awkward. So most blind people have to wear slip-ons. Collies can do it, but you don't see too many collie guide dogs, collies aren't great in other respects. They tend to walk out in front of lorries, so it's swings and roundabouts. No good having your laces tied if you get pancaked by a juggernaut. Jesus, that bus made a terrible mess of him, didn't it? Where's the dog? Oh there he is, under the back wheels; still, they went together, didn't they. That's nice. And his laces are nicely tied and that's the main thing! I often thought it'd be a good idea to return the favour – you know, blind dogs for the Guides. Worn-out sanctuaries for the donkeys, that kind of thing.'

'Piano donor cards,' the red-haired woman adds quickly.

'Sorry?'

'Piano donor cards. Why is it just organs that get donated? Why not pianos?'

'Good one. Yeah, that's it.'

'Spawn shops for frogs.'

'Short grass for small sheep.'

The two women laugh uproariously.

'Primates in the Vatican.'

'Is that true?' the girl asks.

'Is what true?'

'About the guide dogs and the shoes?'

The red-haired woman looks at the young girl and realises she's serious.

'No, it's not true; don't mind her, she's taking the piss.'

'But it'd be a good idea.'

'Yeah, great,' the slight woman says, sneering. "Blind man seeks far-seeing woman. No ties."'

But any irony is lost on the girl.

'I'd hate to be blind,' she says.

The red-haired woman is laughing again. 'Are all Venetians blind?'

'It'd be curtains for the tourist trade if they were!' the slight woman says, standing up suddenly, her laughter competing with the rising birdsong from the ditches around them.

'There's a thing, seriously, that's puzzled me for years,' the red-haired woman says, trying to keep a straight face. 'If it's anal, why isn't it the Royal Canal?'

'Ask my arse!'

And the pair are off again, gasping with laughter.

The fair-haired woman walks away from the other three, skirting the side of the field, until she reaches the river bank. There she squats in a length of early shadow from a whitethorn, watching the river flow, never lifting her eyes from the running water. Behind her, the laughter dies away and she can hear the voice of the red-haired woman.

'I have this friend, my best friend, Alice. We grew up together, started school together, left school the same day, got jobs in the same factory, all that stuff. Got poled the same month – how's that for getting the timing right? The difference was that I got married and she didn't. Wise fucking woman. Anyway, when things started going skew-ways between him and me, when I started looking at other guys and thinking – yeah, well maybe or yeah, fucking too right, I'd ride him – Alice sits me down one night over a few jars and starts on at me about not throwing everything away. But I told her: "You can't wake the fucking dead, Alice; he's not Lazarus and I'm not Jesus. I can't resurrect him." She told me I was only saying that because

I was pissed. She said I'd end up sad and sorry and trying to find someone on one of them computer sites. I hadn't the heart to tell her I'd already met someone that way. "Tall, single, handsome, self-employed, good talker." Bollocks. Married, no hair and a wart like a frog's arse over his left eye. Conversation! Hah! "You've lovely tits. Do you wanna fuck?"'

The fair-haired woman gets up and walks farther along the bank, away from the other three. The slight woman watches her and then says loudly, wanting to be heard, 'Be careful – you might offend someone.'

She then follows the fair-haired woman along the river bank until she's standing beside her, so close they might touch, if touch were possible.

'Just go away, get out of my space, go!' The fair-haired woman's sharp voice rises above the birdsong and the sound of the river. The slight woman giggles and shimmies around her, forcing her backwards, back towards the other two, laughing and pretending to dance erotically as she follows. 'You're a good dancer,' the young girl says. 'I love dancing.'

The slight woman goes on with her performance, dancing about an invisible pole.

The girl smiles.

'Do you like dancing?' she asks.

'No,' the fair-haired woman says, not wanting to be a part of the conversation.

'Why not?'

'I just don't.'

'Her legs are stuck together, that's why,' the slight woman laughs.

'Why are you doing this?' the fair-haired woman asks, her face suddenly animated.

'Doing what?'

'Going out of your way to provoke me? Your attitude – your attempts to shock – your assumptions.'

The slight woman laughs in her face.

'Cop yourself on,' she says. 'The minute I saw you, I knew you were a dry, stuffy, self-opinionated, miserable fucker. I see people like you every day – Plan fucking V for very important in the VHI, house private, Off-Roader with bullbars to collect the milk from the shop, off-shore account, up your own arse. "I have an appointment with Professor Menyamenya – it's a personal matter." We all know, dearie, the whole clinic knows your tits are drooping and your arse is sagging and you think he can do something to help you recapture the youth you never had because your nose was in a book and your mind numbed with information. That's why, since you asked. Three years of frustration and bias and you're the lucky recipient. Next case!'

The young girl stares, mouth open, stunned. 'Are you a doctor?' she asks.

'Some chance, Angel-Arse. I'm Florence Nightingale, the smiling nurse in the nice, tight, white uniform. Sister of mercy and fantasy figure. Bedpans, blow jobs, colonic irrigations, whatever you're having yourself. D'you mind if I put your dick in my mouth? Which reminds me, have you ever noticed the stupid look men get when they're coming? The way their eyes roll up in their heads and their mouths drop open like the door of a dishwasher, you know that kind of Aaaaaah, I'm dying, no one's ever come like me before. Wankers.'

'I'd love to have been a nurse.' The girl's face lights up.

The slight woman sighs deeply. 'No, you wouldn't.'

'I would. I was sorry I left school early. I'd love to be a nurse; it's a nice job, nice doctors. It'd be lovely to marry a doctor.'

'Fuck!' the slight woman says, exasperated.

'Interesting how often education is more valued in its absence.' The fair-haired woman's voice is quiet, not sure the others will hear, or want to hear, her.

'Huh?'

'Think of all the people who say – I wish I'd worked harder or stayed in school.'

'Yeah,' the girl nods. 'I suppose.'

And then the slight woman is talking again. 'Oh, Jesus, spare me your shite talk.'

But this time the fair-haired woman doesn't back away. Instead she stands her ground, face to face with her persecutor.

'What is your problem with allowing other people to have an opinion?'

'Sorry?'

'You have to dominate everything, don't you?'

'Yes, Miss. It's just that I hate hearing people talking bollocks.'

'No, it's more than that.'

'You'd know – of course. You'd know everything. I bet you've known everything all your life; I bet you came out of your mother's cunt knowing everything.'

The fair-haired woman is silent for a moment and when she speaks her voice is quiet, as if she has already withdrawn from the argument.

'There are things that are appropriate and things that aren't. That is inappropriate.'

'Inappropriate?' The slight woman laughs, a dry, humourless laugh. 'Do you think so? Do you think it really matters? We're all in the same hearse here, baby. Nothing's inappropriate here. Do you know how I got here? A pair of my own knickers pulled tight around my neck in a nice warm bed, in a nice detached house in its own grounds, with a nice respectable well-educated man, till my face turned blue and my eyes went pop. I went there for fun, for a shag with someone I knew, someone I thought I could trust, and I ended up dead – now if you were to ask me, that's what I'd call inappropriate. The rest of it is just fucking inconvenient.'

She steps quickly away. The other three women stand in silence, watching her go, absorbing the truth in what she has said, the truth that has hung, unspoken, between them since their arrival. And then she's turning, walking back towards them, her finger pointing, talking loudly.

'What would you call inappropriate now? Seriously, I'm asking you. Now that we're all dead and shoved into some hole in the middle of a fucking bog or thrown in the sea or buried under a field of thistles, what else might be inappropriate?'

'Nothing,' the fair-haired woman says and her voice is a whisper.

'I still think a nurse is a good job,' the girl says.

She and the slight woman are sitting on the bank at the side of the field. The sun is well up now, a vibrant blot on the open sky, its brightness diluting the blue around it.

'Don't you believe it, Angel-Arse. What did you do?'

'I was a cashier in a supermarket.'

'Like it?'

'It was all right.'

'Boyfriend?'

'Sort of.'

'Is that why you're here?'

'God, no,' the girl says, genuinely shocked. 'He's really quiet. I only just started going out with him – first he was a friend, just someone. I was working on it.'

'Good for you. What age are you?'

'Fifteen, but I'm nearly sixteen; my birthday's the end of next month.'

'Not any more,' the fair-haired woman says from the shadow of the whitethorn.

'Sorry?'

'No more birthdays – for any of us.'

'Well, we'll have birthdays anyway. Won't we? Being dead doesn't stop us having birthdays, does it? We went to my father's grave on his birthday.'

'Yeah,' the slight woman says, 'but you were alive – you were going there, he wasn't going there. It's the bloody living who keep remembering, not us. Is he long dead, your dad?'

'Eight months.'

'And you?'

'I don't know, six, seven weeks, something like that.'

'Have you got family?'

'My mam and my brother.'

'Right.'

'They must be sad,' the girl says, as though it's something that has just crossed her mind.

'That's one way of putting it,' the slight woman replies, unable to mask her sarcasm.

But the girl isn't listening; she's miles away.

'I loved my dad. He only worked in the sewerage plant, but when he'd start talking about it, it was like he was talking about something that was so important. The gravity feed and the greaser and the screens and separators and the aeration system. "Two-and-a-half million litres a day coming in there," he'd say, like it was money he'd won in the Lotto, something to be really proud of. And he was proud of it, proud of the treatment plant, proud of the fact that he worked there, proud like it was his. "The bacteria is the boy that does the work," he'd say, "that's the boy to make you hop."'

'They are the boys,' fair-haired woman interjects. 'Bacteria are plural!'

'It was, it was like, like it was all working away there for him, because he told it to. And you'd always know when he was annoyed, really annoyed with someone. He'd say: "There's more than one kind of shite."'

'Man after my own heart,' the slight woman smiles.

'That was the thing about Colin, the guy I fancied. When we got talking, in the canteen in work, he asked me what my father used to do and I told him and he didn't laugh. Maybe because my father had just died, maybe because he thought I'd be upset, but I don't think so – I think it was because he's a nice guy. Kind. It's nice when people are kind, isn't it?'

She looks about her, expecting an answer, but the other three are silent. She's not sure if they're listening or if they've lost interest. But their silence forces her to continue.

'When my father died, my brother, Jeffrey, told me he wouldn't cry. He said my aunt had told him he was the man of the family now and that he wasn't to be crying at the funeral. She said it'd only upset my mother. Jeffrey was only thirteen years old and there he was, afraid to cry! He was a kid, still scared of the dark, of girls, of most things, and on top of that he was afraid to cry because he thought he'd be letting my mother down, letting himself down. I remember him carrying my father's coffin. He's tall but he's as thin as a rake and the coffin was digging into his shoulder, the weight of it pushing him down. That night, I went in to his room to see if he was okay and to say goodnight to him and I was sitting on his bed talking to him and I noticed this welt on his shoulder, where the edge of the coffin had cut into his skin, a big, ugly, red welt where the angle of the coffin had worn it away and it looked just so sore and cruel. I felt so sorry for him.'

Again she is silent. But again the silence of her companions compels her to go on.

'I'm glad he won't have to carry my coffin; I'd hate to think of him having to do that. I'd really, really hate it. I'm better off out here. Never liked graveyards anyway, everything in straight lines, like the way I used to have to stack the corn-flakes when I started in the supermarket. I was a stacker then, before I was a cashier. I reckon I'm better off away from the town. I wouldn't want my mother seeing me go down into the same grave as my father. There's only room enough for two in the plot and it's only right that she'd be buried with him. It's funny, I kind of don't mind being dead for myself; just for them, for Mam and Jeffrey. But then, they don't know I'm dead. Not for sure.'

Only then does anyone speak. It's the fair-haired woman, still seated in the whitethorn shadow.

'I think they do. They all do. I think, deep down, they're as certain as we are.'

'Do you?'

'Yes, I do.'

'How did it happen?' the slight woman asks the girl.

'I was walking home from work, it was about half ten at night. Two guys in a van pulled up, they pulled me into the back. There was this dance music going, you know, with the heavy bass, *badum, badum, badum,* going real loud in the van. Every time I asked them to let me go, they'd tell me to shut my mouth and they'd turn the music up louder. They drove for a long time, out of the town; it got darker and darker and then we turned off the road and down a track and then they stopped the van. When they were taking me out of it, they pulled me by the hair. It really hurt.'

'And then they raped you,' she says, matter of factly.

'Yeah.'

The slight woman laughs again, the same dry, humourless laugh.

'The bastards are always the same. Let them fuck you and they want to show you who's the boss; don't let them fuck you and they're even more determined to show you.'

'They both did and then … again … and then I thought they were going to leave me there but one of them went to the back of the van and got a shovel and I knew. And then he hit me with it, across the face, with the back of it and the pain went right through me and I started praying that they'd do it fast. Then, when I was lying on the ground, he brought the side of it down on my skull.'

She touches the side of her head, tenderly, as though expecting to find blood.

'Do you believe in God?' she asks, turning to the fair-haired woman.

'I believe in something greater than me.'

'I wonder!' the slight woman mocks.

'Do you believe there's a heaven?'

'I believe heaven is a place – no, a state – of being, just being. It's peace and freedom and connection. There's no isolation, no aloneness, no separation, no needs, no desires; it's desire that causes human suffering.'

'I used to nick money from the till in work. I was always worried that if I died without confessing it, I wouldn't get to heaven.'

And then the slight woman is laughing again, standing over the young girl, bending to look into her face.

'If there was a heaven, Angel-Arse, do you think you'd have been taken off the roadside? Or do you think some God, in his fluffy cloudy paradise, surrounded by little cherubs strumming harps, would have said: "Take her, she's fifteen and she'd been robbing the till in the supermarket; get that pair of bastards to pull her into their van and rape her and beat her head in with a shovel. That'll be a lesson to her and everyone else not to pilfer again.""'

'You have no right to say that to her,' the fair-haired woman says, her eyes angry.

'This isn't about rights. She's dead, you're dead, we're all fucking dead. We have no rights. Rights are for the lucky ones. I'm sure you had rights, lots of rights, when you were alive, but not here, not any more. This is the democracy of the dead, Mrs Fucking Look-at-Me-I'm-Great.'

Even the birds have fallen silent in the midday heat. They sit like deeper shadows in the stumped shadows of the trees and bushes along the water's edge. Only a kingfisher flicks over the face of the river, a spurt of colour, there and gone, if it was there at all.

The three women are lying in the yellow grass at the foot of an oak, eyes closed, their palms open to the sky. The young girl is sitting, her back against the tree, staring into the blue above her.

'Will I get to dance in heaven?' she whispers, not sure that anyone is still awake.

'Fucking hell,' the slight woman says, without opening her eyes. 'How did I end up in the place where the crazies go? A dancing wanna-be nurse! At least you'd never be stuck for work in a club! Bring your own pole.'

'Are you a good dancer?' the fair-haired woman asks quietly.

'I think so,' the girl says.

'Go on, show us,' the red-haired woman says, opening her eyes and raising herself on one elbow. 'Go on, do, please.'

Seeing the older woman's smiling eyes, the young girl gets up and moves out of the shadow of the tree. She dances, uncertainly at first, but then with growing confidence, spiralling and pirouetting in the sunlight, closing her own eyes now, nodding to a melody from somewhere, some memory of a rhythm that was life.

'Pity you didn't dance away from the two bastards in the van,' the slight woman says, squinting into the sun.

The young girl stops dead and walks away, out into the middle of the field, away from the women and the shadows of the trees and the whisper of the river.

'What is it with you?' the red-haired woman barks, her rage plain to hear. 'Can you not let anything go? She's just a kid. Why are you so angry?'

'What a stupid fucking question.'

'Right then, why are you angrier than the rest of us? What gives you the right to be more hurt, more badly done by than anyone else?'

'Because I'm sick listening to this shit. Listening to Miss High-and-Mighty talking down to us.'

'Bollocks!' the red-haired woman laughs. 'You were angry before you met her.'

'And what if I was?'

'So why?'

'Is this a fucking inquisition? What are you, a Jesuit?'

'I'm just asking,' she says evenly.

For a moment the slight woman is silent, and then she launches into her reply.

'All right, I'll tell you. When I was growing up, there was a cross at the end of our lane, where it came out onto the main road, a little white cross with a girl's name on it. Margaret Murphy. She was four years old when she ran out in front of a car and her mother never got over the fact that she was dead. She used to wander around the farmyard or the garden or the house all day, talking to Margaret, and she'd shout at me when I was going to school in the morning, and she'd shout at me when I was coming home from school in the evening, and I was terrified of her. I was sorry for Margaret and I hated her at the same time, for getting all the attention and I hated my mother for always talking about her, for being so consumed by her, for keeping this dead little girl alive in her head, for forgetting that I was her fucking daughter too, for not seeing that I needed to be hugged and held and pampered and loved. And I despised my father for not standing up to her, for not telling her that I was important, just as important as the little dead girl in the flowery summer frock. Will that do for starters? And by the time my turn came, that mad woman was dead and buried herself, still raving about little Margaret this and little Margaret that. When I died, when I disappeared, there was no one to look for me, or to talk about the kind of kid I was, or say how well I'd done, or to meander up and down the garden talking aloud to me. Nobody and nothing. People forget the ones who disappear, forget we even lived. And they don't know we're here, still … existing … wandering, fucking wandering, bumping into one another like a game of blind man's bluff, just talking, then drifting away. Listening to little Miss Nijinsky singing and dancing around heaven all day.'

'Nijinsky was a man,' the fair-haired woman says, delighted. And then the slight woman is on her feet, screaming.

'Fuck off, you fucking fuck.'

'I thought Nijinsky was a horse,' the young girl says, from the middle of the field.

'He was one of the foremost ballet dancers of the twentieth century,' the fair-haired woman tells her.

'Thank you for that,' the slight woman says, her tone now controlled and bitter. 'You must have worked as a travelling encyclopaedia in your spare time, did you? I'll bet your husband couldn't wank without consulting your inner pages.

Sorry, darling, don't come just yet, I'm on fourteen across, it's an anagram of my fanny. If you had a husband. If you didn't drive him away.'

The slight woman, the young girl and the red-haired woman are dawdling on the river bank, their toes only inches above the blue water. The trees have begun to grow shadows again in the early afternoon. The red-haired woman is speaking.

'I was never sure ... that life goes on ... for us ... here. I was never sure about that, about what would happen after it was over. I never expected life to go on here, too. I thought it'd be different. Better. Or worse. But different.'

'I thought there'd be choirs singing and that I'd be in one,' the girl says.

The slight woman laughs.

'And you'd have angel wings to match your angel arse!'

The red-haired woman frowns, waiting for her companion to add something else, something even more cynical, something hurtful, but there's only the near-silence of the river at their feet.

'There must have been things in your life, before all this; things that were good.'

'Obviously,' the slight woman says.

'It'd be nice to hear about them.'

'I hate that word – nice – it means nothing.'

'Good, then. Good to hear about the good things.'

'Why?'

'Because maybe that's all we have – memories. Maybe they're the only things we have any control over. Sometimes I think about my husband, about the fact that most people probably believe he killed me. They're walking around the town, pointing him out to their kids, telling them to keep away from that man because he murdered his wife. I laugh about that because there's nothing else to laugh at and sometimes you have to laugh at something, or it just gets worse and worse and drags you down. I used to hate it when my mother said, You have to have a laugh, don't you? But I think she was right; I do now, anyway.'

'I don't see it that way.'

'One time, in the pub, I was talking to some of my friends about a course I was doing, telling them about how the instructor guy told us we had to think outside the box, when my husband pipes up with this pretend thick-o expression: Thinking outside the box, that's foreplay, isn't it? He was just trying to fuck up my story, trying to make me look stupid. But sometimes I think back and it makes me smile. It was funny. He was just acting the bollocks, but it was funny.'

The slight woman smiles and is quiet for a while. And then she starts talking, determined to have her say, afraid almost that she will lose faith in the story she is telling.

'We remember our lives, you know, and the things we remember are different from the things other people remember. Or they don't remember at all. I have cousins and an aunt, but what'll they remember of me? They remember things, but not the things I remember or the way I remember them. No one will remember me as I was. Or you. They'll remember the picture they had of you. My cousins will remember a wild woman that liked to drink and fuck and live life for today. But they won't know about the woman that went back to her home place three weeks before she died, back to the farmhouse, back to the orchard that's gone to hell and the sheds that are falling down. And they won't know anything about the woman that was saving her money to put a new roof on that house so she could move back there and watch the sparrows rising up out of the trees when she opened the back door in the mornings. And they won't know it was her that put the bunch of apple blossoms at Margaret Murphy's cross.

No one will know I was coming home, that I wanted to live there again, to give that raving woman's ghost another chance to be my mother. All they ever saw was the me that couldn't stay; they know nothing about the me that couldn't stay away.'

It's late afternoon; the sun is sliding into the tops of the trees, spiking the highest branches, the listlessness of midday sliding along with it. The river has taken on another shade, a crimson that will lighten to golden red and later to melted flax.

The red-haired woman and the fair-haired woman are walking slowly around the perimeter of the field, stopping now and then to peer at flowers in a gap of the ditch.

'You don't say much about yourself,' the red-haired woman says.

'What is there to say?'

'I don't know – things. Are you married, do you have kids, stuff, things?'

'Yes, I am married. No, I don't have children.'

'Were you happy?'

The fair-haired woman stops and lifts her face to the falling sun. She smiles, a tight smile.

'Yes, I was.'

'Did you get on with your husband?'

'Yes, I did. Really well. He has a beautiful smile. He's quiet but in a reassuring way. I don't think I ever did anything that he didn't fully back me on. Not that he ever tried to confine me, as we actually lived our own lives. I think because he has a great sense of self-worth, nothing shakes him.'

'You were lucky.'

'Yes.'

'Did you have a job?'

'I was a teacher.'

'I'd never have guessed!' the red-haired woman laughs. 'Daughter of teachers?'

'No, my father was a doctor. Is a doctor.'

'I'd have taken odds you were a teacher's daughter.'

'Maybe it's much of a muchness.'

'Maybe. There was a girl in my school when I was in primary whose father was a doctor. I always wanted to be invited to her birthday parties. But I never was. I loved her house. I thought it was real posh. The only time I ever got to go into it was for injections. I loved the smell of it, that antiseptic smell.'

The fair-haired woman walks on, her companion following, only now her face is half-turned away.

'Wherever we lived, my father's surgery was always in the house. In a front room of our first house; then in a converted garage to the side of our second house and then in what had been a drawing room in our last house, the house my parents still live in. From the time I was six or seven, that always played on my mind, having the surgery and waiting room in the same building we lived in. I had some sense of an awful consequence around that fact. I even thought as a small girl that waiting room was spelled w-e-i-g-h-t-i-n-g room. A place where people sat with the weight of the world on their shoulders, a phrase I'd picked up from my parents' conversations. I'd see them coming and going though the hall, sad faces, sick faces, shoulders bent, doubled over. And as I grew up I realised that it wasn't just the elderly who were carrying that weight. I'd see a beautiful young woman and I'd know, from the code my parents used at the dinner table, that she was seriously ill or dying, even. Often I'd go and sit in the waiting room – at night when my parents were out – sit there and soak up that fear and uncertainty. It was an ominous feeling, and I wondered if I was the only one who felt it, wondered if it was telling me something, something waiting for me. When I was fifteen, I had this very close friend in school. We lived our lives like sisters. I'd stay in her house and she in mine. One weekend she came to stay and on that Saturday night when my parents were out, I brought her into the waiting room. We sat there, in the darkness, and I tried to explain to her that there was something there, waiting for Monday morning's patients. For some woman who thought everything was going just right for her. For a little boy that didn't even know why he was being brought there. Something waiting for the next victim. Waiting for someone who thought they had only a cold or a cough or appendicitis. Something waiting to bring the bad news, waiting to write a last prescription. Always waiting for the door to open, to say: That's the one I'll throw my shadow over. But my friend just hushed me and then she kissed me. Perhaps she thought she could exorcise the place by kissing me. Perhaps she wanted to kiss me. Perhaps she was in love with me.'

'Love is a strange thing,' the red-haired woman says quietly.

The fair-haired woman nods. 'My father still sits up every night, waiting for me to come home. You'd think by now he'd know that's not going to happen, that there isn't going to be a tap on the window at three in the morning. That he won't open his eyes and see me at the door, that he won't struggle up out of his chair and hobble over to turn the key in the lock. It's not going to happen.'

For a long time the red-haired woman says nothing, and when finally she speaks, she might be speaking to herself. 'I beat cancer. Isn't that a joke?'

'Not a very funny one.'

'No, but I beat it. I'd just got the all-clear. I was out celebrating with my friend, Alice, who works in a travel agency. We went on the piss and then on to a nightclub, or what passes for a nightclub in our town. That's where I met him. I was out of it and I told him to shag off when he asked me to dance. I was so pissed I walked off and left Alice chatting up some guy, had it in my head that I'd go and get a taxi for the two of us, never even told Alice, started walking to the taxi rank. He must have followed me. He pulled up beside me, told me to get in, and I did. Don't know why, I knew who he was but I didn't expect … this. Who does? But I knew when he started talking, I knew I was in trouble. I asked him to stop, said I wanted to pee, but he just kept on driving. I said, If you don't stop I'll piss on the seat, but he just laughed. I asked him what he wanted from me. I want to teach you a lesson, he said, not to look down on people, not to be ignorant to people that ask you to dance. Just because you're tarted up, he said, that doesn't give you the right to treat someone like dirt. I'm sorry, I said. I'm sorry, I'm sorry, I'm sorry. I'm so fucking sorry. Not sorry enough, he said. Too late for sorry, he said. Time to learn a lesson, he said. And I knew there was no point crying, no point begging, just run for it when I got the chance. He drove into a field. It was October and the ground was hard and stubbled. He parked at the far end, in a dip, where no one could see the car. He knew the place, knew the car wouldn't get bogged down. And then I started laughing, I couldn't help it. What are you laughing at? he said. Everything, I said, the whole thing, everything, life. You're laughing at me, he said. No, I said, I'm just laughing at the whole thing. And I laughed so much I wet myself and I wet the seat of the car and I couldn't help it. You could smell the warm piss in the car and he grabbed my head and started punching me, hard, across the face, punching my nose until I heard it breaking and I didn't laugh any more. Not so funny now, he said. No laughing matter now. What do you want? I said. Do you want sex? You can if you want, whatever you want. I wouldn't touch you with a tongs, he said. I wouldn't dirty myself by stroking you. There was something in that word, stroking, something about the way he said it, softly, like he'd thought about it, like it meant something to him, that brought it home to me that this was it. This was the end. And I started laughing again, laughing at him. I knew there was no way out of there; I just wanted it to be over, just wanted him to finish it. So I thought I'd provoke him into finishing it, quickly. "You're not a hard man," I said, "but you know that, don't you? Real hard men take the chance that they'll be caught, that they'll swing for what they do. They take a risk. They're not afraid of what might happen. No, you're just a fucking gouger, you have no courage, no balls, you've nothing to lose. You're just a scumbag, a miserable, crawling, cowardly little bastard. Fucker, fucker, fucker." I don't know how long I went on. In the end, he opened the door and pushed me out. I was kneeling on the stubble and I could see the motorway lights across the field and it was the saddest thing I ever saw because they were just there. Just there like I could touch them, like I could run to them, across two fields, up the embankment, wave down a car, be safe, be looked after. I imagined it all in my head, the warmth in the car. A man driving, there'd be a woman with him. She'd sit into the back seat with me, put her arm around me, hug me, tell me I was all right, everything was all right. Yet all I could do was kneel there and listen to the cars whistling by. Warm, wrapped-up people looking out at where I was but not seeing me, not even knowing I was there. And I could feel the stubble cutting into my knees and I couldn't get up and I couldn't run. I just couldn't. When I got cancer, when the doctor told me I had it, I was so fucking angry. With myself for getting it, for being the one. I had to tell someone so I told my mother-in-law. I asked her not to tell anyone else. But she did, she told my husband. I didn't want him to know. But she told him anyway. And we talked about it and I tried to be matter-of-fact. And then one night, the end of that week, we were in bed together and we were having sex and he asked me to put my bra back on. I can't touch your tits, he said. I can't look at them, knowing what's in there. That's what he said. And I did, I put it on and he fucked me. And he never mentioned it again, never asked me how I was, nothing, just wiped it out of his mind because he couldn't deal with it. But I beat it. I fucking beat it. Didn't I? After that there was nothing anyone could do to hurt me.'

She pauses for a moment and a smile darts across her face.

'The guy that killed me, he has a family. He takes them out for lunch on a Sunday and then for a spin in the country. Is it a little lap of honour that he has in his own mind? Envisioning where he picked me up, where he killed me in the field, where he buried me in the bog and then back home for tea and a nice quiet night in front of the telly. Does he take me on holiday with him, in the back of his mind? Am I always there with him, like a prize he's proud of? All these questions that I'll never get the answers to. And everyone else thinking my own fella did it!'

The four women are at the gateway to the field. The young girl leans against one of the pillars, the other three loll against the bank, the rays of the sinking sun shining straight into their eyes, lighting up those eyes as if there were life inside them.

'I was in Tramore with my mates on holiday last year,' the young girl says, her brow furrowed. 'I nearly drowned there and it wasn't funny. And all your life doesn't flash before you either, when you're dying.'

'I think we all know that by now,' the slight woman says.

The girl is silent, a furrow still ploughing her forehead.

'So why did we end up here, now, today, together?'

'Maybe this is Purgatory – the halfway house.'

'Do you think so?'

'No, I don't.'

'Do you think we'll be together for ever now?'

'Jesus, I hope not! I can't think of anything I ever did to deserve that.'

'So what do you think we're doing here? Why is it happening now?' The young girl turns to the fair-haired woman.

'I have no idea.'

'We're waiting for Godot,' the slight woman laughs. 'Or the Blessed Virgin-O. Or the Holy Ghost-O. Maybe this is the great Lost and Found in the sky. Where the dumped and dislocated all find their way in the end, limping in with their battered faces and broken necks and stabbed hearts. "The winner takes it all." Bet that's not one of your songs.'

The fair-haired woman shakes her head.

The young girl settles herself more comfortably on the gate.

'Do you believe in God?' she asks the slight woman.

'He hasn't come looking for me, not even a text message.'

'Do you?'

'Yes, I do,' the fair-haired woman says. 'There has to be a God to make some sense of this.'

'Why?' the slight woman asks. 'Why does this have to make sense? I never understood it when people said that and I still don't.'

'Because there are no answers in chaos.'

'Why do you expect answers to everything?'

'There is an answer to every question.'

'Except the chicken and the egg,' the girl laughs.

'To every serious question – about life and death and faith and hope.'

'No, no, no, no, that's waffle,' the slight woman says quickly. 'That's aspiration. That's the kind of stuff you hear on radio breakfast shows, new-age bullshit, crap they throw out at half-six in the morning when you're too tired or hung over to understand, let alone contradict. Nothing has to be.'

'If there's no God, how are we here, in this place, now, talking, continuing to exist?'

The slight woman shakes her head, genuinely amazed.

'You think us being here, in this fucking field, having this poxy conversation is proof of the existence of God?'

'Not if you don't want to believe. But if you have faith, there are answers. To everything.'

'Ah, so I'm a second-class sinner travelling in the last train to Graceland because I don't believe? But you're up there in first class with the Communion of Saints and Scholars? Is that it?'

'I wouldn't put it that way.'

'And just how would you put it?' the slight woman says, standing up and leaning into the fair-haired woman's face. 'Pope Whatever Your Name Is? You haven't really said anything definite about any of this, have you? You just think it should make sense because you've always believed in your gossamer, spirity little life that it should. But none of it has to. We don't have to know where we are or why we're here or any of that stuff. Like your man said, "We can see no reasons, cause there are no reasons." Just like there didn't have to be reasons for any of us to be killed. It was circumstances, that's all. Wrong time, wrong place, wrong turn, wrong bed, wrong house, wrong road. That's all it amounts to in the end – situations, details. That's all, no master plan, no all-seeing eye. Nothing.'

'I didn't realise Bob Geldof was a theologian too.'

'Oh yeah, and a great ride too, I'd say,' the slight woman sniggers, stepping and turning away.

'I believe what I believe.'

'Won't get you anywhere, won't solve anything, won't help you find heaven's gate. And even if you do, you'll find the paint is peeling and the hinges have fallen off and there ain't nobody at home. This is it – we go on existing and nobody knows and every now and then we'll stumble across one another and that'll be it. Human contact in an inhuman somewhere or other.'

The young girl swings on the gatepost, looking to the red-haired woman for reassurance, but she just smiles wanly and shrugs. The slight woman turns to face the other three, her face set and earnest.

'Do you know what I remember most clearly from life? A winter morning at three on Leeson Street, and a guy I knew who was tall and attractive, and a big black car with that shiny, new look and a smell of someone else's perfume in the front seat and Indian music playing and a pleasant conversation about the party we were going to and what this guy would like to do to me and laughter. There's my life, the last hour of it anyway. No blinding flash, no Saviour coming down off his cross to show the bad guys who's really the boss. Nothing, just losing breath, losing consciousness, being rolled into a hole, being covered, being afraid, being breathless, being dead, being here. That's what it comes to, that's what I remember. That and the Halloween night my dad dressed up in women's clothes and did a striptease and I laughed. And the day my dog died. And the day my sister was knocked down. And that's about it. That's the fucking all of it.'

'When I was nine, my dog was run over,' the young girl says quickly. 'I had a picture of him that I drew. I kept it under my pillow for months. I won a prize for it.'

The slight woman laughs. 'Angel-Arse, you never cease to amaze me with the profound way you link one thing to another, completely unrelated, matter.'

The girl smiles.

'If I could go back now, I'd sit on the side of my brother's bed, and I'd sing and I'd say: "I love you so much, scallywallywallywag."'

For a moment she is silent, taking in the field and its length-ening shadows, gazing along the empty roadway.

'Do any of you know where we are?'

'We're at the end of the line, Angel-Arse,' the slight woman says. 'Literally and metaphorically. And if you don't know what that means, ask our learned friend there.'

'Are we ghosts?'

'We're the smell of a dead animal on the side of a mountain, that's what we are.'

It's evening. The red-haired woman and the fair-haired woman are watching the last rays of the sun's afterglow. The light in the field is so delicate it might shatter at any moment, a brittle midsummer crystal in the air. Spirals of gnats gyre above the darkening river, where a trout rises into the air and falls again, the water closing over it.

'Funny,' the fair-haired woman says. 'Whenever I thought about dying, I never dreamed I'd be killed.'

'Can't say I ever thought too much about dying.'

'I did. Often.'

'Maybe that's because your father was a doctor, what you were saying about the waiting room and all that stuff.'

'I think it was more than that. It was like something constantly in my head, like, I don't know … like something I was waiting for.'

'Fear?'

'No, not fear. I wasn't afraid of this thing. I don't know how to explain it properly. When I met him, the man, it was morning, a bright, sunny, summer morning. I was walking along the canal bank and I'd taken a book of poems with me. I saw him sitting near one of the lock gates, watching me walking, peering out over the top of these little round glasses. He was wearing a leather jacket and black jeans. From the first time I saw his eyes, it seemed to me that he knew everything I'd ever thought and done. I know that sounds trite, but it's true. And he had a notebook and pen in his hand, which made me think he was okay. I know our friend over there would laugh at that, say I was pretentious, but it's just something we all do, don't we? We see something about someone and we either like or dislike them for it. Do you know what I mean?'

'Yes, I do.'

'He said something like, "Life is too short" but not in any kind of threatening or dark way, more as if it were a natural thing to say, a natural greeting. Anyhow, I sat beside him and we started talking about nature and life and death and God and meaning, serious things. It was as if we knew each other intimately. Like we'd had these discussions before, like we were comfortable with the conversation. We talked for a long time and then he said he'd walk me to the next lock, his car was parked there. And he took my arm while we were walking, which I didn't like. It was the first thing that didn't feel right. But we were still talking, still discussing, and I was enjoying the conversation, so I thought perhaps it was just a natural gesture.'

'And what happened?'

'Just before we reached the lock gate, it started to drizzle. He said he was meeting someone and asked me for directions. I told him how to get where he was going and wished him well, but just then the heavens opened and he started laughing and said, "Get in the car, I'll drop you to a bus stop." I was wearing a tracksuit, and knew I'd be drenched, so I said okay.'

'And?'

'He drove past the bus stop. I asked him to let me out. He smiled and told me to relax, said he'd drive me home. Told me to trust him. One part of me did, implicitly. And another part told me I was mad. It had stopped raining. I thought – this'll be okay because people don't get harmed at ten o'clock on a summer morning, broad daylight. It just doesn't happen.

'"Listen," he said. "I'm sorry if I scared you. What about we take a walk in the mountains, solve the problems of the here and the hereafter? I am sorry if you got the wrong impression."

'I looked squarely at him and he was smiling. His eyes met mine and I trusted them.

'"All right,"' I said.

'I knew anyone hearing me say that would think I was crazy, but I was willing to take the risk because I felt challenged by the things he had said.

'"Good,"' he said. "Thank you."

'He drove up the mountains. Anyone seeing us would have thought − summer morning, couple out for a drive, a walk through the woods and lunch on the way back. And we did walk into the woods, and he kept talking to me about the same things we'd talked about at the canal.'

'You didn't try to talk him round?'

'No. I just nodded or shrugged. And then he said, again: "Life is short." But this time his tone reminded me of one of those judges handing down a sentence in an old black and white film. I was waiting for the gavel to fall somewhere but all I heard were the birds singing. Then he told me to sit down. "You know what I'm going to do," he said. I nodded.'

'And then it happened?'

'No. He beat me. Just that, just violence, simple viciousness, so out of keeping with the conversation we'd had at the canal. But he didn't kill me. He beat me and then he bundled me down into a dyke. I was in pain, I knew my arm was broken, I knew my ribs were broken, but I was conscious. And I think he knew I was conscious. He threw the book in after me. I started to crawl away from him, away from any more pain, away from whatever it was he was going to do next. I kept crawling along the bottom of the dyke. It was full of dry leaves and bits of broken sticks. And each time I looked back he was watching me, standing on the lip of the dyke, watching. And I kept crawling and then I looked back and he was gone. I lay there, waiting for him, thinking he'd gone to get a gun or a stone or a spade. And the sun kept rising through the sky and there were flies around the blood on my face and I heard voices, not all that far away, but I didn't call to them.'

'He'd come back with someone else?'

'No, no, these were younger voices, girls' voices, laughing.'

'And you didn't shout for help?'

'No.'

'Why not, for Christ's sake?'

'I don't know.'

The fair-haired woman pauses for a moment and considers what she has said.

'I do know,' she corrects herself.

'And?'

'It was as if I had made a decision. Not to try to go back, not to leave that wood. Not to try to escape.'

'Why, for fuck's sake? Why?'

'Because all my life I'd been waiting for something, waiting for that darkness that followed the other people into my father's surgery to find me, to fall across my shoulders. Here was the inevitable consequence that had been shadowing me all my life. Here was my destiny and I had no right to interfere with what had been predestined for me. It wasn't unlike when they told us we couldn't have children, after we'd wanted children so badly. But when they told us there was nothing we could do, we went home and we made love every day for a week, sometimes twice or three times a day, as though we might somehow forget, shed the bad news in the sweat and stimulation of love-making. But of course it doesn't work like that, so I finally accepted it. And my husband accepted it. And I somehow accepted that my life was meant to end in that wood. And I knew my husband would accept it, too.'

'But didn't you want to go back?'

'There is no going back – ever. We think there is; we think we can undo what we've done, or explain ourselves away to those we hurt, but we can't. And it's better to accept what's been laid out for us.'

'I think you're wrong.'

'Most people would.'

'Very wrong.'

'I lay there as my body settled into the ground and the pain became something I could manage, and the day ended and the moon came up like a paper lantern, blowing and catching on branches, then blowing higher and catching again. Right up through the tallest trees, and then down again, falling and catching and falling and catching until it was almost dawn. And I thought of a night when I was young, when I was a student. I had driven up the Dublin Mountains with my husband, who was my boyfriend then. It was summer 1984, a hot summer night in the middle of July. We parked the car and went into the woods and I took off my dress in the moonlight and we made love. I thought about that while I was lying there. I remembered it, tried to be in that time and that place, with my husband, but I couldn't. Like I said, there's no going back. So I waited. I waited for that man to come back. I knew I'd see him again.'

'Fucking hell.'

'The next day he was there, standing above me again. It must have been late in the morning because I couldn't see his face, the sun was behind him. At first I thought I was hallucinating, I was thirsty and hungry, but when he stepped down into the dyke and his shadow fell across me, I knew this was what I'd been waiting for. I saw the blade, but there was no pain. Then he covered me over with leaves and sticks and clay, but I know some day the winter rain running through the dyke will wash all that away.'

Three of the women are standing in the twilit field, looking across the river and up towards the brow of the darkening hill.

The slight woman sits on the low stump of a tree and kicks off her black boots.

'I knew these would cut the feet off me.'

The others are silent. She stands again and looks at them.

'Right, so much for the party spirit! I'm going. I'll see you. See you, Angel-Arse. Keep dancing.'

'Yeah,' the young girl says. 'See ya.'

The slight woman walks slowly across the field and steps through a gap in the ditch, disappearing into another field.

'I wonder if we will see her again?' the red-haired woman asks.

No one answers her.

'Strange,' she says. 'The way we all start out so full of high hopes, when we fall in love, like. We meet someone and we think life is going to be everything that it wasn't for our parents or our friends. We see someone and we think they're gorgeous and we get to meet them and we think they're great and they think we're great and everything is going to be fantastic for ever. And then it just goes … somewhere … away … gets lost, goes missing and one day you realise it's gone. And it doesn't matter if you meet someone else and you think they're great too, and they don't mind that your breast has been sliced open, they just want to love you, to make love to you, and then that slips away as well. There's nothing that lasts, nothing you can rely on, it's not just people or breathing, it's everything, feelings, even fucking love itself.'

The girl looks at her, frowning.

'That's very sad.'

'Yes, it is, isn't it? Bloody sad.'

She's silent for a moment, watching the young girl's worried face and then she says, smiling, 'Alice and me … we were fourteen … we were on a bus, with all these other kids from the youth club … it was a summer tour … just for the day … and the bus came over the top of a hill and there it was … the sea … the first time I'd ever laid eyes on it … Jesus … this blue sheet from one side of the world to the other … flat, blue. I just wanted that moment to last for ever … I couldn't hear anything … none of the singing or shouting or laughing … just me and the sea. I was holding onto Alice's hand, squeezing it without knowing, and she didn't say anything. She realised how special that was to me … the sea … blue … blue and calm, wide, beautiful … the most beautiful thing I ever saw.'

As she finishes, the fair-haired woman moves away into the twilight, becomes something distant and then nothing at all. The night settles about them, neither the red-haired woman nor the girl speaks, until each sees the other as a darkness on the darkness of night. Finally, the older woman speaks.

'It's time to go.'

'Yeah,' the girl agrees, carelessly kicking off her runners, as if ready for her next adventure. They begin to cross the field, towards the gate, but then the young girl turns and goes back to where they had been standing. She scans the ground until she finds the child's wellington boots in the grass. Hesitating, she kneels and picks them up, holding them in one hand.

The red-haired woman comes back and stands above her.

'I think we should go,' she says.

'What about these?'

'I don't know.'

'My brother loved it when I stayed with him. Imagine being a child, being left on your own, left out somewhere like here where no one will ever find you.'

'No different to ourselves.'

'I know, but we found one another, didn't we? And, anyway, we're big people.'

'True.'

'Imagine whoever owns these, how small they are? What if they come looking for them and there's no one here?'

'We don't know if they will come, or when. Maybe never.'

'But what if they do?'

'I have to go,' the red-haired woman says.

'I know,' the girl says. 'I'll wait … for a while, just for a while … just in case.'

The Low Terrace

It was the breathing that made us realise something was wrong, something beyond the ordinary, more a warning than a possibility. A rasping, uncertain, caught-in-the-throat breath that was a statement of intent, that said this was it, there was no going back, no recovery, no hope.

Each time I stepped into her hospital room I'd hear the laboured breathing. And each time I left, it followed and died when the door was closed. The corridor was always a relief after the endless hawing.

And sometimes there was the rambling talk about my brothers. I didn't have any brothers. I'm an only child. But she went on about them and about how we were to take care of them and not let them get cold.

'Keep them warm,' she'd say. 'Make sure they're warm.'

My father would lean across the bed and pat her hand and assure her and sometimes, when I was alone with her, she'd tell me to check that they were warm and I'd do my best to reassure her and pat her hand and massage her temples. And then she'd stop her rambling and, for a while, there'd be quietness.

We'd sit with her in shifts. My father through the day, my aunt in the evenings and myself through the night, sleeping in that hard armchair, a blanket tucked around me.

On the Saturday morning, at four o'clock, I walked the length of the corridor, while the nurses turned my mother.

Outside the day was white and fresh. Summer without the heat. A washed-out day. I walked right to the end of the glass-panelled mezzanine and looked across the car park, with its tarmac boxes and their dinky cars.

And I knew when I walked back, even before they said. I knew by the way the nurses were standing outside the door.

'She's gone,' one of them whispered softly.

I nodded.

'Would you like to spend a few minutes with her?'

I nodded again and the nurse opened the door for me and I stepped inside. She stood a moment watching, the lemon skin of daylight like an aura around her, before she quietly closed the door and left me alone.

The silence in that aching, tortured room.

I stood at the window with my back to her, waiting for some movement, the slightest noise. I couldn't believe that death could be so still.

I remembered us packing the string shopping bag and climbing out through the back ditch and heading for picnics in the River Field. And I remembered Tommy MacMahon.

Jesus, Tommy MacMahon! What put him into my head? There was no silence when he died. When was it? July. Yes, it was July, but what year? Nineteen fifty-nine? No, earlier. Fifty-seven? Fifty-eight? Yes, fifty-eight. He was eight years younger than me and I was ten when he was killed. Tommy and Geraldine and Mr and Mrs MacMahon. They lived in the next cottage from ours. The gardens ran a full acre side by side. Twenty-four semi-detached cottages in a cul-de-sac. The Low Terrace, a village all on its own.

You were in your element that summer and then the world came tumbling down.

And the radio blaring all day long. What the hell was it? 'All I Have to Do is Dream'. But who sang it? I can hear you singing it. Your voice sweet and high as you sang about dreaming your life away. Sweeter even, I thought, than the voices from the radio.

Who was it?

'The Everly Brothers,' my mother says. '"All I Have to Do is Dream." God, they're gorgeous. Your father says they can't sing, not in Mario Lanza's class, but they're gorgeous.' And then she leans across the fence between the gardens.

'Do you like them, Mrs MacMahon?'

'Who?'

'The Everly Brothers.'

'Do I know them?'

'*Dream, dream, dream ...*' my mother sings.

'Oh yeah, yeah, they're good. Geraldine likes them. Don't you, Geraldine?' Geraldine MacMahon, sixteen, lying in the sun, rarely bothering to speak, even when she was spoken to.

'What?'

'You like them fellas that sing *dream, dream, dream.*'

'They're all right.'

Mrs MacMahon gives up on her daughter.

'I see she's still knocking around with Liam; that looks like a strong line,' my mother says.

'He's a very nice lad.'

'And very bright.'

Later, I overhear my mother and father discussing Geraldine and Liam.

'She has one aim in life and it isn't books. She's fella mad, anything in trousers.'

'So long as he stays in the trousers, things'll be all right,' my father laughs.

My mother looks at me and then back at my father.

'Ssshhh,' she says.

'He's ten,' my father grins. 'The bould Geraldine is another matter. And a grand-looking young one with it.'

My mother puts her arms around him and wrestles him against the sink, laughing.

'Don't you even think about that or you'll be out on your ear.'

When I look back, life seemed like that all the time. All happiness and laughter and light. Black and white is how childhood seems from this distance and that summer was all whiteness, all light, all sunshine and my parents laughing in the back garden. It was a summer of finding them kissing in the kitchen. A summer of my father spinning me on the swing, and my aunt coming to stay, and my parents dolled up to the nines for a midsummer dinner dance and waking, the next morning, to three bars of Fry's Cream on the bedside table, and the sound of my mother and my aunt giggling in the back garden and the sight of them on the garden seat, sipping tea. And then watching as my aunt drove away, waving, before going with my mother to pick lettuce and scallions for a salad for the tea. And my father's car in the yard and my parents hugging at the back door.

But there must have been another side.

And the corner-boy voices reassure me, the chorus of watchers, the ranks of seers:

Course there was another side.

We saw. Of course we saw.

Everybody saw.

We all knew.

The whole Low Terrace knew.

The whole town.

We saw the MacMahon one and the Master's son at it.

Conniving under the streetlight was one thing. Going into the River Field was another matter altogether.

No light there!

Never a truer word.

Ha ha!

Never.

The long hot summer.

Long hot young lad.

Young wet wild one.

Sure we all knew.

She wasn't laughing at nothing.

I saw them.

And I saw them.

And so did my brother, saw them down the Back River. Kissing and their mouths wide open.

And him feeling her.

And her with her hand inside his trousers looking for the long lad.

Ha ha!

And then one evening, is it the same evening that my aunt drove away or is it another? No, I'm sure it is that evening. We're walking between the strawberry beds at the side of the garden and Mrs MacMahon comes to the fence and calls my mother.

'Mrs! Mrs!'

'What is it?' my mother asks.

'Jesus, Mary and Joseph …'

'What's the matter? What's wrong?'

'Sacred Heart of Jesus.'

'What is it?'

'It's Geraldine.'

'Is she sick?'

'Four months gone. Jesus, what am I going to do?'

'When did you find out?'

'Half an hour ago. They came and told me, her and Liam. They're gone to tell his mother. What are we going to do? He's all on for marrying her, getting a job, but what age is he? Seventeen. And her only sixteen.'

'How did it happen?'

'She says she doesn't know. And now I have to tell her father. She'll be a laughing stock. Young Tommy is only two and now his sister is having a child. What will I do?'

'God is good.'

'She told me she tried jumping off a wall early on. But too late to hope for it stirring now, it's well and truly settled.'

'God is good,' my mother says again.

'I better go and get Martin's dinner ready.'

And she walks away, her back bent, her head shaking.

Later, my parents are whispering in the garden.

'As though Martin will say anything to her!' my mother says. 'Geraldine's the apple of his eye. He dotes on her.'

I sway quietly on the swing.

'It's not the first time it's happened,' my father says, 'and it won't be the last. They'll get along all right. He's a bright young fellow. He'll get a job. They'll make out.'

'How can he? Isn't he waiting for the Leaving Cert results? He has prospects, the guards or a call to teacher training, something worthwhile. His father isn't going to let a thing like this destroy Liam's possibilities. I know the MacMahons are grand people, but they're hardly the same cut as Liam's people. Farm labouring is hardly the same thing as teaching!'

'It's not the fathers that are in trouble. They're not the ones wanting to get married,' my father laughs.

'Don't be smart,' my mother says and she's not smiling. 'Do you imagine, if you were in Liam's father's boots, you'd want your son marrying a little trollop like Geraldine MacMahon?'

'At least she'd tango,' my father grins, 'and that takes two!'

'Oh, for God's sake. She was never done chasing fellows. We saw her ourselves at the marquee, going outside with three different fellas.'

And, even now, I can hear the chorus behind my mother.

She did.
By Jasus she did.
Couldn't keep her legs together if she tied them.
A whore to go.
But sure, her mother was the same in her heyday.
Doesn't know how it happened, she says.
Doesn't know what it's for!
Or where to put it.
She'd milk an ass!
And come back for more.

A week later, Mrs MacMahon and my mother are at the fence again. Tommy MacMahon leaning against the wire, watching me dawdling on the swing.

'Young Liam was up last night. He says he wants to marry Geraldine as soon as she'll say yes.'

'And what does his father say?'

'I don't know. I'm afraid to go and talk to him. What would I say to a schoolteacher? Martin says they'll come and see us when they're ready.'

'And what does Geraldine say?'

'Little or nothing. She's cool with Liam but I think she's putting that on. Would you talk to her? She'd listen to you. She thinks you're great.'

'If you want me to, if you think it'll help.'

'Do, do. Good woman, Geraldine!'

Mrs MacMahon calls and calls again. Eventually Geraldine slouches from the house.

'Come here a minute,' her mother says. 'Talk to Mrs. She could tell you, advise you on things.'

She sweeps Tommy into her arms and leaves my mother and Geraldine at the fence.

'How are you?' my mother asks.

'All right.'

'You're not showing yet, anyway.'

'No.'

'Your mother says you weren't too sick either.'

'No.'

'That's good.'

'Yeah.'

'So what are you going to do?'

Geraldine shrugs her shoulders.

'What do Liam's parents say?'

'Dunno. His mother just said she'd have to talk to his father. I haven't been back there since.'

'How long ago was that?'

'Two weeks.'

'And what does Liam say?'

'He wants to marry me.'

'You're young.'

'So?'

'Do you love him?'

'Suppose.'

'Something'll happen.' My mother smiles and pats Geraldine's arm.

And it does. But my parents only hear about it second-hand.

Liam's father puts his foot down. No marrying. You have a career, he says. You'll get your call to teacher training. You'll be a teacher like me, he says.

And the voices leak from under doors around the parish.

I'll marry Geraldine, the young lad says.

Over my dead body, the ould lad says.

The mother screamed.

He walloped the young lad.

He was always a dab hand at that in the school. Ha ha!

You've brains to burn, you'll do your training and you'll qualify, the ould lad says.

You won't keep her from me, the young fella shouts.

Well, by Jesus, I'll keep you from her then, the ould lad says.

And he did!

By God he did!

Yahoooooo.

By Jasus, did he what!

Every night, over the kitchen table, my parents talk in riddles.

'I heard all guns are firing on the Western Front.'

'And what about the good woman over yonder?'

'Not a word; she says there's not a word at all. She says they may be moving the young soldier to another camp.'

'I heard otherwise. A reliable source tells me the Right Reverend has been called in.'

My mother frowns. 'Is that so?'

My father leans forward and speaks very seriously. 'Both as spiritual adviser and as manager of the school. He wants the fire brought under control as quickly as possible.'

'And what about the young soldier himself?'

My father runs his tongue around the inside of his mouth and shrugs.

'There's not a word to be got out of her ladyship,' my mother says. 'She just sits out there in the garden sunning herself. But I don't see him about at all.'

'I'd say he's still holding out for married bliss,' my father grins. 'The fool.'

My mother leans across the table and slaps him with the rolled-up newspaper and they both laugh out loud.

After that, everything seems to settle. There's talk of Geraldine going away and having the baby and then coming home and giving it to her mother to raise. And Liam is to go to teacher training college and complete his course. They'll wait and see how things turn out. They won't see each other for three years and then the situation can be looked at.

My mother knows all this because, out of the blue, the parish priest sends for her and asks her to help.

'He brought me down to the kitchen,' she tells my father. 'The table was laid for afternoon tea. The housekeeper must have done it before she went out for her walk. He sat me down and told me the whole story. It was Geraldine's doing! I thought as much. He told me straight that she'd insisted on Liam doing it.'

Her voice drops to a whisper so that I have to strain to hear from the corner where I'm playing with my soldiers.

'He wanted to pull out but she held onto him. A proper little vixen.'

'Isn't it great the way the parish priest has all this inside information,' my father mocks. 'Like he was there, overseeing the whole thing, making all the calculations. Would he not have caught Liam by the legs and pulled him out?'

'Are you saying he made it up?'

'I'm saying nothing.'

'She had her claws in him,' my mother says, and the words come out hard and sharp. 'Anyway, there's more. As the PP pointed out, Liam has a career. It's all well and fine for him to talk of love now, but ten years down the road, when he's stuck working at the bacon counter in Browne's and she's off gallivanting, and there's six or seven children, as there's likely to be with that one, he won't thank anyone for letting him make a fool of himself. The PP put it perfectly. "Youngsters, given the freedom to pursue their passions, are given a loaded gun." If they can't control themselves now, they'll hardly control themselves when they're married.'

'Is that his expert view?'

'You're making a mockery of the whole thing,' my mother says. 'He's right too. Ten years from now Liam will have a house full of children without a mother. He'll be a frustrated and thwarted young man with his life in ruins, and she'll be at it with every Tom, Dick and Harry.'

'And where do you come into the picture?'

'He explained that, as manager of Liam's father's school, he's in an awkward situation. He wants me, as a neighbour, to talk to the MacMahons.'

'And you told him to feck off with himself.'

'I talked to them this afternoon. I explained his side of it. He'll arrange a place for Geraldine and she can decide, when the time comes, whether she wants to keep the baby or give it up. Mrs MacMahon says she'll look after it for her.'

My father shakes his head and says nothing.

A week later, my mother is back in the Parochial House. By the time she gets home she's fuming.

'I can't believe it. He can't be so stupid as to throw his life away on that one.'

'They're gone to Gretna Green,' my father smirks.

'Oh, stop being so smart, you. They were caught. Together. At it. Again.'

Ha ha!

No stopping them.

Like an ass's tool, big when he's out.

Can't get enough of it.

Up she flew.

And where do you think?

In the long grass behind the chapel. Broad daylight. Knickers around her ankles. Stretched to the limit. Driving right into her.

Ha ha!

The sacristan saw the sun glinting on the young fella's arse.

The parish priest met them and they sneaking around by the bell. You're a prostitute, he says.

He never did!

He did. By God he did.

And rightly so.

'"No further discussion," the PP says. She goes next Friday and there's no coming back if she decides to keep the baby. And he's gone already, he was sent to his aunt in Blackrock. "Enough is enough," the PP says.'

My mother is standing at the kitchen sink, as my father sits looking into his teacup.

'And he should know,' he says angrily. 'He should know exactly what to do in this kind of situation. He's the man to put things to rights because he's the man that knows what the world is about. He's God's deputy-vicar on earth. He's the boy to put us all in our places.'

'I'm going to talk to Mrs MacMahon,' my mother says. 'I see her in the garden. I'm going out to talk to her. I feel sorry for her, but Geraldine brought this on herself.'

'Is that what the PP says?' my father asks before he turns on the radio and my mother goes out through the open back door and into the garden. I give her ten seconds and then follow, quietly.

'Will he not think twice?' Mrs MacMahon asks. Her voice is a beaten whine.

Geraldine is standing beside her, gazing over my mother's shoulder to the figures on the distant football field.

'He says it's all arranged,' my mother says.

'I know what she did was wrong. And, God, behind the church! Why did you do it there?'

'The grass was long,' Geraldine says lightly.

'Would he not think again, Mrs?'

'He thinks it's for the best all round. He says they need time apart.'

'But wouldn't he think about changing his mind about Geraldine bringing the child home? She wants to. Don't you?'

'I suppose so.'

'It'd be someone for Tommy to play with,' Mrs MacMahon says, as if my mother has the final say-so. 'There'd only be two years, two-and-a-half years between them. How is she going to live away from home with a baby? Would he not consider that?'

'I think he believes it'd be best for everyone if Geraldine gave the baby up.'

'But she doesn't want to, do you, Geraldine?'

Geraldine shakes her head.

'Well,' my mother sighs. 'Unless you go and talk to him yourself.'

'But what could I say?' Mrs MacMahon asks. 'What could I say to a priest if he has his mind made up? And after him seeing them in the chapel grounds. What would I be able to say?'

'You could tell him to fuck off and mind his own business,' Geraldine says and she turns on her heel and walks away.

Afterwards, as I get ready for bed, I hear my father laugh and say, 'Fair dues to her, she has a point.'

And my mother sighs in exasperation.

'I'm not listening to you. It says everything about her and how she got to be the way she is. A young one of her age and in her condition having the gall to talk like that. Can you imagine the merry dance she'd lead that young lad for the rest of his days? Imagine it! He's lucky to be shut of her. The sooner she's gone, the sooner it'll be mended. Can you imagine her with children streeling out of her? You cannot!'

The following afternoon, I'm kicking football in the garden. Mrs MacMahon is pulling stalks of rhubarb. Geraldine comes down their garden and stands beside her mother. Her voice is breaking.

'Don't let them do this to me,' she says. 'I won't go near him. Honest to God, I won't see him. I'll keep away from him when he's home. I won't even go up that end of the town. I swear, Mam, I swear.'

'There's nothing I can do,' her mother says. 'I can't change the way things are.'

'It's nothing to do with Liam, I swear. I don't want to be shut away for the next four months. I don't want to be with people I don't know. I don't want to be away from you and Daddy. How'll I make out in Dublin? Just let me stay here, please. Please. Don't let them send me away, Mam, please.'

'What can I do, girl?'

'Please, Mam.'

'He said it'll be the best thing in the long run. He said he's seen it a hundred times before. He said it's the only way. And Liam's father says the same.'

'Let me talk to Daddy about it.'

'What can he do?' Mrs MacMahon asks and she puts her arms around her daughter. 'There's nothing any of us can do. Bear with it, child.'

'Please,' Geraldine says and she buries her face in her mother's breast.

I seen her getting on the bus.

Ha ha!

The mother walked her down.

I seen them on the Square, waiting. Stood there with the mother and the little brother, Tommy. Bold as brass.

Her belly like a little hill.

Three little hills, I say three little hills.

Ha ha!

Was the PP there to give them his blessing?

The teacher slipped her a fiver.

Ha!

And his young lad slipped her another.

And a tenner for the ride!

Some whore. I wouldn't go with her if you paid me.

Neither would I.

And neither would my brother.

That's not what I heard.

Ha ha!

Geraldine MacMahon leaves in the middle of July and I have my mother to myself. Mrs MacMahon is there in her garden but she and my mother do nothing more than pass the time of day. She seems never to be at the fence when my mother is about. I'm relieved, glad to have my mother's full attention again.

Now and then little Tommy wanders into our garden and my mother lifts him and swings him around.

'He's a wanderer,' she says. 'There'll be no stopping him when he gets older.'

Apart from that, there are no other interruptions and the days are mine and, in the evening, my father's car is in the yard and my parents are kissing in the kitchen and the three of us are around the evening table.

'Any sign of Mrs MacMahon these days?' my father asks one evening.

'She seems to be avoiding me,' my mother says. 'Maybe she blames me for siding with the PP.'

'I hope not,' my father says. 'Didn't you say she seemed to see the sense in it, if there was any?'

'That's what I thought. But you never know.'

'I met Martin down the town and he was as friendly as ever.'

'He has no say in anything, one way or the other, as far as I can see.'

All those summer days. We play cards in the garden, we laugh together in the shadows of the gooseberry bushes, we go on a picnic to the River Field and I swing on the rope that dangles from one of the giant oaks leaning across the water. Swinging out and back, my bare feet rippling the river of the sky turned upside down.

Until the first day of August. Another sunny day, like all the other sunny days that summer.

We're in the front garden, weeding. Children on the terrace road, the sun shining, the coal lorry turning at the far end of the terrace and reversing into Hayden's gateway, Tommy MacMahon standing, watching as he always does, two dogs fighting in the

Church Field, the high lob of a football in the sky. A game and voices in the air.

'Queenie eye oh, who has the ball?'

Another game.

'Ring a ring a rosy, a pocketful of posies, atishoo, atishoo, we all fall down.'

And another.

'No walking! No talking! No laughing!'

Four o'clock on a summer afternoon, on a peaceful street. The Low Terrace going about its childish business. Children sing-songing, dogs barking, a lorry turning, my mother and I weeding.

Afterwards, there are versions of what happened. All of them, more or less, accurate.

Easy does it, back her up easy.

Two bags of coal for Dinny Smith, a bag of turf for Harringtons, three bags of blocks for Dessie Hayden.

The paraffin. Did he load the paraffin for Whelans?

Easy does it, look behind.

He must have put it in with all the rest, he'd never be that thick as to leave it behind.

He swore to God that he never felt a thing. And then one of the children began shouting.

We hear someone shouting. My mother drops her trowel and starts running. I have no idea why. Children are always shouting. And then I hear a wail and the summer sun and the blue sky can do nothing to check the coldness running through me. I realise the wailing sound is coming from the mouth of a man and his voice is high and lost.

Oh Jesus, Jesus, Jesus.

And my mother is running towards him and there are children everywhere and I run after her, through our open gate, along the road. And I see my mother, on her knees, under the lorry and the driver is kneeling beside her, talking to her, crying, shouting at her.

'I never seen him, I don't know where he come out of, he must've stepped under the trailer. I never seen a thing. I'd have seen him if he walked in front of me. He was that small. I never felt him. What can I say, ma'am, what can I say? Jasus, I wouldn't wish this for all the world. I'd do anything to bring him back.'

A small boy turns to the girl beside him and giggles.

'He was under the trailer. He never heard it starting. The axle caught his head.'

And, out of nowhere, Mrs MacMahon is on her knees beside my mother, driving her fists into the clay-covered road. And then my mother lifts Tommy out from under the axle. He doesn't look dead to me. A small bump on his forehead. The lorry driver looks as if he is the one about to die. His face is the colour of ashes, the colour of sand. He goes on whispering.

'I never seen him, I never seen him at all, I swear to Jesus, I never felt a thing.'

'We'll take him home,' my mother says to Mrs MacMahon.

And the children follow at a distance. My mother with the dead child scooped in her arms and Mrs MacMahon beside her. We follow them up the terrace. Near MacMahon's gate, I look back and the lorry driver is talking to one small boy who stands with his hands on his hips, nodding. And then the festival of children stops and my mother and Mrs MacMahon pass through the gateway and around the side of the house. I hesitate, unsure of what to do.

'Go in,' someone says. 'Your mother's gone in, you can go in, too.'

And so I do.

The days are one long funeral. The wake, the church, the burial. The neighbours, the town, the priest at the graveside.

'We have no words that can repair the hurt,' he says. 'Only prayer and the love of the Almighty God.'

I stand with my parents, beside the MacMahons, and the voices drift in the afternoon heat.

'Sorry for your troubles.'

'You have our sympathy.'

'He was a dote.'

'You have an angel in heaven.' And the priest's voice, again.

'In the name of the Father and of the Son and of the Holy Ghost. Amen.'

Walking home, my father is angry. 'You'd think they'd have let Geraldine come back for the funeral. She was his sister, for Christ's sake.'

'Would it have done any good?' my mother asks.

'She's his fecking sister.'

'It'd only open wounds.'

My father starts to say something but thinks better of it and steps away from my mother, quickly making small talk with someone else.

Once, and only once, after that, do I remember my mother and Mrs MacMahon talking at the fence. It must be a month or more after Tommy's death and autumn is setting in.

'It's not only that I miss him,' Mrs MacMahon says. 'God knows I miss him. But to think of her little baby growing inside of Geraldine and my little baby buried in the graveyard above. Tommy gone and Geraldine gone and her baby to be took from her as soon as it's born.'

'I know,' my mother says. 'I know.'

'No one knows, Mrs. No one.'

'I know,' my mother says again and her voice is dark and breaking. 'I do.'

Some days, that September, I come home from school and find my mother in the garden, crying, and when I ask her if she's sad because of Tommy MacMahon, she nods.

'For him, for them. For all of us.'

Geraldine's baby was born in Dublin and she never came back home. I lived beside the MacMahons until I left the Terrace. I'd see them at Christmas and Easter. And then they died. First him. Then her.

And then my mother died.

That long bleak night and the church and the Mass and the burial. And clearing out her clothes and coats and shoes and my father in the doorway of their room, unable to step inside. And visiting the graveyard and him stopping for a moment at MacMahons' headstone.

'They were nice people,' he said. 'Good, decent people.'

'I remember the day Tommy was killed,' I said.

'It's a long time ago.'

'That was a strange summer, with Geraldine and all. It was a nice summer for me, until he was killed. And then it was like no one recovered. I remember that autumn I'd find Mam crying in the garden.'

'For the boys,' my father said.

'What boys?'

'At least Tommy got a proper burial. A Mass and a grave up here.'

And then the whole sorry story came out. My brothers, dead at birth. Unspoken of, unblessed. A burial in the garden at dawn. My father wrapping them in towels. Their small, still features resting on the grass while he dug deep.

My mother lying inside, in their pale room, waiting for the rasp of the spade in clay. It all came back when Tommy MacMahon was killed, and then again in that hospital room. Children about her bed, Tommy MacMahon and my brothers.

And I hear the voices trickling under the doors again.

That's the way it was.

We all went through it.

Dark mornings and summer mornings.

Gardens and ditches and fields.

The dead are dead and buried and it's best to leave them lie.

And then I hear my mother's voice at my bedside, praying with me. Outside, the sun is going down and I can hear my father closing the shed door and cleaning his boots on the back step and spring is everywhere and that long, bright summer is before us with the promise of picnics in the River Field.

Sacred Heart

He sits in his car. It is late in the afternoon and the last of the autumn light is being tightly wrung from the heavens, dribbling down onto the flaky, rusted stubble of a long, wide field. He watches an old crow flail jadedly across the dull September sky, in search of its rookery, and he thinks of his young daughter running carelessly along the beach, her sun-bleached hair flying like a thousand short kite strings.

And he remembers the shadow of a gull on the warm summer sand.

'Look,' his daughter says. 'Look, there's a bird under the sand.'

'That's a sand gull,' he says.

'What's a sand gull?'

'It's a magic bird. It can fly on the sand or under the sand. You can see it but if you try to touch it, it isn't there.'

She looks at him quizzically.

'See,' he says, pointing to the circling shadow.

His daughter watches the silhouette darken and lighten as the bird swoops and rises unseen above her head.

'What does he eat?' she asks.

'He eats the wind.'

'Does he?'

'Yes.'

'Why don't we see him every day?'

'Because he only appears to children who are very good and even then just once in a blue moon.'

She throws him that look again.

'The moon's not blue.'

'Sometimes it is.'

'I never saw it blue.'

'Do you remember the first night we were in America?'

'Yes.'

'Do you remember the moon when we came out of the airport building?'

'Yes.'

'Do you remember what colour it was?'

'Orange.'

'See. You'd never seen an orange moon before that but there it was. And you've never seen a blue moon but you will.'

'Tonight?'

He shrugged. 'You never know. It'll be there when you least expect it and when you most need it.'

'What does that mean?'

'You're full of questions.' He laughs, swinging his daughter high into the air, twirling her above the sand and sea, throwing her into the sunny sky and catching her as she falls in a shower of laughter.

And out of nowhere, as it always comes, the memory. He is dancing with his wife, her head against his chest, her body warm against his own, her hands light on his shoulders, his arms around her waist, the music moving them in some slowed-down version of a waltz, and he shivers in the burning sun and looks at his daughter and he feels a desperate, surging need to know that she will have happiness in her life.

'The sand gull is gone,' the little girl says.

'It'll be back.'

'Will it?'

'Of course. It always comes back to good girls. Always.'

She smiles and he hugs her and puts her back down in the warm shallows of the Atlantic water.

'You know the way you write in your little book every night?'

He nods.

'Why do you do that?'

'I'm keeping a diary of our holiday.'

'Why?'

'Because it's special – just you and me.'

'Are you keeping it to read to Mum when we get home?'

'No, but I could.'

'What does it say?'

'Lots of things.'

'Like?'

'Like about what we do each day, about the sea and the weather and where we've been and things I've been thinking, and tonight I'll write about the sand gull.'

'Will you read it to me tonight?'

'Okay.'

'Will you read it to me every night?'

'Yes, okay.'

'Promise?'

'Promise.'

They paddle on, the sunlight surging over them like a reassurance.

'Don't forget to look for the sand dollars,' he says and they lower their heads and walk slowly, eyes scanning the shining sand.

That night, as he tucks his daughter into bed in her air-conditioned room, she reminds him of his promise to read from his diary.

'I haven't written today's entry yet.'

'Well read me something.'

'It'll be boring.'

'I'll tell you if I'm bored.'

He goes into his room and returns with a notebook.

'Is that your diary?'

'Yes.'

She settles herself against the soft pillow and waits.

'This is from the first day.'

She nods. He clears his throat.

'"The heat when we came out of the airport building was like a wall. We'd been warned but I wasn't expecting it."'

'That's silly, it wasn't a wall,' his daughter says. 'It was just hot. If it was a wall, we wouldn't have been able to get out, unless it fell, and if it fell it might have squished us.'

'Told you it'd bore you.'

'Read more. I'll see.'

'"I like the way the houses here are built into the woods. When they build, they use the landscape; they don't clear everything. They knock as few trees as possible and then they put up the timber frames and block-build around them. As we drove down from the airport, coming through the tobacco fields, the skies opened and we had a glorious thunderstorm."'

He pauses.

'That's okay. I kind of like that. Read me something about the beach. About us at the beach.'

He leafs through the pages of the notebook

'Okay, here's something, but you may not understand it. "There are several houses strung along the beach, straight out of *Summer of '42*." That's a film, there were houses in it like the houses along the beach.'

'I think I know what you mean. You don't have to explain everything. I'll stop you if I want to ask you something.'

'Yes, Miss.'

'Now go on.'

'"The heat on the beach is intense but the breeze makes it manageable. I've been careful that L doesn't get burned."'

'L. That's me. Why didn't you write Lynn?'

'I was writing fast. I was tired.'

'Oh, okay. Go on then.'

'"The only things that are annoying on the beach are the jets from the airfield down the coast. They come in loud and low and really should be farther out to sea."'

He notices her nod gravely.

'It's just that kind of stuff.'

'Well, why don't you write more interesting things, like about the sand gulls and the sand dollars and stuff. You can write them before I go to bed and then read them to me and I'll tell you what I think.'

'That sounds like a very good idea.'

'Now,' his daughter says. 'I'm tired.'

She reaches up, wraps her hands around his neck and kisses his cheek.

'Goodnight, Daddy.'

'Goodnight, sweetheart. I love you.'

'I love you.'

She turns, nesting her head in the pillow, closes her eyes and smiles.

In the morning they go body-boarding in the shallows but his daughter is terrified by the sound of the breaking waves and he takes her back to the swimming pool near the apartment and that night writes his diary entry while she's in the bath and reads it to her as he tucks her in.

"'I miss trees here – deciduous trees. The sea is pleasant when it's warm but it's too changeable. Trees change, too, but differently, more slowly. And they have the sound of the sea in their leaves. The sea is not so constant, regular yes but capable of great unpredictability and viciousness and the power to swallow. In the forest the change is more gradual, leaves fall, trees fall but there's a peacefulness and a smell of growth, not threat. And saplings, leaves unfolding, flowers, even the smell of cut wood."'

'I'm sorry that you miss the trees,' his daughter says.

'That's okay. I'll get back to them.'

'And I miss Mum sometimes.'

'That's good, too, and you'll get back to her soon.'

Later, he sits in the tarn of light from the reading lamp. Outside, beyond his glassed reflection, the sky flares and fades with distant lightning above the rumbling sea. He turns a page of *Lifting the Latch* and reads of Stow and Adlestrop and Oxford. The names are freshly beautiful in the American heat. He remembers them as villages and cities emerging from the English summer haze and he catches his own slight smile in the mirroring glass.

His daughter is playing in the shallows of the sea. Another young girl, more or less her own age, is playing with her. Together they build a sand dam and giggle as the surging ripples eat the walls away so that they can start again, a foot closer to the high watermark.

He stands with the girl's father.

'You'd think they've known each other for ever,' the man says.

'Yes.'

'I'm Ken, by the way.'

'Al,' he says and proffers a hand.

'Vacationing?'

'Yes. For three weeks.'

'Couldn't have chosen a more remarkably picturesque place.'

'No.'

'Been coming here since I was a kid myself.'

'You're lucky.'

'Yeah, I guess I am, blessed with the good fortune of being born in the land of the true and the home of the brave and the beautiful.'

The girls move again, hunkering in the warm, slow water.

'By the way,' the man says. 'My daughter's first name is Melissa.'

'And this is Lynn.'

'You're European?'

'Yes.'

'English?'

'Irish.'

Ken nods and smiles. 'Always appreciated here.'

'Thank you.'

They stand together, watching the children play.

He watches his daughter building sand castles in the rising morning heat. He lifts a piece of driftwood from the beach and carries it to her.

'Sand only.' She waves him away.

He smiles and runs his fingers along the bleached and faded timber. He thinks about how the sea wears everything to a smoothness – shells, stones, timber, wire and glass. How, by the time they wash up here, every jagged rim has been robbed of its roughness and its edge.

'Homogenised,' he says out loud but his daughter appears not to hear him.

Back in the apartment, making sandwiches for their lunch, he turns on the radio. Judy Collins is singing 'Jerusalem'. He stands transfixed while Blake's words pour over him.

And did those feet in ancient time
Walk upon England's mountains green:
And was the holy Lamb of God
On England's pleasant pastures seen!

And did the Countenance Divine
Shine forth upon our clouded hills?
And was Jerusalem builded here
Among these dark Satanic Mills?

Bring me my Bow of burning gold:
Bring me my arrows of desire:
Bring me my Spear! O clouds, unfold!
Bring me my Chariot of fire!

I will not cease from Mental Fight,
Nor shall my sword sleep in my hand:
Till we have built Jerusalem
In England's green and pleasant Land.

Later, at that time where day and night begin to merge, he walks with his daughter on the orange sand and they find a long scarf of seaweed.

'What's that?' his daughter asks.

'It's a small sea dragon,' he says, lifting the golden green ridges in his hands.

His daughter looks at him, searching for a give-away twist of the mouth but, finding none, she returns her gaze to the puckered shape that rests against her father's arm.

'It's sleeping,' he says quietly.

'Can it make fire?'

'Not the sea dragon. Fire and water don't mix. Do you want to touch it?'

The girl is uncertain.

'It won't bite,' he says.

She lays an uneasy hand against the slippery seaweed.

'It's soft.'

'Yes.'

'And it won't bite me?'

'No.'

Again, she touches the spongy, wet crests.

'Would you like to put it back into the sea? That's where it belongs.'

'All right.'

Gently he drapes the ribbon of seaweed across her palms and she carries it down to the murky sea and lays it delicately in the small waves. Together they watch it blend into the dark water, retreating with the receding waves until it disappears into the wide Atlantic.

'You're a lucky girl.'

'Why?'

'You've seen a sand gull and a sea dragon. Some people live their whole lives and never see either.'

'Do they?'

'Yes, they do,' he says and realises the night has fallen. 'Time for us to head for home.'

'Will we be able to find home?' the girl asks, suddenly aware of the darkness.

'We'll follow the lights.'

Feeling the sand crabs scuttle across his feet, he swings his daughter onto his shoulder, turns his back on the black, uncertain water and moves towards the lighted windows.

He is sitting at the table, writing about the sand crabs, when the telephone rings.

He considers not answering but he knows it will ring and ring, every two or three minutes until he does.

'Hello.'

'Hello. Al?' His wife's voice from halfway across the world.

'How are you?'

'Fine. How's Lynn?'

'She's really well. She's sleeping.'

'At this hour? Is she sick?'

'It's midnight here.'

'Oh right, of course.'

Silence spans the thousands of miles.

'When will you bring her back?'

'Sorry?'

'When will you bring Lynn back to me?'

'Why are you asking this? You know when we're back,' he says quietly, forcing himself to be calm.

'I know nothing. Who's there with you?'

'Lynn. She's sleeping, like I said.'

'Why are you whispering? There's someone in the apartment, isn't there?'

'There is no one else here. I was sitting alone writing my diary. Lynn is sleeping.'

'Put her on to me.'

'She's asleep.'

'There's someone else there.'

'There is no one else here, just the pair of us, as you and I agreed, Lynn and me, for three weeks. That's it. No one else.' 'I don't believe you.'

'It's the truth.'

'Are you feeding her properly?'

'Yes. She's eating really well. Lots of fresh air, lots of good food, lots of sleep.'

'And you're putting her sun cream on?'

'Yes.'

'Factor fifty.'

'Yes.'

Another silence and he imagines the waves rolling over the buried telephone cables.

'You realise how much the legal fees are going to be?' she asks.

'I'll pay them. All of them.'

'You realise this is an act of gross selfishness?'

'Yes.'

'And I don't believe there's no one else there. I don't believe there isn't someone else.'

He scratches his forehead and sighs very quietly.

'We'll talk about it when Lynn and I get home. Back,' he corrects himself. 'I'll have Lynn ring you in the morning at eight, that'll be one in the afternoon your time.'

'Will you?'

'Yes, of course.'

'And there's no one else there?'

'No one.'

'You said once you'd die for me.'

'I almost did.'

'I'm sorry.'

'I know. Me too. We'll ring you at eight in the morning, okay?'

'Okay. Goodnight.'

'Goodnight.'

They sit in a bright, clean restaurant and a smiling waitress comes and stands at their table.

'This young lady will have a burger and fries and a Sprite. And I'll have … could I just have a large salad?'

'My daddy is a vegetarian,' his daughter says.

'Is he, honey?'

'Yes. He was a vegetarian before I was born. Weren't you?'

He nods an embarrassed nod.

'This lady is busy, Lynn. She doesn't need my life story.'

'We saw a sea dragon last night on the beach and we put it back in the sea.'

'Well, ain't you the lucky girl. Been here all my life and I can't say I've seen one yet.'

'My daddy said I was lucky, too.'

'Your daddy's right.'

'And we saw a sand gull one day.'

'Wow. You're blessed!'

'Lynn,' he says, 'the lady is busy.'

'Are you busy?'

'Not so I can't hear about sea dragons and sand gulls.' She smiles a warm smile. 'But I'd better bring your Sprite or you're gonna run dry and then you won't be able to keep me entertained with your stories.'

The little girl giggles.

'And coffee for your dad?'

'Thank you.'

Later, they go to SafariLand but he finds he doesn't have the $25 they need to get in. The woman at the admission booth looks at the $19 he counts out and shrugs and listens to his explanation about having left his money in his other jeans.

'Sorry, honey. No mon, no fun.'

They walk slowly to the car.

'We'll come back another day.'

Across the hedges and fences they can see and hear the people on the water slides he promised he'd bring Lynn on. He knows she's upset but she doesn't cry.

When they get back to the apartment, they play chess in the afternoon heat and, as the sun begins to sink, they go down to the pool and his daughter takes her first, tentative strokes and he remembers the day she first walked.

Later still, they ramble to the edge of the woods and watch the fireflies do their flame dance and they catch one in a jar and bring it back to the apartment and when his daughter falls asleep he opens the jar and releases the fly into the darkness that's beginning to blow a storm.

They spend most of the following day at the pool. His daughter is frightened by the rolling breakers on the beach, by the pounding of the waves after the previous night's slow gale. Only in the early evening, when the sky is clear and the heat is clean and the sea has calmed, do they go walking on the beach.

Mostly, they have it to themselves. Five hundred yards ahead of them the surfers skim to a standstill and then turn and paddle out again, in search of a last few breaking waves, reminders of the previous night's turmoil.

He watches his daughter scrutinise the sea, nervous of whatever violence it still might hold. He inspects the pieces of flotsam and jetsam on the sand: a broken plastic fish box; three battered kerosene cans; a plank of yellow wood; dead fish, their mouths wide open in a series of silent cries, and what looks like a human heart.

For a moment, he cannot believe what he's seeing. His daughter has wandered ahead, dragging a piece of timber from the shallows; she is writing her name in the sand. A giant 'L' and a tiny 'y' and two ill-fitting 'n's.

Bending, he looks more closely and, yes, as far as he can tell, it is a human heart. He feels his own heart pound in his chest, its every throb a punch against his ribs. What to do: lift it and take it with him to the apartment? What then, call the police? Explain why he had moved it from its resting place?

'See my name?' his daughter calls.

'Yes, I see. That's very good.'

He walks to where she's standing, hoping that when he turns there will be no heart on the sand.

'Will I write your name?'

'Yes, do. Can you spell it?'

'Yep.'

She drags the piece of timber through the damp sand, slowly carving the two letters.

'And Mum's?'

'Yes.'

Again, she sets about the task, her tongue between her teeth, concentrating hard, working her way through the eight letters of her mother's name.

'Now,' she says, standing back.

'That's wonderful. You've done a great job.'

His daughter nods and hands him the piece of timber.

'Can we go back now? I'm hungry.'

'Of course.'

He steers her away from the waterline, away from the dark heart resting on the shore.

'Let's see if we can find a sand dollar on the way back.'

He sticks the piece of timber into the sand, well above the high-water mark, an indicator for the morrow. For now, there is nothing he can do. He doesn't want to bring the heart to his daughter's attention, doesn't want to frighten her with this macabre gift from the sea.

That night he dreams the dream again. He sees himself, the second youngest man at the long table, hardly more than a boy. This is all he ever dreams. The reverie never takes him beyond this point and on to the other, darker days that followed. Instead, he sits with the others and someone begins to sing a soft song. He knows this bit of the dream has come from elsewhere, from another time and place, when they would sing together. It comes from one of the nights at a desert campfire or an evening in winter when they were crowded into one room in someone's house. But, in this dream, the singing happens at the long table. It starts at the other end, Andrew's voice running like a low, slow river beneath the conversation, gradually making its way into the ears of the listeners, stopping their speech until the song can run freely, without the word-rocks getting in its way, until each of them picks it up and feels the lightness of its beauty begin to lift them. Always the same dream and the same song that seems about to explode, to drive them from their seats and lead them smiling through the marshalled, silent streets outside. For ever, he sits waiting for someone else to rise; he waits to follow, he knows he will not lead. But the song never quite reaches that pinnacle. Instead, it fades away, the words becoming sparser, the silent gaps expanding to fill the moments between those words until, at last, there is only the silence, and the room is as it was that night, full of fear and indecision. And then he wakes, as he always does, his body a berg of perspiring skin, his hair dripping sweat into his open eyes.

Outside, he hears thunder rising and falling, catches the sheets of lighting through the window of his room and hears the wind begin to rise.

The following morning, he leaves his daughter with her new-found friend Melissa and Melissa's mother at the pool and jogs to the point where the timber marker still skewers the warm sand. His stomach is churning, bile rising in his throat. He tries to remember how far above the tidemark the heart was resting. He wishes it gone but he needs to be sure, needs to go back. If it is still there, he has no idea what he'll do. Chances are the tide or a scavenging gull will have lifted it, yet it doesn't matter if the heart is there or gone. What matters is the fact that it was there.

The sea is calm, the tide retreating steadily. And, indeed, the heart has disappeared. He walks fifty yards in each direction, scanning the sand and the shallows but no sign of it remains. The surge of the sea or some wandering foragers have done their work and there is no longer what Ken might call a situation requiring resolution.

Standing in the shallows, Al vomits, the clear water diluting the green liquid, sucking it out into the deeper waves and the open ocean beyond.

That afternoon they drive to SafariLand. To his relief, the woman at the box office is not the woman who turned them away. Inside, the park is virtually empty. He counts five people on the paths between the rides.

'Right,' he says. 'Where would you like to start – water slide, roundabout, bumper cars, dinosaur, elephant swing?'

'Can we do them all?'

'We can do them all. We have all afternoon. Twice if you like.'

She laughs.

'Really?'

'Really.'

'Mum would love this, wouldn't she?'

'She would.'

'Can we come here some time with her?'

'Let's hope we can.'

And now he sits in his car. It is late in the afternoon and the last of the autumn light is being tightly wrung from the heavens, dribbling down onto the flaky, rusted stubble of a long, wide field. He watches an old crow flail jadedly across the dull September sky, in search of its rookery, and he thinks of his daughter running carelessly along the sprawling summer paths of the amusement park, her sun-bleached hair flying like a thousand short kite strings in the brightness.

And he remembers the shadow of a gull on the warm summer sand.

And the sacred hearts of those he loved and lost.

Friends

I was a fat kid. Does that change the way you think about me?
I'm not asking if it makes you more sympathetic; sympathy
doesn't come into it, sympathy isn't at issue here, as you'll be
the first to tell me. It doesn't raise its head inside these four
walls. But while you're sitting there with your bellies hanging
over your belts, do you secretly have just the tiniest inkling of
regard for me? Do you admire me the way you admire winter
swimmers, from a distance, as people who've done something
you'd like to have done but never could? Do you secretly envy
the way I got myself together, slimmed down through my ado-
lescent years, kept my weight under control by eating sensibly?
You assume it's easier for me to control the middle-age spread,
don't you, just because I have twenty-five years of careful eating
behind me? Secretly you do. It's all about secrets in here, isn't
it? My little secrets and your little secrets, except, of course, that
I may not have the secret you want me to have, the one that
would make your job that much easier.

I'll bet you were surprised when you discovered I sell ice
cream for a living. Surprised that I could walk that line between
selling and eating without ever – and I mean ever – crossing over.
That's not something that comes easily to you, is it? Walking the
line between the things you wish for and the temptations that
make you surrender.

Sorry, maybe I'm doing you a disservice. Perhaps, deep
down, you're not making too many assumptions because you

don't know me, don't really want to know me and couldn't care less about what makes me tick. Perhaps all this is surface stuff. I mean, why should you care? I sell ice cream to the people on the streets, all kinds of streets, your street, your culs-de-sac.

There's a thing! Have you noticed how the phrase 'cul-de-sac' was once used to describe a place like the dive I grew up in. A dirty phrase that meant the bottom of an empty coal sack on a wet Saturday. Now it's pronounced with all the Frenchness people can muster. Now it's okay; it's chic, it's cool.

But I digress. You want me to talk about her.

She's not chic, she doesn't dress to please or tease. She dresses for herself, to feel good, to be comfortable. That's how she dresses. It'd be easy to get sucked into lumping her with the rest, just because she lives on the kind of street they live on. That's the danger, isn't it, lumping people together, making assumptions? At a guess, I'd say you've made assumptions about me. Now, I don't want to tell you your job, but I don't think that's a healthy approach. We need to keep our minds open.

I didn't make any assumptions about her. That's not something I do. I don't want to blow my own trumpet, but I pride myself on my openness to people. It's my belief that we can only live in the hope that people forgive us our trespasses as we forgive those who trespass against us.

That line always appealed to me. Give us this day our daily bread, I could take or leave, never rang any bells, maybe because of the food connotation. And lead us not into temptation, well that's crazy, we need temptation to keep our lives vaguely interesting; temptation is where life is happening; temptation is what keeps you in a job. But the forgiveness and trespass bit, that bit I like.

If, on top of being a fat kid, I tell you I was a troubled soul in my younger days, how do you feel about that? It's my experience that people, ordinary people, split, more or less, sixty/forty against the fat kids, but when it comes to troubled youngsters, it's always trouble was means trouble is.

But if I throw in the fact that I come from a decent, upright, hardworking family, good-living brothers and a sister, does that help redress the balance? I'm talking siblings here, not parents. Parents are random. Think about it. Take two people who, for some obscure reason, believe they suit one another, throw them together in a steamy car or, if you want, in a marriage bed and you never know what you're going to get. And nor do they. But that's only the start of it. Throw in their ability, their need, even, to interfere in their kids' lives and you have a lethal cocktail. They'll give you all the usual excuses – it's for his own good, you can't put an old head on young shoulders, if I'd had someone to advise me when I was his age. What they really mean is – if I screwed up my own life for you, you can carry some of the load yourself. They'll never say it out straight, but you get to know it and, later on, you have to laugh about it, don't you?

But brothers and a sister are another matter, they're the leaven in the mixture. If the recipe comes out more or less okay across the family cake, then the chances are that the slightly wild one will come round. That's my belief. I know I did. I wasn't the fat and lonely only kid. I wasn't the spoilt, overfed brat. I was just a kid. That's all.

If I could tell you I had a happy marriage and a doting wife, you'd probably be a little more impressed. You might look again at your assumptions, at the evidence of your bias, at me. But I can't. Unfortunately, I can't. Can't produce a wife. I lived with a woman once, for three years, but we got tired of arguing; neither one of us had the stomach for it.

I can offer you the evidence of a nice house, no porn magazines stashed anywhere, no dubious stuff on my computer, a reasonable living in the ice cream business, self-education, hard work as proof, if it's proof you want, that I'm an ordinary, decent, upright, law-abiding citizen. But that's not what you want, is it?

And then there's the little matter of what you call my obsession with her. I prefer to call it a fascination. The word 'obsession' has all kinds of connotations. It gets us all off on the wrong foot, doesn't it? So, I'd like to call it my fascination.

It started quite unintentionally, but I realised, very quickly, that it had a consequence in my life. It was an important matter. Even you must understand that; there must have been a time when someone captivated you. Maybe you're still a captive, maybe you still find times and places for your fascinations. You have the ideal job for it, don't you – power, two-way mirrors, long hours, unpredictable situations – to help you pull the wool over your wives' eyes? I see your rings and I see your opportunities.

Isn't it interesting the way fat fingers grow over rings, swallow them the way fat mouths swallow big dollops of food? I've always found that fascinating.

Anyway, you don't want to hear about yourselves, do you? You know all about yourselves. You know yourselves better than most. You don't want an ice cream seller rooting around inside your minds. That wouldn't be fair. That's your business. You want to know about me and her and the matter in hand.

The problem is, it wasn't just me and her. It's never a question of just two people in any relationship. Look at us, four of us sitting here around a table. Coffee cups. Shooting the breeze. But that's just surface stuff, there's so much more going on. And it was the same with us. If it had been just the pair of us, things would've been different. Or even the three of us, her and me and the little girl; that would've been okay, too. I'd happily have settled for that. But children have fathers and men tend not to want someone else in their patch even when they've deserted the patch. What we want and what others think we should have is seldom the same thing.

Actually, the kid was with her the first day I saw her and I didn't mind. That didn't throw me, not one iota. It was one of those days, late spring, when I knew I wasn't going to make any money. It was pissing rain. I remember drinking a cup of coffee at the window, looking out across the garden, watching the trees dripping. The front ring had burned out on the cooker that morning. I'd put the kettle on and gone off to have a shower and come back to find the kettle still cold. Strange the way details blister themselves into your memory, like you have a sense for the things you believe you'll want or need to remember. A sense of occasion, I suppose, even before the occasion happens.

I thought about staying at home, but I'd already been working three weeks at that stage and one of the tricks of the ice cream van trade is that, once the season starts, you never miss a day, hail or rain. People get to know the routine and that's how you build your business. Miss a day and you confuse them. Exact opposite to the way you guys work. Anyway, I did all the usual stuff, mixed the mix, filled the machines, checked the cordial bottles, ran the jingles. I do all that in the garage, don't want to disturb the neighbours with yet another blast of 'London Bridge Is Falling Down'. It was just an ordinary, miserable April day, the kind of day you survive in the hope of better times. Your job must be like that a lot of the time. You must survive the bad days in the hope that one day, some day, people will hit the straight and narrow and not feel the inclination to veer into the undergrowth.

But that's all in the future or the past, you don't want to hear all that. Or maybe you do, maybe you make it all add up.

Anyway, I did my route that morning, drove as slow as I always drive. No one buying, hardly anyone on the streets, a bit of sun, and then the rain coming down like nails, and then another twenty minutes of an excuse for sunshine. It was sunny when I saw her. She was pushing the buggy across the open ground at the end of her road and then the skies opened and she was drenched before she could get under a tree. I drove beside her and she smiled at me and turned her eyes to heaven. I opened the window. Will I play a song to cheer you up? I said.

Do that, she said, and then she started running along the path, pushing the buggy in front of her and the rain was bucketing down and she was soaked. I stuck the 'Raindrops keep falling' jingle in the tape deck. She turned in at her gate and I saw her fumbling in her purse for a key and then she was opening the door. I stopped at the gate.

Would you like an ice cream? I said. She started laughing.

No, she said, but thanks for the song, it's very appropriate.

And then she was lifting the kid out of the buggy, into the hall, and her shirt was stretched wet across her back and I could see her skin through it.

That was the start of it. If you want me to put a finger on a time and a place, that was it, the minute I saw her lifting the child into the hall, the colour of her skin through the wet shirt, the arch of her back, the curve of her shoulders, her hair plastered against her face.

I fell in love with her, there and then. Something about the way she moved. The way she said appropriate. There was something warm about it, something refined and yet friendly, inviting.

The problem is, it's a waste of my time telling you all this because you just want the sordid bits. The things you'd like to believe happened. You imagine there's a who, what, where and when that I can give you. Reasons don't really interest you. And do you know why that is? It's because you lack imagination. You have a limited view and a limited understanding. That's why you miss the things you might otherwise see. That's why you can only react, because you have an underdeveloped imaginative capability. You have it down there, for plodding, but you don't have it up here. Your biggest mistake is in assuming that people are stupid when the opposite is so often the case.

It's all this us and them stuff with you and that's real enough. But you're the ones who've made it that way. Your presumption has put us on the other side of the fence and we'll always be there, out of reach, beyond your comprehension. You think, by bringing me in here, that you're reaching some kind of conclusion.

Not so, my friends.

You're the ones who said that, about being my friends, that you want to help me, that you're here to listen. Trying to make a virtue of your weakness. If you're good listeners it's only because you have nothing to say, no perception of what you're dealing with or if you're dealing with anything at all. That's the sad and pitiable part of all this.

Anyway.

Do you remember that Joni Mitchell song, 'The Hissing of Summer Lawns'? Unlikely. Probably not your kind of music. Not that it matters. I mention it only to bring the summer weather to mind. Nor do we ever truly get that kind of thing here. The odd hose attached to one of those water-driven revolving sprays, but nothing like you get in the States. Have you been to the States? Actually, don't answer that because I don't really need to know and this is all about need to know, isn't it? I'm not boring you, am I? I certainly hope not.

You did ask me to tell you everything, but that's a tall order. What I believe to be important may not seem so to you. And the things you imagine to be important may be of little or no consequence to me. It's a question of perspective and that is not something we share, believe you me. I recognised that fact the moment we sat down together.

And do you know why? Because you want to clear things up, nail things down, tidy your desks, close the file. All those action words. But then that's what you are, isn't it? Action men. And yet, you think there's nothing you can do without me, isn't that right? No action you can take, no response, no operation? Nothing. You're stuck here drinking crap coffee, tapping your feet under the table, wishing you could beat out of me whatever it is you mistakenly believe I know.

A scenario. Your scenario, mind, not mine. Mad bastard becomes besotted with young, single mother. She rejects him. He becomes crazy with lust and anger. He kidnaps her and her child. He leaves the child in a field by a river and drives away. He kills the woman and dumps her body somewhere just out of your reach. You know he did it but you can't pin it on him without a body. If he'll just give you that much, you'll do the rest yourself. Semen stains, skin samples from under the woman's nails. Home and dry. The child's too young to tell you anything, too young to know her mother is gone. You need a body or, at least, co-operation.

Another scenario. This one is mine. Man drives an ice cream van for a living. Wet day, sees this woman. Watches her as she's caught in the rain. He remembers the way her skin shone through her wet shirt. But we're not talking wet T-shirt nonsense here. We're talking about a moment of beauty, a moment that lives in the memory. We're talking about a woman at ease with herself and her body. She's not embarrassed by how she looks or what he sees. She smiles at him and, yes, he offers her an ice cream cone and another to her kid and he chats to her and he looks forward to seeing her and, he believes, she looks forward to seeing him and, yes, he sees her again. Just because our ice cream man fantasises about taking off her wet shirt and kissing her shoulder doesn't mean he's driven by a need to hurt her. What would be the point? Not everything is as crude as you believe it to be and not everyone is as destructive as you imagine.

I appreciate physical beauty and I appreciate sex but I appreciate other things, too. Things like, say, a summer night when the air is absolutely still. You take a night like that and you go and stand in your eight-by-ten garden and you squint up at the stars through the light from the street lamps and you think you're communing with nature.

Me, I'd prepare for an occasion like that. I'd finish work early and leave home before dark. I like driving into the tail end of a summer evening, into the mist and the shimmer. That gives me pleasure. I drive and drive until I find somewhere quiet and deserted, somewhere that doesn't have crying children or radios blaring or foul-mouthed teenagers kicking footballs or drinking. Say, a forest that's miles from anywhere. And, sometimes, I go there alone and sometimes I bring a friend.

Correction, not a friend. You tell me you're my friends, but I wouldn't bring you. I bring an intimate, someone who'll respect the silence and the beauty of the place. And we walk a little distance into the forest, just to be away from car lights and traffic and interruption. And we lie on the mossy floor of the wood or sit against a tree and listen to the sound of the night falling.

Did you know night has a sound that it makes when it falls? I can't describe it. Nobody can. But if you wait long enough and listen closely enough and have patience enough, you'll recognise it. The fall of night. It makes you one with nature, it sucks you into the soil and swallows you among the leaves and you do, actually, become one with the cosmos. I suspect Wordsworth experienced it. And Blake. If they were living now you'd probably have them outside, waiting to follow me in here.

But even the warmest night grows cold and, if you're prepared to allow yourself, you begin to detect the way the woodland shivers as the night goes on. It's a bit like that thing doctors say about the body reaching its low point around three or four in the morning. The earth is the same; it has a low point, a time when it comes close to death. A time when the moonlight is like dead skin. Inanimate. It just seems to lie there, like a corpse, still beautiful but lifeless. Extraordinary, really.

So you see, sometimes we get sucked in by the beauty of the moment and we need to reflect on the things we've seen and the places we've been and the people who've received those moments with us.

You're privileged. I hope you appreciate that fact. This is not something I've shared with many of my friends – ever. And I'm not sure why I'm sharing it with you. It's not something you can understand or even begin to appreciate without undergoing it. And sitting all night in a forest doesn't necessarily mean you'll appreciate it either. The grace of experience is what it's about and even best friends cannot share their experiences through words. You know that.

You could tell me now about the most dangerous times you've lived through. You could talk to me about the greatest risks you've taken. You could give me every detail of your greatest triumphs, the times when things fell into place for you, when circumstance and evidence and that sixth sense you told me about all tumbled together into that something that's compensation and gratification in one. But I wouldn't understand it because I haven't experienced it.

And you can't understand the beauty of the moment I'm describing because you weren't there. You didn't hear the wind whisper, you didn't feel the forest shudder, you didn't see the light of death come down from the moon, you didn't smell the smell of coldness and you didn't taste that particular taste that's like a mortal kiss on the mouth, like an inert tongue on your tongue.

You see, sometimes friendship is not enough, and some things are too personal for sharing, even with friends.

Resurrection

It was the morning of the last day of February when the man at the other end of the phone told Miriam her husband was dead.

'There's no comfortable way for me to put this or for you to hear it,' he said. 'Your husband's body was found yesterday afternoon. No matter how I say it, it doesn't make it any easier for you. I'm sorry to be the one.'

Miriam took a deep breath. There were questions she needed to ask but they were beyond her for now, so she did the practical thing. She asked for the caller's name and a telephone number.

'It must be what, three in the morning – where you are? It's just after eight here; it's still dark outside.'

'Yes ma'am,' the soft Canadian inflection.

'So you won't want me calling you back in an hour.'

'This is a police station. I'll be on duty till eight but my colleagues can assist you any time.'

'Right.'

'Again, I'm sorry.'

Miriam found herself wondering about the policeman, about his age. He sounded young but it was more likely he was in his late thirties or forties, that he'd have some experience of this kind of thing.

'Do you have someone there with you?' he asked.

'Yes, Charlie, my son – he's here.'

'He's an adult?' He put the emphasis on the second syllable.

'No, he's six. But my sister will come.'

'That's good, ma'am. You call her and then you call us back when the time is right for you.'

'Yes.' She hesitated. 'How did it happen?'

'Looks like it was a natural passing. We need to wait for results. But there was no sign of anything untoward.'

'What a strange word,' Miriam said.

'I beg your pardon?'

'Untoward – it's a strange word.'

'Yes, ma'am. I guess it is.'

'If I call back in an hour or two, you'll still be there?'

'I'll still be here.'

'Thank you.'

'I truly am sorry.'

'Yes.'

Putting down the phone, she stood for a moment, not thinking, staring into the shadows of the hallway, and then, picking it up again, she rang her sister.

Suzann spoke to the Canadian policeman and to the embassy and to the travel agent and then rang their brother and arranged for him to travel with Miriam. She contacted the undertaker and the Department of Foreign Affairs and made coffee and lunch. She talked a little about Bart but not too much and then took Bart's photograph from the sitting-room mantelpiece and put it on the kitchen table, where they could see it when they felt the need to see it. Suzann organised everything without it being obvious and she listened to her sister and hugged her and smiled that smile that made Miriam believe things would be all right, in spite of everything. And, the following morning, when Miriam and Michael left for the airport, Suzann stood with Charlie and waved them goodbye.

ii

'Where's Mammy?'

It was late on the first evening of March.

Charlie was sitting at the kitchen table, swinging his legs and trying to kick off his damp runners without opening the laces.

'She's on her way to Canada,' Suzann said.

'Is Uncle Michael gone with her?'

'Yes.'

'How will they get there?'

'They're flying.'

'In an aeroplane?'

'Yes.' Suzann smiled.

'Angels can fly without aeroplanes. They have shiny, bright wings, brighter than the sun. Feathery wings.'

'Do they?'

'Do you know any angel names?'

She shook her head.

'Are angels related to chickens?'

Suzann laughed out loud.

'You're a funny little man.'

The boy nodded and then opened his mouth, as though he was about to ask something else, took a deep breath and was silent for a moment.

Suzann stared through the kitchen window but she could see nothing beyond her other self, gaping back from the rain-pocked glass.

'Your mum and Uncle Michael are going to bring your daddy back home with them,' she said quietly.

The little boy perked up, loosening a shoe against the chair
'When will he be home?'

'Next week.'

'When will it be next week?' 'Five sleeps away. Or six.'

'Which?'

'Six.'

'Is that why Daddy's picture is on the table?'

Suzann turned and smiled at him.

'Yes Charlie, that's why. To remind us.'

'To remind us that Daddy is coming home, so that we won't forget and go out and not remember to leave a key? We did that once.'

Suzann nodded.

'Can I stay up when he comes home? Will he collect me from school?'

'We'll see.'

'I don't like that photograph,' the boy said, holding the framed picture in both hands.

'Don't you? Why not?'

'I don't like the big rocks behind Daddy. They could fall on him.'

'Not in the photograph.'

'But sometime, and then he might die.'

iii

Miriam asked for the policeman by name, the one who had telephoned to tell her Bart was dead.

'He might not be here,' Michael whispered.

'I know that but he might. I want to see what he looks like.'

'Does it matter?'

Miriam shrugged.

They were sitting in a small office in the police station.

Outside, old snow lay like twisted, unwashed dishcloths on the sills of the barred windows. Inside, the faded room smelled of steaming coffee and damp carpet.

A tall man stepped through the open doorway. Michael stood up and shook his hand.

'This is my sister. This is Miriam.'

'Steve Mallett,' the man said. 'I spoke with you on the phone.'

'I wondered how old you'd be,' Miriam said quietly.

'Probably not as old as I feel today.'

They sat, the three of them, and the policeman answered Michael's questions. It looked like Bart had died of a heart attack; they'd know for sure in a couple of hours but they weren't looking for anyone else in connection with his death.

'So this is what it means,' Miriam said. 'When you hear that phrase on the news.'

'This is what it means,' the policeman said.

'Can we see Bart?'

'Yes, of course. A car will take you to the hospital.'

'And he's, you know, he's okay?'

'He's okay.' The policeman smiled a reassuring smile.

'Who found him?'

'Next-door neighbour – old-timer, lives thirty minutes from the cabin. He went to see if your husband needed anything; seems they had any arrangement about picking up supplies from town. He found him and called us. It's about two and a half hours from here to there at this time of year.'

'Where did this man find Bart?'

'He was sitting at his table, ma'am, looked like he'd been working there. I understand he was a writer?'

She nodded.

'He couldn't work at home, said he couldn't concentrate. Never did, always had to live in the places he was writing about.'

The policeman smiled again.

'How long had he been dead?' Miriam was surprised by the calmness of her voice.

'A day, maybe two, I believe. But it's pretty cold out there; the place was freezing. Nothing had happened to the remains.'

'Is it possible for us to go out to the cabin?'

Michael glanced at the policeman and he immediately nodded.

'Of course. Sometimes, people want to see where a loved one passed away. I understand that. I can have you taken out there first thing tomorrow morning. It's a long trip, just so you're prepared for that. And the cabin is pretty isolated but we can get you there, yeah, sure we can.'

'You're certain you really want to spend five hours travelling there and back?' Michael asked.

'Absolutely,' Miriam said. 'I need to see.'

'It'll be all right,' the policeman reassured them. 'Trust me, everything is fine, it's not a problem, not a problem at all. And it's very beautiful out there. That may be some consolation.'

iv

Suzann was sitting on the side of Charlie's bed.

'How many days is it now until next week?'

'Still six.'

'You said that already.'

'Yes but that was this morning. It's still the same day. But it'll be a new day soon. When you wake in the morning, it'll be only five days.'

The boy nodded.

'Have you said your prayers?'

'God bless Mammy and Daddy and Auntie Suzann and Uncle Michael and me. And everyone. Amen.'

'That's it?'

'When Mammy is here, there's more but I think that's enough.'

'Okay.'

Suzann tucked the bedclothes under the boy's chin.

'You're as snug as a bug in a rug,' she smiled, tickling him.

He laughed and squirmed and laughed again.

'Daddy always brings me a present when he comes home.'

'I know.'

'I think this time he'll bring me an aeroplane like the one he'll be flying in.'

She nodded but said nothing.

'Tomorrow, can we paint a picture of an aeroplane for Daddy, a big picture? And I can give it to him when he brings me my present.'

'Of course we can.'

'I like painting in the daytime when the sun is out. You can see things better.'

'Yes you can.'

'Why are you crying?' the boy asked.

'I'm just sad. But I'm happy, too. Happy to be here with you.'

'Will you stop being sad when Mammy and Daddy and Uncle Michael come home?'

'I'm sure I will.'

'Can you be happy and sad together?'

v

'I'm sorry, I can't take you folks up there myself,' Steve Mallett said. 'But Officer Marsh is one of our best. She'll take care of you.'

They were standing outside the front door of the police station, the dark morning traffic slushing past them on the main street of the town.

'I guess everything will be finalised within forty-eight hours. I'll be talking to someone from your embassy this afternoon. Everything will be in place by the time you get back from the cabin.'

'Thank you,' Michael said. 'We appreciate all you've done.'

A patrol jeep eased out of a gateway to the side of the station.

'That's your ride,' the policeman said. 'I'll introduce you.'

Miriam and Michael followed him down the wet concrete steps.

A young, casually dressed woman climbed from the jeep and came to meet them.

'Dominique Marsh,' she smiled. 'I'm sorry about your husband.'

'Thank you.'

She shook Michael's hand.

'Real sorry.'

'Not sure if you folks want to talk or not on the ride out,' Dominique said.

They were clear of the town and, ahead of them, where the road arrowed into the horizon, mountains reared above a thick smear of evergreens. Closer to hand, barns and silos crouched beside farmhouses, their backs pitted against the bitter, churning winds.

'Some folks do. Some don't; people differ at times like this. I brought some coffee and bagels. Best we get out to the cabin and let you have time. We can stop off on the ride back, get something more substantial, if you feel like it. Everything is your call.'

'Thank you,' Michael said.

They drove on, across the snowbound farmland and then, mile by mile, the fences and farmhouses evaporated until they were speeding through a bottle of murky green forest, the low light shattering as it fell between the trees.

'How could he write up here?' Miriam asked. 'He told me it was bright and white and clear. This is darkness.'

'Forty-five minutes on we're into snowfields,' Dominique said. 'And then it's just stands of timber and an eternity of snow. It's everything you don't see here – white, bright, clear, fresh. And mostly just empty.'

'That's what his letters said.'

'How long had your husband been up here?'

'Since just after Christmas. Eight or nine weeks. He'd planned on staying till the end of summer.'

'He was a writer?'

'Yes.'

'A good one, I guess.'

'I think so.'

'That's it,' Dominique said, pointing into the wilderness ahead. 'That's the cabin. Just thought I should tell you that we're almost there.'

Michael leaned forward from the back seat and Miriam squinted into the rosy whiteness.

'To the left of that stand of trees.'

'I see the trees,' Miriam nodded.

As they drove, the cabin began to take a shape within the shadow of the coppice, a low and regular building and behind it what looked like a garage. Bart had told her, in his first letter, that he had bought a small car. It was a necessity out here. A small and simple house and a small and simple car; what else had she expected? Wherever he went, Bart chose to live austerely. He detested ostentation. Sometimes, she thought, he had no choice but to go; even their modest house seemed to hold echoes of affectation for him.

As they swung off the roadway and onto a rough track, Miriam could clearly see the cabin now with its shuttered garage and, behind that, a woodshed precisely stacked with neatly sawn logs. The logs had come with the cabin, Miriam knew. Bart had told her. He wouldn't have had the patience for such orderliness.

She was thinking of Frost's lines about the woods and the frozen lake. Somewhere beyond that stand of trees, somewhere in a hollow in the snow she supposed, was a lake, ice-covered but breathing in the expectation of spring. Without that anticipation, how could anything or anyone go on?

Then, right away, she was overwhelmed by the enormity of what had happened. There were no tears. Instead, the cold seemed infinitely colder and the emptiness of the landscape was immense, and the forlorn, the unlit windows of the cabin were deep, black holes that terrified her.

Michael coughed and only then did she realise that the jeep had come to a standstill and that Dominique was assiduously looking into the distance, allowing her the time to prepare herself.

'I'm sorry,' Miriam whispered. 'I was just thinking how beautiful it is out here. And how lonely.'

Dominique laid a gloved hand on her arm.

'I can go in with you or I can stay out here – whatever way you want it. It'll look just like any other room in any cabin, I promise you. I realise it'll mean much more to you but there's nothing to be afraid of.'

Michael put his hand on her shoulder.

'You okay, sis?'

She nodded, smiled and opened the jeep door.

Inside the cabin it was colder than she had expected, colder than outside, as if the wind had gathered every shaft of iciness and shut it up in the half-darkness of this functional room, dulling its light and congealing its coldness.

Michael stood in the shining doorway. Beyond him she could see Dominique just outside, listening and waiting, on duty. Miriam stood in the middle of the room and, closing her eyes, breathed slowly, deeply, searching for the moment of her husband's death, listening to the ice crack on the gutters, feeling the weak dusk from the small window lean uncertainly on her left hand. But she found nothing of Bart. What had she expected: that there'd be any more of him here than there was in the house they shared? That, secretly, this had become home to him.

Opening her eyes, she moved between the plain kitchen table, with its four sturdy chairs, and the small desk that faced a window filled with distant, drunken trees. Some notebooks sat, neat and silent, side-by-side on a flock of coffee rings. Two loose pages lay together, a pair of redundant wings, feathered with Bart's scrawl, lost now without the force that had made them fly.

She lifted the top sheet and read a list of things undone and groceries unordered.

The second page was tidier, lined and neatly written.

It's snowing here again tonight.

I hope it's snowing there, too.

I like the idea of you sleeping and snow falling outside your window.

I imagine myself standing at that window, looking out at the snow, then turning back to watch you sleep.

vi

On the morning of the day that Bart's body was due home, Suzann told Charlie about his father's death. They were sitting at the kitchen table, low sunlight streaming through the picture window. She said the usual things, the words she had heard others use when they spoke to children about death. She told him something terribly sad had happened, she reminded him of how much Bart loved him, she assured him that his father's love would never stop, just that it would be coming from a different place, about how Charlie would find his father's star in the sky and know he was always there.

'Stars are not people,' the boy said.

'They can remind us of people we loved.'

'What if two people pick the same star to remind them? Whose star is it then?'

Suzann smiled, relieved that this was the question he'd chosen to ask.

When Charlie's father came home, it was in an enormous wooden box and the box was left in the sitting room and people came and went and they kept stepping over Charlie where he was playing with his digger on the floor at the foot of the stairs. All those legs and all that talk and, from time to time, a hand reaching down from the sky to rub his head and, afterwards, the smell of perfume from his hair. And someone gave him money and he squashed it into the little pocket at the front of his jeans and thought for a minute about what he'd like to buy and wondered if his father had remembered to bring the aeroplane he'd promised. And then he went back to his work, digging blocks from the hall carpet and piling them on the first step of the stairs.

Charlie woke while it was still dark. He always woke in the darkness. He liked to wander around the house in the shadows from the landing light. At the foot of the stairs he stopped; there were voices in the kitchen, so he turned right, into the sitting room where his father was still keeping out of sight.

Putting his ear to the box, Charlie listened. His father was keeping very still; he was good at that. Charlie knew what he needed to do: he needed to surprise his father. He waited, silent, unmoving, counting to fifty, counting and waiting for longer than he'd ever done before. Then he knocked loudly on the side of the box inside which he believed his father was hiding, knocked and giggled because he suspected his father couldn't keep still for ever and he knew his father loved to hear him laugh; it made him laugh too.

Suzann was suddenly beside him, her arm across the boy's shoulder.

'What are you doing, little man?'

'Playing hide and seek with Daddy. I know where he's hiding. He's in the box. I can hear him.'

vii

'I'm tempted to pull the fucking lid off the coffin and slap his face,' Miriam said.

She and Suzann were standing in the back garden, drinking coffee, stooped against the black March wind. A few beaten daffodils huddled at the foot of a dividing wall.

Suzann looked again at the sheet of paper her sister had pulled from her jacket pocket.

'All it says is, I hope it's snowing there, too.'

'It rarely snows here. You know that, I know that, he knew that. This is not for me.'

'It's probably just a piece of a story, something he was working on. Notes. He was always leaving notes around the house. You said that yourself, ideas, bits and pieces. That's what writers do. I think.'

Miriam warmed her face in the steam from her coffee cup.

'His notes are on his laptop. I've read them. They have

274

nothing to do with this. And anyway, there was an envelope, with the page.'

'Was it addressed to anyone?' Suzann asked quickly.

'No.'

'There you are then.'

'The page was sitting on the lip of the envelope, ready to be put inside.'

'You don't know that.'

'There was a roll of stamps beside it.'

'This is not a good time to come to these conclusions. This is not the time to decide stuff like this. Honestly it's not.'

'He was expecting some old guy to call. There was a grocery list beside it. He was going to address the bloody thing and have it posted. I know, Suzann. Don't tell me I'm not right. You always try to find the balance in things, but sometimes there is no balance. Sometimes life is totally unbalanced, it's dark, it's disingenuous, it's fucking twisted. The fact is – and I know this in my heart – he just hadn't got around to addressing the envelope. So fuck him.'

viii

Charlie was mesmerised by the priest who was to conduct his father's funeral service. He was a tall young man with a mop of brown hair and a smile that the six-year-old recognised as genuine.

He knelt by Charlie in the church and shook his hand and asked how he was.

Charlie said he was fine. The priest talked about Charlie's father the way Charlie did, as though the game of hide and seek which was going on would end when Charlie least expected it. He let Charlie light the taper from which the candles would be lit.

He asked if Charlie would like to come up and speak about

his father from the altar during the service. The boy looked at the expanse of white marble he'd have to cross and shook his head. The priest showed him where to leave Bart's camera, when the time came to present the gifts of remembrance, on a small table with three of Bart's books, and then he said they'd talk later.

Watching the priest move along the front of the altar space, distributing the communion wafers, Charlie began to believe the marble wasn't so expansive after all.

And when the priest talked about death and life, he listened.

'If we believe in Jesus the Christ, then we believe in the promises he made. We not only believe, we trust. Jesus promised his disciples that he was the way, the truth and the life. We can find our way to that truth through Jesus' life. We can rediscover the joy in life by recognising that death is not the end. Jesus preached the resurrection and his disciples had their faith rewarded on Easter morning when, as the sun rose, they found a very real presence in the absence of Jesus from the tomb. We are four weeks from Easter, the rationale of life and death lies there. We have faith that we shall rise again and, as Paul tells us in I Corinthians: "For now we see through a glass, darkly; but then face to face." We believe, even better we know, that we will see Bart face to face again.'

The priest smiled at Charlie and Charlie smiled back. Glancing to his left, he saw that his mother's eyes were closed. To his right, Suzann was crying. She caught him watching her, took his hand and held it on her lap. Her hand was cold but her clothes were soft and they had a gentle smell of perfume that made him feel warm and wanted. He shifted slightly in his seat, moving closer to her.

ix

'If I could pity the bastard, I would, but I can't. If he'd died a day later, I'd never have known but he wouldn't, would he? That might have spared everyone.'

Miriam was standing at the sink, staring into the solid, sunless garden.

'Have you said anything to Michael?' Suzann asked.

'I have not! I don't want everyone to know what a fool I was. No one knows but me, you and her – whoever she is. I wonder if she's even heard that he's dead. I keep expecting the Canadian police to forward one of her letters to me. If they did, I'd have a name.'

'Well, it's been three weeks and they haven't. Surely that counts for something?'

'Most likely she lived somewhere in that godforsaken town, probably a waitress in the local caff or a fucking pole dancer. She'll have been close enough for him to get to. She'll know by now. They always do.'

Suzann came and stood by her sister. Together, they watched Charlie in the garden outside. He was kicking a ball into the wind, laughing each time it lifted above his head and landed at the other end of the lawn.

'He's taking it well,' Miriam said.

'Seems to be. I'm not sure how much of it has sunk in.'

'He knows Bart's dead, if that's what you mean.'

'Of course he does.'

Outside, the ball soared into the wind, bounced on the narrow lawn and disappeared into the neighbour's garden.

'Got it,' Suzann called.

Charlie could see the top of her head above the dividing wall.

'I'm going to throw it in to you. See if you can catch it.'

The bright, shining ball held in the wind and blew back

into the next-door garden.

He could hear Suzann laughing.

'I wouldn't make much of a player, would I?' she called.

'Throw it again. Harder.'

She did and it bounced beside Charlie.

'Have you got it?'

'Yes.'

'Right. Coming over.'

Her face appeared above the wall and then she pulled herself up and sat on the narrow blocks.

'Humpty Dumpty sat on a wall,' she laughed, rocking puppet-like, backward and forward. 'Humpty Dumpty had a great fall.'

Suddenly she tumbled, all arms and legs, onto the lawn.

'All the king's horses and all the king's men couldn't put Humpty together again.'

Charlie came racing across the garden and jumped on her. Together they rolled, tickling and giggling in the cold grass, their arms about each other, hugging together against the hardness of the ground.

'How long are you going to stay with us?' Charlie asked quietly.

'Till Easter, the week after Easter.'

'When is Easter?'

'Not next Sunday but the one after that. Ten days.'

'I like when you're here.'

'Thank you.' She hugged the small boy close to her. 'I'm going to buy you the biggest Easter egg you've ever seen. It'll take you a month to eat it.'

'And Daddy will bring me an egg.'

'Not this year, sweetheart.'

'Jesus came back. The man said Daddy will come back too.

And he might bring an egg for me, if he can find one.'

x

'I took Bart's photograph off the mantelpiece,' Miriam said. 'I put it in Charlie's bedroom.'

'Why?'

'I thought it would be good for Charlie to have it there. As a reminder.'

'I'm not sure he likes that picture. He's afraid the rocks will fall on Bart. Anyway, the first thing he did every morning was to go into the sitting room and say hello.'

'Well now he can do it when he wakes. And last thing at night. And I don't have to see Bart staring at me when I'm watching telly. A win, win situation, isn't that what they call it? You only have to look at Charlie to see he's flying. He laughs all the time. He's happy, Suzann, that's the important part. I can deal with what Bart did. See no evil, speak no evil.'

'He wasn't an evil man.'

'If you say.'

'You know he wasn't.'

'You're not telling me that what he did was acceptable?'

'You have no idea what he did or if he did anything. A few words on a sheet of paper, a blank envelope, that doesn't amount to evil or anything remotely like it. This has to do with other things, Miriam, things about Bart's being away, and that's understandable but it does not make him an evil man. Just let it go with him. Give him the benefit of the doubt, or don't if you can't, but let it go.'

'Easy to say. If you want to know me, come and live with me. I feel totally humiliated and used and I do not want to see that dark, suntanned, self-satisfied face grinning down at me night after night. Charlie likes having the photograph in his room, whatever you say, so good for Charlie. Like I said, it's all win, win.'

xi

Only after his mother and aunt had tucked him in and read him a story and tickled and laughed with him and promised to help him in the morning to find the places where his eggs might be hidden, after they had kissed him goodnight and wished him sweet dreams and told him he was the best boy in the world and that they loved him more than anyone else, after they had switched on the soft bedside light and closed his door, did Charlie take his dinosaur clock from the shelf above his table, wind it and set the alarm.

xii

'I think I'm going to sell this place,' Miriam said.

She and Suzann were sprawled on the couch in the sitting room.

'Wouldn't Charlie miss his friends, the school, all that?'

'I don't mean to leave the town, just the house. I never liked it. The rooms are too small, too gloomy. Bart said it was big enough, which was easy for him—he was never here. Passing through between books. And women, it seems.'

'Charlie thinks Bart is coming back.'

'What?'

'He thinks he's coming home for Easter.'

'Shit, where did that come from?'

'I'm not sure. From what the priest said, I think.'

'What priest?'

'At the burial service.'

'What did he say?'

'Charlie thought he said Bart would be back at Easter, like Jesus.'

Miriam laughed out loud and then her eyes filled with tears.

'I'm sorry,' she said. 'I didn't mean to laugh. It's just another good reason to keep religion and children apart, fairytales and bullshit. Well at least the Easter Bunny will come. That much we can see to, that much will happen.'

xiii

Charlie dressed quickly by the light from the bedside lamp. It was five o'clock. He wasn't sure if that was very early or just early. He made no attempt to be quiet. It never crossed his mind that he should. He was too excited.

Downstairs, he didn't bother to look for his eggs. Instead, he wriggled clumsily into his jacket, zipped it up, pulled on his cap, opened the hall door and stepped into the melting yellow light outside.

xiv

Miriam woke to the darkness. Pressing her mobile phone, she squinted at the dim, scratched screen.

Bugger, she thought, forgot to charge it again.

Something after five but she couldn't decipher the minutes.

Turning back towards sleep, she considered for a moment the fact of Bart's death. She thought of him on that morning or afternoon or night when the end had come in the isolated cabin. It was like a nightmare to her now. But, in that moment, she allowed herself to forgive him whatever wrongs he might not have done. She imagined him recoiling from the bullets of pain inside his arm and the convulsive explosion in his chest. And she pitied him the terrible hurt of that moment. And then she slept.

xv

Suzann found him.

She had sensed, when he didn't come bounding into her

bed at six o'clock with the egg she had left on his bedroom table, that something was wrong. She had gone into his room and then looked in on her sister's sleeping form before hurrying downstairs. She saw, immediately, that his jacket and cap were missing from the low peg in the hallway.

Upstairs, she pulled on her jeans, a jumper and the jacket with the fur-trimmed hood; it would be cold outside, she knew that.

At the foot of the stairs, she dragged on her socks and jiggled into her boots.

In the street, the windscreen of her car was frozen. Splaying her hands, she pressed them hard against the glass until the ice began to melt in fingers and palms.

And then she was driving, swinging out through the wide and curving crescents of the estate, into the narrow street of the old town, past the voiceless yard of Charlie's school and sharply left onto the avenue, with its cortège of wintry trees, nodding mutely towards the ravenous gates of the graveyard.

Though she doubted Charlie had even noticed her car lights at the gate or heard her running feet on the gravelled path, he didn't seem at all surprised to see her. His knees were resting against the frozen mound of Bart's grave. His face looked pale and tired.

She knelt beside him, aware immediately of the cold and damp seeping through the knees of her jeans.

'I think Daddy will come soon,' Charlie said, nodding towards the eye of a railway bridge. Through it Suzann could see a vein of light against the edge of night.

'Maybe he will,' she said.

They hunkered closer, waiting for whatever it was they believed, separately or together, was about to happen.

'The sun is coming up,' Charlie whispered.

'So it is. Maybe the sun will blow the snow away.'

'There isn't any snow.'

His voice was sleepy and hoarse.

Suzann opened her coat and hugged him to her, taking his frozen hands in hers, letting his rigid frame fold against the warmth of her own.

'Let me tell you a secret,' she whispered. 'Sometimes it snows and people don't even know.'

Absent Children

I moved away from the river when its invitation became too strong. Ironically, that growing temptation coincided with the arrival of summer. All winter I had lived on the banks of the cold, fast torrent without once sensing that its drab and dreary arms might appeal to me. But the arrival of the warmer days and the turning of the water from grey to blue brought a growing fascination that terrified me.

So I packed up and left, driving across country, moving along narrow roads that twisted, or so my map informed me, farther and farther from any significant body of water. When, eventually, I stopped in some two-horse town, my pick-up wouldn't start and the local mechanic was less than optimistic about it ever starting again.

'It might but you'll have to talk nicely to it.'

'How nicely?'

'Hundreds.'

'How many?'

'Six or seven – new engine at least. Maybe more, maybe eight or nine.'

'Right.'

'But you don't have it?'

I shook my head.

'Looks like I'll have to consider the possibility of work,' I said.

'Does that scare you?'

'Not at all. I just hadn't planned on staying anywhere so soon.'

'And definitely not here?'

I looked down the long, empty street framed between a pair of ancient gas pumps, pursed my lips and smiled.

'You don't need to say no more than's been said,' the mechanic grunted. 'If I could get you going, I would, but this lady won't be persuaded.'

He patted the roof of the pick-up. There was something in his tone that made me believe he wasn't trying to make an easy buck.

'I understand,' I said.

He looked me in the eye for twenty or thirty seconds, a long time.

'My brother has work that needs doing; been under some pressure lately,' he said quietly.

'What kind of work?'

'Farm work, tractor stuff. If you can nurse this thing along, then you could drive a tractor. He has timber that needs drawing, hedges that need cutting – nothing too complicated.'

'I could do that.'

'I'll call him.'

The mechanic's brother lived at the end of a long lane in a large, squat house that had a porch that ran around all four sides. It stood on the edge of a pinewood, resting on the top of a hill and eyeing an enormous cornfield that ran away in three directions, for ever it seemed.

His barn and machinery sheds were on the other side of the wood so that, approaching the house along the lane, as we did in the mechanic's car, there was no hint that this was a farmhouse. Instead, the building looked like it had sprouted from the trees, finding its own form and making itself available to the humans who had, eventually, found themselves beneath its roof.

The mechanic dropped me at the garden gate and waved me away.

'They'll be inside; they're expecting you. I'll call you about the pick-up.'

'No hurry,' I said. 'I won't be able to pay you for at least a couple of weeks.'

He shrugged.

'If I get it going you can drive and pay later.'

'I might do a runner.'

He shrugged again.

'I don't think you're the kinda fella that would.'

And he was gone, the wheels mounting the low bank near the gateway as he turned his car.

I lifted the latch on the garden gate and stepped into a patch of ground that might once have been a garden. It still had the contours of a garden – with the outlines of paths and beds – and there were straggling pockets of flowers, beaten flat by the weight of incessant sunlight, but nothing had been sown there in years.

The dominant smell was of stock. Night was falling fast and the air was suddenly thick with its scent. I had always imagined the scent of stock to be red and blue and I tried to visualise those colours as I climbed the six steps that took me onto the wooden porch of the unlit house. There was no sound – no radio or TV playing, no dogs barking, none of the noises that I'd have expected from a lived-in house.

For a moment a series of awful thoughts crossed my mind. The mechanic had dropped me here knowing the place was empty. My pick-up was already on the back of a low-loader, heading for a scrapyard. The guy didn't even own the garage in which I'd met him. This was all a swizz and by the time I walked or hitched back to town, I'd be too late to do anything about it.

'You the fella looking for work?'

The voice was gloomy and came from a dim, deep doorway. Peering into the twilight, I could just make out a figure in what seemed like a hallway and then a light was suddenly switched on and a middle-aged man towered above me, backlit, his features shadowed.

'You the fella?' he asked again.

'Yes. Philip.'

'Jake.'

I offered my hand but it was left unshaken.

'My brother dropped ya?'

'Yes.'

Jake stood aside and I stepped into the long hallway.

'Nice smell of stock out there,' I said.

He didn't answer. Instead, I was ushered along the hall and through a doorway into a large room. The man flicked the light switch as we passed from one room to the other and I found myself in an enormous kitchen. He indicated a chair at the rambling table and I sat there.

'You want coffee?'

'That'd be good.'

'You eaten?'

I shook my head. 'There's something we had for dinner. I'll heat it up.'

'Thank you.'

A gas ring went click click click and then spurted into life.

'You drive a tractor?'

'Yes.'

'Combine?'

'Yes.'

'Okay. I got maybe twelve weeks' work here. You on for that?'

'Yes. My pick-up is kaput. Your brother is going to fix it.'

'He said.'

'Yes.'

A spoon rattled in a saucepan and a plate was taken from a cupboard.

'You have a fine place here.'

'Six-hundred acres.'

'Nice.'

'Work.'

'Course.'

'Just work.'

The spoon rattled again, followed by the sound of food slopping onto a plate and then a rattling in a cutlery drawer.

'You wanna beer?'

'No thanks.'

The plate arrived, piled high with stew. A knife, fork and spoon were laid beside it.

'Bread?'

'No, this is great. Thanks.'

I ate. The food was tasty.

'You make this yourself? It's really good.'

'No.'

I ate some more and the man sat opposite me.

'Have you been farming here a long time?'

'Long enough.'

I nodded and went back to my food. The man was silent, watching me eat. When I'd finished, he took the plate and cutlery away and led me out, across a small yard, to a low building.

Inside, there were four sets of bunks.

'Take your pick,' he said. 'Blankets and the like in the cupboard over there; shower and the rest through there. Breakfast at seven.'

And then he was gone, the door closing quietly behind him, leaving me in the sparse bunkhouse that seemed, suddenly, full of the ghosts of long-lost cowboys.

I woke before six the following morning, showered and then loafed around the bunkhouse for half an hour before tapping on the kitchen door and stepping inside.

A slight, fair-haired woman was standing at the stove, her back to me.

'Good morning,' I said.

'Good morning,' she said quietly, turning and smiling. She was in her forties, I guessed. Her face was pale and drawn, her eyes a dull, dead blue.

'I'm Philip,' I said.

'Emily.'

Her husband lumbered into the room and nodded towards me. We sat at the kitchen table, eating for the most part in silence. Whatever conversation happened revolved around farm work. Jake seemed anxious to assure himself that I could do what needed doing.

'Don't need a sidekick,' he said. 'Gotta work on your own.'

'I can do that.'

'Good.'

I did work on my own and day by day, week after week, through that first month, Jake came to trust me. In the beginning, there were tasks he set for me and then checked. Then there were tasks that were set, with which I was entrusted, and, by the end of that month, I was allowed to get on with the work that I thought needed doing.

In the third week, my pick-up was returned and I paid a quarter of what I owed Jake's brother.

While the summer unbolted its door, my evenings were occasionally filled with work but sometimes offered freedom. When that happened, I drove into town, caught a movie, drank a few beers and came back to the farm.

One evening, as I pulled into the yard, I saw Emily sitting on the porch, a book in her hand. I parked the pick-up and went and sat on the step below her. By then, the book had disappeared.

'That your garden?' I asked, nodding at the ragged collection of overgrown colour.

'It was.'

'I could do something with it, if you want. Dig it over, weed it.'

She shivered and shook her head.

'Well, if you change your mind. I have time on my hands.'

The evening sun rinsed the enormous wheat fields in a profound, rich gold and the sky deepened from a light to a darker blue.

'Enough to look after.'

'Okay. But the offer stands.'

'Thank you.'

Sometimes we ate together in silence. In the first few weeks, I'd try to make conversation but it seemed like a pointless exercise, so I stepped into the silence that was Jake and Emily's natural habitat, accepting what I couldn't change. Some days we met for breakfast, lunch and dinner and never spoke at all and, when we did, I found myself drawn into the disconnected monosyllables that passed for conversation or didn't. I could never decide whether they despised or delighted in their lake of silence.

Nothing in their eyes or mouths gave any inkling, nothing in their physicality betrayed love or hate or like or boredom. Emily's eyes remained the same lacklustre blue, picking nothing of the summer light from the sky. Jake's taciturnity bordered on the obsessive. He behaved as if a word would shatter whatever it was that held his world together. He never looked me in the eye, not even for a moment. Instead, his eyes constantly ploughed the ground around him, afraid the earth might dissipate or disappear if it slipped out of his sight. Even when he drove the tractor, he never seemed to trust the horizon. His gaze fell ten feet ahead of the front wheels, constantly checking that the world was not flat, that it wouldn't suddenly reach a precipice and slip from beneath him, sending him tumbling into nothingness.

One Sunday afternoon, as I was turning the pick-up in the yard, I saw Emily take her place on the porch, book in hand. Slowing, I leaned through the open window and shouted across.

'Do you want me to bring you a book from town?'

'What?' She frowned.

'A book. You must be close to finishing that one.'

'I don't read books,' she said, pushing the book behind her.

'Okay,' I said. 'Anything you want? Provisions? Anything?'

She shook her head.

'You want to come for the ride? Won't be too long.'

Another shake of the head.

'Okay,' I said again, but not so she could hear.

One morning after breakfast, when Jake had gone out to check the wheat for cutting, I went back into the kitchen to get my hat. Emily was sitting at the table, her back to me, her book lying open on the scrubbed wooden boards.

Passing the table, I saw, before she had time to close it, that the pages of the journal were covered in neat, copperplate handwriting, the lines indented, numbers and words like mathematic poems.

She blushed – the first colour I'd seen in her face – and swept the book into her lap, closing it as she did.

'I wasn't trying to read it,' I said.

'No.'

'Just came back for my hat.'

'Yes.'

'It's burning up out there, even this early.'

'Yes.'

'I thought you heard me come in.'

She smiled a half-smile and then quickly looked away.

I took my hat from the chair and angled it onto my head.

'I'm sorry,' I said. 'I hope you believe me.'

'I do.'

'That's good. I wouldn't want you thinking otherwise.'

It was two or three evenings later. I was washing the cab of the pick-up when Emily came down the yard.

'There's some coffee inside, fresh brewed,' she said.

I had never been invited into the house in the eight weeks I'd been there, other than to eat, never spoken to her other than out of necessity, never encouraged to believe there might even be a cause for conversation, so I didn't move. As far as I was concerned, she was, for reasons best known to herself, imparting this information. I had no cause to believe this was an invitation.

Halfway back to the house, she seemed to realise I wasn't following, so she stopped and turned.

'There's apple and cinnamon pie too.'

Her soft voice carried in the still evening air.

'You mean for me to come in?'

'If you want.'

'Thank you,' I said, dropping the sponge back into the wash pail.

Inside, the kitchen smelled like one of those patisseries that draw you in and won't let you out. I closed my eyes and breathed deeply.

'Reminds me of the bakeries in Paris,' I said, but there was no response.

On the kitchen table a pie bulged and puffed, cinnamon steaming off its pastried back.

'Sit,' she said and I did.

She brought coffee, cream, sugar and plates to the table and then went back to get knives and forks.

'Can I help?'

'All done,' she said, sitting across from me.

'Jake not joining us?'

'He's gone to town. Needs something from his brother for the combine. Reckons the time is just about right.'

'Could be,' I said. 'Don't think that wheat will get much riper.'

She sliced the pie and a gust of steam rose and hung a moment above the table, pastry wrapping itself around the steaming fruit, the fragrance of cinnamon stronger now, catching the nose and resting on the tongue.

'You can taste cinnamon before you taste it,' I said. 'One of those smells that lands in your mouth like a ... butterfly.'

She laughed, the first time I'd ever seen her laugh, but her eyes were still indifferent and flat.

'I hope this don't taste like butterfly,' she said.

'I have no doubt it won't.'

She lifted the coffee pot and poured, first for me, then for herself.

I lifted a forkful of pie and held it beneath my nose, relishing the scents, allowing the fruit to cool, anticipating.

She watched as I slipped the pie between my lips, waited for me to taste and smile and chew and swallow. Only then did she lift her fork and break a morsel from the slice on her own plate.

We ate and drank in silence and the sun sank lower, its light stretching and lengthening the shadows of the window frames across the kitchen floor, catching the side of Emily's face and her hair.

I wanted to say something, to tell her what I was seeing, but I didn't dare.

'This pie is indescribable,' I said. 'Best I've ever eaten. Hey, I'm not even eating it; it's melting in my mouth.'

She smiled her half-smile again.

'You want some more?'

'What about Jake?'

'Don't eat it.'

'Well then, I will.'

She cut another slice and poured more coffee and then she took her book from somewhere down the side of her chair and placed it on the table, pushing it gently, fractionally towards me.

'That's it,' she said. 'All in there.'

'May I read?'

She nodded.

I reached across, lifted the hard-backed journal and pushed my plate to one side. I opened the book and found myself reading a recipe for bread. Overleaf, there was one for asparagus soup and then one for a beef stew and another for chocolate cake and so the recipes went on, page after page after page, the book bulging with neat, well-thumbed pages of good food.

'Your life's work?' I asked.

'Seven years,' she said.

'You ought to try to get these printed – sell copies in town.'

She laughed again, a hard and charmless laugh that was at odds with the care that had gone into the book I was holding.

'Where's the recipe for that apple pie?'

She reached across and flicked some pages, her hand brushing mine.

'There,' she said, and I read the words that described what I'd just smelled, tasted and eaten. Words shaped with care, as if they were a poem or a song or something, like they were meant to be enjoyed for themselves, never mind what they were describing.

'You write a lovely hand.'

'Thank you.'

'And bake angelic fare.'

'It's just a pie.'

'What I buy in the store is just a pie. This is the reason Eve got kicked out of Eden. And I'm glad she did.'

She arched her hands beneath her chin, nodded and looked at the remnants in the pie dish. I leafed through another few pages but I wanted to talk, I didn't want to read.

'How many recipes?'

'About six hundred.'

'You've got to do something with those.'

'I don't think so. I dream 'em up, sometimes I make 'em and then I write 'em in this book. That's enough. That's it.'

We sat in silence and the sunlight retreated through the windowpanes and then Emily stood up, turned on the lights and began clearing the dishes.

'Let me help,' I said.

'No, you go. Jake'll be home soon. It's getting late.'

'Thank you again,' I said.

'It was an apple pie, that's all.'

'For letting me read your book.'

'Just recipes.'

I knew she didn't mean that, but I said nothing more.

A couple of days later, Jake was out in the barn – I could hear the combine engine turning over – and I came up to the yard to collect a tool box.

Emily was sitting on the porch again, her book on her lap, head bent, but she was crying. From twenty yards I could see her tears when the sunlight caught them, thin little rainbows slipping from under her hair.

I crossed the yard and stood at the foot of the porch steps.

'You okay?'

She looked up. Her eyes were red nicks, like wounds that might never heal.

'Can I do anything to help?'

Her head turned slowly from side to side, as though she hardly had the energy to move it.

'Just say if there is,' I said.

She stared but I knew she was neither seeing nor hearing me, so I backed away, picked up the toolbox from inside the shed doorway and followed the cranky sound of the combine, back to work.

That night, after dinner, while Jake was outside checking the night sky for weather, I asked again if she was all right.

'Not sleeping is all,' she said.

'Awake all night?'

'I sleep at dawn. Dawn is whenever tiredness comes.'

'That's a nice way of putting it.'

'Is it?'

'Yes it is.'

The kitchen door opened and Jake blustered in.

'Start cutting tomorrow,' he said.

I nodded.

'Weather's gonna hold. Gonna call Timber, get him to organise the trailers. You and me, we'll do the combining in shifts. Twelve on, twelve off.'

And that's how it was, Jake and me in turns in the cab of the combine. He worked days and I worked nights, the big sallow moon sitting above the enormous, uncluttered cornfields. The tractors and trailers beside me in the darkness, the cab a glass box filled with music or simply with the familiar throbbing of the perpetual engine noises, the hum and whine; the saw and grind; the tension and release, hour by twilit hour through the half-dark night. Sometimes swinging the cabin door open to let the tractor noises and the cooler air of night come in. Sometimes lost in the songs from the radio. Sometimes beguiled by the sinking moon or the blush of dawn. Sometimes fighting sleep by shouting and laughing to myself. Sometimes stopping and climbing down to share a coffee and smoke a cigarette with a tractor driver before we both returned to the work that waited impatiently for us.

And sometimes I imagined how that work might look from space, two machines, their headlights furrowing the earth before them, travelling slowly but methodically across the vast spaces of these malformed fields that had once been buffalo prairies. The viewer would see a pair of toy machines, driven by two lunatics whose waking and sleeping vision was riven by relentless lines of high, dry wheat.

In the morning, just after seven, Jake's truck would come across the vast field like a sheepdog in search of lost sheep and I'd climb down and he'd climb up, without a word, and I'd drive his truck back to the yard, roll into bed and sleep until midday. I'd eat and afterwards I'd sleep or read until an early suppertime and then go back to work.

So it went on for three days: sleep and eat and work and sleep and eat and work. I dreamt of wheat fields and the rise and fall of certain sections of the land, the way a field would gradually tip the combine to one side without ever threatening to flip it.

On the afternoon of the third day, I went into the house to have my lunch. The kitchen was empty, so I poured coffee and took food from the stove. Emily's recipe book had been left on the table and, as I ate, I casually opened and flicked quickly through it. There were pages marked with pieces of paper and newspaper cuttings and a few photographs acted as bookmarks at the beginnings of sections, but I didn't believe it was my place to look at them or read the cuttings. Instead, I ran my eyes over the recipes: Watermelon Wine; Stuffed Peppers; Pasta Penne.

I poured more coffee and put the book on the table beside me. A moment later, Emily came downstairs and into the kitchen.

'You're awake,' she said quietly and then, seeing the recipe book beside me, her tone changed. 'Have you been looking in my book?'

'I've just been daydreaming about your recipe for strawberry jelly,' I laughed. 'I could taste it off the page.'

'You had no right,' she said sharply.

'I'm sorry.'

'No right whatsoever.'

'Are you annoyed?'

'Annoyed isn't the word I'd use.'

'Angry then?'

'Very, very, very angry.' She spoke slowly, calmly, emphasising each syllable of every word.

'Why?'

'Why?' Her laughter was cold and hurt. 'If you have to ask, then you have no idea about anything and it's not my place to explain. The fact that you even ask that question is an answer in itself.'

'Right.'

I waited for her to continue but instead she picked the book from the table, crossed to the armchair near the window and sat there, her back to me. I saw her open the book, watched her head drop, imagined her eyes welded to the lines before her. I might not even have been in the room, such was her concentration. I recognised that intensity of absorption from a couple of days earlier and felt compelled to try to undo whatever wrong I'd done.

'You don't want to talk about this?'

Her only response was the very definite turning of a page. Who would have thought a sheet of paper could cut like that.

'Who would have thought the old man to have had so much blood in him?' I said for no better reason than that it had come into my head, but, again, no response, neither a sigh nor a movement.

I walked into the garden and sat in the shade of a buddleia. Butterflies rose and then resettled above me. From where I sat, I could see her through the kitchen window. Another page turned and still no break in her concentration. I closed my eyes and listened for the distant wash of passing traffic. The waves of early afternoon noise rising and falling, like the waves on the shore of that other sea a long time ago.

It was late in the afternoon when I took a bicycle from the barn and cycled down the long lane to the road. Passing the house, I saw that the armchair by the kitchen window was empty and I was disappointed. I wanted to apologise, wanted to wave and cross to the window, ask if she would like to cycle or walk with me, or at least have her exchange some words that I might take as a token of forgiveness. I didn't want to be at war with her. But the chair was empty and the window looked in on a neat and vacant room.

Reaching the end of the laneway, I turned right, away from town, and cycled quickly along the dusty roadway. It was good to be out and moving. In the last few days I had fallen into a pattern of sleep and work, forgetting that I needed relaxation too. As I rode, I promised myself two things – I would get some exercise every day during harvest time and I would mend the fences I had broken with Emily. I didn't believe that what I'd done was very wrong – it hadn't been my intention to be intrusive – but she obviously did and that was reason enough to apologise again.

On a bend at the head of a steep hill, about two miles from the house, I saw a small burial ground at the foot of the incline, half-hidden by an overgrowth of saplings and brushwood which formed an uneasy support for a low picket fence that had seen better days. Here and there the fence had collapsed entirely but mostly it hung in the summer air, supported by a sapling or a rotting post at one end and a tangle of dogwood at the other.

As I gathered speed, flashing between the hedgerows, a cloth of butterflies rose in the breeze and my face was washed and dried in the noiseless, rising rainbow of dying wings. Faster and faster I went, the air flecked and dappled with the plumes of swirling colours, the butterflies tumbling and turning in their outrageous and beautiful dance of death. And then, at last, the road levelled out and the bicycle slowed, giving the butterflies time to open their curtain and let me safely through. The bicycle slowed and slowed, the sound of its spokes becoming more methodical, their click click click returning to a regular pattern as I pedalled the flat, dusty road, eventually falling silent when I came to a standstill outside the gate of the decrepit burial ground.

I didn't go inside. Instead, I lay on the dry, burnt grass by the roadside, my hat tipped over my eyes, the bicycle lying beside me, and listened to the hot, tired songs of resting birds. Everything, it seemed, had wound down into the pit of this late summer afternoon.

An hour later, as I made my way back to the farm, the hill road was petalled with dead and dying butterflies. They lay still or broken-backed, their wings waving goodbye to the gift of flight. I tried to weave a way between them but it was impossible; their slaughter would not be ignored, their colours already losing lustre in the dust of the lengthening shadows.

Life is short, I thought, and the very banality of the idea was, in itself, a moment of epiphany. I was determined that I wouldn't allow what had happened that morning to destroy the delicate but definite connection between Emily and myself.

Back at the farmhouse, her armchair was still empty. I returned the bicycle to the barn, knocked at the kitchen door and walked inside. The room was empty, as it had been when I'd arrived for lunch.

I made some coffee and a sandwich. In two hours I'd be back in the combine cab, the falling darkness stretching itself across the wheat fields. I was determined not to begin the night without speaking to Emily. And then I heard her in the hallway and I called her name.

She came into the kitchen and I asked if she'd like some coffee.

'Okay,' she said.

We sat across the table from each other and I told her about the butterflies. She winced.

'I wanted to say I'm really sorry about your book. I just took it up without thinking.'

She nodded.

'I didn't mean to intrude. I'd never do that. I'd never barge into your life. I like you too much to do something like that.'

'I won't sleep with you,' she said quietly.

'That wasn't my aim.'

'No. But it would be. In time.'

'Would it?'

'Yes.'

'And yours?' I asked.

'It might have been.'

'It honestly hadn't crossed my mind.'

She arched an eyebrow.

'I just wanted you to know.'

'Too late for all that.'

'Because I opened your book?'

She laughed.

'You really don't know much, do you?'

I drove the combine through the night, trying not to think about Emily. I ordered the figures in my head, worked out that I'd be ready to pay off Jake's brother when the harvesting was done and I'd have enough to get me through the winter if I was careful. I examined the possibilities of staying a little while longer, maybe seeing out the winter. That would depend on whether or not Jake had work for me. But it would also depend on whether or not I wanted to stay.

One good thing had come of all this – I'd almost forgotten the river and the river's call. I knew I would never live near water again. And then I stopped thinking. I don't like to think too much. Thinking leads to the past and the past is not a healthy place for me to travel. I need to live in the here and now. When my heart says go, it's time to go. Thinking about the future inevitably leads back because the future and the past are equally uncertain. So I concentrated on the job in hand, tried to estimate where I would be when the tractor driver next stopped for a break.

Every couple of hours we stopped for coffee and a cigarette, and I and whichever one of Timber's men happened to be on the service tractor sat on the steps of the combine and shot the breeze. Sometimes we talked about movies or music or sport or the women in the town bar.

'You cutting any corn in there?'

I shook my head.

'Good-looking guy like you. I am surprised.'

'Nice of you to say so,' I laughed; 'nothing doing.'

'Women love that European accent, specially out here where they don't get much of anything they ain't got before, one way and another.'

He stubbed his cigarette carefully on the step, gargled a mouthful of coffee and spat it into the light from his tractor.

'I'm telling ya, you just talk low and slow and you'll have more pussy 'n you'd get in a cattery.'

'Sounds attractive.'

'Don't knock it, buddy; it's wet and it's willing,' he said, swinging down onto the stubbled earth. 'Guess we better get moving or Jake'll be saying we stole his time. I reckon that guy can hear in his sleep.'

'You think so?'

'See, that's just what I mean,' the driver laughed, pointing at me. 'You talk like that, low and slow, the way you said "think" so, to any woman in this town and the gates of Eden will spring open faster'n you can get your belt unbuckled.'

We finished the harvesting at the end of that week and, when I got my money from Jake, I drove into town and paid off what I owed on the pick-up. Driving back to the farm, I noticed a change in the evening, a subtle alteration in the sky, reminding me that the season was ending.

That night, over supper, I asked Jake if there was work enough for me to stay on for a couple of months.

'You want to?'

'If there's work.'

'Stay on a time. I'll tell you when the work runs out.'

And that was it.

We set about the ploughing. This was less frenetic than the harvesting. We worked a normal day and if something didn't get done, it could always get done the next day. A couple of times a week I'd go into town for a beer, meet one of two of Timber's tractor men, shoot some pool, chat to the girls in the bar. I took one of them out to dinner a couple of times and we caught a handful of movies, but that was it. Something might have happened but neither one of us ever seemed to want to take it beyond a goodnight kiss in my pick-up truck.

'We could go on like this,' she said one night. 'But that's just habit.'

I nodded.

'You're a nice guy and I'm a nice girl but that's about it.'

'Nice and nice makes nothing.'

'You prepared that line.'

She laughed.

'Yes, I did. See that's the thing: I can admit that to you and you won't get mad. We're too polite to have fun.'

'Just me?'

'No, me too. I need someone down and dirty.'

'I could try,' I said but neither of us was convinced. So we kissed goodnight, said we'd see one another around and left it at that, knowing we wouldn't.

Thanksgiving came and Jake and his brother drove the five hundred miles to see their mother.

'Do it every year, expecting it to be the last but seems it never is,' Jake told me.

I was helping him clear out the year's accumulation of bags from the back of the barn. We took them out onto a headland and made a bonfire before he left.

'Some folks live beyond their time and some folks only get half a life. They're only getting out in the sun and then the sun goes down. Don't seem like there's any justice in that. Never seen the fairness in it. You take my mom. She's a bad-assed, nasty lady. Is why me and my brother is living five hundred miles from her. Be farther 'n that if we could find that place. And there she is, seventy-nine and still dipping life in a bucket o' shit for anyone she can.'

I'd never heard Jake talk so much at one time and, as if he noticed my surprise, he added: 'Get like this every Thanksgiving – just the thought of seeing her. Me and my brother'll relax and smile when we pull out of her driveway and head for home. Always the best feeling of the whole damn holiday.'

I was sitting at the kitchen table that night, dawdling over dinner, and Emily said: 'You don't seem to go to town so much anymore.'

'No.'

'You were goin' in a lot, for a time.'

'Yes.'

'She dump you?'

'Hard to say,' I shrugged. 'Think we each dumped ourselves.'

'People expect too much from life. From love.'

'I don't think we came close to love,' I smiled.

'Sex then.'

I shook my head and laughed.

'You still want to sleep with me?' she asked.

'Yes,' I said but the word got lost in my throat.

She looked me straight in the eye, her dead blue stare holding me in its gaze.

'Yes,' I said again and this time the word came out too loud.

'I won't sleep with you,' she said quietly. 'But we can come to some arrangement, if you want, some kind of mutual satisfaction. You can watch and I can watch. That's all I can offer. No touching, no kissing, no lovemaking.'

'Why are you saying all this to me?'

'I've seen all the books you have down on the bunk house window,' she said. 'Reading books doesn't make you a better person. I used to read a lot of books and they had nothing to offer when it mattered. They were just mountains of letters; they meant nothing. And me saying this doesn't make me a bad person.'

'That's not what I meant.'

'What I'm offering you is the best I can offer. You don't know how far I've had to come to say what I've said.'

'I appreciate that.'

'Good of you.'

'We don't have to do anything,' I said, crossing my leg under me and leaning my chin on my hand.

She smiled that frozen smile.

'I'm not here to be analysed. Words mean whatever you want them to mean and that might, in the end, come down to absolutely nothing. If you want to do this, we'll do it. If you don't, that's okay. But it's not a negotiation. Some things are beyond all that and I'm not gonna sit here and talk about it.'

'I'm sorry.'

'You say that a lot. It's another word.'

We held each other's gaze for a moment, two gunslingers on an empty street with nothing to lose and nothing, it seemed, to win.

'I'm going upstairs. If you want to follow, you're free to do that but I meant what I said.'

And that's how it began. It was easy for the four days Jake was gone, but afterwards, when it might have been more difficult, we found ways to make it possible. I'd go up to Emily's room, at the opposite end of the landing from her husband's room, and she'd lie on her bed and I'd sit in the big easy chair across from it and we'd masturbate. Sometimes it was mechanical, sometimes one or other of us got lost in the moment and occasionally we both forgot the distance between us, or were engrossed in the presence of the other, and were almost one or totally alone and it didn't seem to matter which. I never instigated anything; sometimes I wanted to but one look in Emily's eyes told me that I was the one who needed to wait; I would never be the one to drive this liaison.

Some days Emily was more reckless than others. She would bring me to her room while Jake was working in the barn and it was my responsibility to watch for his return. Sometimes this meant my rushing back downstairs and out the front door before he reached the yard door. And some days I'd see his tractor on the far horizon and know we were safe. Then I could look carefully at Emily, watch her fingers between her thighs, watch her breasts tighten and her nipples harden and listen to the chaos of her breathing as she came.

'*La petite mort,*' I said once as we were dressing. 'It's how the French describe this.'

'What does it mean?'

'The little death.'

She shuddered.

'I don't like that. Don't say that again. Please.'

I wondered, long after I'd left the farm, if our being caught together by Jake was inevitable – intentional even. Did I want him to find us? Did I fool myself into believing that discovery would force the moment and make Emily decide between

307

her twilit world and the possibility of some other life, with or without me? Did she want her husband to know that not only had she rejected him but that she was being intimate with a stranger? Was what we were doing meant as a punishment that would, in time, find its target? Whatever our separate motives, he did find us.

An afternoon in early January, darkness falling, Emily and I lost in pleasure because, even then, those moments seemed of no consequence beyond their own fulfilment, minutes of isolated enjoyment taken out of ordinary lives, devoid of any connection to the past or the future, a time of engrossment.

What did Jake hear as he slowly climbed the stairs, his day's work done? At what point did he become aware of the urgent breathing from his wife's room? The bedroom door was open so he must have seen our figures from the turn of the stair, silhouetted against the picture window and the flat acres of land beyond. And as he reached the landing, he must have heard Emily moan and sigh, her body tightening like a fist and then exploding into relaxation as she came, and he must have heard me say oh, fuck, fuck, fuck as I came.

I thought about all this afterwards but, in the moment of discovery, all I knew was that Emily's room was suddenly electric with light and she was lying naked on her bed, her hand still trapped between her legs and I was sitting naked in the easy chair by the window, my hand covering my limp, wet cock. And Jake was standing in the doorway, his face wearing an awful, wounded expression of disbelief and disappointment.

Emily looked her husband up and down and then rolled slowly on her side, her back to him. I froze. I waited for Jake to say something, to lunge across the room, but instead his gaze seemed to have strayed past his wife, past me and out onto the wintry landscape beyond the window.

I remember the awful uncertainty of that silence, and the feeling that he and Emily were less concerned by it than I was. And then Jake seemed to refocus, as though his mind were retracting like a telescope, changing his focal point and becoming aware, again, of what had been happening in his wife's bedroom.

He flicked off the light switch, turned and his heavy tread retreated along the landing. A door opened and a door closed and then there was an absolute stillness that seemed to mirror the stillness of the day outside. As the twilight settled in the room, the sky beyond became brighter. Through the window, nothing was moving. The trees were severe against the grey evening sky. I believed that if I reached out, I could touch the barn roof or open the bright red windows of the bunkhouse or run my hand along the chrome fender of my pick-up. Such was the stillness, such the clarity of that time.

Standing up, I began to twist into my jeans. Emily turned, flicked on her bedside lamp and picked through her clothes in that languorous way that women have, unhurried, considering each item as though it were brand new.

'Best you go,' she said quietly.

I nodded.

A door opened and there were footsteps along the landing. Pulling on my boots, I prepared myself for whatever was about to happen. Should I take my beating or put up a fight, try to run for it or talk my way out? Jake was standing in the doorway now. I stepped closer to the window, my shirt and jacket in my hand. And then I saw the bottle, a whiskey bottle, almost full, the neck tight in his fist. Emily went on dressing slowly, ignoring him. She stepped out of bed, pulled on her skirt and slipped her feet into her shoes. Jake watched her every move and only when she was dressed and ready to leave the room did he raise his arm and smash the bottle against the jamb of the door. The stench of whiskey flooded the room and Jake extended his arm, the jagged bottle top pointing first at me and then at Emily and then he smiled at her and said: 'Are we quits yet?'

She laughed – a low, dry laugh – and bent to lift her scarf from the floor.

Jake's arm angled slowly at the elbow and he buried the broken bottle in his throat, turning it this way and that, working the serrated glass into his flesh until the blood began to flow.

I shouted at him to stop and rushed across the room, grappling the bottle from his grasp, pulling it from his flesh as gently as I could and stuffing my shirt against the open wound.

'Call 911,' I said, but Emily didn't move. In that instant I realised she wasn't in shock; she simply had no interest in saving her husband's life.

Jake's body began to slide slowly down the jamb of the door. I moved with him, keeping the shirt tight against his neck, until he was sitting, his back against the wall, and I was kneeling beside him.

'Can you hear me, Jake?' I asked quietly.

He nodded.

'Can you hold the shirt if I call the medics?'

He nodded again.

'Keep it tight,' I said.

There were tears in his eyes and I wanted to hug him.

I ran down the stairs and dialled, gave the address and was back upstairs in under a minute. Jake was slumped against the wall but still conscious, the blood-soaked shirt pressed against his throat. Emily was sitting at her dressing table, slowly combing her hair.

I knelt beside him and whispered: 'You're going to be all right. Medics are on their way. Hang in there.'

His eyes were glazing over, breath stuttering through the wound in his throat.

'I'll turn the porch light on,' Emily said, stepping over him.

I stayed on at the farm for ten days more, until Jake was ready to come home. In that time I'd gone to see him twice at the hospital. I'd sat across the table from Emily and asked her why she had laughed at her husband when he'd found us together. I asked her a dozen times but she refused to speak to me.

In the middle of the second week, Jake's brother drove out from town to tell us Jake was being released the following day. Emily shrugged and carried on with what she was doing.

I walked Jake's brother back to his car.

'I don't know how much you know about what happened,' I said.

'Don't matter. That's not why he done what he done.'

'I wish I were that sure.'

'There's a history here,' he said, sitting on the hood of the car and opening a pack of cigarettes. He offered me one, took one himself and we lit up.

He drew deeply on his cigarette, scratched the back of his neck and surveyed the bunkhouse and the roof of the barn.

'No one to blame – just the way things catch up. Maybe now she'll be satisfied.'

He sucked again on his cigarette and it burned halfway down, the paper glowing and darkening.

'Was a little girl here one time, was killed in a wreck, Emily's daughter, not Jake's. He was driving. Too fast I reckon.' He pulled again on his cigarette, sucking it close to the filter before flicking it across the damp clay. 'She never got over it. Never forgave him. Guess the girl would've. She was a cute little thing. Smart as a lash.'

'So what's going to happen to them now?'

'Guess they'll pick up right where they left off. Wounding themselves and one another. What they been doing well for a long time now.'

'I'll move on.'

'Best for you. How's that pick-up of yours running?'

'Smooth.'

He smiled.

'I done a good job.'

'You did.'

'Best to leave all this kinda shit behind. Ain't no one ever gonna sort it.'

'I know.'

'You've been through it before?'

'Something like that.'

'Well you take it easy,' he said, pulling open his car door and sitting heavily in.

'You too.'

He turned the key, the engine hummed quietly, he waved, and then he was gone.

I packed my bags that night, threw them in the pick-up and walked up to the house.

Emily was sitting in the chair by the kitchen window.

'I'm going to move on,' I said. 'I think it's best for all of us.'

Her eyebrows arched.

'Jake's brother told me. About what happened.'

She nodded.

'Maybe now is a good time to forgive …'

'Don't,' she said sharply.

I stood in the middle of the kitchen and Emily sat where she was, looking out into the night.

'Right,' I said finally. 'Well then ... I'll be going.'

I moved towards the door.

'Jessie,' she said, so quietly that I almost didn't hear.

'Nice name,' I said and then I opened the door and stepped out into the darkness.

My Beloved Son

I remember the evening well; it was in the winter of the sixth year after the Captain had been killed. We were in the library together, my young son James and me. Same name, same blood. And the librarian, a really nice woman, always smiling, always saying hello when we came in to play chess, was gathering up the books and I had one eye on the clock, knowing the place would close in fifteen minutes.

'It's lovely to see you here with your boy,' she said quietly.

She looked at James.

'You and your dad are really close,' she said.

He smiled and nodded and then his attention went back to the board.

'Anyway, I just wanted to say that,' the librarian added. 'I've been meaning to say it for weeks.'

I noticed that she had a really warm smile and her dark hair fell around her face as she stooped to pick up some books from the table beside ours.

'You keep playing,' she said. 'I won't be finished tidying till ten past, so take your time and enjoy your game.'

'Thank you,' I said.

Did she know, I wondered? How could she – it's a big town with a lot of people coming and going. She couldn't know.

'Check,' James whispered.

I studied the board but there was nothing I could do; no move I could make that would get me out of the noose he had made for me.

'Looks like you might have me caught.'

He smiled and sat back, folding his arms, and it was worth being checkmated to see that satisfaction, that smile.

'I'll just make sure,' I said, though I knew it was a hopeless task and James knew that I knew. He clasped his hands behind his back, looked nonchalantly around him and went on grinning. I examined the board, piece by piece, possibility by possibility, but there was nothing to be done.

'You got me again,' I said.

'Again. What's that, four in a row?'

'Five.'

'Is it?'

'You know it is.'

We began to put the pieces back in the box, carefully laying each one in its compartment, James the white pieces, me the black.

'All done?' the librarian asked, coming back to our table.

'All done,' I said.

'Who won?'

'Need you ask?'

'Five in a row, between last Thursday and tonight,' James said.

'You're obviously a very good player.'

James blushed.

'And thank you for putting the pieces away,' she added.

'We always do,' James said.

'I know. I've noticed. Not everyone does.'

'And thank you,' I said. 'You make us welcome.'

'We'll see you on Thursday,' she said.

I nodded and pulled on my jacket and hat.

'Cold outside,' she said. 'Freezing again.'

'Yes.'

'Well, take care. See you on Thursday.'

'Thank you.'

'Thank you,' James said.

'Some night you'd better let your daddy win,' the librarian winked as we headed for the door.

'Should I let you win, Dad?'

We were walking the bitter street, the wind tunnelling into our faces, an ambulance screaming in the distance.

'No, you should not. The lady was just being kind to me. You're a good player, James. You keep working on your game. You deserve to win. You think things through.'

'I'm glad you came back,' he said.

I took his small, gloved hand in mine and squeezed it.

'Me too.'

'Was it warm in that country?'

'Very.'

'Did you like that?'

'I liked the heat but I missed you.'

'Do you miss the Captain?'

'Yes,' I said. 'I do miss him but not in the same way I missed you.'

'And I wasn't dead. I was only in a different country.'

'You're right.'

I rubbed his head, tousling the hair beneath his woolly hat, pushing it down into his eyes while he laughed uproariously, his sweet ten-year-old voice ringing in the empty street.

We walked on, hand in hand, James peppering me with questions about the Captain, as he often did. What was he like? Were you there when he was killed? Was he ever funny? Was his mother very sad when he was killed? Was he very brave? Are you braver than he was? Did you nearly get killed too? Were you afraid?

I answered truthfully the questions I could. The rest I glossed over.

And then we were at the gate of his mother's house and we were hugging and he held me tightly, his little arms trying to encircle me, his hands making fists of the back of my jacket.

'I'll be here on Thursday night. At the gate. Six o'clock. You can count on it.'

'Sharpish.'

'Sharp.'

'Sharpest.'

'On the nail.'

'On the button.'

We had this rigmarole we went through every time I left him home.

'Can I come and stay with you some night?' He hadn't asked me that in over a month.

'Soon now, yes, soon.'

'That'll be nice. We can watch TV.'

'Yes.'

'Goodnight, Daddy.'

'Goodnight, my son.'

We hugged again and he galloped up the path and I waited till the hall door had opened and closed before I turned away from the gate and retraced my steps along the avenue, leaving the multi-coloured houses behind, crossing the bridge and out onto the street that would take me to the other side of town.

I was living in a shed back then. But, as far as I was aware, only three people knew: James's mother, the elderly man who owned the shed and myself. The man had made it as habitable as he could. He'd put a stove in the corner and a bed beside that and a padlock on the door. It was the best he could do and I was happy to have it. He didn't charge me any rent and the place was secure, all the more so because no one else knew I lived there. I showered at the swimming pool and spent my days on the move, looking for work, taking whatever odd jobs came my way, sometimes finding two or three weeks on a farm or as a builder's labourer in other towns, not letting things get to me, always coming back on the nights I was due to collect James. But it wasn't the kind of place his mother would ever allow our son to stay and she made that perfectly clear, as though I'd ever think of bringing him there and didn't have any pride left.

So, on Tuesdays and Thursdays we went to the library and played chess. Saturday afternoons we went to a film or, if the weather was good, we cycled or walked out into the country. And once a week I'd go to the bank and lodge what I'd saved into my account.

Sometimes I offered rent to the man who owned the shed but he'd just smile and tell me not to be crazy, that I was keeping it aired against the future. So once a month I'd drop something to his house – a bottle of whiskey or a box of strawberries or a cowboy book. He liked westerns. And he'd say: 'There's no need.' And I'd say: 'Least I can do.' And he'd say: 'You're keeping that place aired against the future.' And sometimes I'd come home and find a piece of furniture outside the door, an armchair or a table or a locker. He'd never unlock the door, never intrude into what he saw as my place, just leave it outside, wrapped in plastic if the day was wet.

So, week by week and month by month, I put money aside and by the end of the year I had enough saved to lease a flat but I didn't. I went on saving and I started telling James about the house I was going to rent. It would have a bedroom for me and one for him when he came to stay, but I never told him about the shed.

'And can you have a TV in your bedroom?' he asked excitedly. 'And can we watch it in bed at night? Late. Sometimes Mammy lets me do that, sometimes we watch TV together. At weekends.'

'Course we can.'

'When will you get your new house?'

'At the end of winter.'

'And will we stop going to the library?'

'What do you think?'

He shook his head.

'I like it there. I like the lady.'

'I agree, but when the library closes, we can go back to my house for hot chocolate and you can stay there at weekends, if your mum says it's okay.'

And that's how it was. I found a place to rent and when I approached the owner of the shed about doing a deal to buy the bits and pieces of furniture he'd provided, he wouldn't hear of taking any money.

'Not a question about it. They're yours.'

And on the day I was moving, he brought his van down to the shed and loaded the furniture with me. On the last run, after he'd gone home, supposedly to have his lunch, he returned with a three-piece suite in the van.

'It was doing nothing where it was,' he said. 'You'll get some use out of it. The young fellow can sleep on the couch when he comes to see you.'

'Thank you.'

'No need, no need.' He waved away my thanks, not dismissively but because he was embarrassed. '"From each according to his ability …"'

'"… to each according to his need,"' I finished.

'I knew you were a good man,' he said and then we got on with unloading the furniture.

When the work was done, we sat on the back step, looking onto the small garden. I pointed out what I was going to plant and where.

He got up and walked across the garden, digging it with his boot heel, rubbing the soil between his fingers.

'Needs manure,' he said. 'Dead as a doornail. I'll drop some up.'

'You have enough to do.'

'Well it won't grow anything otherwise. Dig it in, dig it well in. Let it break down, it'll make a big difference.'

The following evening, when I got home from work, there were eight plastic sacks of manure stacked against the side wall of the house and a fork laid across them.

I smiled at that. Typical, I thought. He won't brook any excuses.

I hadn't dug in years but I enjoyed the work and during my working day, while I was barrowing blocks for the block layers, I looked forward to the evening and the work I'd be doing in my garden. I couldn't wait to go out and get the sods turned; the grass piled and dried in a corner, ready for burning; the soil turned and the manure dug in. One evening, a young couple with a baby next door came and stood at the fence and chatted while I rested between digging and spreading.

'I must do something with this place,' the young man said, eyeing the wilderness on their side of the fence.

'You renting or do you own?' I asked.

'Renting,' the young woman said quickly.

'Same as myself.'

'Ah, right.'

'I'll give you a hand, if you like,' I said. 'Once I get this place done.'

'Not at all,' the young man said. 'I'll get stuck into it next week. You have enough to be doing there.'

'Well, once it's sown, there won't be much else I can do, apart from keeping it weeded. So just say the word.'

'Well, I might do that. Thanks.'

The young woman looked at him and then looked away.

By the time James came to stay for his first overnight, the garden was a glorious flicker of browns, reds, blues and greens, the sun picking shades and shadows in the late spring evening. And a week later the drills and beds were made and a week after that we worked together, kneeling in the warm soil to sow seeds and then raking beds and dreaming of the crops that lay, still curled inside their seed pods, beneath the ground.

I never did get to help the couple next door. I saw them one morning, early the following week, loaded down with suitcases and plastic sacks, pushing the baby's buggy out the front gate. It was six o'clock and they were heading for the early train.

I pulled on my jacket, went out and took three or four of the bags and walked with them to the station. They didn't speak and neither did I but I knew, by the way they were laden down, that this was a flitting. At the station, just as the train pulled in, I stuck a fifty note in the young woman's hand and legged it. The last thing I saw was the couple loading their bits and bags onto the train and the young man lifting the buggy through the open doorway.

Another evening, early that summer, when the plants began to grow, I invited the Shed-man, as I thought of him, to come to dinner. He inspected the drills and beds and told me I'd done myself proud and that the garden was a credit to me.

'Your dad is a hard worker,' he told James. 'You're a lucky young man to have him for a father and to share his name with him too. Doubly blessed. And he's lucky to have you.'

Later when I talked about the Shed-man, James asked me why I called him that.

'I stored some furniture in his shed once,' I lied. 'He's a nice man.'

'Why don't you ask him his name?'

'His name is George.'

'So why don't you say George?'

'You're right, I should. I will.'

And I did. The next time he visited, I called James from the garden.

'George is here. He has something for you.'

The old man had brought a bag of sweets for James and a box of strawberry plants for me for the garden. While we planted them, he nodded towards the house next door.

'I hear they did a runner?'

'They did,' I said. 'To tell you the truth, I felt sorry for them. I carried some of their bags to the station. I guessed they were getting away.'

'Good man.'

He settled a plant in the soil and firmed the earth about it, took another from the box and did the same.

'Never liked the fellow who owns that place,' he said, sitting back on his heels.

'You know him?'

'I do. I saw him shoot one of his dogs one time because he thought it was ugly. A man that'd do that deserves no sympathy. A man that'd do that would do anything.'

That spring, two magpies lived their joyous life on a quiet country road and every morning I'd see them, black and white, while I cycled to work. By the time June came, my garden was productive enough to promise food for the rest of the summer. I had built a small greenhouse from bits and pieces of timber and a few old window frames that I'd taken from an out-office we were demolishing on the building site. Green tomatoes bunched against the glass, lettuces and scallions were a month ahead of the lettuces and scallions in the open drills. Potatoes and peas and runner beans flowered at the far end of the garden, away from the house. Closer to the back door, I had sown onions, parsnips, turnips, beetroots and carrots in a sandy bed.

'You'll never eat them all,' George had laughed and I knew he might be right but I'd found it hard to pass a seed packet without wanting to try another variety.

'And you won't go hungry,' I promised.

Along the fence, between the still vacant neighbouring house and my own, I'd sown sunflowers. They, too, were pushing up and each weekend James had the job of measuring them. There were ten in all and we'd given them the names of other flowers.

'Pansy is leading,' he'd tell me. 'But she gets more sun and later in the day.'

'So that's why!'

He nodded.

'And why is Lily coming last? She's in the middle, not brightest, not darkest.'

He thought about that for a moment.

'Soil,' he said. 'Bet there's a concrete block under her.'

I laughed. He sounded just like George.

'Am I probably right?'

'You're probably right,' I said.

One evening, in the middle of July, as I was about to take my bike out and cycle up to collect James, the phone rang. It was his mother. I hadn't spoken to her, nor had I heard her voice, in more than five years. We had communicated through her solicitor, arranging access and collection times and dates. But the moment she said my name, I knew who she was.

'You're due to collect James,' she said.

'Yes. Is everything all right?'

'Everything is fine. I just thought I could save you the journey. I could drive him over. If that's acceptable.'

'Of course. That would be fine.'

'We'll be there in ten minutes.'

I left the front door open and each time a car slowed, I stepped out onto the front garden path. Eventually, her car drew up at the gate and I saw James in the passenger seat. To my surprise, his mother got out and walked up the path with him, smiling.

'I've heard great things about your garden. James tells me you've been working hard.'

'Can Mum see it?' James asked.

'Of course she can.'

I'd been lost in the fact that for the first time in five years I was having a civil conversation with this woman who had once been my wife and lover and had, with good reason, come to hate me.

I led them through the house and into the back garden and, as we stepped into the sunlight, I felt proud of the work I'd done over the previous months. Everything was growing, everything looked healthy.

'And we have sunflowers,' James said.

'So I see,' his mother said and then she turned to me. 'You've done a wonderful job. You should be proud of it.'

'I suppose I am,' I said and I tried to smile but no smile came, only a sense of abject self-loathing.

'Will I put the kettle on, Dad?'

'Do,' I said. 'I'm sure everyone would like a cup of tea.'

He scampered inside and his mother walked between the drills and beds.

'You've packed an amazing amount into a small space.'

'Thank you. There's more than I'll need. You're welcome to anything you want.'

'And James says you're well.'

'I'm well, thank you.'

'Good,' and then an abrupt silence that sprawled awkwardly.

We stood in the evening sun, the full light of July breaking over us in one long, warm wave. She leaned across suddenly and lifted my T-shirt, looking at the twisted scar that seemed still raw after all these years, the place where a blade of bullets had ripped my flesh and left me bleeding on the roadside, my blood running with the Captain's into the ground.

'How's the pain?' she asked tentatively, as though she were afraid the answer might be the one she had heard in the years before we parted.

'The pain is manageable. It's never going away but I cope with it, on my own, without anything. I'm not just saying that ... I appreciate your coming around with James.'

As though on cue, our son appeared at the back door and called us. We went inside together and sat in the kitchen, drinking tea, eating biscuits, perhaps even happy in the moment. And afterwards I walked James's mother down the path and thanked her again for visiting.

'You don't have to call but I'd be happy if you did,' I said, as she sat into the car.

'We'll see,' she said. 'And it's good to see you so well. I'm glad you're well.'

I nodded. She pulled on her seat belt.

'And I'm glad you let me find James again and get to know him.'

'You're a good man,' she said. 'You just did things I couldn't handle. I know it was the pain and the medication and all that stuff but it wasn't up to me to deal with it. You were dangerous, you were vicious and not just that night. I'm not saying that to make you feel guilty. I just need to say it.'

'I was. I hope I never am again.'

'I hope so too.'

Later, after we'd watered the plants and measured the sunflowers and I'd dropped James to his gate, I sat in the open back doorway of my house, cradling a mug of tea, and I thought about the last time, before this evening, that I'd talked to James's mother.

It was a wet night and we were sitting in my car in the car park of a rundown hotel and, in the end, not because of the pain or the medication or the loss of love, not because I had run out of words but simply because I could think of nothing else to do, nothing that would make her see how badly I needed her not to go, because the anger overcame the pain, I hit her. My fist caught the side of her face. Not my hand or my fingers but a closed fist that bounced back off her cheekbone. It took her a couple of seconds to recover from the blow and by then blood was trickling from a cut beneath her eye and I was thinking of the Captain's blood and my blood on the sandy yellow road.

'Now you know,' I said. 'Now you have some fucking notion of what it feels like.'

And then she opened the door of my car and stepped out into the rain. I didn't try to stop her, didn't say anything, didn't laugh or cry or shout. I just sat there and watched her walking. The dribbling rain on the windscreen began to melt her form but still I did nothing. When she reached her car, I saw her fumble in her bag for her keys and then I saw her wipe her cheek with the sleeve of her jumper before the hazard lights flashed and she sat in.

It took her twenty or thirty seconds to start the engine but I knew she wasn't waiting for my apology, wasn't hoping I'd cross the car park and try to explain away this new cruelty. I knew she was catching her breath, feeling the tender skin and the bruised bone beneath the blood. She was trying to gather the strength and the courage and the calmness to drive away. And then she did, as she had done on a hundred other nights when we said goodbye – sometimes kissing; sometimes touching; sometimes embracing in the cold or warm night air; sometimes, lately, fighting about the painkillers I couldn't live without. And the car drifted out, an unsteady haze at the hotel gate, and then it disappeared. I leaned across and pulled the passenger door closed and took a packet of tablets from my pocket and a bottle of brandy from under my seat and I swallowed the tablets and drank the brandy until there was only a cupful in the base of the bottle.

Stepping out of the car, I splashed what remained of the brandy on the driver's seat, struck a match and waited for the flames to catch. Only then did I close the door and walk away, not looking back, not buttoning my coat against the rain, not doing anything. An hour later, I lay down in the deep porch of a church and the Captain's words came back to me. A man's enemies will be in his own house.

I had no memory of when he'd said it but I knew the words were his and I knew, with the terrible clarity that sometimes came out of the haze of pain and numbness, that this was what he had meant, that this woman would never understand what we had been through, not just the Captain's death and my fes-tered wound but the years of camaraderie, the months when our belief was not just a dream or an aspiration but something achievable, something of significance and consequence.

And then I fell into a deep, satisfied sleep and I dreamed, and in my dream there was no rain, no woman walking away, no tomor-row when she would have to invent a story about her wounded face for our son, no years when I drifted out of his life and he grew from childhood to being a small boy, nothing of the years of violence and jail and anger and dependence, nothing of the realisation that the next step would be my last – none of that. And nothing of my slow rehabilitation and the years living in that shed which became a place of unexpected redemption, nothing of the tentative approaches to see our son again, a handsome boy of eight with the weight of my absence laid heavily on his heart – none of that.

And, for that minute, sadness drained me, sucking every morsel of hope and happiness from my heart. Then, looking over my shoulder, I saw the three cups and saucers, the biscuit plate, the milk carton and the sugar bowl, domestic promises on a kitchen table, and I allowed anticipation and desire to lodge again within me.

In late July, George and James and myself dug the first potatoes, cooked them and sat in the kitchen eating them, smothered in butter and sprinkled with salt. James watched as George and I ate them, skins and all.

'Can you eat the jackets?'

'Best part,' George smiled. 'Try one.'

I laughed while James tentatively tasted a piece of skin and then another, chewing uncertainly but surprised, it seemed, by how tasty it was.

That night, when I dropped him home, he took a bag of potatoes with him for his mother.

'Will Mum know you can eat the jackets?'

'I think she will.'

'They taste okay.'

'They do.'

'And we sowed them, Dad, didn't we?'

'We did. You and me.'

He smiled and gripped my hand a little tighter.

In early August, James's mother came to see the sunflowers open and follow the sun. She spent an afternoon with us and we ate in the garden, James and myself carrying the table onto the small patch of grass and serving a meal that consisted only of produce we'd grown ourselves. George joined us and charmed James's mother with his courtesy and gentle humour.

'That man is good for you,' she said as she was leaving.

'And good for James.'

She nodded.

James walked ahead of us, carrying two baskets of vegetables to the car.

'Thank you,' she said and she kissed me lightly on the cheek.

Despite the warmth of the setting sun, I felt myself go cold and she noticed the shiver flooding through me.

'I'm sorry,' she said. 'I shouldn't have done that. Are you okay?'

'Yes,' I nodded. 'But sorry ... so sorry.'

And that was all I could say because it was the truth.

In September I brought James with me when I collected a second-hand car from the garage on the edge of town. The number plate said it was seven years old but the smell inside was the smell of a new car. We drove to his mother's house and she came out and said all the things we wanted to hear and told us we looked the right pair in it.

'Like pilots ready for take-off.'

'Isn't it cool, Mum?' James asked.

'Super cool,' she said. 'It was made for the two of you. And it seems like it's been well looked after. Well wear.'

'Thank you,' I said and I knew, in that instant, that we were both thinking of the night I'd burned my last car and I was hoping she could believe that I was truly different now, that although the pain in my body and the pain in my soul would never go away, I could live with them and not be at their beck and call.

'You should come in for a cup of coffee,' she said when she'd walked around the car a few more times.

'Is that a good idea?'

'I think it's something we can do.'

And we did, we sat again, the three of us, and she and I listened while James talked about the places we could drive to.

'The zoo, the sea, the mountains, somewhere no one has ever been, the place where the country ends, loads of places and we could all go and one time we could take Mum's car and the next time yours and then when I'm big enough to have my own car, I can bring the two of you in my car.'

I said nothing.

'Sounds good,' his mother said. 'We'll talk about it.'

Maybe we only know heaven when we've left it. Maybe that's all it is, a point of reference that crops up in our lives. Perhaps that's why it's not a lasting kingdom. All it ever can be is a place we look fondly back on or a place to which we aspire but not a place we're ever permitted to stay.

It was the first Friday in September and I'd collected James from his mother's house. We were driving back to my house to do a final measurement on the sunflowers. George would meet us there to act as arbiter, in case of any disagreements.

'Who do you think will win?'

'Iris or Pansy or Lily. They've all made a late burst.'

'But Pansy has the biggest face!'

'She has, no doubt about that.'

'It's exciting.'

'It is.'

We stuttered through the evening traffic.

'Would you like some fish and chips?' I asked.

James's face and eyes lit up and his fingers spread wide, his teeth gritted in a mock grimace. I fumbled in my pocket and found a note.

'You hop out here and order three cod and chips and I'll find a parking space and meet you at the chipper.'

He opened the door.

'Does George take salt and vinegar?'

'He does.'

'Okay.'

I watched him cross carefully to the opposite path and disappear inside the shop. The traffic budged and stuck and budged and stuck until, at last, I could turn onto a one-way street and find a parking space behind the library. I locked the car and ambled back the way I'd come, past the railings outside the bank that made a zebra of the sunny evening road. Past the empty, broken window of a derelict shop and out onto Main Street. And then I heard the screaming. At first I thought it was the high pitch of a girl's laugh, but it went on, unrelenting. A scream that was pitted only by someone catching their breath before it gathered force again, rising and faltering between desolation and horror. The traffic had come to a halt and some people were standing by the open doors of their cars, staring down the length of the street, as though they were waiting for some great mystery to be resolved. And the screaming went on and on and I followed its reverberation across the street and into the open doorway of the chip shop.

The screaming woman was standing at the deep fat fryer, her face the white of lard. A second woman was on the phone at the back of the shop. There was no one else behind the counter.

The owner and two other women who worked in the shop were on their knees outside the counter, bloodied tea towels in their hands. One of them was bent low, pushing air into someone's lungs. And then I saw James's jeans stretched between the shapes of these three people, his blue runners angled clumsily, one of his legs shuddering spastically. Abruptly, the screaming woman stopped screaming, as though she had lost all the energy she needed to carry on, and there was silence, apart from the sound of the kneeling woman breathing into my son's mouth and the dull hum of cars in the street.

'Did you call the ambulance?' the owner shouted.

'Yes,' the woman who'd been on the phone said. 'It's on its way.'

'That's my son,' I said.

The man looked up at me, terrified.

'The guy came to get money. I gave him the money,' he said. 'I gave it all to him.'

I could see the hole in James's shirt and the dark blood on the black and white tiles of the floor, and the red blood on his skin, and the awful colour of his face, a colour I'd seen only once before.

'The guy was turning to leave,' the man said. 'He was turning to walk away. I don't know why he fired, I don't know why. He blew the little boy off his feet. I gave him all the money. Gave him everything. I didn't even argue, they'll tell you.'

'That's my son,' I said again, as though neither of us was hearing the other. 'That's my little boy.'

After the funeral, we went back to my house, the three of us. For no better reason than that I was driving. And we sat in silence in the kitchen and then George got up and made three mugs of coffee and they went cold on the table between us.

I don't know what the other two were thinking but I was trying to figure out why a man with money in one hand and a gun in the other would shoot a small boy dead, and I couldn't find even the beginning of an answer.

After the little box had been buried, with our son inside it, the shop owner had come up to us at the graveside. For a long time he said nothing and when he spoke the only words that came out were the ones he'd said before: 'I gave him all the money. I gave him everything.'

'I know,' I nodded and his hands opened and closed as though they were the only part of his body that could speak any more. And then the woman who had tried to breathe life back into James came and hugged his mother and hugged me and led away the owner. And, lastly, the woman from the library came and held our hands and said nothing because there was nothing to say.

I thought about this for a long time and when I looked up, George had left, slipping quietly away, leaving us to our separate and united grief. And a while later James's mother got up and opened the back door and went out into the garden and I heard her moving between the drills and the raised beds and I knew, without looking, that she was pulling everything from the ground, every living thing. I heard the glass crack in the little greenhouse by the end wall; I heard the sunflower stalks snap and then I heard her breath, coming heavy as she tugged their roots from the earth; I heard her sobs and I knew she was on her knees near the fence, that her face was pressed against the hard, dry earth. And I knew, of course I knew, that she had always been a good woman and that our son had been a good and beautiful boy and that I had tried to be a good man, but I understood, too, that goodness is not always enough.